The Serpent's Mark

THE
SERPENT'S
MARK

Robert L. Duncan

St. Martin's Press
New York

This novel is a work of fiction. Names, characters, places, and incidents are the product of the author's imagination or are used fictitiously. Any resemblance to actual events or persons, living or dead, is entirely coincidental.

THE SERPENT'S MARK. Copyright © 1989 by Robert L. Duncan. All rights reserved. Printed in the United States of America. No part of this book may be used or reproduced in any manner whatsoever without written permission except in the case of brief quotations embodied in critical articles or reviews. For information, address St. Martin's Press, 175 Fifth Avenue, New York, N.Y. 10010.

Design by Amelia Mayone

Library of Congress Cataloging-in-Publication Data

Duncan, Robert Lipscomb.
    The serpent's mark / Robert L. Duncan.
        p.   cm.
    ISBN 0-312-03424-5
    I. Title.
PS3554.U465S4   1989
813'.54—dc20   89-35345

First Edition

10 9 8 7 6 5 4 3 2 1

To John Hawkins,
the best literary agent in the business,
and my good friend of many years.

Acknowledgments

I want to express my appreciation to the generous individuals listed here who have shared their experiences and technical knowledge:

First, to my wife, Wanda, for her invaluable aid and absolute integrity.

To Maj. Bruce M. W. Shaw, Executive Officer of the Investigations Bureau of the Oklahoma City Policy Department, for sharing his considerable knowledge of the use of computers in police work, an area in which the OCPD is rapidly approaching the state of the art.

To Trooper Ric Robinson, Public Information Officer for the West Virginia State Police in Charleston, West Virginia, for his gracious cooperation.

To the men and women of the Las Vegas Metropolitan Police Department for their wholehearted cooperation and technical help in the days before the Crime Lab was moved, particularly Lt. Les Simmons, formerly Public Information Officer, Lt. John Connor of the Homicide Detail, Richard Renner of the Criminalistics Bureau, Richard Good in Ballistics, and finally to Detective Dennis Zenda for updating me on the activities of his department.

To Clyde A. Redding, Jr., Security Chief for La Mirage Hotel and Casino, for his cooperation.

And finally, to my editor, Charles E. Spicer, for his boundless enthusiasm and seemingly limitless expertise.

Alas, the sin of Adam's fall,
The serpent's mark has touched us all.

—*Anonymous*

The Serpent's Mark

BROOKLYN, NEW YORK

Gavilan was tired, and he found a corner of the psychiatric emergency room and leaned against the wall, ostensibly studying a clipboard with the admission records for Emilio Perez, one of the seventeen young men handcuffed to their wheelchairs in the bedlam of the waiting area. Gavilan had no idea which Latino Emilio Perez was. Maybe he was the guy who looked to be all murder and straining tendons, who was doing his best to grab one of the nurses with his free hand while screaming in Spanish that he was going to kill her. Or maybe he was one of the passive crackheads like the seventeen-year-old who had thrown up all over himself and had been lying in the street for seventy-two hours, during which time a car had driven over his right wrist and hand; or the fat thirty-year-old (so goddamn strange to find a fat crack addict; they were all thin, emaciated).

Frankly, Gavilan decided, he didn't give a shit about any of them. He was a psychiatric resident, thirty-three years old, and his wife Marie had given him an ultimatum that morning. Either he was home by six for dinner, in time to take her to a movie, or she was leaving him and going back to her parents in Cleveland. All over a movie, for Chrissakes, but not really over a movie, of course, but because he was never able to keep his word and always so damn tired he sometimes fell asleep at the dinner table. And now, here he was, propped up against the wall, people screaming and yelling around him, and he was actually dozing off with a clipboard in front of his face. He came to with a start as Nurse Falanga touched his arm.

"Doctor," she said. "Mr. Burr wants to talk."

"Burr?" he said. "Who in the hell is Mr. Burr? I don't know any Mr. Burr."

"He's Dr. Smith's patient."

"Then let Dr. Smith talk to him."

The irony was not lost on Nurse Falanga, because they both knew that Dr. Smith had a practice on Fifth Avenue and made a half-mil a year and Mr. Burr was one of his *pro bono* charity patients. Dr. Smith would be out on his boat at the moment, sails catching the summer wind, taking some visiting shrinks around to see the Statue of Liberty, no beepers to interrupt. It was exactly where Gavilan wanted to be, would be, for God's sake, given another ten years and the breaks, but right now, this was a way out of the larger loony bin for a half hour, maybe an hour, if he was lucky. "Okay," he said to Nurse Falanga, handing her the clipboard. "Give this to Dr. Squires and then stand back when he explodes. And where is Mr. Burr?"

"The Green Room."

He went down the corridor, wending his way between wheelchairs and gurneys, and he wondered vaguely whether there was any correlation between the coming of warm weather and the flowering of psychoses in the city. Because the fruits were ripening and falling off the metaphorical trees into his emergency room, and in this one stretch of hallway, he could see classic examples of every condition from catatonia to six varieties of schizophrenia, not to overlook the drug-induced crazies and a handful of normal people Gavilan classified as "those who had used up their cope." Some were naked, curled into fetal positions; others watched with wary eyes as he passed. Others sang to themselves or with long fingernails picked pieces of flesh from scabrous hands.

He paused at the desk where no-nonsense Nurse Jenkins maintained her fiefdom. She was a large and matronly R.N. who had witnessed thirty years of nuthatches and was immune to anything.

2

"Burr," he said to her, and immediately the chart was in his hands and she was telling him about W. W. Burr, who had been sent over from the South Beach Psychiatric Center two weeks ago. The number stopped him dead in his tracks. *Two* goddamn weeks ago? Fourteen goddamn days? He read on. Dr. Society Smith had conducted only a couple of sessions with Burr in that time, and Gavilan scanned his notes, his dashes and snatches of language and phrases, written in the same semi-illiterate script he used for prescriptions. Gavilan realized Nurse Jenkins was leaning on the counter, watching his face with bemused anticipation, as if waiting for the fireworks that were bound to come. Instead, Gavilan gave her the gentlest of smiles, the most placid of voices. "Perhaps you would like to tell me about our guest in the Green Room? We seem to have a shortage of papers in his folder."

"The guest *is* a pay-per," she said with a benevolent smile. "Dr. Smith intends to write up his case for a journal, but Dr. Smith was at a meeting in Los Angeles last week and then went on to a mental health symposium in Washington after that, lunch with the Prez, you know. But he'll get around to Mr. Burr presently, I'm sure."

A woman had begun to howl like a wolf down the corridor, a high moan interspersed with yelps. Gavilan had difficulty thinking. The howling woman had been parked in the hallway for sixteen hours at least, because she had bitten an intern last night. She had just reached out and grabbed his arm and snap, dog teeth puncturing flesh. Sixteen hours for the wolf lady in a high-traffic area, nonsense, since the Green Room (so called because Smith's wife had picked a shade of green designed to be most calming to the mentally disturbed) had been occupied as a private facility by the subject of one of Smith's future papers.

"Background," Gavilan said, eyes on the chart, and Nurse Jenkins was more than happy to oblige. "An ax man," she said. "He dispatched a number of young ladies in Pennsylvania a few years back. You remember the case?"

"Why should I remember a case from a few years back?" Gavilan asked sarcastically. "I had a guy who gutted his grandparents last month and barbecued his landlord, and I don't even remember *his* name."

"Mr. Burr was judged incompetent to stand trial. He's floated from hospital to hospital. He's a model patient."

"Thorazine," Gavilan read from the chart.

"Enough to pickle him," she said. "You couldn't draw blood without hitting undiluted Thorazine."

He checked his watch, shit, as if time mattered, and went into the secured Green Room, the orderly locking the door behind him. Burr was in his late forties, but his prematurely gray hair lay like sparse strands of silk across his shining scalp. His flesh was pale, obviously from long confinement, Gavilan concluded, but he had good muscle tone despite his thinness, and his gray eyes were clear, well focused, no telltale traces of erratic movement. He was sitting in an easy chair next to the barred window, fully dressed in a sport shirt, slacks, and street shoes. The soft strains of Mozart flowed from the radio next to the bed. Burr rose from his chair in a fluid motion, putting aside the magazine he had been reading, extending a hand to Gavilan as if he were the host here. "I'm W. W. Burr," he said.

"My name is Dr. Gavilan."

"An interesting name. It means eagle, doesn't it? I'm delighted to see you. Would you like me to ring for coffee?"

I'll bet you could get room service, Gavilan thought. "No, thanks," he said. "How are you, Mr. Burr?"

"Please sit down," Burr said. "And take the easy chair. I really prefer the straight chair." He sat down and crossed his legs, his manner earnest, lucid. "Physically, I have a touch of bursitis," he said. "Psychologically, I've never been better. Frankly, I'm bored, but I would leave any interpretation of my condition to you, Doctor."

"And what would you be doing if you had the choice, Mr. Burr?"

"Dr. Smith suggested I might make a good librarian or go into inventory control. I seem to have a gift for classification and organization. He was going to ask at Columbia concerning courses I might take."

"I see," Gavilan said. "Do you have any relatives in the city, Mr. Burr?"

"Unfortunately not. I think Dr. Smith had a halfway house in mind. Would you care for a cigarette?"

"No, thanks," Gavilan said.

"Would you give me a light?"

Gavilan lit his cigarette. "I would like to ask you some questions, Mr. Burr."

"Certainly."

"Do you know why you're here?"

"In this hospital specifically, or in hospitals generally?"

"Generally."

Burr inhaled the smoke, blew it out. "I was a very sick man. Schizophrenic. Delusional, convinced I was hearing voices." His face was sober. "I committed atrocities, Doctor, and although I've come to accept the processes that brought such terrible things about, I'll never be able to accept the fact that I took human lives."

"The voices," Gavilan said. "Do they still speak to you?"

"No," Burr said. "And frankly, I don't remember any of the psychotic episodes at all."

"Are you aware of your legal status?" Gavilan said.

"Yes. I never came to trial, but now there's been a sanity hearing, two weeks ago, it was. I was given a clean bill of health. I'm sure you have the findings in my records. Dr. Smith intends to do some further research, so he asked me to keep myself available. He's making a study of the delusional personality, I think."

"A study," Gavilan echoed. He heard the wolf lady howling again and his nostrils prickled with the smell of urine, sweat, feces, and marijuana smoke prevalent in the hallways, and in his mind's eye he planted a bomb in Dr. Smith's boat and watched the explosion send a shower of teak planking high into the air, the boat emitting a terminal gurgle as it slid beneath the surface, leaving Smith to splash for his life. There was an urgent rap on the door, and Barrett, the squat security officer, was in the hall, scowling, and Squires was red in the face and ready to kill.

"I'll be right back," Gavilan said to Burr. He went out into the hall and thrust the clipboard at Nurse Jenkins and was immediately caught up in dispute. It seemed that a paddy wagon had just pulled in with a dozen teenagers out on crack, picked up in a raid, wild animals, and there was literally no place to put them. Squires was yelling that the cops would have to take them to Bellevue, and as Gavilan led the party down the corridor, the wolf lady reached out and grabbed the cop's hand and locked her teeth on his thumb and he yowled and backhanded her, dancing away, demanding that the wolf lady be tested for AIDS, and another cop was trying to herd the crackheads through the glass doors.

"Shit, shit, shit," Gavilan chanted to himself and then set about the impossible task of restoring order.

Burr waited a few minutes after Gavilan had left. He finished smoking the cigarette and then he tried the door and found that the knob turned easily in his hand. They had forgotten to lock it behind them. He opened it slightly, peered down the hallway at the bedlam of activity near the entry doors, and then pushed the door open far enough to look across the hall at the nurses' station. Empty. The girls had gone down to help the doctor and the police.

He stepped into the hallway and went in the opposite direction, and in the act of rebellion and escape, some of the old feelings began to come back, the excitement, and he knew that the electricity was affecting his brain, coming into his system from the electric wires in the ceiling overhead. He took the first right, found himself at a service entrance where a janitor had propped a heavy metal exit door open to empty wastebaskets into a dumpster outside. The old man looked at him warily. "Now, if you come to get me to help with all that shit in reception, you wasting your time," he said. "I work my ass off around here just trying to keep this place clean and I sure as hell ain't going to get mixed up with the mean kind of crazies."

"I don't blame you a bit," W. W. Burr said. "I've just been visiting my cousin."

"I got me a union," the old man muttered, half to himself. "I work hard, but I ain't no cop." He picked up another trash container and Burr went past him, into the fresh air and the clear day, the first time in years he had been out by himself. He could feel the vibrations of all the people around him and some of the old instincts began to come back to him in full force. He wasn't going to be able to enjoy his freedom until he was a long way from here, because the doctors would sense his disappearance before long and the front of the building would be swarming with cops.

He quickened his pace to a half-run down the alley, stopping when he reached the street, momentarily overwhelmed by the screech and blur of traffic, the heavy trucks, drivers yelling, brakes squealing, horns blaring, and from somewhere far off, the wail of a siren. Out to confuse him, yes, and God only knew what they had done to him in all those hospitals; they could have put something in his blood that sent out signals so they could track him down. He could not afford to stay outside.

He scurried down the sidewalk and ducked into the entryway of a clothing store, forced himself to be calm, to pat his pockets and take inventory. He had nothing on him except a pocket comb, a handkerchief, and ten cigarettes left in his pack. He wanted a smoke and he didn't even have a match. He wasn't going to get anywhere without money. He started down the street again, glancing over his shoulder at the crowds of pedestrians to make sure nobody was following him. He saw a police car turn into this street two corners down and he immediately went through the door of the next brownstone.

Inside, he made a cursory survey of the lobby, saw a uniformed elevator dispatcher on duty, white thatch of hair poking out from beneath the cap. It was an old building with a checkerboard of black and white tiles on the floor, all the elevator doors decorative brass. He was about to ask the old man for a light when his breath caught in his throat. Because right there in front of him, mounted on the plastered wall, was an old-fashioned emergency firebox with brass rims to hold the glass labeled BREAK GLASS IN CASE OF FIRE. He shaded the reflection on the glass with his hand while he peered inside.

Perfect. A length of canvas fire hose, coiled. He felt a shiver of excitement. An old-fashioned fire ax with a perfectly polished silver single-bit head and a hook on the head opposite the blade. He squinted at the honed edge of the bit, and even though it was partially hidden in shadow, he knew it was razor sharp. Magic, yes, transcending any medicine they could ever have pumped through him. He felt the murderous fury in his veins and he took off his shoe and, with the leather heel, smashed the glass, which shattered and showered onto the marble floor. The elevator dispatcher came across the lobby in a limping run, raising an ancient hand as if trying to hail a taxi. "Hey, you," he yelled. "Hey."

W. W. Burr reached in and expertly seized the ax with his right hand, yanked it free of its mount, and when the old man got close enough, yelling for him to stop, W.W. let loose all the anger that had been building within him for years. He swung the ax. The blade caught the old man in the side of the head and dropped him against the wall in a shower of blood and brain matter. Breathing heavily, Burr put his shoe on, and then, holding the ax in his left hand, he went through the old man's pockets with his right. He took the wallet from a rear pocket, flipped it open. Three or four twenties, some fives and ones. He put the wallet in his own pocket, was going through the old man's front pockets for change when he saw the middle-aged man in a business suit come through the door, stop for a startled moment at the sight of the blood before he grabbed a revolver from a shoulder holster.

"Freeze," he yelled from a shooter's crouch, both hands aiming the pistol. "I'm a cop. Drop the ax."

W.W. smiled at him, jiggled the change in his hand, knowing that as long as he held the ax he was invincible. He put the coins into his pocket, then took the cool wooden shaft of the ax in both hands and moved toward the man.

The man yelled a second warning, and just as W.W. took another step toward him, he squeezed the trigger, a sequence of four shots. W.W. seemed to absorb the first three without moving, his chest blossoming red. But the last one caught him in the face, just to the right side of his confident grin, blasting the flesh away from the bone, and he collapsed in a heap, the fire ax sliding across the floor, leaving a smear of blood to the point where it came to rest against one of the highly polished elevator doors.

QUEENS, NEW YORK

My father would have liked the day, Stein thought as he walked across the grass toward the casket suspended above the open grave. His father had always enjoyed the days of early summer when the trees were full leaved, and in the first rest home in Queens, before he went to Yonkers, he would sit on the porch and watch the jets making an approach into La Guardia from the south, flying above the screen of trees on the lawn like birds descending to the nest.

Today there was only a handful of people at the cemetery. His father had outlived all his friends and in his final days was completely withdrawn into a private world, totally inaccessible to anybody, including his son. At one time, he must have looked the way I do now, Stein thought, and the old man was always looking at him as if seeing his own youth and middle age in the mirror of his son, a tall, lean man with an unruly thatch of salt-and-pepper hair. "A spitting image," the old man would say, cocking his head to one side as if to gain perspective. Not handsome, no, but "presentable," as his father used to put it. And now his father's frail body was going into the ground and Stein had his own son and a curiosity about how six-year-old Barney would look thirty-nine years from now. He pulled his collar up against the chill of the day and the thoughts of his own mortality.

The rabbi was a young man in his twenties. He conducted the service impersonally because Stein's father had last gone to temple three rabbis back, and the ceremony was mechanical. A mousy woman from the nursing home stood in the group of mourners next to the official representative of the NYPD, a spare old man in a dark suit that showed years of use at unofficial functions like this one.

Stein's mind wandered, projecting ahead, five hours until his plane left La Guardia and in seven hours he would be home. He was jolted into the present by the bearlike man who arrived toward the end of the service, balancing on his cane, lop-gaited with arthritis. His old friend Teddy Fleischman, by God, the aging gadfly of a columnist for *The New York Times,* who had lost none of his sting. He was six years older than when Stein had seen him last, hair grayer and more ill-kempt beneath his battered fedora, the lenses of his spectacles a little thicker. He looked as if he still wore the same gray suit he had always worn, even more rumpled now.

When the service was over, he went up to Stein and engulfed him in a bear hug, smelling of tobacco and brandy, then pulled away without a word of greeting and regarded the casket with rheumy eyes.

"Never easy," he said. "Did he suffer?"

"No, he went in his sleep. I'm pleased you came out. He would have liked that. He liked you very much and he had a great admiration for the written word."

"It's hell to grow old," Teddy said. He nodded toward the police department representative, who was lighting a cigarette before he got into his car. "I see old Thayer doing all the funerals now. He was a fine cop back in the old days. But this gives him something to do in his retirement. It's not my idea of a hobby." He looked up as another jet approached La Guardia. "You had any word from Captain Thornton?"

"No," Stein said. "But then, he never knew my old man."

"This wasn't about your father," Teddy said. "How long before you catch your plane back to West Virginia?"

"Five hours."

"Plenty of time. I'd like to get your reaction to something, have a drink and an interview, if you don't mind."

"I haven't been newsworthy in a long time," Stein said. "But I'd enjoy a drink."

He dismissed the funeral car and settled back into the Mercedes the *Times* had provided for Teddy, who directed the driver back into Manhattan. "I've thought about you often," Teddy said to Stein. "And I've kept up with you in a way. I read the article about your government grants in the *Washington Post* about a year ago. It's difficult for me to buy the notion of you, the city dweller, finding happiness in the bucolic sticks. How long did it take the photographer to get the picture of you pushing your son in the swing, with Karen in the background, everybody looking so damned happy?" He grimaced slightly, obviously expecting no answer to his rhetorical question. "None of that sounds like the Peter Stein I knew. Aren't you bored silly with your computers and your telephones? Or have you really withdrawn from life in the raw?"

"I don't see it as withdrawing from life," Stein said. "I've just changed my way of living."

"And you don't miss being a cop?"

"I'm still a cop."

"Not really." Teddy looked out the window as the car crossed the Triborough Bridge. "And perhaps it's time to discuss the irony. You came up to bury your father and it's one of those cruel streaks of coincidence that something from the past should rise up to confront you while you're here."

"What's going on, Teddy?"

"An Irishman named Mickey Waters was working as an elevator dispatcher in the old Conklin Building. He was seventy-two years old, much loved in his parish, in perfect health, and an Irish musician. He played the pipes at the commissioner's funeral last year. He has a wife, ten children, two of whom are cops, and seventeen grandchildren. Yesterday at two in the afternoon, a mental patient took advantage of a frantic day in the loony bin, found a door unlocked, walked into Mick's building, and cut him down with a fire ax, just to get seventy-nine dollars from his wallet and a pocketful of change."

"So?"

"So Detective Flannery, Midtown South, off duty and coming into the building to pay on an installment loan, witnessed the killing, drew his service revolver, and when the ax man kept coming, blew him away."

"What does this have to do with me?" Stein asked.

"The ax man was W. W. Burr."

"Ah," Stein said, and for a moment he felt a breathlessness, as if a nightmare expunged from his life over a long period of time had just returned in full force. There was a saying among detectives that if you allowed a case to get under your skin, it would be with you forever, and now he realized it was true. "How in the hell did W.W. ever get out of maximum security?"

"How do bureaucratic mistakes ever happen?" Teddy said. "Burr slipped through a crack as a result of overworked doctors, sloppy paperwork, and Burr's own gift for improvisation."

"Incredible," Stein said. He did not want to deal with this but he knew that he must. For Teddy was not so much a columnist as he was a conscience made flesh. For many decades, he had been a confessor who insisted that the questions be asked, even those to which there were no answers. He sat now, polishing the twin lenses of his heavy spectacles with an Irish-linen handkerchief he carried for no other purpose, as if the philosophical problem confronting him required the keenest vision. In all his years as a New York City cop, Stein could not remember a single major case where Teddy was not there, always asking the hard questions, always pushing for his single-minded definition of justice.

Stein had had enough of death for today, yet there was always hope that the specter of W. W. Burr, which continued to unsettle his marriage and give Karen nightmares, could finally be put to rest.

"I want to see the body," Stein said.

Teddy leaned forward to instruct the driver.

"What was the victim's name again?" Stein said.

"Mickey Waters."

"I knew his son. Eddie, isn't it? At the Seventeenth Precinct?"

"Detective Edward Waters now."

Yes, of course, a lot of years since Stein had been on the force, long enough for all sorts of changes to have taken place, and he remembered Eddie Waters as a beat cop, a boy with an easy grin, rather slow-witted actually, but tough as a boot physically and dedicated to the blue uniform.

The car parked in front of the M.E.'s office and Stein crossed the sidewalk to the steps with unaccustomed slowness, waiting for Teddy, who limped along with the aid of his cane, nodding and speaking to clerical help leaving the building for the day. They were all strangers to Stein. Stein followed Teddy downstairs to the cold corridors of the morgue and the smell of formaldehyde. They signed in and had an attendant call around to find Elmo while they stood among the gurneys lined up with bodies draped in sheets, nothing exposed except waxen feet, old, young, arthritic, battered, scarred, calloused, graceful, nothing in common save the same pallor and the identification tag tied to the big toe. No autopsies were in progress, all of the the pathologists absent. Teddy simply flipped his cane around and rapped on the tile floor with the wooden crook, a sharp, staccato sound, and a young black attendant came snapping around the corner. He grinned when he saw Teddy.

"Hey, Mr. Fleischman," he said, shaking hands with Teddy. "I made it as fast as I could."

"Elmo, I want you to meet my friend, the legendary ex-detective Peter Stein, who was known around here for many years as the monster catcher."

"Well, hey, Detective Stein," Elmo said, shaking Stein's hand, slightly curious but not wanting to display ignorance. "You was a bit before my time, I bet."

"A bit," Stein said. "I would like to see the body of W. W. Burr."

The name rang no immediate bells for Elmo. "Burr, Burr, Burr," he said, trying to jog his memory.

"The ax man," Teddy said. "Blown away by an off-duty cop."

"Yeah, yeah." Elmo led the way into a larger room and moved down the rows of gurneys. "Burr, Burr, where you be? John Doe, John Doe. Okay, baby. Think we got you made." And he waited for Teddy and Stein to catch up before he grasped the corner of the sheet between thumb and forefinger and expertly peeled it back.

It was W. W. Burr all right, the mortal shell of him, Stein thought, whatever spirit that had occupied that cold, dead flesh now gone. He felt a jolting shock he had not expected, strong enough to click off any feeling in him. Dead meat, a cadaver, a thing, certainly no longer a man. Even the ripped face was bloodless, pale, like a medical drawing, with white flesh peeled back to reveal a smashed and splintered cheekbone and the open cavern of a mouth with shattered teeth. One eye swollen, the other recessed, the undamaged part of the face almost masklike, as if it had always been in rigor.

Stein remembered the day when Burr had sent him the severed foot of a murdered woman, involving him in a nightmare of a case that had persisted for months, the obsession to find this killer of women, a dark battle that eventually saw Karen terrorized by the man with the ax in the darkness of her backyard while Stein was gone. The grotesque figure had made a slow, keening whistle, as if summoning her, the ax swinging in front of him like a pendulum, moving toward the house while she watched from the kitchen window until she fainted. That time, Burr had suddenly departed, leaving her unharmed.

But Stein the husband had not been able to shelter her, because Stein the cop took precedence, always away from home, always tracking elsewhere, until that final bloody night when Stein was home and W. W. Burr had come for vengeance, smashing into the kitchen with his ax. Stein had tackled him while Karen fled the house, screaming for help. The lunatic Burr, bloodstained, more animal than human, his sharp blade slicing Stein in a bloody and terrible finish, ending with Stein battered, wounded, and close to death but hanging on to consciousness long enough to stand over the fallen Burr, holding the ax above him, ready to bring it down on the head of this crazy who had dared to invade his home. He had not killed Burr; his moral instincts had prevailed over his anger, and Burr had been hauled off by the police, locked away for years, but not forgotten, no.

Karen had nightmares, and for months she sat bolt upright in bed in the small hours of the night, certain she had heard the whistle and that W. W. Burr had come back to kill her. She had been totally dependent on Stein for a long time, unable to let him leave her, and at the same time consumed with the heat of a banked anger that he should have allowed this to happen to her in the first place. She had gone through years of therapy and still saw a psychiatrist occasionally. With a total change in lifestyle, she was beginning to trust again.

"I want to see his hands," Stein said, on impulse, and Elmo gave the sheet another expert fold, halfway down the naked torso. Stein looked at the oversized hands responsible for the deaths of how many people? He would have to count them if he truly wanted to know; the facts had receded; he had wanted to forget. All young women, chopped up, pieces missing, frozen for use in obscene ceremonies. The large spatulate fingers were cupped in toward the palms, the thumbs stiffly extended, nails white. "Cover him up," Stein said. "I've seen enough."

Elmo pulled up the covering sheet. "So you was a monster catcher?" he said, flippantly, to Stein. "This ole boy, he was a monster?"

"Yeah, he was a monster," Stein said.

As they walked back to the car, Stein was aware of the opalescent sky, pinkish before twilight. Teddy unwrapped a cigar and put it between his teeth without lighting it. They drove on to Sullivan's, which had been a cops' bar in the old days, catching trade from One Police Plaza. But no more. Now Art Deco, exposed air-conditioning pipes along the ceiling, painted orange, wide stripes of color zigzagging along the walls, everything upscale, young men in suits, gorgeous, brassy young women. The maître d' obviously knew Teddy, clicked his fingers for a waiter, who led them to a circular corner near the rear, where Teddy had an unobstructed view of the place.

"I swore when they remodeled and crowded the cops out, I would never come here again," Teddy said, unfolding his napkin, eyes screening the room to see who of interest might be there. "But it's been taken over by Yuppie attorneys, male and female made he both, God's gift to the old hounds like myself, because it's become fashionable for them to be quoted in my column, and I mention Sullivan's name, and so it goes." The waiter had perfect teeth and obvious theatrical ambitions. "A double bourbon and water, Randy, for my friend," Teddy said. "And my usual, if you please." He held up a hand to hold the waiter in place. "If you're hungry . . ." he said to Stein.

"Nothing for me."

Teddy nodded and the waiter disappeared into the noisy crowd, to return momentarily with the drinks. Teddy lifted his glass. "To the memory of your father, may he rest in peace," he said. And drank. He ate the onion off the toothpick, settled back in his chair. "I've known you a long time, Peter, and your father before you. I should know what you think, but I don't."

"Are you interviewing me?" Stein said.

"I'm always interviewing. If there's anything in our conversation you don't want me to print, just let me know."

"I don't think I have any reservations," Stein said. "There aren't a hell of a lot of people in Charleston, West Virginia, who read *The New York Times,* and even if they did, your column would be much too esoteric for them."

"That's too bad," Teddy said without rancor. "I do like to think that what I write will be understood by everybody."

"Most people don't care to understand," Stein said. "That's the reason so many cops I know think in terms of black and white, because it simplifies life for them and lets them sleep at night."

Teddy sipped his freshened drink. "I really write because I'm in search of my own answers," he said. "And inadvertently you have provided me with a perfect illustration of the kind of dilemmas that fascinate me. You served with distinction on the NYPD for many years and you specialized in psychotic criminals—I use that term advisedly, knowing that there is a whole school of thought that classifies all criminals as psychotic. Nevertheless, you distinguished yourself as a monster catcher. And then came the time when your own wife was threatened and you ended up in mortal combat with one W. W. Burr. He almost killed you and you had the opportunity to kill him, and given that opportunity, you declined." He stirred his martini with his toothpick. "Is that a fair summary?"

"With some modification," Stein said. "But what's your point?"

"I'm coming to that. Had you killed W. W. Burr then, you would have saved the life of the innocent man he killed yesterday. So why did you back off when you had the chance?"

"I subdued him," Stein said. "That was my job. It wasn't my job to execute him. On top of which, he was crazy."

"But had you been given the gift of foresight, had you known that he would kill again if you gave him the chance, would you have done differently?"

Stein drank his bourbon. "It's an impossible question. I couldn't have known the future."

"You're saying that it wasn't your job to remove W. W. Burr from this planet. But you're also saying that you think he was too crazy to be fully responsible for what he was doing. So who's responsible for the death of Eddie Waters's father?"

Stein was tired. "I haven't missed these arguments with you in the slightest."

"Not arguments. Dialogues."

Stein shrugged. "Burr never questioned the voices that he heard telling him to do the things he did, any more than I question the fact that I'm sitting here and having a drink with you. When I got some distance from it, I hoped that medical care would make a difference in his life. I've come to believe that most mental illness is a matter of chemical imbalance."

"You think sanity can be restored by pills?"

"You're getting too simplistic, but yeah, in the broadest sense, yes."

"So we can dismiss evil as a chemical accident."

"I'm talking individuals, not good and evil," Stein said. "And if you want to look at it in that light, a hell of a lot of psychotics I stopped were made crazy by chemicals they took—pot, crack, booze, uppers, downers, you name it. And a lot of psychotics have been cured by drugs."

"And what went wrong with W. W. Burr?"

"After the medical establishment took him over."

"Yes."

"I haven't the slightest idea." He finished his drink. "But whatever happened, they messed up."

"I think he was just plain evil," Teddy said. "I believe in evil as a force of nature, a force quite capable of infecting individuals and nations alike."

"And there you lose me," Stein said. "End of argument. I'm good at what I do and I have a wife and a son and a business to run. I'll leave the larger issues to somebody else."

"I'll send you a copy of the column," Teddy said.

"I don't think you have enough material for a column," Stein said with a tolerant smile.

"I've been accused of being wordy," Teddy said. He was silent a moment. "Don't you ever miss it?"

"Miss what?"

"The city. The sense of being in the center of things."

"No. I've nailed twenty times as many people with my computers as I ever did on the streets. And it's good, clean, safe work in a beautiful part of the country. No, I don't have any bad dreams. I don't miss it in the least."

Teddy ran thick fingers through his unruly thatch of hair. "Maybe I'm being too goddamn old-fashioned," he said. "But I don't find very much that's heroic to write about anymore. No man against man, no demonstrations of raw courage. 'Serial Killer Trapped by Computer.' That doesn't light my fires. The age of machines."

"Speaking of machines, my plane leaves in about an hour," Stein said. "And we haven't talked about you yet."

Teddy shrugged. "I'm old and crotchety," he said. "But my curiosity keeps me alive. I want to see how it all comes out."

Stein smiled. "Come down to West Virginia. The country air will do you good."

"I might do that sometime," Teddy said, but Stein knew that he would not. Because Teddy was a fixture here, surrounded in a bar by frantic people who were his audience as well as his subject matter. He was miserable, with a feeling of total uselessness, whenever he was away from the city.

And at the same time, Stein realized that there was nothing left for him here at all, and that with the death of his father, the last link with the city had been severed. He would not be back.

LAS VEGAS, NEVADA

Detective Picone crawled out of a cruiser on Tropicana Avenue before the morning warmth had turned to scorching heat, and he had difficulty even thinking about the case at hand, having left his ex-wife Mimi at the apartment, right in the middle of an argument. She had been defiantly and vocally angry at the unfairness of her life, of which he was the major cause. She poured coffee from an aluminum pot while she clutched the flowered silk wrapper around her and listed the sins of which he was guilty.

Unfortunately, Mimi had been born just on the edge of things. She was almost pretty enough to be a showgirl, but not quite, and her legs were well shaped but not quite long enough for her to make the line at the old MGM Grand. She had married Picone at the age of nineteen, intending to settle into a life of domesticity and children, only to learn that she couldn't have kids. By the time she realized that her marriage was going no place, some years had passed and she had begun to lose her figure, so she had left him in desperate pursuit of a career that had taken her no further than a short time as a keno runner, a cocktail waitress, and finally a blackjack dealer, where she wore a badge that said MIMI—CALIFOR-

NIA in deference to California customers (although she was originally from Rhode Island).

He wanted her back and she wanted to go back to him, but only after differences were negotiated, and there was never time to finish anything, never enough time to sort things through.

He stepped over the yellow Mylar ribbon that marked the crime scene, thinking that there was never time to finish a conversation with Mimi. He nodded to the boys from forensics, clicking along as they always did, led by the meticulous Adamson, who nitpicked everything to the point that everybody went crazy. Someday an impatient cop would break and shoot Adamson dead for taking just one minute too long, and no jury would convict. He was a fussy old maid of a man who was kidded behind his back for the labels on the baskets and drawers of his office desks—PENCILS here, FORMS F I there, everything in its place. He wore a dark serge suit despite the heat, the white collar of his shirt too large for his thin neck, his narrow face in a perpetual frown as he made sure the cameras got every angle of the bodies that were concealed from Picone by a hummock of sand, or with the slight waggle of a finger directed a team laying down resin in a tire-tread mark. Picone watched him roll his wrist, pull back his cuff to check his exposed watch. That meant Adamson was almost through here.

Picone studied the sand dunes topped with clumps of wiry grass against a brilliant blue sky. The sand occupied the greater part of a square mile, surrounded by apartments and a shopping center to the east and a large sign soliciting tenants for another shopping center to be built on this site. Just outside the Mylar line stood a twelve-year-old kid, sandy-headed, wearing a T-shirt that said UNLV and blue jeans cut off at the knees. He held a leash attached to the collar of a white mongrel that was a cross between a female English sheep dog and an unclassifiable sire. Picone would interview him shortly. He could tell the boy was bursting with the excitement and the drama of finding the bodies. This was as close as he would ever get to participating in the kind of bloody action he saw on the VCR movies with chain-saw massacres and murderous monsters loose on Halloween night.

Picone drifted over to where Rizzuto was studying the bodies laid out in the sand, three in a row. Rizzuto and Picone had worked together for seven years now, never socializing away from the job but treating each other with an easy professional respect. Picone was a tall and rangy man, quite content to process information and follow a by-the-book approach, always working toward the end of something, a case, a solution to a problem. Rizzuto was his opposite, a short, dark-skinned, third-generation Sicilian who wore heavy sunglasses and Italian silk sports coats and did a lot of standing around.

He scratched his chin, nodded at Picone, watched Adamson's crew packing up while the boys from the coroner's office waited impatiently with body bags and stretchers. Rizzuto always needed time at crime scenes. He claimed he could pick up vibes, having come from a superstitious family that believed in wizards and witches and the evil eye. Picone was tolerant because he halfway believed in Rizzuto's supernatural powers. After all, Rizzuto was excellent at spotting small things that proved to be significant and would have gone unnoticed by anybody else.

Rizzuto squatted down now beside the bodies, two men, one woman, all disparate types; the man on the left end of the row was Hispanic, fiftyish, purple sports coat, broad mustache, hair plastered down, new shoes of black patent leather, his face broad. Mestizo, Picone thought, a working man. There was a plain yellow pin in the lapel of his coat. He had died with a grimace, face all screwed up when the bullet went through his forehead. He had been sitting up when it happened. Rivulets of blood had snaked down his face, following natural lines to the right of the broad and protuberant nose.

Rizzuto turned his attention to the woman in the center, purse beside her in the sand, hands folded across her chest. All three bodies were parallel, laid out, hands on chest. The woman, wearing pale blue culottes and a matching polyester top, was in her fifties, heavyset, hair dyed brown, ringlets of a tight permanent coiled tightly against her scalp. She was obviously a woman who had not had an easy life and yet had retained a strong streak of vanity right to the end. The misshapen toes visible in the open vinyl sandles were tipped with vermilion to match her fingernails.

With the eraser end of a pencil, Rizzuto pulled up the little finger of her left hand to examine a red streak along the edge of her hand. He grunted, moved back slightly to examine the left hand of the Hispanic, then used the same pencil to slip back the lapel of the purple sport coat. No wallet in the inside pocket. He probed the inside of the woman's purse.

Picone looked at the face of the dead woman, expressionless, empty, vacant. The bullet that had killed her had entered the temple, loosed blood on the entire left side of her head, which had clotted in the matted curls and ringlets.

The third person in the line had obviously resisted dying. There was a scrape on the knuckles of his right hand, where he had struck at something or somebody and connected. He was Oriental, Japanese, Picone surmised, his features almost delicate, black hair cut short and bristly, and he was wearing a three-piece linen suit, the vest of which had been ripped in a struggle. He wore off-white leather loafers. He had been shot lying flat on his back. The blood had run from the forehead wound to collect in the hollows of his eyes, two caked and reddened spots like Kabuki makeup. Was there the faintest of residual scowls, a trace of irritation in those lifeless features?

Again, Rizzuto used the pencil to examine the left hand and then laid back the lapel of the linen jacket before he stood up with a grunt and nodded to the deputy coroner that he was through with the bodies. He moved to the beaten drive-path and cracked his knuckles.

"Okay," Picone said. "Run it down for me."

"We got us a real squirrel working here," Rizzuto said. "The lady's got a couple diamond rings, not top quality but hockable, and the Jap's wearing a presidential Rolex, good for a quick three grand on the street. But nobody's got a wallet."

"Gang," Picone said. No question, a prompt.

"Uh uh," Rizzuto said, shaking his head negatively. "This is compulsive shit we got here. We got a triple roll for cash and credit cards and the shooter leaves the goodies. But why the layout side by side? Why the execution style, two in the forehead, one in the temple?" Rizzuto lit a cigarette. "This guy's no ordinary squirrel. He marked his victims. Lipstick cross on the left palms."

Picone looked off toward the apartments gleaming to the west, at least a quarter of a mile away. Not a chance in hell anything would have been seen from there. Then across Tropicana, more apartments, and a half-mile east, the shopping center. "There's an all-night market down there," he said. "We'll canvass apartments, taxis, delivery services. Might get lucky."

"Yeah," Rizzuto said. He looked at the mobile crime van

pulling away just as a television van made a turn into Tropicana off Pecos Boulevard.

"One shot in the head?" Picone asked.

"A stingy shooter. Just one. Close range."

Picone went back to the boy, who was obviously waiting to be interviewed, and flipped open his small notebook and clicked a ballpoint pen, more to make the kid feel important than from any need to record information. The first officers on the scene would have the kid's name and address, but the boy would work a lot harder if he thought his words were being written down. "I'm Detective Picone," he said. "What's your name?"

"Harvey Attenborough," the kid said and proceeded to spell it slowly, as if he were used to having people stumble over the letters. And then he gave his address, an apartment off Tropicana, and volunteered the information that his father was a truck driver for United Van Lines, and his mother worked as a cashier in the grocery store down the street. It was no wonder the kid was starved for talk, Picone thought. He had but to grunt or nod his head and make marks in his notebook and the stream of words flowed out of the boy.

His dog was named Queenie and had something wrong with a leg joint, which meant that Harvey had to walk her slowly, keep her from getting in fights, see after her. Harvey had walked his mama to work this morning at six, and then he had come west on Tropicana. Queenie had begun to bark frantically, and Harvey had held her back and had seen the three bodies in the sand, from an angle, only their feet. He'd thought they were sleeping and was afraid Queenie might awaken them and they would raise hell. But Harvey had moved five feet closer and then had seen the blood.

"Did the blood frighten you?" Picone asked.

"I thought at first they were kidding. I mean, I saw some television people on the Strip one day, lots of shooting, you know, fake blood."

Picone drew a squiggly line in his notebook. "How did you know these people were really dead?"

"I didn't. I ran back to the store and Mama called the cops."

"And that's all of it?"

"Sure. I mean, what else would there be?"

"I was a kid myself," Picone said, improvising now but so smoothly he could have passed a polygraph, he had done this so often. "Once I saw a drunk on the street, I mean, out cold, and I figured, what the hell, somebody was going to roll him if they hadn't done it already. So I took his wallet out of his pocket, a couple of bucks in it, and I figured I'd hold it for him and maybe give it to the police. But I needed the two bucks more than he did, so I kept them and dropped the wallet in a trash can."

Harvey looked at him blankly.

"If you'd done the same with these people, I could understand that," Picone said. "You wouldn't get into any trouble, not if you admitted it to me."

Harvey shuddered slightly. "I didn't take nothing off them. I mean, what if they had been zombies, not dead at all?"

"You got a point," Picone said. He looked out over the hummocks of sand, crowned with sparse grass, an occasional thorny shrub. A squad of uniforms was making a sweep of the whole undeveloped area in the distance and a last man was rolling up the Mylar tape. "You ever play out there in the dunes?" Picone asked the kid.

"No," Harvey said. "I don't like sand."

"You walk your mama to work every morning?"

"Most of 'em."

"You ever see people sleeping out here in the dunes?"

"You mean the homeless," Harvey said.

A definite television kid, Picone thought. Savvy to the truth in some areas, overly imaginative in others. "Yeah, the homeless."

"Once or twice," the kid said. "Last winter. A man, a woman, and a couple of kids. They used to build a bonfire. But nobody since then. Most of them sleep closer to downtown."

"You're right. Anything else you can think of?"

"Like what?"

"You seen any moving vehicles out here?"

"Only land-moving equipment, the big dirt movers, but they was over closer to the shopping center."

"I see. Well, if anything comes to you, I want you to give me a call. Anytime. Night or day." He took a card from his pocket, wrote his home number on the back.

Harvey looked at the card like a relic from the true cross. "Yes, sir. I will."

Picone turned back to the deserted crime scene, where the bagged bodies were being loaded into an ambulance while the TV

24

minicam operator scampered to get coverage. Rizzuto had already gone and Picone recognized the good-looking woman from Channel 5 with the fantastic body and the Ann-Margret smile. Her name was Barbra, without a middle *a*, at least publicly, and she had been here for three years now. He liked her because she reminded him so much of Mimi. She was always pleasant, with a gift for ad-libbed phrases developed in twenty years before the news cameras in Des Moines and Albuquerque and Waco, Texas. Las Vegas was probably going to be the last stop for her, so the cameras avoided tight close-ups of her face, not only to avoid the tracery of lines around the eyes but the subtle and constant hint of desperation. She spotted him and came across the sand.

"Good morning, Barbra," he said.

She balanced on a high heel in the loose sand, looked down at the impressions the three bodies had made, almost indistinguishable from the surrounding hollows now that the forensic crew had literally scooped off the top layer and sifted down six inches. "Want to make a picture?"

"I'd love to, honey," he said. "But you know the rules."

"We could always get pictures and I can do a voice-over later."

"And my lieutenant would have me for breakfast," he said with a smile. "Anything you had would look like it came from me."

"Can you fill me in off-camera?"

"Three bodies," he said. "Shooting victims. No leads. But you got a first-class source in the kid over there." Her eyes moved to Harvey, who still stood gawking at the prowling cameraman.

"He found the bodies, right?" she said. "I know that a woman at Safeway called in. That's her kid, right?"

"You got it," he said. "He's a perfect interview, a real walking TV addict."

"How long before your lieutenant puts out a release?"

"This afternoon sometime."

"You're a sweetheart," she said and she touched his shoulder and was off toward Harvey in a second, waving to her cameraman to gather him in.

Picone headed for his car, feeling melancholy, not because of the murders particularly—the victims were beyond feeling—but for Mimi, who was bereft because she felt she had missed the illusive "it" she had wanted so desperately, and for this Barbra with the missing *a*, who had now slipped from the prestigious evening news to the throwaway noon slot and would not make it back. And finally, although he tried to avoid self-pity, for himself, because in this business, there were precious few clear-cut answers and no happy endings at all.

Rizzuto had already ordered his eggs *ranchero* by the time Picone went into Denny's and sat down at the table in the smoking section. Rizzuto had a cigarette going even as he ate, occasionally taking a drag between bites. Picone ordered scrambled eggs and ham and then nursed a black coffee. Rizzuto chewed and swallowed, washed down the bite with coffee, took a drag on the cigarette.

"That's going to kill you," Picone said. "You know that?"

"The caffeine neutralizes the nicotine."

"Bullshit."

Rizzuto sipped his coffee again. "I just got a prelim from Adamson."

"How'd you do it? You blackmailing the son of a bitch?" Picone said. Adamson was particularly tight with information until his final report was perfectly typed, three-hole-punched, and placed in a perfectly labeled black notebook.

"He's got a puzzler and we're going to unravel it for him and make him look good."

"Nothing can make him look good." The ham was rubbery but mercifully thin. Picone finished chewing, swallowed. "What's the puzzle?"

"A killer who goes for cash and credit cards and leaves merchandise is usually in a hurry. This guy took his time. But this guy was also handy with a knife."

"How so?"

"He cut crosses into the left palms of the victims."

"Crosses?"

"That's not all of it. He made a shallow cut all the way across the left hands and from the junction of the second and third fingers down to the end of the thumb pads. But then he took a lipstick and marked over the cuts." He took a drag on his cigarette, exhaled the smoke. "All three the same. First the crosscut in the skin and then the lipstick lines over the cuts."

"Jesus."

"You're the gang expert. Any of them leaving markers like that?"

"No way," Picone said. "It's not even possible. I think we got us a nut."

Rizzuto shrugged. "Adamson's going to go bananas on this one. He goes out of his gourd when he's got evidence that doesn't have some kind of logical explanation."

"If it was a nut, how did he work it?" Picone asked, almost to himself. "How did he haul the Mex and the woman in without a fight? The Jap evidently made a try. There might be scrapings under his fingernails." He doused his eggs with Tabasco and had another go at them. The incongruity of the moment was not lost on him, that he should be talking mortal struggles, skin and hair caught beneath fingernails, while he wolfed down eggs and Tabasco and tough ham. "Has Adamson made the tires?"

"The tire's a 23575R15 Goodyear Vector," Rizzuto said. "Fits a hell of a lot of cars. Pickups, vans, too."

"Why don't we fade into the background on this one and let Adamson make the calls?" Picone said. "He needs a chance to look good."

"You're all heart," Rizzuto said. "Letting him have the credit."

"I have a feeling this case is going to be a real bitch," Picone said. "If anybody's going to have his ass burned on this one, I can't think of a better man. Besides, I'm in this business for the money."

Picone was fond of the new city hall, which he liked to think of as an architectural handmaiden among the glittering neon whores of the nearby casinos. The city hall projected a tall white half-cylinder of a tower to the world, topped with a floor of smoky glass, and on the straight side, a reflecting pool and the glass-fronted floors of the building that housed the police. He enjoyed his space in the squad room on the third floor, a desk and files with wall space, where he thumbtacked newspaper clippings, departmental orders, and reminders to himself.

He like to spend his time on the streets, among the transients, the bums, who were his particular assignment. There were occasional bursts of violence among the floaters, killings from drugs, robberies, and recently a death of a sleeper in the sand who had been too drunk to be aroused by the roar of a giant earth mover that slowly rolled over him. He spent a few hours running his informants. The word of the triple homicide had spread through the streets, but he was willing to stake his career on the sure belief that none of his people had any information. There was not even a hint of gang involvement, no leads on any new transients who were exhibiting crazy behavior.

He put in a call to Ramona in the crime lab. He couldn't remember her last name, but she was a study in contradictions, a big and showy blonde who always dressed in flaring skirts and wore her hair in outrageous hues of pink and blue. She gave the impression of an irresponsible scatterbrain, yet when she sat down with a microscope and her chemical tests, the end result was as perfect a report as a prosecutor could wish.

She called back to let him know that she had analyzed the cuts in the hands of the victims and could give him a time sequence. The woman had definitely been cut first, because her blood type was O and the Mexican's was AB and there were traces of O in the AB wound. The Japanese had been cut last. In her expert opinion, all three cuts had been made by the same person. The depth of the wounds was approximately the same; an equal pressure had been applied to the knife each time. Too, she had found in the wounds microscopic particles of a glue made from a resin base, plus traces of cellulose. This meant that the knife (for she was certain it was a type of two-edged stiletto blade rather than a razor) had been used to cut through the tape that sealed shipping boxes. She couldn't identify the glue formulas, which were too similar to isolate any single box company. The lipstick was Revlon, a shade called Orange Glow, definitely from the dead woman's lipstick.

"I could kiss you, Ramona," he said. "Splendid work."

"Promises, promises," she said, and such was the warmth of her voice that he almost believed her.

Early afternoon and Picone and Rizzuto sat opposite each other at a conference table. They were the detective team assigned to this case and they had long since learned not to sit together where Sergeant Jones could bracket them with his glare. Jones was a beefy man in his forties whose jaws were in constant motion against a wad of gum as he fought the urge to smoke. He had a way of fixing the person in front of him with a slightly hostile look, unblinking blue eyes fixed on the subject while his jaws continued to move in a slow, grinding motion, and many were the men who were broken by that stare.

He sat at the right hand of God the Father, who occupied the end seat—Captain Owenby, commander of the Detective Bureau, an *éminence grise* who loved the position in which he found himself, between the hierarchy above him and the foot soldiers below, a man wise to maneuvering who was currently in the center of the battle with the city council to raise the police budget. His head was square; his hair, a short-cropped iron gray; he had a special alertness about him, as if no pertinent fact, however small, was going to get by him. The second most important person in the room was Homicide's Lieutenant Farley, who sat at the opposite end of the table, lean, intense, tanned. His right hand doodled circles on a yellow legal pad, nesting circles that resembled bullet holes on the paper.

There were screwed-up undercurrents in this meeting, Picone thought, influences that could not be spoken but that had to be coped with anyway. And paramount was the effect of this zappy mass murder on the people who lived here, the city council, and the budget. The gambling interests wouldn't give a damn because nothing could hurt them. Even a massacre in the middle of Fremont Street wouldn't break the rhythm of the slots, and the casino drops would not suffer at all. Not one tourist reservation would be canceled, but to city residents, already fretting over a CBS documentary that had pictured the police as good-natured dolts adrift in a sea of unchecked teenagers, drifters, and perverts, this crime would have significance and be used either for or against the increased budget.

"All right," the captain said, opening the meeting. "What we got?"

"Triple homicide," the sergeant said, laying out the essential facts, consulting the field interviews plus the preliminary coroner's report. Picone listened intently. No drugs had been found in any of the victims. The reports covered the cause of death, the recovery of one 9-mm slug that had remained in the skull of the Japanese. The three had been killed separately, elsewhere, then hauled in one at a time and the bodies placed in a line. There were three separate sets of comparatively fresh tire tracks, some of them overlapping, plus remnants of a fourth made sometime earlier, probably when the shooter was looking around for a display site in the sand. The murders had been punched into the computer keyed to the address on Tropicana, but only three felons had kicked out of the data base, none of them for homicide. Two of them had moved out of the apartments on Tropicana within the past couple of years, and the third was an old woman who had been convicted of stealing Social Security checks and had done her time.

The sergeant turned his glare to Rizzuto. "You got a pair ID'd, right, Detective?"

Rizzuto consulted his typed sheet. "We got lucky with the Mexican. His name was Federico Gonzalez, Whittier, California, and he came up on an all-night freebie from L.A. called 'Bunch of Fun.' When the bus began to load to go back, his wife got panicky and the tour leader tried to calm her down, but she insisted on calling the police. The rest of the group went back to L.A., but she stayed behind, and when her husband was found she identified the body."

"You get anything out of her?" the lieutenant asked.

"They argued all the way up on the bus, so he split when they got here. I got a request out for the names of the other tour members. Detective Picone got a make on the female victim."

The collective eyes swung toward him. "Mary Alice Phillips," Picone said dryly. "Age sixty-two, a member of the Gambling Girls Senior Tour from Sioux City, Iowa. Made her on a fluke. She was diabetic, missed her insulin; tour leader called in for help in locating her. Last seen at the Dunes progressive dollar slots at ten o'clock on the night she died. We made her room. Absolutely nothing. I talked an hour ago to her only relative, a sister in Iowa. No troubled waters there, no exes, no kids, just a lady living on her pension and hoping for jackpots."

The captain seemed to hum, lips pursed. "What about background on the Mex?"

"Nothing," Picone said. "Janitor at a municipal building for thirty years. Never in any difficulty. Good marriage, three kids. The Mex met his trouble here. He didn't bring it with him."

"The Japanese," the captain said.

"Nothing," the sergeant said.

"What you mean nothing?" the Captain asked. "My God, we got two low profiles that you made in nothing flat, no secrets, and you got one high-rolling Oriental wearing gold chains and a Rolex, eight grand retail, and five-hundred-dollar shoes and you don't know anything about him?"

"You got it right, Captain," Picone said. "We notified the Japanese consulates in San Francisco and L.A., as well as the feds, but you know the snags. If he's here on his own, it may be weeks before we have any unhappy relatives tracking him. If he's on a tour, we may get a break. I've circulated ID flyers to the major Asian tour operators coming into Vegas."

"The weapon?" the Captain asked.

"Nine-millimeter Beretta," the sergeant said. "The Jap also had a hard blow on the head."

The captain leaned back in his chair, patted his fingertips together soundlessly, went down his mental check list, methodically. Picone had worked with the old man long enough to read his mind. He wouldn't miss anything. Forensics had been thorough. The depths of the tracks implied a truck or van, light load. Hand cuts definitely made with a stiletto sharpened on both sides of the blade. Crime site unusually clean, not even the normal amounts of wastepaper, empty cans, bottles, and condoms. The captain blew his nose, doubled over his handkerchief before he returned it to his pocket.

"Gang involvement?" he asked.

"No, sir," Picone said. "Whoever did this didn't even try to make it look gang-related."

"How many men we have on this?"

"Seventeen," the sergeant said.

The captain nodded, looked to the lieutenant. "Media requests?"

"It's drawn a hell of a lot of attention. Networks, local TV, wire services, both newspapers."

"Channel Five has minimum tape coverage," Picone said. "Barbra without the middle *a* showed up just as we were cleaning up. Her noon coverage had standard shots, bodies into the ambulance, interview with the kid who found the victims."

"We won't sweat that," the captain said. "We're going to need a press release, Lieutenant, and we're going to play it down. There was no money on any of the victims, so we can assume robbery. Let it out that we expect a break in the case at any time. Nothing big or out of the ordinary and definitely nothing kinky. Hold the details about the slashed hands. I don't want any satanic cult shit getting started and we have to have something to screen out the compulsive confessions." He lit a cigarette with great care, taking a match from a matchbook that he closed before he struck a flame. "Now, you have a man who's good at fielding confessions, Sergeant?"

"Yes, sir. Abernathy."

"Get him started on this. All calls through him. And you boys are going to be approached for inside information by council members, civic groups, maybe even the governor himself. And you're going to toss the ball to Lieutenant Farley, politely, frankly, because this is a well-run, well-disciplined department and that's the way things are done. One source of official information. No gossip, tips, or leaks. No interviews, no verbal asides. We accumulate questions and Lieutenant Farley issues written releases. So we always know exactly what goes out. Clear?" He looked from man to man for assent, then stood up. "Let's get this goddamn time bomb defused," he said. "Let's put this fucker away. Would you say forty-eight hours, Lieutenant?"

"We'll do our best, sir."

"Then put that in the press release," the captain said just before he left the room. "We expect a break within forty-eight hours."

CHARLESTON, WEST VIRGINIA

I t was three weeks before Stein received a copy of Teddy's column, folded neatly into a triptych and inserted into an envelope along with a note in Teddy's cursive writing, "Argue with me if you disagree," then signed with a simple *T.* The envelope came to the office and Stein meant to read it, but he was totally blitzed at the moment. The control board showed a document coming in from Atlanta on the facsimile machine, additional data from Atlanta on one computer, and data from Chicago on another.

He could hear Thatcher going into the main computer room, the heart of the operation, where the large units known as "jukeboxes" were kept at a constant temperature and humidity, metal cabinets seven feet high and nine feet long, loaded with hundreds of large optical discs that held billions of bytes of information in permanent storage.

Stein was fascinated by the machines and what they would do, but from the moment Thatcher had left the Pennsylvania state police and come to West Virginia to work with Stein, he had regarded the power of the machines with reverential awe and was constantly scouring the country for new software to feed into the system on a trial basis, staying late at night until Alice had issued her ultimatum. If Thatcher wanted to preserve his marriage of long standing, he would have to show his wife as much care as he lavished on the machines and admit that there was a world outside the walls of this building.

Stein shared his enthusiasm, even though he kept his work in balance with his life at home. He knew that he and Thatcher were part of a revolution in police work, and it was possible that in the next few years a detective seated at a terminal anywhere in the country would be able to solve a complex multiple-state case in minutes that would have taken months to break before computerization, if it was ever broken at all. Their operation was almost fully automated, and around-the-clock data was being fed into their computers from around the country by a government mainframe known as the Big Hummer, holding data banks so large they were unable to store them in this building.

Thatcher came stalking into the control room, mumbling to himself. He flopped his lanky body into a leather chair in front of a work station, started a printer chattering, glanced over at the FAX.

"I'm printing out the FI's on the Atlanta lady-killer. The incoming FAX should be a mug shot of our suspect." He fiddled with his pipe, a leather pouch of tobacco, the whole business of smoking that Alice hated passionately and that was strictly forbidden at home and in the larger computer rooms, leaving Thatcher to light up whenever he had the chance.

Stein checked the FAX, the picture quickly emerging. "It's coming through," he said. The first stray dots near the top of the page elongated into a thatch of hair, and miraculously the whole face emerged onto the sheet, a broad forehead, a widow's peak, two horizontal thickets of eyebrows that almost met in the center, and then the eyes, large, oval, with a hint of the Mideast. The lady-killers always seemed to have large eyes. Now the bags emerged beneath the eyes, puffy cheekbones. No young buck this. The mouth had a hint of a smile, as if even the police camera coaxed forth a faint charm.

When the picture was finished, the Atlanta ID number was printed across the bottom. Stein tore off the picture and stuck it into a scanner that would break it down for the computer and compare it with hundreds of composite faces drawn of suspects in multiple cities and stored in his memory banks over the years. He had the feeling they would pick up a number of matches. This man had a name, of course, perhaps a dozen of them, but in the system here, he would be 779-A, the numerals identifying him and his crime, the letter code for the city in which he had been apprehended. So 779-A was a man who married elderly females and killed them. *A* was the code for Atlanta.

Thatcher sighed, puffed his pipe once more, and abandoned it to an ashtray before he approached the keyboard again. "I'll run it through," he said.

Stein nodded and retreated to his office, where he poured himself a cup of coffee and sat down at his desk, looking at the racks that held the computer printouts like linen hung on a line. Through the open door, he looked into the deserted reception room with its glossy desk of chrome and glass and walls of books on forensics and computer applications. Originally, when they had first leased the small building on the hill up from the river, the reception room had been occupied by a glossy girl named Helen, who was to answer the telephone. The names STEIN AND THATCHER had been painted in gold on the glass door. Both Helen and the names had since been removed. The telephone calls came in to be recorded on an answering machine and all the substantial messages arrived by electronic mail. The names on the door were useless. The police departments in need of their services knew where to find them; the names had attracted nothing but inquiries from people looking for CPA's or lawyers.

He removed Teddy's column from the envelope, smoothed it out on the table with his fingers, and from the first word, realized he was reading it on two levels, not only as Teddy had written it, objectively, but as Karen would react to it when she eventually saw it. And she would see it, of course. What he had told Teddy was not exactly true. Few people in Charleston read *The New York Times,* but among those who did would be one who eventually would mention it to Karen and save her a clipping.

Teddy had written:

Three men died this week, one in a nursing home in Yonkers and the other two in the lobby of a Brooklyn building. Isaac Stein was a very old man who survived the Holocaust in Dachau, only to spend the last five years of his life in

35

what we may presume is the dream world of the very old, where reality is ephemeral and few differences in the environment are perceived at all. One of the men who died in Brooklyn was Mickey Waters, an elderly man who worked as a part-time elevator dispatcher, and his death was brutal and heinous, killed by an ax in the hands of a psychotic named W. W. Burr. Burr was the third man to die, killed by an off-duty policeman shortly after the murder.

Two of the dead men had something in common. The old man was the father of former detective Peter Stein, who left the NYPD a number of years back to set up a law-enforcement consultancy service in the peaceful countryside near Charleston, West Virginia. W. W. Burr was the last psychotic brought in by Stein, a New York cop who specialized in attacking the increasing problem of the random killers, the psychotics, the often flamboyant and always publicized criminals who seem to kill for reasons only fully understood by psychiatrists. Stein became known on the force as "the monster catcher," and perhaps would have continued his career except that in a final attack made by W. W. Burr, Stein was severely wounded. This happened before he wrested the weapon from Burr in the kitchen of a modest Pennsylvania house, and then—inexpicably in the eyes of many—allowed this verminous murderer of young women to stay alive, when, with a single stroke of the ax, he could have dispatched him and thereby eventually spared the life of a gentle man who worked only to supplement his Social Security.

But the point of this column, the subject under consideration, is not the personalities involved as much as it is a look at evil as a philosophical concept, whether it truly exists, and how it should be treated in modern society. To Isaac Stein, evil was a certain reality, for evil men implemented an individual belief, and his relatives were gassed in German showers and turned to ashes in German crematoria. You could read his belief in his eyes, long after he lost the ability to speak. It was only logical, therefore, that Isaac Stein's son should have become an official combatant of evil, having seen its existence so tragically confirmed in the death of his relatives.

Yet this week, when Peter Stein was in Queens for his father's funeral and I talked to him about the death of W. W.

Burr, I was startled by the basic beliefs of the man responsible for apprehending scores of the bloodiest villains New York has ever seen. "I don't believe in the existence of evil, per se," Stein said. "In all my years on the force, I never believed that a murderous psychosis was any more than a chemical imbalance, a condition that can be cured."

"And if you had it to do over again," I asked him, "you still would have allowed W. W. Burr to live?"

"Yes," Stein said. "It's tragic he was allowed to walk away from a hospital and even more tragic that he should have killed again, but I'm more certain than ever that sooner or later, science would have come up with a treatment to return W. W. Burr to normal."

Stein sighed and scanned the rest of the article, a long one that asked a rhetorical question that Teddy was only too anxious to answer. There was indeed a class of people in the world who were best described as evil, people who had done so much harm, created so much havoc and human suffering, that even if a so-called corrective cure was found for this condition, they should be forced to pay for their crimes. Peter Stein had begged the question by removing himself from the streets and the arena, as it were, but his father certainly would have given his solution to the problem without hesitation. For as this one psychotic had slipped loose and murdered again, there were nations that could not be trusted, as well. The only sure cure for evil was its eradication, swift and certain retribution, which, if it had come in time from the democratic nations of the world, would have spared history the Holocaust.

Ah, Teddy, he thought without rancor. You always have to tidy up, don't you? Even if it involved moving Stein's words around somewhat to make the point Teddy had in mind. And this time, Teddy had included Stein in one of his summing-ups—as a man who had chosen to avoid the problem by removing himself from it. He had to admit that Teddy was at least partially correct. After the Burr incident, Karen needed the healing quiet of a place like Charleston, where she had found a good therapist and had no bad memories. He had picked West Virginia to establish his new company because many of the government computers had been installed in the West Virginia mountains and he could be assured of a pool of qualified technicians to keep them running. His choice had nothing to do with good and evil. Only incidentally had come the bonus with his choice—a home in some of the loveliest countryside in the world.

He went home early and found Karen in that part of the solid cherry-wood barn that she had converted into a studio with a huge Thermopane window looking down a timbered valley toward the river. The studio was in disarray, canvases and drawings everywhere. On a drafting table was a sketch for the greeting card company in New York that bought her drawings of stylized children and nature scenes and paid good money for them. But now, she stood in front of an easel and a canvas decorated with swirls and loops of raw color, a painting that he enjoyed because she took such pleasure in it. She kissed him briefly and then stood back and studied the canvas carefully. He opened the small refrigerator and took out two bottles of beer for their afternoon ritual.

"Where's Barney?" he said, popping the lids.

"Over at Jeff's house, where they have a new colt," she said. "The mare dropped a foal this morning. Barn was awed by the whole process." She added a final touch of white to the painting. "He's going to hit you up for a horse."

"How do you know?"

"He takes it for granted that I'm on his side. He asked me to plan his strategy."

Stein smiled. "You give him any advice?"

"I told him to use a direct approach. Cards on the table. Just ask the question."

"You ready for a beer? If you are, kindly lead the way."

"After your comment on the painting."

"Spectacular," he said.

"You said that on the last one."

"No, I said the last one was stupendous."

She opened the French doors onto an attached deck, and he handed her a beer, suddenly very pleased with his life. The sunlight caught in her finely spun brown hair. She had become prettier with each year that passed, although she didn't believe it and protested whenever he told her so. There was an ease about her now that had been lacking even before the trouble with Burr, which had sent her into a deep shock. No, he had made no mistake in bringing her into these hills. He sat down in a canvas deck chair with Karen next to him. "Now, what do you really think of my new paintings?"

"I love 'em," he said. "I'm no connoisseur of fine art, but I look at your paintings and they make me feel good."

"That's the best kind of praise," she said. She took a long pull from the bottle. "Mr. Johnson came by to see you this afternoon."

"Johnson?"

"The man who puts up the crosses."

"Oh, that Mr. Johnson," he said. The beer was cold. Johnson was a marvelous, soft-spoken old man with one good eye and a sense of mission. He had followed the example of a man upstate and had created hundreds of groups of three Christian crosses on prominent hills and ridges all over West Virginia and into Kentucky, a vocation that Stein considered to be a fine eccentricity. "Did he say what he wanted?"

"Nope," she said. "Typical country gentleman. He wasn't about to confide his business to the missus of the family."

He was quiet a moment, drinking his beer, looking down into the cool shadows of the valley. "Are you happy here, babe?"

"Very," she said. "What woman could ask for more?"

"And the past?"

"You mean the nightmares?"

"Yes."

"They're gone. Knock wood. It's been six months since I had one."

"Teddy wrote another piece about me in the *Times,*" he said quietly. "It just came out."

"Good old Teddy," she said with a smile. She put her hand on his. "And you're afraid it will upset me, aren't you?"

"The thought occurred to me," he said. "But somebody's bound to mention it to you sooner or later."

"What does Teddy have to say?"

"You don't want to read it?"

"No. I want you to tell me."

"W. W. Burr died."

She was suddenly silent. She shivered, almost as if she had been jolted by an invisible electric current. She shook her head back and forth, slowly, as if this were something it would take a while to absorb. "Are you sure?"

"Yes." He told her: the escape from the mental hospital, the killing of the elevator dispatcher, and Burr's being shot to death. And then he was aware of changing the subject and shifting the emphasis. "Teddy's still dealing with his struggle over good and evil."

But she was not diverted. "You're absolutely positive he's dead."

"I saw his body. Does it upset you?"

"Some," she said. "This is going to take some time to sink in, I guess. The therapists have all helped me move past the fear of his getting loose and coming after us again, and I've done that." She was quiet a long moment, the sunlight rich on her fair skin as she looked off down the valley. "I've been conditioned to work against the fear, and now there's no reason to be afraid anymore, is there?" She tasted her beer. "He's not even in this world anymore. So we're finally safe."

"Yes. Absolutely."

She nodded, accepting. "Then we won't ever mention him again. Now, I want to talk with you about my paintings."

He was surprised at the intensity of the relief he felt. He had dreaded mentioning Burr at all and was enormously pleased that she had adjusted so quickly and was ready to move on. "Shoot," he said.

"I don't have any pretensions toward great art," she said. "But when I was talking with Andrew the other day about the new card designs, I asked him what he knew about the market for corporate art, not the Wyeths and the Motherwells but the kind of paintings I call office decorator art, and I sent him a Polaroid of some of the new paintings and he thinks they're great as well as commercial. He wants me to take some samples to a dealer in Washington who buys for new company headquarters' buildings."

"Wonderful," he said. "I'll have to go over in a couple of weeks. Why don't we take Barn to the zoo while we're at it?"

"I'd love it," she said. She looked at him, her face radiant. "That will give me time to pick the best of the lot to take with me."

He finished his beer, relaxed. The shadows of the past were indeed gone.

You're wrong, Teddy. I don't miss the old world at all, he thought.

Barn came home just before dark, with Wolf running in wide circles around the yard and barking wildly, as if to let the world know that he and Barn had arrived. After checking with his mother to find out that supper would be ready in fifteen minutes, Barn went out to the utility shed, where Stein was dipping a coffee can into a bag of dry dog food while Wolf circled the small metal building, his way of announcing that he was hungry.

"I hear you've had an exciting day," Stein said. Barn followed him back outside and watched Stein fill Wolf's dish and then put the empty can back on a shelf.

"Yeah," Barn said. "They got a good deal, Dad."

"What kind of good deal is that?" he said.

All the way back to the house and through the ritual of hand washing and sitting down to supper, Barn's pitch was relentless and indirect. Stein looked at his amused wife with an expression that said, So much for cards on the table. For a six-year-old, Barn was amazingly articulate on the subject of horses and how practical they were. You never had to feed one because horses ate grass and they mowed the lawn for you, and if your car ever broke down, they provided transportation. The horse talk lasted all through dinner and Stein finally agreed to look into the possibility of a pony (no promises). Barn was pacified enough to settle down to arithmetic flash cards before watching television. Stein carried his briefcase into the pine-paneled den to deal with the day's mail. Generally, he spent the hour after dinner filling out the reports that were always attached to government grants. Tonight, he had a questionnaire from the Bureau of Justice Administration to complete, but the telephone rang before he could open his briefcase.

"Stein here," he said.

The voice on the line was hesitant, troubled, steeped in caution. "Mr. Stein, my name is Father John Rowan. I'm associate priest at St. Justin Martyr in Las Vegas, Nevada."

"What can I do for you, Father?"

"I'm not quite sure," the priest said. "I'm on my way to see

41

my sister in Washington, D.C., but I had to stop here. On a hunch as it were. This may seem very peculiar to you, sir, but I need to know if you received something in today's mail which you found puzzling."

"I was just getting ready to go through it," Stein said.

"Then let's put it this way. If you find that you want to talk to me, I'm staying at the Ramada Inn and you can call me back. If there is no such troubling mail, then I'm sorry to have disturbed you."

"What's this all about?" Stein asked. "Is this some kind of joke?"

"I wish it was," the priest said. "But I'm afraid it's not."

"I'll call you back either way," Stein said. He leaned back in his chair and thumbed through the letters, the big majority of them from the FBI or Justice, a few mail queries from departments too small to have computers yet. Then he picked up a manila envelope, eight by ten, which had been folded over and held in place by Scotch tape. On the front was written—in large block letters—DET. PETER STEIN, and no address except CHARLESTON, WEST VIRGINIA. But the boys at the post office were used to mail addressed to him in peculiar ways and it had been delivered to his home.

He slit the tape with his penknife and opened the envelope to find a packet of Polaroid pictures, a brown stain on the corner of each. He felt a twitch of visceral revulsion. He did not touch the face of the pictures but used a pair of tongs from the desk drawer to separate them. The first shot showed three bodies, side by side in what appeared to be a desert, and each of the victims had been shot in the head before being laid out as if for viewing at a funeral parlor. The other pictures were close-ups, bloodied faces in varied degrees of distortion. He used the tongs to open a paper wrapping that contained three driver's licenses, two of them laminated state cards and the third the green paper of an international driver's license, made out in the name of the Japanese man in the pictures, who would have no further need for it.

He heard Karen laughing in the other room as she kidded around with Barn, and the presence of these pictures felt infectious and obscene. The sickness had spread into his home via an envelope and he was willing to bet that the brown stains on the corners of the photographs were blood, as if the murderer had taken a picture of each of the victims and then dipped each photograph into the subject's blood. He searched through the desk for a supply of glassine envelopes, and then used the tongs to bag the pictures and the licenses individually, even placing the wrapping paper into a larger glassine container of its own. He examined the collection for a written message that might explain why these things had been sent to him, but there was none. It made no sense.

He was suddenly cautious. He dialed Las Vegas information for the number of St. Justin Martyr. When he rang the church, a nun answered. He asked to speak to Father John Rowan.

"He's on vacation, sir. He should be back next week."

He thanked the nun and then dialed the Ramada Inn, and when the priest came on the line, he wasted no time. "You obviously know what I received in the mail," he said. "Now, what the hell is going on?"

"Along with the photographs, did you get three driver's licenses?"

"Yes."

"Can you meet me down here in half an hour? I'm sorry to inconvenience you, Mr. Stein, but something terrible has happened and I don't know how to handle it."

"Have you notified the police in Las Vegas?"

"I'll explain all that when I see you. I won't take much of your time."

"All right, then. Thirty minutes."

"I'll be in the restaurant."

He would not tell Karen about this because it would only upset her. It was his duty to check in with the West Virginia state police on the infrequent occasions when he learned about an unreported crime, but it could wait until after he had talked with the priest. He put the glassine envelopes into his briefcase, told Karen he would be back in an hour, promised to bring a half-gallon of Heavenly Hash ice cream as the price for allowing his work to interrupt an evening.

He had no trouble spotting the priest in the restaurant, a middle-aged man in a blue suit, showing signs of a long journey. He had a long face, tanned, short brown hair, and the most troubled expression Stein had seen in some time. He stood up as Stein approached and shook hands, then sat down again. "I'm feeling as pale as I look and I'm going to have a drink. Can I buy you one?"

"Not at the moment."

The priest ordered a Scotch and soda as Stein sat down across from him.

"Okay, Father," Stein said. "Now, what's this all about?"

The priest took a newspaper clipping from his pocket. After he had unfolded it, he pushed it across the table. It was an account of a crime in Las Vegas, Nevada, from the week before, a picture of the same three victims whose pictures he had in his briefcase.

He read the story, nodded, then removed the glassine envelopes from the briefcase and waited until the priest had been served his drink before he placed the pictures and the licenses on the table. The priest looked at them wearily, shook his head. "My God," he said. "He really did do it. I thought he had but I couldn't be sure until now."

"He?" Stein said. "You know who did this?"

"In a sense."

"What does this have to do with me?" Stein asked. "Why have I been singled out?" And now the thought occurred to him, improbable, but he had to know. "You can tell me this much. Is there a possibility the man is from here? There's an old man who puts up crosses . . ."

The priest shook his head. "No," he said. "This isn't an old man. He doesn't have an accent. I can tell you that much."

"Then what's his connection with me?"

"He said that would become clear to you after a while."

"And?"

"I'll talk about that in a moment, but first, I have to know if you're a Catholic."

"No."

"Do you believe in God?"

"That's a discussion that can wait until another time."

"No," the priest said. "It's very germane to what's happening, to your understanding of it."

"I haven't the slightest idea what you're talking about."

"Then perhaps I should explain my predicament." The priest ran the tip of his index finger around the rim of the glass. "Have you ever heard of the poison in the chalice theorem? It's something that young priests drive themselves crazy with at seminary, but it makes an important point."

"Which is?"

"The posed question is what a priest would do if a man told

him during confession that he had poisoned the wine in the communion chalice. The proper answer is, of course, that the priest would have to hold the confession in such sacred confidence that he would have no choice but to drink the poisoned wine, because he has a sacred commitment not to act on any information gained in the confessional."

Stein ordered a bourbon and water. "Are you telling me that somebody confessed these murders to you?"

"I've never been faced with this problem before," the priest said, sipping his drink. "So I have to be very careful how I word this. But on the Friday after the murders, a man came to confession. He sat on his side and I sat deep in the shadows on mine. That's the point, after all, strict anonymity if the person confessing wants it. Anyway, the person told me certain things and I tried to persuade him to come forward for the good of his immortal soul. He refused. But he did tell me that he was going to send you some material. And he gave me permission to talk with you. He was very agitated and he said he had to see you."

"Ordinarily, I'm a very tolerant man," Stein said. "But I don't see how you can observe confidentiality in this case. Have you reported your conversation with this man to the police?"

"If I'm questioned by the police, I won't admit that there's been any conversation to talk about."

"And why does this person want to see me?"

"I don't know."

"How soon are you going back to Las Vegas?" Stein asked.

"A couple of days."

"I am going to put these pictures and licenses in the hands of the Las Vegas police. I am also going to tell them of our conversation."

The priest finished his drink. His face showed acute distress. "You're not taking my predicament seriously, then."

"Very seriously," Stein said. "But the larger issue takes precedence. Three people have been slaughtered and the psychopath who did it confesses to you and then sends me evidence to involve me in whatever fantasy he's created for himself. This isn't the first time that's happened. Sometimes the psychos write to me because they want to be caught and other times they write me because they want to play games with an ex-cop who's an expert in this particular field. It's a kind of crazy mental game of hide and seek. Only I won't play."

"This is no game."

"I don't have any sympathy with your point of view. This man obviously sat within two feet of you and confessed to bloody murder. And you could have opened that screen and taken one look and identified him."

"At the cost of my immortal soul."

"Then we damn sure have different priorities, Father. Because if I had the chance to save the lives of the people this nuthatch is going to kill at the cost of my soul, I'd make the trade."

The priest shook his head as if the whole business was too much for him. "Suppose the Las Vegas authorities ask for your help?"

"They'll get the same cooperation as any police department in the country would."

"Which is?"

"The most sophisticated computer workup available anywhere," Stein said. "I'll cross-reference this crime with any similar homicides nationwide. Plus personality assessment and profiles and whatever else we can do, since this crazy contacted me."

"But you won't go to Las Vegas?"

"No."

"I see," the priest said. "I want to ask you a favor then, Mr. Stein. It's up to you, of course, but I would very much appreciate it if you could forget that we talked. Believe me, the police would get nothing out of me and they probably wouldn't even try. They respect the seal of the confessional. But I want to continue my ministry in Las Vegas and that will be impossible if the word gets out that I've even told you as little as I have."

Stein considered a moment. "All right. I can live with that," he said. "Tell me something, Father. If this person ever contacts you outside the confessional, does the confidentiality still hold?"

"No. He's fair game outside the confessional."

"And the police can count on you if that happens?"

"Absolutely," the priest said. "As a matter of fact, I'd feel a great sense of relief. And now, I'd better be on my way." He stood up, bowed slightly rather than shaking hands, and Stein watched him leave the restaurant. He put everything back into the briefcase to send to Las Vegas by express mail in the morning. He found himself fretful. He would be relieved to get this package out of his hands as soon as possible and to free himself of this potential entanglement. He thought briefly of Teddy's accusation and admitted to himself that it was quite true. He had no desire to put himself in that grungy world again, one to one against the scrambled, unbalanced minds that expressed their grievances against society in bloody acts.

He paid the bill and then went in search of heavenly hash.

LAS VEGAS, NEVADA

Desmond opened the window of the small apartment across from the Convention Center and let the hot air ride in over the cold current from the air conditioner. He sat back in the cracked red vinyl of the chair in the room and willed a storm, wanting the warm air to roll into a visible cloud and rise toward the gray ceiling, where the rain would condense and begin to fall. But even though he squinched his eyes shut and rocked back and forth with his large fingers interlaced in a knot clamped beneath his knees, it did not happen.

Finally, he stood up and wandered through the small apartment, the single bedroom with a bath, where the plastic tile was beginning to peel from the wall above the tub, the linoleum worn in the tiny living room. He caught a glimpse of himself in the mirror, a large man, lumpy, ugly. He did not like looking at himself as he was now. Ugly. But at the moment, God needed an ugly man. Later, when he had done everything he was supposed to, God would let him look like Tom Cruise or maybe a younger Paul Newman.

He was restless, yes, and it was about time for him to do *it* again.

God was insatiable.

Desmond's mind was razor-sharp, and he tested it by adding a string of numbers without writing them down, certain his answer was correct. Razor-sharp, and so turned in upon itself he could feel the pain of his mind being cut by an imaginary blade. He should take the medicine but he did not want it. It dulled his thinking.

He stood by the window, pulled it shut, lit the last cigarette in the pack, carefully pressed the empty pack flat against the windowsill, smoothed it over with his fingers, folded it over once, absently, pressed it again. Had he sufficient power in his hands, he would have been able to keep folding the empty pack forever, condensing it until at last it was no larger than a speck of dust, but there were forces at work within the world that kept his power in check.

Nothing was happening across the street in the vast parking lots of the Convention Center, where the heat rose in waves from the burning concrete and the furnace of the desert beyond the city. He cooled himself in the blast from the air conditioner and then opened his wallet and counted the money he had left. Two hundred and eighty dollars, with a single one-hundred-dollar bill and the rest in twenties. He had to make up his mind how much he would put in the poor box at the church. He counted the money again. The hundred was crisp; one of the twenties was filthy, no telling where it had been, but it represented his pay after all, money for services rendered, albeit against the will of those he served. The Jap had paid his share, contributing the hundreds, but the Mexican had been flat broke save for a quarter in his pocket, and Desmond had put three dollar bills in his shirt pocket, only a gesture, of course, one for the Father, one for the Son, and one for the Holy Ghost.

Finally, he walked down to the Strip and onto the moving sidewalk that carried him into the cool dark of Caesar's Palace, through the slots and back to the roulette area. There were only three players at the table, a blond woman in a tight dress and two Japanese men in business suits who had smoked their cigarettes so short that their faces shrank from the heat and their fingers burned. He could smell the scorched flesh. He took the hundred out of his pocket, mentally asked the question, and then approached the table, where he put the hundred-dollar bill on the red.

"Play the hundred," he said to the bored croupier, who called into the shadows, "Playing the hundred." When the blonde had distributed her chips, he started the ball in its orbit while Desmond waited, staring up at the smoked glass above the table, at the reflection of the two Japanese. He wondered whether he should take another of them, but he was not so sure that God liked the Japanese, and besides, the one he had sent over to the other side was overly strong and wiry for his size, and Desmond had been lucky to be able to harvest him at all.

The ball bounced into place and the croupier pushed out the chips to match Desmond's bet. Desmond picked them up, enjoying the feel of them against his palm. He had received his answer, an obvious yes. He cashed them in at the cage and then walked down the Strip toward the church, looking for further messages in signs and bumper stickers and the names of streets. They were there for his benefit, of course, a mental puzzle waiting for a solution, letters in clusters by the dozens, waiting for him to find the answer to the larger question that haunted him.

The instructions were there, if he could just pick them out of the babble—HAVE A NICE DAY . . . WE ARE SPENDING OUR CHILDREN'S INHERITANCE . . . JESUS SAVES . . . TEXAS SUCKS. At the church, he stood outside the kitchen entrance for a long time, waiting until there was a break in traffic on the street, no pedestrians on the sidewalk, nobody to see him. Then he went in through a service door, approached the confessional from the blind side. He waited until a woman left before he slid into the small booth, dark, smelling slightly of sweat and perfume. He felt safe, very much at home, and he willed that the right priest should be on the other side of the filigreed screen. Then he said in a low voice the magic words, "Forgive me, Father, for I have sinned . . ."—the miracle words that would seal everything he said within this booth.

"You," came the muted voice from the other side.

"You were away for a long time," Desmond said. "I was beginning to get worried about you."

"You've had a lot of time to think about my suggestions," the priest said in a tight whisper. "You have to give yourself up."

"I don't have to do anything," Desmond said. "I'm waiting for a message from God, so don't tell me what I have to do."

"I've thought a lot about your problem," the priest said. "As a matter of fact, I haven't thought about much else."

"I don't have any problems you could understand."

"You murdered three people," the priest said. "You're in danger of losing your immortal soul."

"Don't worry about my soul," Desmond said. "Someday you're going to consider yourself lucky that you knew me. But I've been watching the papers and I haven't seen anything about Stein's coming here."

"He's not coming."

"He didn't remember, then. Or he pretended *not* to remember."

"Remember what?"

Desmond ignored the question. "Did he get the pictures?"

"Yes."

"He'll catch on sooner or later. And this has to come from him. I know things about him that nobody on earth knows."

"You've got to let me help you. I want you to give me your name and talk with me openly. Or at least give me permission to tell Stein everything about our conversations."

"You're giving me shit now, Father," Desmond said with a chuckle. "You ought to know I got a built-in shit detector when it comes to the Church."

"You will not use language like that here," Father Rowan said harshly.

"Okay, then I apologize."

"Perhaps if you come out into the open, he'll decide to come to Las Vegas."

"That's not very likely," Desmond said, disappointed. "And you know it. You don't encourage a sense of trust, you know that? There are times when I think you lie like a dog, but then, that's on your head. I'd give up trying to lie to me if I were you, because I get most of my questions answered directly."

There was silence from beyond the screen. Desmond examined his fingernails. He tried to keep them clean and well groomed, but his work kept his hands so dirty that sometimes he scrubbed them with Lava soap until his fingers bled and still he couldn't say his hands were clean. "One of these days, when I get ahold of the business, I'm going to buy myself a decent house. My job really doesn't pay enough to keep me going."

"And what kind of job is that?" the priest said in frustrated anguish.

Desmond ignored him. He sighed. "What will it take for me to get Stein here?" he said. "Would he come for a thousand dollars, ten thousand, what?"

"He's a very busy man."

"I know what he does and how busy he is," Desmond said, suddenly irritated. "I tell you what I'm going to do. You tell Stein that I'm going to harvest a soul every three days until he comes out here. And give him a clue. Tell him the answer is in the hands. If he doesn't get that, an awful lot of people are going to die."

"For the love of God," the priest said.

"Just tell him," Desmond said. "Now give me penance."

He listened to the priest's desperate voice, the number of novenas and Hail Marys, and then he slipped out of the booth, soundlessly, making certain he was unobserved as he went back through the kitchen to the street. He looked at the hands of his watch, which had stopped at a quarter of two, the hands like the transverse bar of a cross, slightly askew. It was time for him to go to work. He decided to walk to the warehouse rather than drive his car because he was getting his body used to the heat and walking more miles each day, for when his instructions came, they might involve walking across the desert, and he had to be ready.

The warehouse was old, decrepit, the walls thick and stout. The building had been put together in the old days, when things were built solid, and the kids had scaled the broken-down chain-link fence that surrounded the old loading dock and had sprayed graffiti on the stucco walls. The roof was made of corrugated tin that had lasted without rust in this desert climate for the past fifty years, and the loading dock was put together from old railroad ties that would be here even after the world had ended.

The interior of the building was a maze of corridors that connected a small office with windows, an unused cold storage room, a large, dark warehouse that was empty most of the time, and various smaller rooms quite sufficient to hold the declining inventory of this diminishing business.

Desmond walked up the steps by the old van and into the back door off the dock. Old Swanson was asleep in the small office. The air conditioner in the window sputtered along, working against the heat in the room, and an oscillating electric fan did its best to spread the cool air around the room. Swanson's big, veined hands were laced across his round belly, his feet propped solidly on the footrest of the wheelchair, legs useless. He was snoring when Desmond awakened him. Old. Seventy-five at least, two front teeth missing, still in business because he took accounts with which nobody else would bother. Some of his vending routes went back to the days when Las Vegas had been a dusty little fly speck on the map. Swannie came partially awake, waved a hand at a fly that buzzed across his face.

"I got it all on the list," he said. "You're going to need a couple cases of cigarettes, assorted. Then run the machines out near the dog track."

"How about booze?"

"I wrote it down. The liquor business is going to hell in a handbasket. We're getting undercut all the time. The little man ain't got the chance of spit on a griddle anymore." He fumbled with a pack of cigarettes, lit one. "And I want you to drive that van like it was a goddamned limousine, you hear? I sure as hell don't want to put on no new tires until fall."

"Yes, sir."

Swanson drifted back to sleep and Desmond just stood there, watching that tight, round gut of Swanson's, willing it to burst open like a watermelon, but he wasn't going to have that much luck. Swanson had no children, and ever since Desmond had gone to work for him the old man had promised that when he died, Desmond would get a crack at the business. But Desmond didn't believe him, because Swanson had a nephew and a sister who checked on him from time to time, and he pictured them as vultures wheeling around occasionally to see how close the old man was to the picking point.

Desmond took the list and wheeled the cases out of the warehouse to load the van. He counted out the cartons of cigarettes and added one for himself. The old man's remarks about the van were unfair, because Desmond took excellent care of the vehicle and saw that it was serviced regularly. Some nights when he couldn't sleep, he went down to the warehouse and, by the light of a full moon, scrubbed down the cargo area with a stiff-bristled brush and soapy water, then lay on top of the van and looked at what stars were visible above the polluting light of the casinos.

Once he had started the van, he put his hand underneath the front seat and took out the blue metal pistol, a 9-mm Beretta with a silencer, which he had bought three years ago from a young man who had lost everything at one of the downtown casinos and was willing to let the pistol and the silencer go for twelve dollars and fifty cents. Desmond checked the magazine. Full. He put the pistol back under the seat and for the next few hours made his rounds, ending up at a small casino named Old Roy's Place, where he delivered a brand of cheap whiskey that Old Roy couldn't buy anywhere else. The long twilight had begun and he sat down at the bar facing the window and the desert, where, in the distance, Sunrise Mountain had turned blood red.

He ordered himself ten dollars' worth of quarters to play electronic draw poker at one of the machines built into the bar, and he was given a free beer, which he nursed while he sought answers in the machine. He was convinced that Satan himself existed beyond that horizontal glass window where the faces of the cards flipped up so quickly, always leaving him hard choices to be made, whether to draw to a pair of tens in the hope of three of a kind, or whether to wipe out one of the tens in an attempt for a straight. He won and he lost and won again, then began to lose consistently, quarter after quarter, always guessing wrong, until finally he was down to his last quarter and convinced that God did not want him to win tonight. He put in the final quarter, saw a king, jack, ten, eight, and ace, and then he let the machine sit blinking at him, waiting for his choice. He was aware that a man had sat down at the bar next to him, watching him play. When Desmond looked at him, the man grinned as if to say that he meant no harm. Suddenly, Desmond was aware that this was one of those moments when the forces of the universe came together and God and the Devil were locked in mortal combat in the circuits of that electronic machine in the counter, and the man next to Desmond was the prize at stake.

Desmond had no choice except to take the gamble and then abide by the decision. So he pressed the buttons to hold all the cards except the eight and then pressed the button to redeal. And immediately, the queen of diamonds appeared and the shower of quarters began to clang into the metal dump next to the screen. He was aware that everybody was looking at him and a bell was ringing, and the bartender, a dapper little man named Al, was beaming at him. The stranger on the next stool was laughing.

Desmond was faced with a dilemma. There were perhaps a dozen people in the bar and only one or two of them could be considered regulars here and likely to remember him, and the tourists would be gone within a couple of hours. But Al would certainly remember. Desmond would have to work his way around that handicap. He took all the quarters out of the bin and Al dumped them into a coin counter while the man next to Desmond struck up a conversation.

"Jesus," he said. "That's great. I never seen anybody hit a jackpot like that. How much did you win?"

"A hundred dollars," Desmond said. He could not make out exactly what the man was doing here, because he was wearing a dress shirt and suit pants, black leather shoes with a spit shine. His face was slightly puffy, a pasty complexion, and his hair had been combed from right to left in a vain attempt to cover a growing bald spot. "You just passing through?" Desmond said.

"Not exactly," the man said. "You ever hear of the SGS Paper Products Company?"

"No," Desmond said.

"You will. It's growing like crazy. My name's John B. Chance, Jr. I'm the new vice-president in charge of distribution, or I will be as of Monday. I just drove out from Des Moines to look for an apartment so my wife can join me." The smile was overeager. John B. Chance wanted something. "I'd like to buy you a drink."

"Sure," Desmond said. "Just let me collect my winnings here."

"How you want it, Des?" Al said. "Twenties okay?"

Desmond nodded and the twenties were counted into his out-stretched hand, all crisp bills, no dirty ones. He moved to a booth with John B. Chance, who ordered himself a Scotch neat while Desmond had another beer, making no move, just waiting until he learned how he was supposed to carry out God's decision.

The drinks were served and Chance hoisted his glass, showing off a Masonic ring set with diamonds. "Here's to good luck all around," he said. "You must live here, right, buddy?"

"Yes," Desmond said. He sipped the beer.

Chance's bright eyes roamed the room, fixed on a waitress who was wearing a short dress. "It's a goddamned shame when you think about it," he said. "I mean, the wife and I are close and I've been what you'd call an honest husband, very little messing around, if you know what I mean, and here I am with a few days off the leash and not against finding a little action, if you get my meaning, but it's not safe anymore, is it? I mean, what with AIDS and all."

"I guess not," Desmond said. He did not look directly at him, not wanting to influence him, even indirectly.

"But I hear that the state of Nevada has all the girls in the houses inspected, I mean, so there wouldn't be much danger if you went to an official house."

"I wouldn't know about that."

"But you would know where the official houses are, wouldn't you?"

All right, Desmond thought. He has made the move and it's all right for me to respond. He would not tell the man that the brothels had been abolished in this county a long time ago, because it wouldn't make that much difference anyway. He looked at Al behind the counter. Al was facing the other way, talking to a pair of senior citizens. "There's a house near here in the desert," Desmond said. "It's kind of hard to find."

"I'd be willing to pay you to show me," Chance said eagerly.

"I don't want your money," Desmond said. "You just follow my van."

"I'm grateful to you, partner," Chance said.

"I'll meet you outside in five minutes," Desmond said.

Chance winked at him conspiratorially. "You got it."

Desmond went outside, excitement growing within him. He threaded his way through the parking lot to the van, then started the engine and pulled around to intercept Chance as he walked out the front entrance, a little unsteady on his feet. Too much to drink, probably. Just as well. Easier to handle. He saw Desmond's van and motioned toward the second row of cars and Desmond nodded. He waited until Chance reached a Cadillac convertible and started the engine before he drove the van out of the parking lot, the Cadillac following.

Desmond drove up the Henderson highway for a few miles, then cut back into the desert, past the fringe of businesses and residential districts, until the lights disappeared, and finally turned on to the road toward Overton, a small town many miles to the north and west. He kept his eyes on the mirror to make sure that Chance was following and that there was no other traffic. When he came to a side road—scarcely more than a rutted trail into the desert—he turned off and waited until Chance turned in behind him. Then he shifted into second and followed the bumpy road for a couple of miles until he was well hidden from the highway before he pulled to a stop. He could not drive any farther. Inner lights had begun to flash behind his eyes now. He knew God was trying to communicate with him directly, but the sounds were jumbled and came into his head in a whisper like the rustle of feathers.

Chance stopped his Cadillac, got out, and walked up to the van window. "Hey," he said with a smile. "You sure we're not lost?"

"Postive," Desmond said. His hand groped beneath the seat for the pistol.

"This is a hell of a rough road to be leading to a popular place," Chance said.

"Most of the customers at Little Chicken fly in," Desmond said.

"Little Chicken," Chance said with a laugh. "Is that really the name of the place?"

"Yeah." He was slowly raising the pistol from the floor.

"Little goddamn Chicken," Chance said. "That's really funny. Sounds sexy. Like a real trip."

"A trip to glory," Desmond said. And casually, with no change of expression, as if it were the most natural thing in the world to do, he raised the pistol, pointed it directly at Chance's forehead, and pulled the trigger, even while Chance's face was beginning to furrow with the effort of figuring out what was going on. The bullet punctured the skull. Chance dropped like a stone, as if all the electrical energy had been drained from his body. Desmond was breathing heavily from the excitement. His heart skipped a beat. He hesitated until he was sure it was going to continue to beat, then he took a deep breath to calm himself. He put the pistol back beneath the seat, then took the flashlight out of the glove compartment and the remnants of a lipstick he had found in a rest room. He opened the door, then shone the light down on the body so he would not inadvertently put his foot on it as he stepped down from the van.

The body was in a grotesque position, lying on its stomach, the legs all akimbo, one arm twisted behind the back. Gloves, Desmond thought. He went back to the rear of the truck and took a pair of gloves out of the repair box. He straightened out the body, keeping clear of the blood. He checked the pockets and pulled out Chance's wallet, knowing that his reward was great this time, because the leather billfold was fat. He shone his light into it. A couple thousand at least.

He put the wallet in his pocket, then set to work with great reverence, squatting down to pick up Chance's left hand to examine the palm. He took a knife from his pocket, pressed a button, and allowed the long, thin blade to spring free, then he made a careful cut one way in the palm of the hand, and then a crosscut, not deep, no. The depth was unimportant. The blood seeped out of the wound.

Desmond used the lipstick to make a line over each of the two cut marks and had folded the hands in a traditional position over the chest. As he stood up, the terrible thought hit him. He had almost been extremely careless, because Al might remember this man, his face, the connection between Chance and Desmond, their having a beer together. He would certainly remember the Masonic ring with the diamonds. Desmond worked the ring off the right hand and then, after thinking about what he should do with it, he walked on down the road a full fifty yards, beyond the limits the police would search, and then he dug a shallow hole with a twig and buried it.

Still, there was the problem of the man's face, distinctive even in death, but he could take care of that. He took the spare gasoline can from the rear of the van, removed the lid, and carefully poured gasoline on the features of the late Mr. Chance. He struck a match. The face sprang into flame with an eerie light and for a moment held a glorious glow before it charred and began to disintegrate. Then Desmond did the fingers.

Another one, Desmond thought. One more.

He drove his van back around the convertible, then left his lights on while he doused the convertible with the rest of the gasoline from the can. He took his flashlight and examined the vehicle tracks on the desert road. Where there was sand, the surface was too loose to hold an impression, and where there was shale, the track was too hard. He filled a Coke bottle with gasoline and stuffed a rag into the top. He drove the van down the road toward the highway a hundred yards before he walked back. He lit the handkerchief and then threw the bottle into the center of the convertible, which exploded with a muted whomp and began to burn fiercely. He jumped into the van, drove quickly but carefully back toward the highway, and had just pulled onto the blacktop when the gas tank exploded in the distant convertible, a burst of light like a exploding supernova.

Back into Vegas, he cruised past the church, where a bingo game was in progress in the recreation hall. He hung around, noticed by no one, invisible. He bought a card but did not play. He went to the kitchen and with a black stub of pencil blocked out words on the back of the card: TELL HIM TO HURRY!

He went into the corridor, saw the confessional, deserted. He put the bingo card and Chance's driver's license on the priest's side. No one saw him leave.

When Father Rowan entered the confessional the next day and saw the driver's license and the bingo card, his heart turned over. He felt giddy, light-headed. He sat down in the chair, turned the license over and over in his fingers, studying the picture, knowing without proof that this man, this John B. Chance who displayed a vacuous smile at a DMV camera in Des Moines, Iowa, was dead, and all because of a rule that, however rooted in Scripture and tradition, held the priest to a deadly silence.

Wrong, all wrong, Father Rowan thought. All wrong, and I should go to the monsignor or the police or somebody in authority and tell them there is a maniac loose who has pinned me to a silent acquiescence with his crime and made me an accomplice. Or he wanted to wait until he heard that voice again, that distinctive voice with the lilt of madness to it, and then he would leap from his chair and tackle the man before he could leave the confessional.

He heard the rustle of movement from the other side, a woman's voice. "Forgive me, Father, for I have sinned." Without listening, he heard the drone of venal sin, a lie told, a glistening of envy in the eye, a touch of covetousness in the heart, and he gave penance.

After an hour, when there were no more confessions to be heard, he went to the office of his superior. Monsignor Mahoney, a strapping, handsome man ten years his junior, had long since finished the five-o'clock mass and was dressed in his expensive casual clothes. The monsignor had been a rising star from the moment he had been brought into St. Justin Martyr to become the parish priest. Ordinarily, the position would have gone to Father

Rowan, but Mahoney was sharp and an excellent fundraiser. He was at home among the wealthy celebrities and the high rollers, where Father Rowan was not, and when the bishop of the diocese came down from Reno, it was always Monsignor Mahoney who met him at the airport.

The monsignor was an excellent after-dinner speaker with a sharp wit and he had the Italian casino owners in the palm of his hand. When the Pope visited San Francisco, Mahoney had been granted the privilege of a personal audience. And now, as Father Rowan entered the monsignor's office, he was stacking the casino chips that had been collected in the five-o'clock offering. He held up three silver and black chips with a dazzling smile.

"You ever seen these, Johnny?"

"I can't say that I have."

"You'll probably never see another in a collection plate. Most people don't even know they exist. They're five-hundred-dollar chips."

"I didn't know they had chips that large."

"I'm still not sure they're real. But I'll find out tonight. You look pale. Are you feeling all right?"

No, I'm feeling rotten as a matter of fact, rotten and guilty. He did not say it. Instead: "Do you have time to talk for a few minutes?"

"Sure." The monsignor poured two cups of coffee, placed one in front of Father Rowan, who could not help but notice the grace of his superior's hands. He had the perfectly tapered fingers, the hands of a pianist or a surgeon. "I'll tell you frankly, I've been concerned about you lately, Johnny. You seem—what's the best way of putting it?—you seem distracted. Is the weather getting to you? The heat can do that."

Leave me room, for God's sake. Just listen. "No," Father Rowan said. "I like the desert." The coffee was hot, bitter.

"You having trouble with the KC?"

"Nothing like that. I want to give you a hypothetical."

"All right. Shoot."

An unfortunate choice of imperatives. "Suppose that a man came into confession and admitted the Tropicana murders, the ones in the paper."

He was aware of a subtle change in the monsignor's face, the pleasantness still there but frozen now, suspended, as if the skin had grown cold. "Go on," the monsignor said.

"And further, suppose that this man wanted you to contact a police officer who lived in the eastern part of the country to ask him to come here."

"For what reason?"

"Unstated. Assume the man is psychotic."

"Since this is hypothetical, assign a reason."

"We're dealing with insanity, Monsignor," Father Rowan said. "The man is crazy, pathological."

"This hypothetical man," the monsignor corrected.

"Yes."

The monsignor sipped his coffee, eyes fixed on a Lalique madonna on a teak pedestal, which caught the light streaming in through a narrow window, trapped it, transformed it. I would have believed once that there was meaning in the figure of Mary and the way it shone, Father Rowan thought, but now it's only glass. The monsignor cleared his throat. "Just what are you getting at, Johnny?"

"These," the priest said. He put the driver's license and the bingo card on the desk and the monsignor frowned as he looked at the message on the back of the card. "What's all this supposed to mean?" he asked. "A driver's license and a bingo card?"

"They were left in my confessional chair. There's no doubt what it is. It's a message for me."

The monsignor picked up the laminated driver's license. "You know this man?"

"No."

"I don't see what you're getting at."

"I'm trying to walk a very fine line, Monsignor."

"I'm not talking lines, Johnny. I think I know what you're getting at," the monsignor interrupted. "But I'm talking reality. A Mexican girl named Antonia cleans the confessionals. Now, supposing that this gentleman"—he consulted the license—"this man named Chance had been dating Antonia and wanted to leave her a message."

"A message like this?" Father Rowan protested. " 'Tell him to hurry!'? If it's the psychopath, then it makes sense to me. But I can't think of a situation where it would make sense to Ramona."

"Have you asked her?"

"No."

The monsignor waved his hand vaguely, as if they were off track and he was irritated by the diversion. "I was just using her as an example. You probably wouldn't get a straight explanation out of her if you did ask. But I'm simply saying that there are a dozen different possibilities here, any of which could be as valid as any other." He sipped the coffee again, thoughtfully. "What had you intended to do?"

"My duty seems clear to me," Father Rowan said. The sunlight had shifted and the statue of Mary had dimmed. "After all, neither the bingo card nor the driver's license are a part of any confession I've heard. So I thought I would send them to the police."

"Saying what?"

"I don't know. But I suspect that Mr. Chance is in grave danger if he's still alive at all."

The monsignor leaned back in his chair and rubbed his chin thoughtfully. "You're on thin ice here. Think about it, Johnny. You know exactly what's at stake."

The priest felt his face flush with anger, looking at the younger man, who was treating him as if he were a recalcitrant seminarian faced with an obvious truth. And Father Rowan was brought up short by the thought. Perhaps there was something to the monsignor's admonition; perhaps his own stubborness was only partially because he was caught up in the rebellion on the part of an older man passed over for a younger one. "You make me think," he said quietly. "You make me consider exactly what it is I'm fighting for. I've never liked you, you know."

"I know that," the monsignor said without a flicker of animosity. "I never expected you to. Human nature is such that no man with experience likes to be passed over."

"I think about that from time to time," Father Rowan said. "But I don't believe that has ever interfered with the performance of my duties."

"You're a good man," the monsignor said. "And eventually, I hope that you will come to like me."

"I don't believe you really grasp my point," Father Rowan said thoughtfully. "It isn't important whether I come to like you or not. It is only important that my dislike for you is not causing error in my thinking. And in this case, I'm sure of it. I have to balance my own beliefs, the practicalities against the doctrines. There is a sacred rule here—"

"More than a rule, a sacrament—"

"Which I have to take into account," Father Rowan said, ignoring the interruption. "But I have to take the responsibility. This is a man who has committed murder, not only before admitting the fact but afterward as well. And if I do nothing, he's not going to stop. And the blood of his victims will be on my hands."

The monsignor fell silent, studying him, his hand pulling at his chin as if stroking an invisible beard. And Rowan knew that this bright young man with the shining eyes was trying to sniff out weakness he could exploit. He would be excellent at it, and many years from now he would become a bishop. Father Rowan was sure of that.

"Have you ever had anyone lie to you in confession?" the monsignor asked.

"Yes, of course."

"I'm not speaking of the person who minimizes a sin and later confesses to the larger one. I'm talking of the person who invents a sin in order to get attention."

"I've had some admit to doing that, yes."

"And have you ever persuaded one to seek counseling for a lie of that nature?"

"Yes."

"And yet, hypothetically speaking—and we must speak hypothetically because to violate the sanctity of confession is a mortal sin for which there is no forgiveness—hypothetically, you have no proof that any given confession will not contain falsehoods. And if a man were to admit murder and give you details, he could have gotten these details a dozen different ways, and that doesn't prove he ever killed anybody. Perhaps he could help the police and perhaps he couldn't, but in any case, you're not free to tell them about him. You could hand the police this scribbled message on a bingo card and the driver's license, but you would be prohibited from saying a single word because all that knowledge came to you in the confessional. Without your comments, these things would mean absolutely nothing. Am I correct?"

"I suppose so."

"No supposition. What I say is absolutely true. Neither of these things would have the slightest importance without privileged information to back them up. You'd throw the card away and turn the driver's license in to lost and found."

"Yes. But the police would know that the driver's license was found in this church. They could make their connections with no help from me."

The monsignor stood up, hands laced behind his back, obviously irritated. "You're not that naïve, Johnny. You're not that stupid."

"I won't have you insult me. You will speak to me with respect."

"Only when you deserve it. You're about to cop out and take the easy way. Christ didn't come into a peaceful world. He was willing to mix it up with whores and thugs. He knew the score. And if you wanted a vocation without conflict, you should have gone into a monastery and taken a vow of silence and spent your days tilling a garden and contemplating the glories of the Almighty." He opened a glass door in a bookcase and took out a thin ledger, which he slapped down on the table. "Do you know what this is?"

"I have some idea."

"It's a list of donations, not only to this church but to the diocese and to the Holy See at Rome and to foreign missions. Do you have any idea how many African children this one church, our congregation, saved from starvation last year? Any idea at all? Seventy-six thousand and some odd. Seventy-six thousand people, human beings, innocent children who would have died otherwise."

Ah, the monsignor was boiling mad now, firing his full batteries of artillery, and Father Rowan took refuge in silence, waiting until the bombardment passed and he had some clear idea where the monsignor was going with this outburst. The monsignor had picked up a stack of multicolored chips from the desk and riffled them from his left hand to his right. They made a rustling noise, a distinctive clicking.

"Now, who do you suppose donates all this money, Johnny?" A rhetorical question, Father Rowan thought. No answer expected or required. "You know the answer as well as I do. Casino workers, whores, pit bosses, dealers, housewives, hoods; and do you suppose I examine the checks that come in and then call a donor and say, 'I'm sorry, but I can't accept your money because it's tainted. Because it's not pure. Because it was made through sin'?" He made stacks of the chips on the desk, anger fading, the shells no longer aimed in the priest's direction, back to logic again. "Do you think Christ would let a child starve because the money to feed him came from the wrong place?"

"No, but . . ."

The monsignor shrugged, calmed himself. The bombardment was over but it had succeeded. Father Rowan felt obliterated by the pounding. "Now, I'll give you a hypothetical, Johnny, and you give me an answer. Suppose you go to the police and hand them these things and let them know that they had been left in the church. Now, suppose the police ask exactly where in the church you found these items. Would you feel free to tell the police this driver's license and this message were left in a confessional?"

"Absolutely."

"And if they asked you what you knew about this communication, would you lie? Would you tell them you had no idea what these things meant?"

"No. I would tell them absolutely nothing."

"And what kind of conclusion do you think they would come to from that information?"

"That wouldn't be my responsibility."

"You're not thinking," the monsignor said with a frown. "They would know you were withholding information, undoubtedly from a confession." He pressed the fingertips of both hands together with great pressure. "What kind of person do you suppose drops a five-hundred-dollar chip in the plate?"

"A good Catholic."

"Undoubtedly. And he has money. Maybe he's a high roller and maybe he owns a casino or he's hit it big temporarily. The odds are that he's a member of the parish and that he comes to confession here, and if he's rich, he has sins in his life, daily sins for which he needs forgiveness, sins that might be abhorrent to either one of us, but sins that can be forgiven by God."

He held a single chip up to the light as if it were the Eucharist. "We work in the modern counterpart of Sodom and Gomorrah. During my first year out here, I yearned for a parish back in Illinois where I would be the channel to God for good Catholics who lived and died with no knowledge of what terrible things one man could do to another." He began to sort the chips according to color. "All right, we come down to it. Can you see what would happen once the police began to investigate the membership of this parish? The rumors would be out, you can count on that, and everybody would believe that the seal of the confessional had been broken. And suddenly, there would be a great shudder up and down Fremont Street and in a hundred places along the Strip, where individuals who had counted on the confidentiality of the confessional and the resultant forgiveness of God would begin to worry that their secrets would not be respected. They would want assurance that their pasts would not come out and I could not give them that assurance. Because once violated, the trust would disappear. They would avoid the confessional as the trap it had become. And just coincidentally, the money would dry up because we violated a sacred trust and they would feel betrayed."

"You can't be sure that would happen."

"I don't think we can even take the chance. Do you?"

"I'm not sure. What do you think I should do?" Father Rowan said, subdued.

The monsignor pushed the driver's license and the bingo card back across the table. "Do what you know is right."

"Yes," the older priest said, feeling wrung out. He had been pounded, then inundated by words. He longed for nothing more than silence. "I'll take care of it."

"I'm sure you will." And now, with capitulation would come the monsignor's restoration of peace. "I've been meaning to ask you if you would like to plan the retreat at Tahoe this year?" It was the granting of favors, a plum, three weeks in the green mountains, a crystal blue lake, time for meditation and escape from the harsher realities of his vocation.

"Thank you, Monsignor," Father Rowan said. "I would enjoy that very much."

"Fine." The monsignor gave Father Rowan a reassuring pat on the shoulder. "You might want to mention it in the newsletter next week. It's none too early. And about this other, you're doing the right thing. You're allowing God to take care of the situation."

"Yes," Father Rowan said.

He made hospital calls that afternoon, picked up the local papers for any news about a man named Chance. He found none. That evening, he examined the bingo card again and thought about throwing it in the trash. He did not want to make difficulties for himself here. Yet in the end, he made a compromise. He could not contact the local police, so he put the bingo card and the driver's license in an envelope and mailed them to Stein.

CHARLESTON, WEST VIRGINIA

A marvelous Saturday afternoon, Stein thought. He opened a beer and lowered himself into the hammock in the shade next to the house, looking with a sense of accomplishment at what he had done with the morning. He regarded the ache in his back and the general fatigue as the reward for his labors. For he had been using his body, not his mind, cutting trees with a chain saw in a grove east of the house, hauling the timbers behind a small tractor to the front yard. He trimmed them with an ax, notched them, worked up a sweat as he added to an ornamental rail fence around the boundaries of his acreage.

The fence would stop nothing, of course, neither man nor beast from entering or leaving his land, but that was not the point. For this one day of the week, at least, he did not have to use his mind, and he had no mental responsibilities at all. He could lie here and drink beer and listen to the ball game on the radio, totally relaxed, knowing that Karen was out painting and Barn would be with her, dabbing globs of paint on paper with great seriousness.

As he reached for the radio, he did not turn it on because he saw an ancient Ford truck pulling around the house to park in the shade of a hackberry tree, and Mr. Johnson crawled out. He was a lanky old man in overalls and he came across the lawn with a vigorous lope, grizzle-headed, a growth of stubbly beard on his chin.

"Don't you get up now, Mr. Stein," he said as he approached.

"It's good to see you, Mr. Johnson," Stein said, reaching up to shake the old man's hand, startled as he always was at the strength of Johnson's grip. "Would you like a beer?"

"No, thanks. Beer gives me gas. It don't agree with me. But I'd like a favor of you. I just put up three crosses over on Favor's Ridge. Maybe you seen 'em."

"Matter of fact, I have."

"I don't know how you feel about them, but I consider cross-building to be my calling and I'd like to make a trade."

"What kind of trade?"

"I notice you're thinning your grove, building a fence. Now, you got a bunch of trees on the far side and I'd like three of them, eight inches in diameter, maybe twelve feet high. I'll clean out the underbrush in the grove and I'll cut you a dozen logs for your fence and drag them in place."

"You're welcome to the trees," Stein said. "But I'm really building the fence for exercise."

"Then I'll cut and stack you a cord of hickory," Johnson said. "It's been laid on my heart that I pay my own way."

"That's not necessary. You can just consider it my contribution to your project."

"No, sir," Johnson said. "You got to do your fence your way and the crosses got to be done with mine. No charity."

"I respect that. The firewood would be more than enough."

"I'll do it next week if that's all right with you. And you'll want the firewood next to the stack by the house."

"That would be fine."

Johnson shook his hand again, and shortly his old truck, knocking and smoking, pulled down the road and out of sight. Stein had a great admiration for what Johnson was doing because his personal crusade totally occupied his life. And long after the old man was dead and gone, those hundreds of crosses he had spent his life erecting would remain as his memorial, and even after the crosses had decayed and were no more, the old man's lifework would be a part of the folklore and the history of these mountains.

He lay back in the hammock, drank the beer, and dozed, to come awake at the sound of Thatcher's apologetic voice as he approached the hammock from his car parked in the driveway. Thatcher was perfect for the business, Stein thought. He was a perfectionist, and when anything came in, however small, he could not rest until it was taken care of. Alice had threatened him for the past six years with everything from divorce to murder to get him to lighten up on his work occasionally, but now she only muttered and endured that which could not be changed.

"What's up?" Stein said.

"It's quite obvious you're not." Thatcher took a beer from the cooler, uncapped it, and took a long pull. "We have another murder in Vegas."

"You bring me a breakdown?"

"We're in the middle of a download at the office," Thatcher said. "We're printing out their transmission. But you also have another letter from Vegas."

"What's in it?"

"I didn't open it. You need to decide if you want to send it to LVPD Forensics."

Stein moaned slightly, crawled out of the hammock. "I'd better go down and have a look. I'll have to leave a note for Karen. I was supposed to barbecue."

"I tell Alice she wouldn't dare do me in," Thatcher said. "She's got too much motive. But she says she wouldn't try to hide it because there's no jury in the world that would convict her."

Stein grinned. "Let's go."

The printout from Las Vegas was complete by the time Stein reached the office, and he accepted a mug of hot coffee from Thatcher and then sat down in a comfortable chair to study the text, fascinated by a case that was at this point full of non sequiturs and disconnected events. For here, it seemed, was a white male Caucasian, forty-two years old, who had been killed in the desert outside Las Vegas.

The cross slashed across his hand had been covered with

lipstick. Certainly the work of the same killer, yet there was a wrinkle here. For this victim's face had been burned beyond recognition, and his fingertips had been dipped in gasoline and set afire as well. The victim had been ID'd the hard way. The Iowa license plate on the car had provided his name, and X rays of the dental work had confirmed that John B. Chance of Des Moines, Iowa, was indeed the man who had died in the sand. LVPD Homicide was completely up the wall on this one because this man named Chance had driven out onto a desert road that led nowhere and dead-ended in a wash just four miles beyond the spot where the car had been found. It was doubtful he had turned off on the trail by mistake. The highway was in excellent shape and the side road was in such disrepair that no one could mistake it for the main route.

Puzzles within puzzles. What had lured Chance out into no-man's-land? Where had he met his murderer? And why had the killer burned the face and hands, unless it had been to delay identification of the victim?

He sat down at the computer and sent a query to Las Vegas asking for pictures of the victim alive and dead. The answer was immediate. Photographs of the crime scene began to arrive within twenty minutes on the FAX. The LVPD had requested a photograph of Chance's family in Des Moines through the DMPD. They expected one within the hour.

Stein turned his attention to the manila envelope on his desk, his address penned in, a hurried scribble, postage applied by a metering machine. Not from the killer, no, for there was the logo of St. Justin Martyr in the upper-left-hand corner and the initials of the priest immediately below the address. Nevertheless, Stein was careful. He slit the end of the envelope with a penknife and let the contents slide out onto the desk. The driver's license, yes, and here was a picture of the victim, but certainly not a good one. White, middle-aged, with a bemused expression.

Stein examined the bingo card. TELL HIM TO HURRY! the message said.

There was a piece of notepaper in the envelope, unsigned, but it was obviously from the priest. It said:

> I'm sorry that I can't be more involved than this. If it is at all possible, I would ask you to come here before more innocent

people are slaughtered. I have no doubt that this man was killed to force you to come. He told me to tell you he will "harvest" somebody every three days until you come. He implies that you know him and he also told me to inform you that the answer would be found in the hands. I don't know what that means, but perhaps it will strike a responsive chord.

Shit, Stein thought. Another crazy dealing in puzzles, enigmas, riddles. The compulsive was applying the pressure, having to feel as if he were in control of the whole world. He looked up as Thatcher came into the room.

"Las Vegas Metro wants to retain us," Thatcher said. "What d'you think?"

"That's what we're here for. Give me a perp number," Stein said.

Thatcher consulted the list. "That would be 1066-LV," he said.

Stein entered the date into the computer, making a search of any crimes remotely resembling the ones in Las Vegas. He followed the unknown killer's advice, keyed on the hands, the slashed crosses, and the lipstick marks. He requested pictures where available, or autopsy descriptions where pictures were lacking. He set the cutoff date at ten years, knowing that past ten years, the records entered into the computer tended to be incomplete. He included the whole country in the scope of his search. Once the search procedure was activated, he leaned back in his chair, aware that the processing units and the jukeboxes in the computer rooms were accessing The Big Hummer, making millions of comparisons a second, tracking through the thousands of cases that had been entered into the data bank.

"Why not dump all this on Picone before we start anything intensive?" Thatcher asked. "Give him the name of the priest and let him do the tracking. That's SOP, isn't it? You got someone with direct knowledge, you hand the information to the locals and let them take the lead."

"No good," Stein said. "The priest won't confirm or deny anything. And if our killer's using him as a conduit, that'll end the second the cops go into the church." He sipped the coffee. "Why don't you go home?" he said. "I'm going to finish the search and then see what we have."

"Alice is already steamed."

"Blame it on me." He wanted Thatcher out of the office because he was beginning to feel something that he did not want to admit. Thatcher was a hundred percent right. According to his own rules, he should turn everything over to the authorities in Nevada and let them call the shots and request specific services. But Stein was beginning to take this personally, intrigued by a killer known only as 1066-LV who was hinting at some past connection with him and determined to involve him in the most deadly of games. Stein had promised Karen as well as himself that he would never be hooked again. Even now, as the computer began to respond, he made a silent vow. He would stay with this only long enough to complete the initial search and then he would release the direction of the case to Las Vegas.

The telephone rang. "What happened to you?" Karen said. "You have a couple of hungry artists here waiting to be fed."

"A semi-emergency with one of the computers," he said. "Would you mind starting the coals? I'll be there as soon as I can."

"Only because I'm a forgiving, loving, cooperative wife," she said. "But get a move on."

"Will do," he said.

He examined the data streaming in, and he was startled by what he found. The computer had located thousands of homicide victims in the last ten years with cut palms, slashed with swastikas, initials, obscenities, gang markings, a large proportion of double crosses, literal renderings of the axiomatic expression. But there were only five cases in which a slash had been covered with lipstick. He had the locations and dates printed out, three in Connecticut within a three-month period nine years ago, then nothing, followed by two cases in Southern California seven years ago, and then nothing until the Las Vegas killings. But, according to the descriptive entries, none of the cuts before Las Vegas involved cross marks. Pictures were available on all the victims, and he instructed the computer to give him a close-up picture of the mutilated hand of one of the Las Vegas victims next to the hand of one of the Orange County victims, both male. The pictures flashed onto the high-resolution screen and he was startled by the match. In both cases, the first cut had been a short, precise, transverse straight line across the center of the palm, approximately an inch long, located about an inch and a half beneath the base of the middle finger, the cut covered with a single stroke of lipstick. But in the California case, the first cut had been the only one, and it was only with the three murders in the sand of Las Vegas that a vertical cut had been made to form a cross on the palm of each victim.

He went through all the photographs prior to Las Vegas. There was no doubt the cuts had been made by the same killer.

Hands.

A straight line before. Crosses now.

What the hell are you trying to tell me? Stein thought, frustrated.

He took the time to run an extra computer program he had developed just for cases such as this, using the computer to compare all the victims and find out what they had in common or what an unbalanced mind could perceive as commonality. Many serial killers chose victims with a common profile, all females within a certain age range, or women with long dark hair parted in the middle, or members of a certain ethnic group, but in this case, the computer came up with a blank. Some of the victims were as old as seventy, some as young as fifteen, a nonsignificant sexual or ethnic mix, no correlation of profession or appearances.

So now Stein shifted into those elements that a psychotic might consider, the number of letters in a victim's name, various methods by which that data could be manipulated to add up to a magic number; the letters themselves, whether there was any letter of the alphabet that was predominant beyond the norm. He inquired into colors to determine whether there was any shade or hue in clothing or accessories or even makeup that was common among all the victims. The program took a little less than a half hour to run and in the end came up with nothing more than a common MO. The victims were dissimilar but the killings had all been made with a single shot to the head, and the bodies had been laid out in a dignified manner. And, of course, the computer repeated the finding of the slashes in the hand, and the lipstick.

Crosses, now, Stein thought.

The meaning escaped him, but it was obviously significant to the faceless 1066-LV.

One thing was abundantly clear. This was a random killer. If there was any pattern, it was not evident and existed only in his own mind. He copied the data to send to Picone in Las Vegas, and instructed the computer to access every scrap of data on the other crimes. Then he sat back, turning a pencil over in his hands, thinking things through and making a difficult decision.

He dialed the church in Las Vegas and asked for Father Rowan. The priest was on the line within a minute, his voice subdued and immediately apologetic when he realized Stein was calling. "I'm sorry, Mr. Stein," he said. "But the note and the driver's license were left for me to send you as a message. I'm sure of that."

"Have you talked with him again?"

"I'm not free to discuss this with you anymore," the priest said.

Stein was silent a moment, making a difficult decision. "I'm not asking you to," Stein said. "I just wanted to call and let you know what I'm doing so you won't have any unpleasant surprises. I'd like to be able to keep your church totally disassociated with this, but I can't do it anymore. I'm going to let the Las Vegas police know everything you've told me. I won't use your name and I'll keep the source confidential. But they have to know that the killer has frequented your church."

"And what will the police do here?"

"They'll probably put your church under surveillance. They'll make an investigation, hopefully discreet, and when they have a suspect who fits the profile, they'll talk to him."

There was silence on the telephone. Stein could feel the priest's silent misery. "I shouldn't have told you anything," Father Rowan said finally.

"You had no choice, Father," Stein said. "This is literally a matter of life and death. I'm not asking for your approval. I'm just letting you know what will happen."

"You can put an end to this, you know," the priest said. "He never would have approached me except to get in touch with you. If you came here yourself, he would talk with you, I'm sure of that. And it would relieve me of responsibility."

"You don't have any further responsibilities in this matter," Stein said. "I can arrange it so that you won't even know what happens, if that's what you want."

"I beg you not to do this, Mr. Stein."

"We all do what we have to," Stein said. He severed the connection and thought about calling Picone but decided against it. That conversation would be a long one. He would call when he had finished the computer sort. But now he was going home.

LAS VEGAS, NEVADA

Desmond had the shakes. He sat at the window, watching the parking lot of the Convention Center, where trucks were unloading animals in the shimmering heat rising like distorting waves from the concrete, and he knew he would have to take the pills very soon or his mind would fly all to pieces, the fragments spinning off into space, and he could not allow that to happen, not now, for something was to be revealed to him. He could feel it. The revelation had been coming to him in stages, and now everything was coming together for him, and Stein would be here soon, so he had to know what God had in mind. Otherwise, Stein would not help him.

The final part of the revelation would come in some obscure way, perhaps in these animals, the ponderous elephant rumbling down a ramp, a gray monster led into the yawning mouth of a building entrance by a man with a hook on a stick, and then a giraffe, that long neck, swaying like a palm tree, and he was entranced, because all these animals were God's freaks, God's hallucinations, perhaps his mistakes.

And then he saw the apparition emerging from a separate truck, a bird he had seen pictures of when he was a kid, an ostrich, enormous, with thick spindly legs and the whiplike neck. As he watched, the bird kicked up, the handlers moving backward and the giant wings spread with a great whir, the dark underfeathers shining with wrath. When it came down, it strutted forward, then made one more jump, wings beating against the hot air, and at that moment Desmond was sure the bird was looking at him with sharp, knowing eyes that collapsed the distance, saw through the veil of curtains.

An angel in disguise, sent to give him the message, which made sense to him instantly, and he knew what he was to do. The shaking was so intense now that he was seeing jagged lightning across the front of his brain. Finally, he took the two pills, threw them into his mouth and washed them down with tepid water from the tap. He sank back into his chair, panting like a dog until the calming influence of the pills took hold, and then gradually his eyes grabbed objects with a fresh focus and he knew exactly what had happened to him. He looked out the window again. The ostrich-angel had already gone into the building. It made no difference. The meaning of the revelation was quite clear. He had been promoted from harvester to messenger and now Stein and his powers were even more important than ever.

He stood up, unsteady on his feet at first. He made it to the bathroom, where he doused cold water on his face and brought himself more alert. He went to the closet to get his work shoes and glanced at the newspaper and magazine clippings concerning Stein that were pasted on the wall. He had collected them over the years, ever since the summer of the anointing. He had his name on the mailing list of the Charleston, West Virginia, Chamber of Commerce (not his real one, of course, for the odds were too great that someone would find out and backtrack him). In their most recent brochure, he had found a message from God, so subtle he had not fully understood it before the three harvestings on Tropicana. The brochure had a picture of Stein in its pages, looking almost the same as when Desmond had seen him last, a tall, dark man with intensely curious brown eyes, standing in front of his building, the river in the background. The article told of his work with computers, the technology of the future. And on the very next page, immediately opposite the story about Stein, there was a story on the cross-builders of West Virginia, and a picture of three crosses Desmond had seen when he was there. Everything had come so clear to him that he shuddered with the marvelous knowledge of it, and remembered the darkness, the light, and the piercing pain that purged him of mortality, the voices whispering "miracle" and the sacred paint on the face of the man who had brought him back from death.

He pulled a rack of clothes over the clippings and sat down to put on his socks and then the heavy boots he wore on the job. He tested himself, focusing his eyes on the pattern of the wallpaper, the little yellow flowers. His mind cleared, became sharper, almost as if it were a knife being honed.

I'm going to be tested now, he thought. Satan doesn't want this to happen.

He went out to the van and took the cardboard sun shield out of the front window, but the steering wheel still burned his hands when he touched it, especially his one injured hand. He grabbed the wheel anyway to prove his tolerance for pain. He drove past the church to the parking lot. It was almost time for confession and the priest would be there this afternoon.

He was about to turn in when he saw the ice cream truck parked down the street, the sides folded down, and he caught a glimpse of something shining from the cab, a sharp metallic glint. He did not stop but went on past the parking lot and the ice cream truck that sat facing the church. There was something awry here; Desmond could feel it. The man in the cab wore dark glasses and a white billed cap. He put out one cigarette and lit another even in the short time Desmond observed him. Having a couple of cigarettes on his break; that was the way it was supposed to look. Desmond's skin prickled. This man was not in the business of selling ice cream. And he was not on a break, not unless he was crazy, because the thermometer sat at 108 degrees and he would be burning up, sitting in that truck.

As Desmond turned the corner, he looked back to see the man lift a pair of binoculars and study a group of people entering the church.

Cop.

The bogus ice cream man had the word written all over him.

He drove the street in back of the church. He saw two men working on an electric pole near the playground, one at the top and the other at the bottom, standing next to a pickup truck.

Neither was doing anything. The top was a lookout and the bottom was a chaser. He smiled to himself.

Confession could wait.

Desmond drove down to the warehouse, where Swanson was pouring whiskey into a stained jelly glass and really knocking it back, grimacing, wheezing, coughing as if the whiskey burned a hole through the congestion in his chest.

"Sit down, Des. Take a load off your feet," Swanson said, wheeling his chair around, extending the bottle toward Desmond. "Have a drink."

Desmond looked at the amber liquid shining in the sunlight. He could see the atoms and the molecules that made up the whiskey, a universe in a bottle. "No, thanks," he said. "I got to run the route pretty soon."

"All the more for me," Swanson said, rubbing the back of his hand across his toothless mouth. "I ain't got nothing that works right anymore. I tell you, Des, it's simple hell getting old and having everything go bust at the same time." He refilled the jelly glass, drank. "You still interested in buying my business? Hell, I'll give you a good price, the best kind of terms."

"I never really thought you wanted to sell." His mind was racing again. Was this building a part of the bigger design?

"Well, think about it now. One day you going to be an old man like me and you don't want to end up with nothing. I ain't saying the business is all that hot, but you got the energy to build it up."

"What all you including?"

"Hell, you know what we got," Swanson said, frowning. "The warehouse, a couple of trucks, the furnishings for this piss-poor office, and a bunch of damn dumb accounts that don't buy a hell of a lot but pay regular."

Desmond's eyes narrowed against the layer of cigarette smoke hanging in the room. "How much?"

"Shit, I dunno." The lips and jaws worked over the toothless gums. Swannie's eyes consulted the cracked ceiling. "Oh, say you give me twenty grand down and five hundred a month."

"For how long?"

"Rest of my life. In cash, so I can keep my Social Security and

don't have to pay tax. Hell, you wouldn't be paying any interest
and I got so many things wrong with me, the payments wouldn't
go on all that long. You think I'm lying, talk to my doctor. Leonard
McGee. Dr. Lennie McGee. Out at Humana. He'll tell you." He
jabbed a bony finger through the cigarette smoke. "What say?"

"Give me a day or two."

"You want to risk it, that's fine with me," Swanson said in a
resigned voice. "And if I kick off this afternoon, you're going to
be shit out of luck. Arnold, that snotty son of a bitch, will get the
whole works."

"Just a day or two."

As he was loading the van, he looked around the warehouse,
old but sound, high-ceilinged, composition roof, timbered sup-
ports high in the windowless twilight. The flutter of wings. The
cooing of pigeons. A feather drifted down in front of him, onto a
case of Black Label. A definite sign. He imagined the room filled
with angels, wings fluttering, stirring the air, a faint riffle of harps,
a sound like wind chimes, so distant he could not be sure it was
real. The warehouse might do, but only as a first temple for the
initial required miracle. He could put the throne at the far end of
the room, suspended in air. He was pulled back to reality by the
sound of old Swanson's coughing. The old man was right. He
didn't have much time.

But twenty thousand dollars was a lot of money and it would
take him a long time to get it through harvesting.

He loaded the van with the deliveries he had to make in Henderson and then drove back by the church again. The ice cream
truck was still there, the cop with the binoculars broiling in the
afternoon heat, and the bogus men from the power company were
still around. If he had had the power to do it, he would zap the
skinny cop with the mustache off the power pole, and send a bolt
of electricity down into the ice cream truck and the cop with the
dark glasses would run screaming into the street. And then, with
his knife, he would harvest them.

He drove past Sam's Town Casino to a Thai restaurant, where
he delivered a couple of cases of Chinese beer and twenty cartons
of kretek cigarettes, the kind with cloves in them that could really
rot your lungs out. Then he ran six more cigarette machines at gas
stations. He drove out toward Boulder City and stopped at a convenience store, his mind dwelling on the warehouse and how he

could fix it up. Someday, a picture of that place would be in a Las Vegas brochure. The caption would read SITE OF THE MIRACLE. All he needed was twenty thousand dollars.

"You got any more original Trident gum in the blue package?" he asked a girl clerk who was staring through the window at an imitation Elvis filling his motorcycle at the gas pump.

"If it's not out on the shelf, we don't have it." Her voice was a petulant, put-upon whine.

"You might have some in your storeroom."

"We won't have any more until we get a delivery on Tuesday."

He paid for the single pack of gum and then sat down in front of a slot machine near the door, feeling flushed and antsy, knowing that he was about to receive another message. He put in his quarter and pulled the handle. The cylinders spun in the machine, an orange clinking into place, followed by a second and then a third, clink, clink, clink, all lined up, just like that, and the ten quarters clanked into the bin. He had no doubt the coins had been given to him for a purpose.

He gathered up his quarters, took them out one at a time, and looked around, and there she was, a little girl, seven or eight years old, in an orange dress, standing at the counter and paying for a candy bar with two quarters.

He looked through the window toward the parking lot. There was no car waiting for the little girl, no parents who had sent her in for candy, so she must live somewhere in the neighborhood. He went outside and stayed in the shade close to his van. Momentarily, the little girl came out of the store and he dropped his quarters, a shower of silver, the coins bouncing on the concrete and going in every direction. She stopped short, startled. He started to bend over to retrieve his quarters, then grimaced and put his hand on the small of his back.

"I'll give you a dollar to pick up my quarters," he said to the little girl. "My doggone back don't work."

The girl hesitated, measuring him with a glance, and then, solemnly, she started to pick up his quarters. Shortly, he had made a game out of it, pointing here and there to where the quarters had rolled, talking to her all the time. "I bet you don't know who I am," he said. "So I want you to obey your mama. You don't have to say nothing to me because I'm sure she don't want you talking to strangers. I just moved in down the street from you, in the next block, and I don't want to get on the wrong side of your mama."

He pointed out the silver crescent moon of a quarter protruding from under a newspaper rack and she scampered to get it. He watched her eyes, brown, wary, because children were, after all, trained little animals with a high startle reflex, and he had but to say the wrong thing and she would be scampering away. "And I bet I can guess your name," he said, smiling. "I bet your name is Kim."

"No," she said, on her knees, her hand searching far back under an ice-vending machine. "My name is Betsy but I don't like it." She managed to bring out the last of the quarters, then stood up and brushed herself off. "There's a Betsy Wetsy doll. They make fun of me at school."

"Then what do you like to be called?" he asked.

"Bitty," she said.

"You mean Betty."

"No, Bitty. My brother calls me that. I like it."

"All right, Bitty. How many quarters did you find?"

It took her a while to count them. "Ten," she said.

"That's fine. You keep four and give me the rest. And since you've been so helpful, Bitty, I'll give you a ride home."

The eyes grew wary again. "I don't get into cars with strangers."

He gave her a tender smile. "We're not strangers," he said. "Your name is Bitty and everybody calls me Mr. Sunshine."

"I never heard of anybody named Sunshine."

"You have now. When I was about your age, everybody called me Sonny." He opened the van door, looked around to see whether there was anybody watching, but the girl at the counter was now talking to the imitation Elvis and it was as if Desmond had surrounded both the little girl and himself with a shield of invisibility. "I'm sure your mama didn't tell you to be afraid of neighbors, only strangers."

"Well," Bitty said, handing him his quarters, "I guess so."

"Sure," he said. She climbed up into the van and he closed the door behind her. "Sure, sure, sure," he said to himself, a small chant of triumph.

Father Rowan sat in the confessional and tried to keep his mind on Mrs. Flora's repetitive sins, which she dutifully recited to him every week with no variation at all. She had stolen money from her husband's pants pocket when he was asleep and put it in the bank, because otherwise he would gamble it away at a sports book, and she had lied to her sister, Constancia, and told her that the Plymouth was broken rather than let her borrow it.

His mind drifted, aware of the police outside and the sense of guilt he felt about the whole business. The monsignor was icy with anger, and when the police lieutenant had come in this afternoon, the monsignor had done his best to dissuade the cops from taking any action at all. He had friends in high places and he wasn't going to let the church be compromised. But his intimidating manner didn't work, and the lieutenant said he wouldn't put any of his men on church property but that the monsignor didn't control the streets and there was a crazy killer out there.

And Father Rowan knew the monsignor would take it out on him, consistent with Church policy. If Father Rowan had been completely obedient, none of this would have happened. He tried to concentrate on the scrollwork of the sliding screen that separated him from Mrs. Flora. A cross had been worked into a motif of winding vines through which Mrs. Flora's voice penetrated with its high nasality.

"So I slapped Vinnie, Father. I mean I just lost my temper and slapped him across the face."

Father Rowan remained silent and she droned on until she was finished. Then he gave her penance and absolution and heard her footsteps moving away in the slow clicking gait that was distinctively hers. He braced himself, hoping beyond doubt that the man would show up one more time and, under the priest's persuasiveness, give himself up.

But there were no more people waiting for confession. He went outside the church, looked down the street as the cop in the ice cream truck drove on up, face drenched with sweat. "Didn't show, then," the cop said. It was not a question, and the priest allowed no expression to show on his face that would either confirm or deny. "When's the next time you hear confessionals?"

"It's confessions, not confessionals. And the schedules are posted inside," the priest said.

The cop frowned. "If a guy walked in and said he wanted you to hear his confession, say, like ten o'clock in the morning, I mean, you'd listen or do whatever it is that you do. Right?"

"Under certain circumstances," the priest said.

"Okay," the cop said, absorbing, eyes looking off down the street. "And a confession, does it have to take place in that little booth?"

"No," the priest said. "As a matter of fact, most people like confession in a more informal setting—an open room, face to face, instead of using the traditional booths."

The cop shrugged, face pained as he lit another cigarette, shook out the match, and flipped it away. "Let's cut the crap, Father, okay? I want to know what we can count on. Sometimes you can talk and sometimes you can't. So which is which? If this guy contacts you, do we hear from you or what?"

"If I get any information outside the confessional, I'll call the police instantly," Father Rowan said.

"Okay, fine." He wiped at his sweating face with a handkerchief. "Were you the one who talked to this guy in the first place?"

"You have your rules and I have mine. I can't answer that," the priest said.

"Can't," the cop echoed, the exasperation shining in his eyes. He inhaled the smoke, blew a cloud into the hot afternoon air. "You know, sometimes I think it would be a good idea if you guys would come down and sit through an autopsy, maybe on somebody this crazy kills. I mean, religion is religion, and I got as much respect for the cloth as the next man, but your on-and-off business could get another dozen people killed down the line."

The priest blinked. He was beginning to develop another headache. He had no more answers. He turned away from the frustrated cop and went back to his office in the church, leaning back in the soft leather seat his mother had donated for his benefit. He looked up at the crucifix on the wall, Christ hanging there in pain, able to bring Himself down and escape the suffering, except that there were higher values and a destiny that was his to follow. The priest realized these things intellectually but wished with all his heart that he could feel them just once, to share the pain or the vision, or to become so caught up in the mass that he would transcend himself. But it had never happened, and so many years had passed, he was certain that it never would.

He remembered giving the last rites to a dying nun who was in her nineties. She had clutched her rosary with such fervent strength that her knuckles turned white, and she had whispered to him with the dying light in her eyes, "I wish the Blessed Virgin had visited me just once." Without missing one beat, he had been so glib in his ritual of comfort that he was able to say, "Now you will be visiting her, Sister." And the old woman died with a great sigh of comfort.

Mine is a dry religion, he thought. I have never had an overflowing heart.

The intercom buzzed. He was not surprised. He had expected it all day. He flipped the switch. "Yes?" he said into the machine.

"Do you have a minute, Johnny?" the monsignor said in that perfectly modulated voice of his, all emotion controlled. The words came out as a pleasant request.

"Certainly, Monsignor," he said.

The monsignor sat behind a desk made of polished wood from the Holy Land. He was going over the text of an after-dinner speech he would be making that night.

"I appreciate your coming in, Johnny," the monsignor said, tapping the eraser of his pencil against the desk. "The bishop has been on the telephone all morning in Reno, and I'm sure you realize he doesn't like it. A lot of influential people have called him today as to why the police have staked out our church."

"I take it the bishop knows what's going on."

"Of course." The pencil made a steady sound, like the slow drip of water from a leaky tap. "The bishop has referred all his callers right back to me. And I have reassured people that the presence of the police has absolutely nothing to do with our church. I have also called the mayor and county officials to demand that the police be removed, and I haven't gotten anyplace."

"Perhaps I should call the bishop personally and apologize."

"That isn't what I would call a good idea, Johnny. The bishop is a Catholic of the old school, pragmatic, certainly, but a firm believer in the rules."

"Technically, I haven't violated any of the rules," Father Rowan said.

"Technically," the monsignor echoed. The drumming became faster, more accentuated, then stopped abruptly, and the monsignor rolled the pencil between his palms. "The bishop can really do as he pleases," he said. "Without any explanation, without any excuse. But you have created a dilemma that distorts the mission of the Church. A good many non-Catholics might not be sympathetic to our reasoning, and it might seem that we are purposely blocking the apprehension of a criminal."

"Can you tell me precisely what I've done wrong, Monsignor? Can you show me where I've misinterpreted my duties as a priest?"

"You don't have a bit of common sense, do you?" the monsignor said. "Does it ever occur to you that you might have dramatized what you heard, perhaps misinterpreted?"

Father Rowan shook his head. "I didn't misinterpret anything. The Las Vegas police have the evidence to prove it."

"Which is where the evidence would have ended up anyway, had you taken no part in any of this. I think you overreacted. The bishop holds the same opinion."

"Does he want me to leave the priesthood?"

"Good heavens, no," the monsignor said. "That hasn't even been discussed, but it would be impractical in any event, because it might seem that you are being punished for putting the Church into controversy. The bishop has decided that we should resolve this on our local level here."

"I want to suggest something," Father Rowan said. "It's apparent that this person has attached himself to me, and obviously, I've mishandled the whole affair. But it occurs to me that if I was to be transferred to a different parish, a different diocese, then perhaps the furor would end, at least as far as the Church is concerned. I know this is an act of cowardice, but I can't separate myself from his crimes. I keep thinking that if I was a better priest, if I knew more, if I had the gift of persuasion, I could have talked him into giving himself up."

He had said exactly what the monsignor wanted to hear, spoken the exact words that the monsignor would have had to expend diplomatic energy to utter, and now the monsignor was at ease. "You're being much too hard on yourself, Johnny. But I think you're showing great wisdom in your attitude. How does D.C. sound to you?"

"My mother's in Washington. And I have a sister, Paula, back there as well, Paula and her family. My father lives in Hawaii with his second or third wife."

"Despite this little mix-up, you've done an excellent job here."

"Thank you."

"And I'm aware that there's a need for communication skills

in the archdiocese offices in Washington. The actions of the government profoundly affect the Church. You would be putting out press releases, talking with congressmen."

Then the monsignor had already discussed this with the bishop in Reno. Father Rowan's future had been set before he came into this office. "I'd prefer the duties of a parish priest," he said.

"I'm sure we all have preferences," the monsignor said. "But we go where we're needed. For the sake of the current situation, I'll make the announcement that you will no longer be performing your sacramental duties. You'll concentrate on reports that are coming due and put together three or four future newsletters. Your pastoral duties will be assumed by Father Shumate, who will be sent in from Reno."

"Yes, sir."

"You've shown excellent judgment in this matter," the monsignor said, glancing at his watch, clearly dismissing him. "You can count on going to Washington in about a week. Is that satisfactory?"

"Yes, thank you."

Back in his office, he felt a combination of shame and relief that he was out of it now. He would give his mother a ring shortly. She would be delighted to have him back in Washington so she could gossip with her friends at the church and be one up on them again—my son in the hierarchy. His mother's health had not been good since his father had fled to Hawaii years ago, and she haunted the National Cathedral, where she lit candles and prayed to be relieved of her afflictions. His sister, Paula, had never been a person to display caring for longer than a week at a time, and her husband, Harold, doing hard manual labor ten hours a day, looked upon the priesthood as a scam, a refuge from what he considered real work. He always absented himself from the house whenever Johnny came to visit.

Well, family problems offered him nothing he couldn't handle and he would be pleased to be out of the desert and back east again. After a year or two with the archdiocese, this minor transgression here would be forgotten and he could maneuver himself back to the parish level, knowing that the situation that had confronted him was an anomaly, a nightmare that would never happen again.

He was about to leave the office when the telephone rang, and he picked it up. "St. Justin Martyr," he said. "Father Rowan speaking."

He was momentarily chilled when he recognized the voice. "Cops," the man said. "Didn't you know I would see them?"

"I'm glad you called," the priest said. "I'm being transferred and I want to make a last appeal to you, for the good of your soul." There was no sound on the other end of the line and at first he thought the man had hung up. "Are you still there?"

"Yes. But you can't leave."

"I didn't make that decision. But give me your name. Let me set up a meeting with the police for you."

"You don't understand," Desmond said. "I've been anointed as a messenger now. I have been told that God is coming to the earth, not Jesus, no, but God himself. And I have to make things ready for him."

"There's a certain peacefulness in not having to deal with you anymore," the priest said. "I'll be going back east, so it doesn't make any difference if I give up all pretense as far as you're concerned. I believe you're sick and you need help but I don't like anything about you. You're a murderer. We're not in the confessional now. So I am about to hang up on you and then I'm going to relay this latest message of yours directly to the police."

"You can't quit," Desmond said, his voice harder than the priest had ever heard it. "There's no way you can drop out of this now."

"Watch me."

"Don't hang up, not yet. I want you to take down a name."

"I'm through with you."

"Call the police and find out about a little girl named Bitty Williams. I'll call you back."

The line went dead. The priest sat with his hand on the telephone and dread in his heart. By all rights, he should report the call to the monsignor and let him make any decisions. He should back off, finding refuge in the words of an inane column that would do nothing more than fill space in a newsletter noted for its bland conservatism. But he would make this one last call.

He dialed Metro, and momentarily he had Picone on the line. "I finally have something I can tell you. But first, I need some information," he said. "Does the name Bitty Williams mean anything to you?"

"Jesus," Picone said. "What do you know about her?"

"Then you do know someone by that name?"

"She was abducted from her neighborhood out near Henderson yesterday. She's eight years old and somebody snatched her. Now give. What do you know?"

"I had a call from the man you want," Father Rowan said. "He told me that God is coming to earth and he says he has to get things ready. I was about to hang up on him when he said to ask the police about Bitty."

"He has her," Picone said, the pain evident in his voice. "Are you supposed to contact him? Did he give you a number?"

"No." The priest took a deep breath. "He'll call back."

"Get any information you can," Picone said.

"I'll talk to you later," the priest said. He severed the connection just as the telephone rang again.

"Your telephone was busy a second ago," Desmond said. "You gave the police an earful, right?"

"What have you done with her?"

"I want to meet you tonight."

"No. I won't do it."

"Sure you will. One more time and you'll be rid of me. You know a casino named La Mirage?"

"No."

"It's at the corner of Paradise and Flamingo. Listen carefully. There's a bank of nickel slots down from the cashier's cage. You sit down at the middle one on your right."

"I won't meet you."

Desmond ignored him. "At nine-thirty, you get yourself a bunch of nickels and you sit down in front of that machine and start feeding it. When there are no more players on that short row, I'll move in behind you. But you won't even look at me. You just keep on playing and we'll talk. And you won't have any police around and the security people won't know of our meeting. Because I'm going to leave this little girl tricked up. If I don't get back to her in an hour, she'll strangle to death. And if I even think I'm being followed, then I just let the little girl die. You understand me?"

The priest was quiet a moment. "All right. Nine-thirty," he said.

He dressed in a T-shirt and jeans and drove his old Ford down to Tropicana and parked on the west side of La Mirage, walking through the warm night into the air-conditioned lobby. La Mirage was a small casino hotel undergoing expansion, with its rooms surrounding verdant gardens and its gaming rooms old enough to have been bypassed by the flashier places on the Strip. A young man and woman were singing in the small lounge next to the bar. He got ten dollars' worth of nickels from the change girl and sat down at the proper machine.

Merciful Father, let me handle this right. He realized he was praying even as he peeled the paper from a two-dollar roll of nickels and put the first one in the slot. He pulled the handle. He played the whole roll, a nickel at a time, allowing his winnings to accumulate in the bin, aware that the payback was less than his investment. He found himself making a personal metaphor of the act of gambling. He had the feeling that he would continue to expend his energies in life, receiving diminishing returns, until at last he had nothing and would end up as a senile priest puttering around a garden somewhere, a gentle and automatic smile on his face, making empty benedictions in the air. There was a good homily here someplace. All gone, except for the love of God. Even if he had been allowed to stay here, he could never mention gambling in any homily, because gaming supported the church and the town.

He played all his money, surrounded by a tour of Japanese women who chattered like birds, and he grew anxious. For one of them had found a machine that was paying off, the bell ringing with irritating regularity, and the other women had settled in at the machines around it. An hour passed, then an hour and a half. He knew he should have notified the police before he came here. They would have posted men outside and surely they could have spotted this man as he surveyed the casino, perhaps even had a drink at the bar and hung around awhile before he realized the Japanese women were not going to leave and he decided to cancel. Well, this

93

was the end of it as far as Father Rowan was concerned. He felt a great sadness for this little girl, and he would pray for her, but he also felt a guilty sense of relief that his part in this grisly business was now over. Someone else would have to handle it because he could not.

He went to the men's room, washed the black residue from the coins off his hands, then went out and got in his car, thinking that he would call Stein after he had talked with Picone. He would cut all his ties tonight and be rid of them. He turned down Tropicana and suddenly felt something cold poke into the back of his head, just above the neck, and he knew instantly that the man had intended to make contact this way all along, hiding in the backseat of the Ford.

"Just keep driving," came the voice, high, strained, like a wire under high tension. "Don't even think of turning your head around. God would love to have me harvest a priest."

"I came alone," the priest said. "There weren't any police around the casino."

"But you *thought* about having the police there, that's the important thing. You considered it because I'm in the open now, no longer protected."

"I don't care anymore," the priest said. "I don't care about any of it. I should, but I don't."

Desmond jabbed the pistol harder against his neck. "You'd better care. One little squeeze of my finger and you'll be dead."

"What more can you possibly want from me?"

"You aren't excited by the news?" Desmond asked.

"That you've kidnapped a little girl?"

"That God is coming to earth."

The priest ignored him. "I'm being transferred back east," he said. "It will be a quiet life, a glorified public relations job. I won't have to deal with you or your delusions anymore."

"I can kill the little girl, you know."

"I have no doubt you can kill her. But I'm equally sure that your God doesn't want you to hurt little girls."

"God rarely asks me to harvest children," Desmond said. "But it happens. I don't want her to be hurt, but this is the only way I can be taken seriously. I want you to call Stein in West Virginia. You tell him I'll be calling him because God is coming and I am God's messenger and I know Stein's true identity. He has to do what's required of him. You can tell him that the first thing I want is a million dollars for the return of the little girl."

Father Rowan continued to drive. He was suddenly very tired, wishing that this crazy man had found another priest for his confessions, someone with more tolerance and more ability. "I'll call Stein one more time," he said finally. "But he doesn't want to have anything to do with you any more than I do."

"He'll want to pay attention this time." Desmond dropped something in the front seat beside the priest. "Turn left at the next corner," he said. The priest turned into a dark street in a residential district. He had driven less than a block before Desmond spoke again. "Stop here."

The priest stepped on the brakes. "The second I get out of this car, you drive on. Tell Stein I'll call him." And then, as if by magic, Desmond opened the door and stepped out, to melt into the darkness. And as Father Rowan looked around, he could see nothing except the shapes of bushes and trees and a row of houses across a small park.

But for the first time, he had something tangible to offer the police. The killer had been in the backseat of this car and he was bound to have left something of himself behind, fibers, dust, fingerprints.

He drove toward the police department, but at the next stoplight, he picked up the item that had been dropped into the front seat, a small package wrapped in brown paper. He opened it, felt sick to his stomach. Against the wrinkled wrapping paper lay the little finger of a small girl, the nail painted with fresh polish. He rewrapped the finger in the paper, put it in his pocket, then opened the car door before he threw up, racked with pain and, God forgive him, hate.

CHARLESTON, WEST VIRGINIA

"**I** appreciate your taking the time to see me, Mr. Stein," Phillips said, raising a hand toward the waiter, and Stein was surprised that he felt provincial in the presence of this glossy man from New York. Stein had known money men before, and Anthony Phillips had all the physical markings of success, from the presidential Rolex on his wrist to the gold cuff links, the tailored suit, the handmade British shoes. He had the patina of the very rich. He was a short man, brown hair thinning slightly, but he showed the effects of being waited upon, touched by barbers and manicurists and masseuses so that he fairly shone with grooming.

He was no older than thirty-five, perfectly at home running the waiter and the lunch as if he were in his private dining room, not the least uncomfortable at being in West Virginia instead of Manhattan. After all, money was where you found it. He had a pad and calculator on the linen tablecloth next to his martini. "And I take it you must know something about my group," he said, "or you wouldn't have agreed to take a meet."

"I'm flattered at the attention," Stein said. "I had no idea our business was even known outside police circles."

"They're not incompatible, you know," Phillips said. "Public law enforcement and the private sector. We currently operate correction centers in seven states and we're a hell of a lot more cost-efficient than public prisons and we have a recidivism rate that's six point nine percent less than any public facility. We're also the largest supplier of law-enforcement computer software in the country and we're anxious to get into the area you represent."

He wants it all, Stein thought, and if his luck holds out, he might get it. "You may be wasting your time, Mr. Phillips," he said. "Thatcher and I run a small operation and that was one of the purposes of the operation from the very beginning, to show it could be done with a minimum staff. We depend on government grants to stay in business. We maintain a data base of our own, stored on our computers and the Big Hummer, and we can operate with comparatively little expense because everything we get is downloaded from police departments and government agencies. They feed us information to keep us current and we process that information and serve as a national clearing house in areas the FBI doesn't cover. I think we run a valuable service but we're never going to be candidates for the Fortune Five Hundred."

Phillips's tanned face projected sincere enthusiasm. "You ready to order, Mr. Stein? Is there anything on the menu you recommend?"

"Catfish," Stein said. "Hush puppies."

"I think I'll take a chance on the KC steak," Phillips said. And he ordered another round of drinks from the waitress and told her to hold the food for another ten minutes. Then he leaned across the table to Stein, moving closer because he was going to be talking money.

"I'll be up front with you, Mr. Stein. We could talk financial statements and play the game, but I'll tell you straight out what we're prepared to do. I know your fiscal situation as well as I know my own. I'll be frank with you. I've had a net-worth study run and I know the value of your computers, your real estate, the whole works. I know your equity position, who you owe and how much. To make this simple, we want your company, and I'm ready to assume all your corporate obligations and pay you a million dollars apiece," he said in a low dramatic voice. "A million for you and another million for Mr. Thatcher, after taxes, spread any way you like, stock options if you want them, and then we hire you at a quarter-mil per for two years and Mr. Thatcher at a hundred thou per to make the transition."

"Why?" Stein said. "How could you possibly make out with a deal like that?"

"We intend to expand the operation," Phillips said. "Eventually we'll include thousands of smaller police departments with computer services that simply won't quit, ten times more efficient than any public agency, including the FBI. We can collect enough government grants to start off debt-free and we'll get our services written into the budgets of every state, county, municipal, and small-town law-enforcement agency in the country, as well as private security firms, which, by the way, represent a potential gross of a hundred mil in two years. We network the whole damn country. If a perp sneezes in Frisco, it's *gesundheit* in Miami."

Stein ate his catfish and listened, in a state of wonder, to the continual and undiminished font of enthusiasm across the table. His own imagination was insufficient to take in the vast sums that Phillips was throwing around so casually. But he realized how smart Phillips was with this offer of his, for the round figure of a million dollars was the fruition of the American dream, an amount that overshadowed everything else at the moment. A million dollars, certainly enough to support him and his family for life, as well as to change the landscape of the future. Barn could have a whole herd of horses if he wanted and Karen could certainly have the summer of painting in Cuernavaca about which she had always dreamed.

After dinner, Phillips ordered a cognac, relaxed, confident, doodling with his Mont Blanc on the pad of paper. "We don't expect any immediate answer, of course. Talk this over with your partner. I'd like to finalize as soon as possible, but don't think that the bottom line here is engraved in stone."

"And where would the new company locate?"

"Someplace close to D.C.," Phillips said. "Tyson's Corners, McLean, Alexandria. We already have one corrections branch operation in Alexandria. Government access is all-important."

"I see. And what about the cases we're carrying now?"

Phillips shrugged as if the subject was relatively unimportant. "Let me give you a proposed time frame. This is only a suggestion, of course. But we'd like to get this new branch on-line within three months, which would mean that you'd have to start setting up within thirty days. I have a list of men ready for interviews and I'm sure you have people you'd like to have on board. We can outbid any public agency for personnel. And you can start delegating some of your current cases as soon as you begin staffing."

They finished dinner and Stein drove him back to the airport, promised to get back to him within a week. Then he returned to the office, knowing he should give Thatcher a call or stop by home and tell Karen what had happened. But he found himself depressed at a time when he should have been elated. He thought he knew why and wanted time to think it through.

He poured himself a cup of coffee and sat at the window overlooking the river. He considered the past. From the day he left New York and the department, he had never looked back nor suffered the slightest regret at leaving. He had never been a team player, and despite his accomplishments in New York, there had always been a gulf between him and the governing hierarchy, the mayor's office, the commissioner's office, the governor's office.

And even in Pennsylvania, as chief of police in a small town, the scale of the political game had been reduced, but not the politics themselves. There were merchants to mollify, a mayor who wanted preferential treatment toward motorcycle riders because his son owned a Harley dealership. The man with the ax had tipped him into his present business, but Stein would have moved on anyway, sooner or later. Because here he had no bosses, no useless reports to fill out, only the paperwork required by the government grants. He could live with that.

He grew restless. He checked the material that had come in since noon. The New Orleans PD had nabbed their ice-pick killer, who had robbed seventeen old men of their pension checks before he stabbed them. Stein would have to notify Seattle, Portland, and San Francisco, where they had similar unsolved crimes dating ten years back. And he found a printout of all the data on the Las Vegas killings that Thatcher had prepared this morning and left on Stein's desk.

He clicked on his gooseneck lamp. Tomorrow he wanted to run a statistical program on two hundred army officers at a base in South Dakota, seeking matches to a personality profile of a rapist who had murdered four young women in the past six months. He sat with his fingers laced together in the oval of light cast by the lamp, and he knew Phillips would abandon a lot of the

100

current projects as unprofitable—cases such as the small-town strangler outside Denver who had killed one person every five years and was now a year overdue, perhaps dead, perhaps in some other part of the country. Stein doubted that the new company would go to the expense, however minor, of a screen on strangler MO's over the country, just in case this one turned up again. This was a nonfunded project, something Stein was doing on his own.

I'm not a businessman, Stein thought with a sigh, just a cop. And that's not only the way it is, but the way it should be.

The telephone rang and he picked it up. It was the priest and his voice teetered on the edge of hysteria. "I'm sorry to disturb you, Mr. Stein, but something terrible has happened here." And he proceeded to tell Stein of the kidnapping of the girl, the surprise of finding the man in his car, and finally the severed finger wrapped in a piece of paper. Something in Stein closed down, automatically, any sense of feeling or personal involvement.

"What do you want from me?" Stein asked.

"He demands that you come here and talk to him," the priest said. "He says he is a messenger from God."

"There's nothing to be gained by my going there," Stein said. "Believe me, I've been through this kind of thing before."

"I'll send you the air fare personally."

"Tell you what I'll do," Stein said. "I'll check into it and get back to you." He hung up, got rid of the priest on the telephone, knowing he could better deal with a trained policeman. He called Picone in Las Vegas. "What's going on?" he asked.

"I figure we'll close to a full moon," Picone said. "Our crazy snatched a kid on the east side of town, chopped off one of her fingers, and sent in a demand for a million bucks."

"You get a make on him this time?"

"Nope. He was in the priest's car and he's one savvy son of a bitch. He didn't leave one shred of evidence in the backseat, not a fiber, a hair, dandruff, lint, a fingerprint, not even dust. Nobody saw him in the park. But we're bound to turn up something. We're doing a door-to-door in the neighborhood where she disappeared. We've got a full task force on it."

"I've been running some studies," Stein said. "He doesn't kill

101

at any time intervals I can make out. He was killing in Connecticut nine years ago, Southern California a couple of years later, and then a gap until the Tropicana killings. It's my bet he's been a local in Las Vegas for a long time."

"Any idea what kicked him off?"

"Nope."

"The priest says he knows you."

"Possible," he said. "We may have a history but I don't know about it. He could have been a bystander or a relative in any one of a couple hundred homicide cases. He obviously thinks I know him and maybe I do. I haven't made any connections yet. And it's also possible he has a fix on me because I got a lot of publicity when I was working the NYPD psycho squad."

"You think you can get him out of the woodwork?"

"No," Stein said.

"We got a fund if you want to fly out."

"I think he'll surface on his own, especially now that he's made a demand for big bucks. He wants media attention. So give it to him. Splash the papers full of it, the grieving family, the appeal for the girl's safety. Don't mention the severed finger and no hysterics about a crazy maniac. If I were you, I wouldn't even connect him in the press with the other crimes. And start a campaign to raise the money, cannisters in convenience stores, appeals on television. That's going to make him believe he'll get paid and show him it's going to take time to raise the ransom. But emphasize that the money's only going to be paid for the girl if she's alive. If he's really after a million, he'll cooperate."

"We've got time pressures here."

"Hell, who doesn't Help the crazy let off steam. Encourage him to get in touch. Since he's got a religious streak, make it possible for him to get his message out. The whole point is to bring him into the open."

"Sometimes I think I'll go to work in casino security," Picone said with a sigh. "Just run the whores and look out for the slot fixers."

"Keep me current."

He locked the office before he went home. Barn was looking at a cop show on television and Wolf raised his head to yawn toward Stein, his big tail thumping a welcome on the carpet. Karen was at the kitchen table, putting gesso on some canvases, looking happier than he had seen her in some time. She had pulled back her hair in a ponytail that set off her delicate features. She was wearing an oversized paint smock over her blue jeans, which tended to make her look even more delicate and fine-boned than she was. She raised her face to be kissed. "Thatcher's been calling every half hour," she said. "He seems to think we're all going to be rich. What's going on?"

He went into the kitchen for a beer, smelled the stew she and Barn had had for supper, and had the sudden wish he had never seen Phillips at all. He sat down at the dining room table with her, took a pull at the beer, watching Barn sprawled out, and he thought how much the kid had grown. "We've got a lot of talking to do, babe," he said. "What would you do with a million dollars?"

"A real million or a wishful million?"

"Real."

"A million before taxes or after?"

"After."

"I think I'd get rid of the station wagon," she said, holding a freshly gessoed canvas at arm's length. "The transmission is shot."

"What else?"

"Barn wants Reeboks. He says everybody in first grade has seventy-five-dollar tennis shoes."

"I can see that you're taking this very seriously," he said.

"As seriously as the odds of our ever getting our hands on a million dollars."

"It's possible," he said.

"If it is, you're not very excited about it."

"I'm not sure how I feel about it," he said. And he told her about the meeting with Phillips, the offer, the conditions. She was quiet a long moment, continuing to stroke the white gesso on the canvas with a broad brush. "Well?" he said.

"I don't know what to think," she said quietly. "I know it's a lot of money, but my first feeling is that I'm happy and content here and protected, dear God, don't forget protected. And I can't think of anything I really want that money would buy."

"You've always wanted to go to Mexico to paint," he said.

She smiled gently. "There's nothing like the possibility of big money to make me question what I really want," she said. "I think

103

Mexico was just a pipe dream. It doesn't seem important." The brush went back and forth. "But the money would ensure Barn's future, wouldn't it? College, whatever he wanted."

"Yes," he said.

"We'd have to move to Washington?"

"Yes. For two years."

"That wouldn't be so bad." She paused thoughtfully, continuing to work, then the significance of what was happening seemed to hit her all at once. "The money really would change things, wouldn't it? Suddenly, my commercial paintings don't seem nearly as important as they did when the money made a difference. I might even get serious. I could make the rounds of the galleries there and maybe do some illustrating for the Smithsonian. And I've always wanted a better school for Barn, where he can learn French while he's in elementary school."

"And if I decide to turn it down?"

"Are you tempted to say no?"

"I know it's unfair," he said, sipping the beer. "But I didn't like Phillips from the minute I saw him. He's too glossy, too smooth. That's beside the point, though. I don't see how we can pass up a deal like this. Thatcher will go for it like a shot. But I don't know that I really want to be a salesman for the next couple of years. They'd have me on the road working all my contacts. And when I wasn't selling city councils, I'd be making pitches to the Justice Department. And I'm dead sure Phillips would junk all the parts of our operation that aren't money-makers."

She put the brush in water, wiped her hands on a cloth. "What would they pay you for the first year?"

"I'd say a quarter-million, plus benefits."

"And by the time you're fifty, you could go right back to doing what you're doing now, couldn't you? I mean, we could afford to close down the house here for that long and hire a couple to look after it."

"Yes, we could."

"And we could still come out here on long weekends and holidays."

"Then the money does tempt you after all," he said.

"Only over the long haul," she said, but suddenly he was picking up something between them that was just under the surface, a discontent, as if his emotional sonar had just outlined the shape of a negative feeling deep within her. "It's the cop business, isn't it?" he said.

"I have no complaints," she said.

"But no complaints doesn't mean no feelings," he said. "You'd feel a lot more comfortable if I was in a different business, wouldn't you?"

"I won't lie to you," she said. "I would miss you mightily if you were out on the road selling the services of the new company, but I'd be sure you were safe, that you'd come back to me alive."

"So you cast your vote for selling."

"Yes, but it has to be your decision, not mine. I don't want you to do something that leaves you full of regret two years from now. But if I had my way, I'd cut you loose from a world full of crazy people. I'm not talking about people who are just mentally ill, but violent and deadly as well."

True, he thought, and he could not deny it. He was still dealing once removed with the same kind of man who had almost frightened her to death. At the moment, she looked terribly fragile, sitting there with the paintbrush in her small-boned hand, a contradictory woman, delicate, fragile, and yet immensely resilient at the same time. She had gone through a hell of a lot.

Barn started flipping the control on the television set before he finally turned it off. "There's nothing on except reruns," he said, bouncing to his feet, coming into the dining room, the perfect distraction.

"Are you still hungry?" Karen asked with a smile.

"Yeah."

"Cookies?"

"Yes, please." They trooped off to the kitchen and Stein thought how much Barn took after his mother, the same fine features, the same quiet laugh, the love of the outdoors. Stein would not be surprised if the boy became an artist when he grew older.

The doorbell rang. "I'll get it," he said, and he found Thatcher on the porch, face ashen, the envelope in his hand. "This came to the office express mail. You better take a look at it. There's no telling what the son of a bitch will do next."

He opened the envelope, removed a Polaroid picture and a note, the same block letters.

YOU CAN'T IGNORE ME, STEIN. THE NEXT TIME I'LL SEND A PIC-
TURE TO YOUR WIFE. WAIT FOR MY CALL. GOD IS COMING SOON.

He looked at the picture in the glare of the porch light. He flinched. The picture was a close-up of the little girl's hand. A spike had been driven through it to pin it to a wooden plank while the crazy chopped off her little finger with a meat cleaver. The sharp metal blade splintered the bone while the crazy snapped the picture with his free hand. The pain leaped out of the photographic emulsion; the silent scream rang in Stein's ears. He felt as if he had been hit very hard in the stomach. He had difficulty breathing.

"You all right?" Thatcher asked.

"No. Let's walk. I need the air." He slid the picture and the note into his pocket, put of sight, tried to put it out of his mind. Change the subject. Let it rest. They walked down to the syca-mores that flanked the road. "I met with Phillips today," he said.

"I figured nothing happened or you would have called."

"Not exactly," Stein said. "I'm not sure what I think or feel about it anymore." He felt the pain again. "The goddamned son of a bitch," he said. "A child."

"That's what our work is all about, isn't it?" Thatcher said.

"You ever talk to Alice about any of the cases?"

"She doesn't want to know. And I know she and Karen avoid the subject of our work when they get together."

"The deal," Stein said. And he told Thatcher what Phillips offered. Thatcher stopped short, rested his broad palm against the trunk of a tree.

"A million dollars?" he said, startled.

"After taxes. Plus benefits and bonuses and a salary for two years."

Thatcher lit a cigarette, a sad expression on his face. "I've never had any interest in training people or selling programs. Jesus Christ," he said softly. "I like it down here, Pete. I like what I'm doing. I mean, that's a hell of a lot of money, but what would I do with it?" He exhaled the smoke into the warm night air. "I guess we could get a job in town, take up fishing, some damn thing like that."

"We don't have to do this at all," Stein said.

"And what happens if we don't?"

"They have a large corporation," Stein said. "They're determined to get into this business."

"So you're saying they'll go ahead without us, start from scratch."

"Yeah. And inside of five years, they'll be competing for the government grants, offering a hell of a lot more services."

"They'll never find anyone with your background."

"That doesn't count anymore," Stein said. "The computers are doing the heavy work, and we don't have a corner on the machines."

"If we stayed," Thatcher said thoughtfully, "could we compete?"

"It's a big country," Stein said. "We could probably hold on to a share of the business."

"Enough for a living?"

"For a while. Eventually, I don't think so."

"Let's leave it this way," Thatcher said. "If you decide to sell, fine. But I won't go to Washington. Alice and I will stay here and I'll take my money at so much a year and see if I can get in with the state police. I'd like a job in the crime lab."

"We have a week to decide," Stein said. He heard his name being called and saw Karen waving from the porch. "Telephone, honey." And then to Thatcher: "How about coffee?"

"Much obliged, but I have to be getting home," Thatcher said. He said to Stein, "We'll talk later."

Stein went into his study to take the call. "This is Stein."

"Did you get the picture?"

"Yes," Stein said, and he slipped his mind into a different gear, even managed to smile up at Karen as she put a hot cup of coffee on the end table beside the chair. She closed the door behind her as she left the room. "I have the picture."

"I didn't want to do something like that," Desmond said. "Do you think I wanted to do it?"

Cool the mark, Stein thought. Keep him calm. "No, I don't think you wanted to do it," he said. "What do you want me to call you? You know my name. I have to call you something."

"D," Desmond said.

"D-E-E? Or just the initial *D*?"

"It's a sound, not a word. I'm not going to give you enough to ID me."

"But you say I already know you."

"Sure you do."

The voice was calm, but Stein could feel the frenetic mind, racing, looping, spiraling, running on some crazy logic he would have to tap into if he hoped to understand. "What can I do for you, D?" he asked.

"You have to come out here, to Las Vegas."

"Why would I do that?"

"You'll know if you think about it. You have the power and you have the credibility."

"The credibility for what?"

"You'll find that out later. But I got your attention, didn't I? Three in the sand, one for the Father, one for the Son, and one for the Holy Ghost."

You're giving yourself away, Stein thought. Keep it up. "You got my attention all right." He made a stab in the dark. "Are you having trouble, D? Are you supposed to be on medication?"

"I don't need medication anymore," Desmond said. "I never needed medication. Did I tell you that God is coming?"

"No," Stein said.

"It was in the note with the picture."

"It may have been."

"God himself is coming. Not Jesus. God. And I'm the only one who knows it. But I have been delegated the responsibility of preparing the way. And you will be helping." He had the rationality of the schizophrenic, the even voice that might have been discussing the stock market or the weather, except that the mind itself was terribly and murderously awry.

Stein concentrated on the voice, trying to remember it, but it was not the least bit familiar to him. "I'm no doctor," Stein said. "I think you should go to your regular doctor and ask him about the medication. You do have a regular doctor, don't you?"

The voice was edgy now, suspicious. "You're trying to trick me."

"I wouldn't do that. You've had a pretty heavy trip laid on you. If the medication helps, then I'd use it."

"It doesn't help. You gave me the power yourself, don't you remember that?"

"No," Stein said. "Maybe you can prompt my memory. How did I give you the power?"

"Don't jerk me around."

"I'm not going to play mind games with you," Stein said. "I'm sorry, but I can't help you."

"Oh, but you will," Desmond said. "I thought about harvesting more people, but this way's better. You don't want to see the little girl hurt any more than I do. But you're going to make me do it. The ring finger will be next, then the middle finger. You don't want that, do you?"

"No, I don't," Stein said. He steeled himself against the anger, the rage that was threatening to leak through the wall of resolve he had erected against it. Keep cool. For God's sake, keep cool. "Tell me exactly what you want with me, D," he said.

"You're going to help me and in return I'm going to give you the bargain of the year. I've offered the girl to the police for a million dollars and they're raising the money. But if you show up with twenty thousand, she's yours. She won't suffer anymore."

"I can get twenty thousand for you in the next half hour."

"Pay attention to what I say," Desmond said, exasperated. "I expected you to be brighter than this. The bargain is only for you. You come out here and we talk for a half hour and you walk off with the girl for twenty thousand dollars. You might even make some money. Like you tell the LVPD that you can get the girl for a hundred, then you give me twenty and pocket eighty."

"I can't get away from here just like that. It'll take me a couple of days."

"That's fine with me. Three o'clock tomorrow and I cut off another finger. The day after, the same thing. And maybe I'll mail one to your wife."

"Why would you do that?"

"She loves kids. I think maybe she'd give you an extra push in my direction."

"Then give me two hours. Where can I call you?"

"Do you think I'm dumb? I'm calling from a phone booth. I'll call you. Two hours sharp." He hung up. Stein called the LVPD and got Picone, told him to trace the long-distance number from which D had called. Long-distance numbers were always recorded automatically, both origin and destination. When he put down the telephone, his hand was trembling. He opened the door and asked Karen to come into the study and then he closed the door behind him. She took one look at him and became alarmed. "You're white as a sheet," she said. "Who called?"

"I have to go away for a few days."

She shivered slightly, as if she was suddenly very cold. "Tell me about it," she said.

"I don't think I want to tell you and I'm sure you don't really want to know."

"I want you to tell me anyway." She sat down across from him, and when he told her part of the facts, he was not prepared for her response. She showed him a combination of disbelief and anger, no, a rage beyond anger, all expressed in a shake of the head and a nervous, humorless laugh. "I don't believe this," she said. "Not after the talk we just had. No more dangers, wasn't that what it was all about? We talk and then somebody finally breaks through your wall, is that it? Some goddamned crazy who's finally hooked you beyond your computers. Don't you have any sense, for God's sake? Don't you remember that son of a bitch with the ax who almost killed you and drove me crazy?" She was crying now, tears of anger beyond calming. "How could he possibly involve you?"

"I can't turn him down."

"You don't want to turn him down."

"Believe me, I don't want to go to Vegas."

She checked her tears, her anger, picked up a Kleenex, held it to each of her eyes in turn. "All right," she said. "Convince me. Make your case why I should let you go off and risk your life and break your word to me."

"I don't want you to know why," he said. "We'll make a bargain. I'll go for three days and when I get back, I'll sell the business. We'll move to Washington until I can train the new managers and make the transition and then we'll come back here. I'll do something else—computer programming, sales, I don't know. But you have my word."

"Don't make the mistake of thinking that you've cooled this mark," she said, voice shaking. "I'm mad enough to kill you or walk out on you and take your son. This is serious goddamned business. So convince me or lose me. Tell me all of it. Where are you going? Who will you see?"

"A religious psychotic in Las Vegas has killed four people. He claims he killed three of them just to get my attention because I'm supposed to know him from somewhere. And I think he'll kill a lot more people unless I go out and talk to him."

"How does he know you?"

"I haven't figured that out."

"And you've been involved in this for some time."

"Yes."

"Then why the sudden need to go out there?"

"He's like a critical mass, ready to blow," he said. "But specifically, he kidnapped a little girl. He cut off one of her fingers."

"My God."

"He'll continue to cut off fingers until I show up."

"Maybe he's bluffing."

"No."

"You don't know that for sure."

"He sent me a picture. Thatcher brought it to me tonight."

"Show it to me."

"You don't want to see it."

"Show it to me anyway. If I decide to risk losing you, it has to be for something real."

Reluctantly, he drew the picture out of his pocket and handed it to her. She studied it carefully, as if it were evidence, her face pale; then she handed it back to him. "If he's that crazy, then maybe he wants you out there to kill you, to take revenge on you for something."

"The pattern doesn't run that way," he said. "The profiles—"

"God, how I hate that word."

"He knows me from somewhere and I represent some kind of authority to him. He claims I have given him some kind of power and can shape up the world for God's first visit." Ah, he was close to lying now, the sin of omission, for this personality type also sometimes killed authority figures, but he slid past that fact. "If I go out and talk to him, he says he'll release the girl without hurting her any further."

"Is that true?"

"A fifty-fifty chance."

"Does the bargain still hold?"

"What bargain?"

"If I stay in this marriage, you sell out the business. And there can't be any possibility that something like this will happen again."

"Yes," he said.

She did not look at him. "All right," she said. "Where will you be?"

"I'll call you when I get located."

"Can I leave Barn with Alice and come along?"

"No."

"Which means there's some danger."

"Yes."

"That's honest." She snuffed out the cigarette. "When will you go?"

"As soon as I can get a flight."

"At this moment, I love you and I hate you," she said. "I may not even be here when you get back. I'll try to live with this, but you get no guarantees. I'll try, but that's all I can promise."

LAS VEGAS,
NEVADA

Desmond turned onto Nellis Boulevard and then, when he came to a grocery store, he turned in very quickly. He jammed the shift into neutral and sprang out the door and looked off toward the roof of the Alpha Beta. He caught a glimpse of it this time. He laughed aloud, nervously, because he knew it was following him. He had almost seen it a dozen times, but now that form had been unmistakable, the wings flashing in the late-afternoon sunlight before the figure concealed itself beyond the ridge of the roof.

He got back in the van, shifted into gear, and moved back into the stream of traffic, biting at his underlip. It had been twenty-four hours since God had told him to flush the Thorazine down the toilet. He had listened and believed and complied, and now he was rewarded with second sight, a heightening of his senses and the knowledge of the angel that followed him. No need for drugs, for chemicals.

He drove out to a restaurant near Nellis Air Force Base, a hole in the wall called My Place, run by a flashy black man named Big Lester, who wore a ten-carat diamond on his pinky finger. Desmond did not believe the diamond was real. And when Desmond delivered the booze, the weight of the cases was nothing to him. God had increased his physical strength as well as the sharpness of his mind. He opened the cases and watched Big Lester pull the bottles out one at a time to make sure the seals were unbroken.

"Not that I don't trust you, Des." The voice rumbled like distant thunder. "But that sumbitch, Swannie, one time he dint have no Jack Daniels, so he filled up a J.D. bottle with Jim Beam." The last of the bottles slid back into its cardboard partition. "Okay, les go into the office and I give you a check."

He opened the door from the stockroom to the office and then Desmond saw it sitting next to the window, the most magnificent chair he had ever seen, no, not a chair at all, a throne of carved wood covered with gold winged cherubs gamboling up either side to a golden sun that seemed to be rising from a velvet back pillow. The throne had a red silk canopy and beneath the seat were inlaid panels of angels with folded hands and adoring expressions on their faces. Desmond could not take his eyes off it. "Where'd you get it?" he asked.

"Hell, when MGM sold out, they sold all the props from *Hallelujah, Hollywood.* And I have a brother-in-law used to work there, so I says to him, 'You see any chairs or deevans for sale, you get something for me.' " His face cracked into a gold-toothed grin. He wrote a check for the whiskey. "That sumbitch got me good. He say, 'I got just the chair for you, only three hundred dollar,' so I say, 'You sure it big enough?' and I give him the cash and he laid it off on me. But he dint come himself. Some big guy pulling a trailer come, because Bud knowed I'd bust his ass."

"How much you take for it?" Desmond asked, and immediately he realized he had used the wrong choice of words, the wrong tone of voice, with too much interest shining through. Big Lester went on writing the check, but Desmond could see the quickening of his eyes, the pricking up of his ears.

"Hell, I been thinking I might run an ad in the paper," he said. "Bud tole me Marilyn Monroe parked her sweet ass in that chair. Marilyn Monroe and maybe lots more famous people. This could be a pretty goddamned famous chair, you know what I mean?"

"You paid three, I'll give you five," Desmond said, trying to cut him off before he really whipped himself up.

"Five?" Big Lester said scornfully. "Why, you ain't even going to buy the gold paint for that."

Desmond looked him straight in the eye, beyond the black pupils and into the brain, and he sent the thought right to the middle of Big Lester's mind. Because Desmond had not harvested for the Lord for some days now, and he wanted Big Lester to know he was standing on the edge of that scary cliff of eternity. You make things hard for me and I'll take you out in the desert and put a bullet through your head. "Five fifty. My last offer," Desmond said.

Big Lester shrugged. "Hell, why not? When you pay me?"

"Three fifty now. Two hundred next week."

"You got yourself a chair."

He got a couple of men from the bar to help load it into the van and Desmond gave him three of the hundreds he had taken off the body in the desert.

As he drove off, he laughed aloud. Things were coming together. It was almost like a balancing act at the circus or working a jigsaw puzzle when all the pieces were constantly changing shape. Stein would be flying in tonight and all of Desmond's powers would have to peak when he arrived. The devil would be running loose and trying to take over.

He drove the van into the warehouse. He worked up a sweat, sweeping the debris away from one wall. He washed down the concrete with a pail of soapy water and then, using a dolly, carefully wheeled the throne into position, slightly away from the wall, where nothing could touch the surface of its perfect back. He did not sit down on it. This was God's throne, after all. Swanson had already gone home. Tomorrow, Desmond would tell him not to use this section of the warehouse. Desmond would get a large plastic sheet to cover the throne.

He drove back to his apartment after stopping at an Alpha Beta for a can of chicken soup. The little girl lay on an army cot, all doped up with Valium and painkiller, her hand bandaged. Desmond heated the soup on the stove and then sat down by the cot and propped her head up, talking to her all the time he tried to coax the soup into her.

"Now, you got to eat to keep your strength up. We're all sorry about your finger, terribly sorry, but it had to be done, and as a reward, your heavenly Father is going to let you grow a new finger. How about that? A new one." Slowly, one spoonful at a time, she allowed the soup to be inserted through her lips. And finally, he dissolved two blue Valium in a spoonful of soup, and when she had taken it, he put her head back on the pillow and watched her until she fell asleep.

Two hours to go and then the tricky part would begin. He did not trust Stein for one minute. Stein was an ex-cop, after all, still doing cop's business, and despite his agreement to say nothing, he would have notified the local police by now. From the time his plane touched down at the airport, the terminal would be swarming with lawmen. Desmond closed his eyes and rocked back and forth, willing the angel to acknowledge his presence, ordering the angel to comply in the name of the Father and the Son and the Holy Ghost. Then he ordered the angel to watch the airport and let him know how many cops were there.

Speak to me. Answer me in the name of the divine Jehovah.

He waited, listening intensely, sweating. Then he heard the voice, the whisper of mystical vocal chords that had not spoken before.

Seven.

The first report. Seven there already, but more important, Desmond had established direct communication with the beyond. He would not have to look for signs and portents anymore. And by tapping it, the source of all things, he was now partially divine himself.

The jet landed just after dark, giving Stein a breathtaking view of lights just before the jet cleared the last range of mountains to the east. He was immediately on guard. D did not think like ordinary men and he could have boarded the plane at Denver, just to keep an eye on Stein as he arrived. Or, as Stein went through the terminal that resembled a casino with its rows of slots, he knew that D could be anywhere and Picone could not make direct contact.

Outside, he took the first taxi in line and told the driver to take him to La Mirage, the casino hotel that D had specified.

"Yes, sir," the driver said. "Welcome to Las Vegas, Mr. Stein. I'm Picone, LVPD." And he flashed his badge.

"How the hell did you manage to be in the taxi I picked?"

"Every taxi in line has a cop at the wheel," Picone said with a grin.

"You boys are thorough."

"We try." He peered into the rearview mirror. "Hold on to your ass. I'm going to see if our boy has decided to tail." He whipped across three lanes of traffic and made a hard right, cutting in front of a tour bus, to a blast of air horns. He went up a side street, parked in front of a 7-Eleven. "Go in and buy a pack of Winstons."

"I don't smoke."

"I do."

Stein went into the store, the night air warm but not unpleasant. He used the time to check the streets for an obvious tail. Nothing.

Back in the car, he handed the cigarettes to Picone. "I think we're clear," he said.

"What time are you supposed to get your call?"

"About an hour from now."

"You eat on the plane?"

"Yeah."

"We'll have a drink." Picone drove to the rear of a line of apartments, led Stein into a living room that gleamed of polished chrome and sparkling mirrors.

"Nice place," Stein said.

"Yeah," Picone said with some irony. "I keep it because my ex liked it. I'm hoping to get her back. You might say it's bait." He opened the doors of a wet bar. "Name it."

"A little bourbon. A lot of water."

Picone handed him his glass, sat down on a modernistic couch, rattled the ice in his glass. "You said on the phone you'd figured something."

"Maybe, maybe not," Stein said. "But I think there's a pattern to his killing in one way. He said he offed the three people on Tropicana just to get my attention. I think he's murderous when he's off his medication. That would account for the short runs of murders in Connecticut and Southern California."

"How about the guy in the desert?"

"My bet is that he was killed for the money he had on him. D rationalizes, claims he's harvesting for God, but I think he goes off his tranquilizers, gets pissed off or needs money or just kills for the hell of it. And he's off his medication now, that's for sure."

"Then we have ourselves a bloody handful."

"Without a doubt."

"You have a sidearm?"

"No."

Picone opened a drawer, removed a 9-mm Beretta, and placed it on the table carefully. "I want you armed for the meet."

"He wants something, so he won't try to kill me unless he goes berserk and loses it," Stein said. "I've thought that through. He's building pressure and he's going to blow all to hell before he's through, but he has specific business with me."

"There's nothing lower than a child molester," Picone said. "Especially the ones who chop them up. Our priority is the return of the little girl. If he's already killed her, we won't blink if you blow him away."

"I don't work that way. If I find out the girl's dead, I'll take the son of a bitch and hand him over to you."

Picone shrugged. "We got your line tapped at the hotel. We'll play this any way you choose. But I want you to have backup."

Stein picked up the pistol, balanced it in his hand, put it in his jacket pocket. "This is your territory, but I'd like you to stay clear tonight. He's going to be high as a kite because he was able to get me here when he knew I didn't want to come. He knows we'll be out to trick him. He's already edgy. With the slightest excuse, he'll kill the girl."

"How you want to play it?"

"I'll bargain for the girl and make a deal. We'll set up a meet. When I make the buy and have the girl, then he's all yours, any way you want him, but only after the girl's clear."

Picone downed half his drink. "We've already raised eighty-three *g*'s. He's bound to know that. It's been in all the papers and on TV. Why's he giving you a cut-rate price?"

"To get me here."

Picone shrugged, stood up. "I better deliver you to La Mirage."

"Just one agreement up front," Stein said. "Whatever you do, you let me know about it first. No surprises."

"Deal," Picone said.

He drove through the portico at La Mirage and Stein made a great show of paying him and adding a tip, all the time surveying the people getting off an excursion bus from L.A. The crazy could be mixed in with that crowd and Stein would never know it. He checked in and was given the key to Room 422, at the back of the gardens. He carried his single bag down the winding path and unlocked the door, flipping on the lights as he let himself in. The room had a kitchenette with a minifridge. He put his bag in the bare dressing room, the pistol in a bureau drawer, and only then did he spot the folded notepaper with the penciled block letters on the outside: MR. STEIN.

He opened it. The message was in the same block letters.

THANK YOU FOR COMING. I HAVE SOMEBODY WATCHING YOU ALL THE TIME AND I KNOW YOUR TELEPHONE IS BUGGED. PLEASE CALL ROOM SERVICE AND ORDER A POT OF BLACK COFFEE. BLACK. NOTHING ELSE. NO SIGNALS TO ANYONE.

There was even the grace note of a suggested signature, a simple capital *D*.

You're a very bright man, Stein thought with a touch of inappropriate sadness. It was as if some accident of nature had warped a mind that was capable of subtle thought, and D did not perceive the world as anyone else saw it. His sense of proportion was distorted; his whole world was unbalanced. His note was polite, appreciative, and paranoid.

Stein picked up the telephone, dialed room service, and ordered a pot of black coffee. He gave his name and room number and sat down to wait. Within fifteen minutes, there was a slight rap on the door and a middle-aged man stood there with a tray. The waiter's eyes were impersonal. He wore a name tag with CLAUDE printed on it. He was definitely not D. He set the tray with the coffee and a split of champagne in a bucket of ice on the table.

"I didn't order champagne," Stein said.

"A gentleman sent this with his compliments," Claude said.

Stein signed the ticket and handed him a ten-dollar bill. "What did this gentleman look like?"

Claude accepted the money. "I don't know. Average. Maybe forty years old. Wearing a sport coat."

"What color?"

"Kind of greenish blue, something like that."

"What color hair?"

"I'm really sorry but I wasn't paying that much attention. He just handed me a twenty and told me to bring you a split of champagne. He said you were doing business together, something like that." His face furrowed. "Is anything wrong?"

"No," Stein said. "I'm here for some meetings." He took the note from Claude. "I'll figure it out. Thank you."

When Claude was gone, Stein slit the envelope open with a penknife.

THANK YOU FOR FOLLOWING INSTRUCTIONS. NOW PLEASE GO TO THE LOBBY. CALL THE NUMBER WRITTEN IN BLUE INK AND TACKED TO THE WALL NEXT TO THE PUBLIC PHONE. YOU ARE BEING LOOKED AT ALL THE TIME, SO PLEASE DON'T DO ANYTHING FUNNY.

He took the pistol out of the drawer and put it in his belt, concealed by his jacket. He wanted to call Karen and let her know that he had arrived safely, but he dare not try it from this telephone. For the moment, he would do as he was told. He went back to the small lobby, found the pay phones and a number in blue on a card tacked to the wall. He called the number and it answered on the first ring.

"What's your name?" came the voice.

"Stein."

"Good. There's no telling who would call a number on a wall. Now this is what you do. Walk back down toward your room and go on past it and out the back exit into the parking lot. Walk east, toward Flamingo. Once I'm sure you're not being watched, I'll follow you."

"I want some proof the girl's alive."

"I can always cut off another finger and bring it to you." There was no irony in the voice, no hostility. It was a flat statement, a chilling suggestion.

"No, I wouldn't want you to do that."

"She's alive. I wouldn't lie to you."

"All right, I believe you. But maybe we'd better put this meeting off. I don't have the twenty thousand yet."

"That's all right for now," Desmond said. "Besides, I'm sure I could get a couple hundred thousand from the police reward fund, if money was all I wanted. I don't really need money because God provides it for me. It's always there. Like, how much do you have in your wallet right now?"

"Maybe two hundred in cash."

"And if I asked you for a hundred dollars, then you'd give it to me, right?"

"Sure."

"You see? God does provide. I wouldn't lie to you about the little girl. She misses her mama. But there are a lot of things I want to talk about. So start now. And remember, I got somebody watching you all the time."

"I'm on my way," Stein said.

The telephone went dead. Close, Stein thought. He has to be someplace near here. He walked out of the lobby and down the dimly lit path, pausing at the exit into the almost deserted parking lot, the gables of condos rearing above the wall on the far side of the lot like a surrealistic range of mountain peaks against the distant glow of the airport. A half-dozen tour buses sat in the darkness like giant boxes. Temporary parking for the casino was on the other side of the compound and he saw no more than a couple dozen vehicles here.

He walked east, in the shadow of the hotel maintenance shops, and he was just thinking how deserted a place could be in the middle of all the frantic activity that was Las Vegas when he saw a movement from the corner of his eye, a shadow against shadows, something swinging at his head with such swiftness that even his reflexes had no chance to respond. A stunning blow, thoughts fragmented, an awareness that he was blacking out, and then nothing at all.

He came awake slowly, head splitting. His hands and feet were bound and he was lying on the floor of a vehicle bumping over an unpaved road. He heard a man's voice humming over the clatter of the engine. He opened his eyes. He was in the back of a van, and he saw the shape of the man's head above the front seat. Stein could see no lights through the windshield. Suddenly, the driver looked around, clicked on a flashlight. The glare was blinding.

"I'm sorry I had to hit you," the man said in a flat voice. "But I wouldn't have found your pistol otherwise. Why in the hell would you bring a gun along with you? You know I can't be killed, because you made me immortal. So there's no reason for you to pretend. But maybe you're afraid, right? You can put that out of

121

your mind because we have work to do and I'm not going to let anything happen to you. You want an aspirin?"

The words spilled out of him, a tumbling brook of sounds, hyper, and Stein would have to slow him down, keep him cool, nonvolatile. "No thanks," Stein said. He took his time answering, knowing that he must select his words with great care. "If you want me to help you, you're going to have to clue me in. My memory isn't as good as it once was."

"That's not very clever. Ignorance won't cut it." Desmond turned his attention to the road in front of him again. He drew to a stop and killed the engine. The silence was broken only by the sound of hot water gurgling through the van's engine. Desmond climbed out, opened the side door, and pulled Stein out, helped him to his feet. "You sit over there, on the flat rock."

"My feet are tied."

"Not tied. Hobbled," Desmond said. "You can take short steps." He held the light in front of Stein and guided him to the rock. "Sit down," he said, and then as Stein sat, Desmond took a bottle from his pocket. "Whiskey?"

"No."

"You're probably wondering how I can drink alcohol," he said. "But God has nothing against it. Alcohol clears the bloodstream, scours out the arteries, kills all the germs that the devil plants." He uncapped the bottle, took a long drink, and capped it again. He looked to the west, where the lights of the city stained the clouds over the hills. "Now, you may be trying to get me to kill you because you know that would be the greatest honor you could ever have. I am God's harvester. The people I send on are transmogrified immediately, changed from the body to the holiest kind of spirit. They go straight to the throne of God." He shone the light on Stein's face.

"Let's get down to business," Stein said. "Why did you bring me to Las Vegas?"

"I know how I look to people," Desmond said. "Hell, I'm supposed to make the advance arrangements for God's triumphant trip to earth, but who's going to believe me when I tell them that? Nobody. So it's going to be up to you. You're going to have to let the world know who you really are and what you did to make me immortal."

"What makes you think anybody gives a damn what I think one way or the other?"

"I have the clippings at home to prove it. The magazines write about you because you're important and they trust you." He took another pull from the bottle, looked in Stein's direction. "You're the big expert, right? You say somebody's crazy and people believe you. But you tell them that somebody is sane and that you gave them a divine gift, and they're going to believe that, too."

"The best thing you can do is to show compassion for the little girl," Stein said. "You show good faith and turn her loose and people will believe you."

He had said the wrong thing and he knew it instantly. The pistol in Desmond's hand jerked up, pointed straight. Stein heard the click of the hammer. Desmond's voice was tight, immediately on edge. "You try to horse me around one more time and I'll blow your fucking head off." And then, before Stein could say a word, Desmond chuckled, lowered the pistol, stuck it in his belt. His anger had switched to humor in the flick of an eyelid. "I keep forgetting. You know the score. You'd like a swift trip to sure glory, wouldn't you? But you don't have to provoke me, because you can trust me," he said in a low voice. "Because things are happening."

"What kind of things?"

"Do you know who's watching you at the hotel?"

"No."

"Of course not. He wouldn't make himself known to you. He was just assigned to me and he's reluctant about it." Desmond sighed. Stein's eyes had adjusted to the darkness now. Even though he could not make out definite features, he could tell that D was a large man with a thick square head and big arms and legs. Desmond lit two cigarettes, but his head was turned away, his face concealed. Automatically, he kept one cigarette and put the other in the corner of Stein's mouth. "Thank you," Stein said, and the illogical thought hit him that after the ordeal of giving up cigarettes, he had no choice but to accept this one. The first rule of dealing with a crazy was to cross him only when there was a strong and definite reason for doing it. "Now, I ask you again. What did I do for you?"

"You brought me back from the dead."

"When? How?"

"You have to come up with that yourself. Are you afraid to reveal your true identity?"

There was a trick to obsessives, Stein thought, because they would turn any words into what they wanted those words to mean. Right now, he needed time. "I'll have to think about that."

Desmond sucked on the cigarette. The flare of the coal illuminated a broad and spatulate nose, big mouth in a half-smile. "At least you're not denying it anymore," he said. "That's progress. I know the risks you'd run in revealing yourself. So what's it going to take?"

Stein thought a moment. "You release the girl and we have a deal," he said.

"How about this?" Desmond said, obviously on a high. "You're not the only one who has powers. What if I deliver the girl, what if I persuade God to restore her finger so it's whole again?"

Stein was dizzy. His head hurt and yet he was tracking now, his mind on the same wavelength, playing Desmond like a fish, trying to get him hooked before he spooked and darted away. "You're talking a miracle, then," Stein said quietly. "You're going to do this in public?"

"Sure. A public miracle."

"You do that and I'll admit who I am and you get my full cooperation."

"Ah," Desmond said gravely. He nodded, lit a fresh cigarette from the glowing butt of the first. "That still doesn't take care of everything."

"What else is there?"

"I want the cops off me."

"Listen," Stein said. "They'll never tag you for those people in the vacant lot, not if you bring off a miracle. But there's the guy you burned in the desert. Why'd you do that?"

"God gave me the signal. He was a big nothing."

"You got nothing to worry about then."

"You guarantee that?"

"Yes."

"How do I know I can trust you? You're not even Christian, after all."

"You know you can trust me or you wouldn't have called me in the first place."

"I still want the twenty thousand dollars."

"The twenty thousand gets delivered when the girl gets turned loose, however you work it."

"No, the twenty thousand is paid up front. I need the money."

"How do I know she's still alive?"

"She has to be alive for me to produce the miracle. Besides, you can have Polaroid pictures whenever you want."

"Can I talk to her on the telephone?"

"No," Desmond said. "She's doped up to keep her quiet. And I want the twenty thousand tomorrow."

"You'll have it."

Desmond reached into his pocket, and in the darkness Stein could not see what he was doing. Then abruptly, deftly, Desmond swung around and Stein felt the sting as the needle punctured his shoulder.

"What the hell . . ."

"Valium," Desmond said. "If I know about anything, it's Valium. Far easier on you than a hit on the head."

Stein felt himself slipping away, phasing out, a peculiar sensation and not unpleasant. And then he dropped away into darkness.

"Okay," Picone said, wadding up a stick of Juicy Fruit and popping it into his mouth. "So what we got?"

"He's coming around," the doctor said. He leaned over the bed and rolled back Stein's left eyelid with his thumb. "Can you hear me, Mr. Stein?"

Stein moaned slightly, made a move as if to sit up, but his head cleared the pillow no more than an inch before he fell back. He brought the doctor into focus, a young resident with a mustache, and then Picone, his jaws flexing against the gum. "I can hear," Stein said.

"What you on?" Picone said.

"Valium." Stein tried to keep his voice from slurring. "Injection."

"Will it hurt him to talk?" Picone asked the doctor.

"Not if he feels like it."

"I feel like it," Stein said. "Help me sit up. And I want black coffee." He struggled to sit up in bed. The coffee made him more alert. "Where was I found?"

"Sitting propped up next to the emergency room door," the doctor said.

Picone took a tape recorder from his pocket, clicked it on. "You saw him, then?"

The doctor drifted off and Stein finished a cup of coffee. "Hard facts first. Caucasian, approximately forty years old, one ninety to two hundred pounds, maybe six feet, large square head, wears cowboy boots, jeans, plaid shirt, no hat, broad face with a prominent nose. I couldn't fix an accent. Not uneducated. Hair shaggy, dark. Drinks from a pint bottle in a paper bag. Smokes Winstons."

"You see enough to make a composite?"

"No," Stein said. "The van. Eighty-three Chevrolet. Side door. Dark color, probably royal blue. Backseats removed for a cargo area. Carrying boxes. No smells. Very clean. I was tied with rough hemp rope, not smooth."

"Any idea where you were?"

"In the desert. Northeast. I saw the Big Dipper, the city lights."

"How far out?"

"I don't know." He swung his feet to the floor, establishing a tentative balance, headed for his shoes and socks, which sat on a radiator.

"License plate?"

"Never in a position to see it."

"I'll get the description out. We'll pick him up."

"You won't find him," Stein said. He put on his shoes and socks with difficulty. "He may be psychotic as hell but that doesn't mean he's not clever. He follows a logic that makes perfect sense to him. He has his own set of rules, thinks he can't be killed. He believes he's a messenger from God and that God is going to protect him. He wants the twenty thousand up front and he wants me as his personal intercessor."

"His what?"

"He trusts me. He intends to perform a miracle and have God restore the little girl's finger. And then I arrange things so he goes free to set up for God's return to earth."

"Shit," Picone said.

"We pay the cash first. He delivers the girl later."

126

"No can do," Picone said. "If he gets twenty with no delivery, he'll ask for fifty more."

"He started off at a million."

"And he knew he wouldn't get it."

"This is your territory," Stein said. "But I have to tell you what I think. He's got the tunnel vision of a religious fanatic. I believe he's playing this straight. I don't think he'll bump up the price because he's gone to such a hell of a lot of trouble to get me here and we have a deal."

Picone shrugged. "You have any idea the number of crazies we deal with?"

"I'm not talking con games."

"You're not and I am," Picone said. "Let me tell you something about this town. It's got some of the best people I ever met, but let's face it, the whole place lives on the seven deadly sins. I'll give you a scenario. Some guy loses fifty grand at the tables, borrows from a shark who's going to bust his legs because he can't pay back. So our loser turns into a crazy, kills a few people to let us all know he's serious, kidnaps a sweet little girl because the public will go apeshit to donate money to get her back, and he pulls in the country's biggest psycho catcher to make it all legitimate. Then he fucks us all around with the amount of money he wants. We end up paying a couple hundred grand, and he pays back the shark, stiffs the kid, and it's off into the wild blue yonder."

"I talked with him," Stein said. "He's out of it, believe me. Nobody can fake that kind of conversation."

"I wouldn't say that. You can fake it. I don't want to get crossways with you but I have procedures to follow. You feel like leaving the hospital?"

"I feel like hell," Stein said. "But he's going to call the room at the hotel."

"Fine. When you giving him the money?"

"Today."

"I'll give you a ride." Picone was quiet a moment, thoughtful. "We'll stop downtown and pick up the cash."

"You going to let me handle him my way?"

"Nope."

"Then you're going to jump him."

The morning air was hot and dry in the parking lot and the detective's car was an oven even as he started the car and turned on the air conditioning. "Sure we'll jump him," Picone said. "Any way you slice it, the money is bait and he's the fish."

"What about the girl?"

"If he's playing level with you, then she's alive and we'll get her back. If he's lying to you, then odds are that she's already dead, so he won't have to mess with her."

Stein shook his head as Picone edged the car into traffic. "A twenty says you're wrong."

"You got it," Picone said. "But my way's going to work. This psycho won't even know he's being observed."

"He'll count on being watched," Stein said. "He's thinking two moves ahead."

"I saw the people he took out. I want to make this grab myself."

"If," Stein said.

"I wouldn't bet twenty dollars if I wasn't sure," Picone said, a trace of smugness in his voice. "Ask around. Anybody will tell you. This may be Las Vegas, but Arnie Picone don't gamble."

"Goddamn," Swanson was swearing. "God-d-doubledly-damn. How in the hell could you do that?" He spat tobacco into an old coffee can.

"Do what?" Desmond said, checking the invoice. "How come you lowering the price of kretek cigarettes?"

"Because that goddamn Thai testurant won't buy our booze unless we come down on the cigarettes. But don't change the subject." His eyes were fiery. "What kind of big shit you think you are? Who give you permission, huh?"

"For what?"

"This ain't no used-furniture store. And you ain't going to make it one. So you get that goddamn chair out of there by dark."

Desmond didn't look up from the invoice. "I'm buying the place from you. I'll give you the twenty thousand cash tomorrow and pay out like you want."

Swanson spat again. "You shitting me?"

"No. I had an aunt. She died and left me the money."

"I'll believe that when I see it."

"Oh, you'll see it all right," Desmond said, making another

check mark on the invoice. "And if I was you, I wouldn't even mention that piece of furniture I left in the warehouse. And I sure wouldn't lay a hand on it. Because it's sacred. It belongs to God."

"Shit," Swannie said again. "Until I see the money, this is my business."

Desmond turned his eyes toward the old man, glacially cold. He put the paper down, leaned over with both hands resting on the desk. "God already took your legs," he said in a voice that was little more than a whisper. "You make trouble for God and he'll yank your arms straight out of their sockets. He'll puncture your eyeballs and fry your brain with electricity." He shook his head slowly back and forth, but the cold eyes never left Swannie's face. "Zap!" He snapped his fingers. "Just like that and you're dead meat or worse."

Swanson was shaken. His face was white. A thin stream of tobacco juice trickled down from the corner of his mouth. "Okay," he said, his voice a croak. "Okay. I ain't going to bother the chair."

"And apologize to God."

"I got nothing against your religion," Swanson said. "You know my nature. I don't mean nothing."

"I got to go load the van."

He went into the warehouse and took the plastic sheet off the throne to make sure Swannie hadn't touched it. He took out his handkerchief and ran it over the gilded features of a cherub, heard a whisper of wings, and squinted up into the semidarkness of the rafters. The angel was sitting there, features dim, wings glowing dully, almost invisible against the shadows and the pattern of the roofing.

Have you brought a message? he asked the angel without speaking.

The angel made no sound.

Desmond covered the throne, his resolution stronger than ever. He loaded the van and then, making sure that Swanson had gone to the toilet, put in a call to Stein's hotel. He watched the second hand on his watch and began to count from the moment Stein lifted the telephone.

"This is Stein."

"You have the money?"

"Yes."

"There's a McDonald's on Tropicana. Put the money in a

brown paper bag. You get yourself a cup of coffee and then sit at the back. When you get up, you leave the paper bag on the table."

"When?"

"One hour."

"Don't make a mistake." He drove the loaded van a couple of blocks from his apartment, then he transferred to his eighty-one Ford. He looked in the mirror and put on a false mustache and a pair of horn-rimmed glasses that had no lenses. He drove down Tropicana, smiled to himself because a cop car seemed to be making a routine traffic stop a block down the street from McDonald's. But the young cop was leaning against the door of his own car, a walkie-talkie against his face, and that meant he was not talking to headquarters; no, he was checking in with a whole crew of walkie-talkie cops woven into McDonald's.

Desmond passed on by, drove to a convenience store, and bought a warm case of Coca-Cola Classic. He drove out to La Mirage, parked in the lot, and carried the case into the compound. He stopped by the Coke machine, where he could see the door to Stein's room. He took a special key from his pocket, opened the machine, and started putting cans in the dispensing racks while he studied all the windows within sight, one at a time. He listened to chattering Mexican maids as they passed by, pushing their cleaning carts. A pale-skinned couple went out of the casino and headed toward their room, the husband riding the little woman because she had played five dollars a shot at blackjack. Desmond had a keen sense of smell. He could pick up a cop from a half-mile away. There were none around here. No, they were all down at McDonald's, waiting for Stein to arrive and leave the paper bag—to draw him in. They would have allowed him to get outside, away from the kids, before they shot him dead.

He took his time. Plenty of time. He owned all the time in the world. He put another can in the rack, looked up to catch a brief glimpse of the angel settling down on the side of the roof away from him. He saw a beefy man in a business suit coming down the walk, obviously hotel security. "Hey," the security man said. "What's cold?"

"Coke's cold," Desmond said with a crooked grin meant to answer and disarm. "That's what I sell. No other drink except Coke." He took a cold one from the machine, handed it to the security man.

"Much obliged." The tab hissed. The can tilted against his mouth. He wiped his mouth with his handkerchief. "How come you guys pulled such a dumb one?"

"What dumb one?"

"All that shit about changing Coke."

There was movement down the walk as a familiar-looking man went through the garden to Stein's door. The priest.

"Why mess around with a good thing?" the security man said. "I mean, what the hell, I been drinking Coke all my life, but if you would've changed it for good, I wouldn't give you a dime a can for it."

Desmond sighed, a long exhalation of breath, listening without hearing the security man—because the priest had knocked on Stein's door, which opened to admit him. Desmond knew there was no way he was going to get at that money tonight but, he thought, he would wait around, just in case. He finished loading the machine, studied the face of the security man, the broad forehead with two deep vertical furrows. He visualized the brain encased in the skull, the two halves coming together like the sections of an orange. He could always draw the security man out to the parking lot, offer him a free case of Coke, because everybody was on the take here, and when there were no witnesses, place a bullet straight down that obscured cleavage of the brain.

He was short of breath. The thought occurred to him that perhaps he needed to harvest more people who were busily consuming oxygen and water and the resources of the earth, in order to make more room for the presence of God.

"So what you think?" the security man was saying. Desmond realized he had missed something leading up to the question.

"Well," Desmond said, stalling.

"I mean, you think Coca-Cola's a good stock to invest in?"

"Not now," Desmond said, lowering his voice as if imparting highly sensitive information. "But look for something big to happen about a month from now, cataclysms, natural disasters, famines in foreign countries, and then buy Coke stock, because people always drink Coke in nervous times." He stopped, grinned abruptly. He had been about to say too much, about to tell this broad-faced man that God was coming and he was going to shake things up. And still the thought lingered that perhaps he should harvest this man, that maybe it was predestined, because he was still hanging around, swigging the Coke out of the can. You don't know how close you are to seeing God this very day, Desmond thought. A living example. Close to being a dead example.

"Yeah," the security man said. "I'll remember that. I sure as hell will." He drifted back toward the casino, paused to lift the can in Desmond's direction. The movement on the roof caught Desmond's eyes again, the flutter of wings. Something prickled within him. The angel was just out of sight, but Desmond felt as if the creature was mocking him, accusing him of a loss of nerve for not harvesting this security man, and it began to occur to him that the angel might not be a blessing after all.

"I've been doing a lot of thinking," Father Rowan said. He swallowed two aspirin, washed them down with the glass of water Stein had provided. "I realize I have to do something."

Stein counted the money for the last time, put rubber bands around the clumps of bills before he put them in a paper sack. "I don't have time to talk, Father. I'm running on a strict schedule."

"This will only take a couple of minutes."

"That's literally all the time I can give you."

"You have to understand my position," the priest said, a part of his mind waiting for the aspirins to affect the headache. "I have a niece about the same age as the girl he took. And he went too far when he cut off the finger, when he mutilated a child. And I don't believe that Christ would approve my position for a minute. So I want to make you a proposition."

"I'm listening."

"I'll cooperate. He won't go anywhere near the church, but I can help you in other ways. The monsignor has strictly forbidden any cooperation with the police, but if it will help, I'll get you a copy of the church rolls. You can talk to people at home. Maybe one of them has seen this man and can give you a lead."

"And in return?"

"A *quid pro quo.* You hedge the facts about where you got your information, enough so that no one ever connects the information with me or with the church. I'm being reprimanded anyway, transferred, but the Church is my life and I don't want to risk losing what I do have. Can you guarantee me confidentiality?"

Stein folded the top of the bag with the money in it. "We may not need it."

"That would be a great relief to me."

"Right now, I have to go." He stood up.

"Can you tell me what's happening?"

"I'll walk out with you."

The afternoon heat was intense in the parking lot. The priest was driving a modest Ford. "I'm being transferred back to Washington," he said, squinting up toward the cloudless sky. "I'm supposed to consider it as punishment, because I'll be pushing papers around and writing innocuous reports. But I'm getting used to the idea. I won't be on the spot back there. I can say that in favor of it."

"We all suffer dilemmas," Stein said. "I hope things go better for you."

He left the priest and walked to the red Chevrolet that Picone had loaned him for the day, the paper bag under his arm, taking nothing for granted. But the adrenaline was pumping and he felt jazzed up, a welcome feeling. Because he was in the middle of things once more, in the center of the action, vulnerable, excited. He walked around the car before he unlocked it and removed the cardboard sun screen. He left the door open to release the trapped heat while he studied the outside of the compound wall. Three Mexican workers were moving what appeared to be bed frames from a truck into a repair shop. Stein was certain he was being watched.

He was going through the motions and he knew it, because he was in Picone's territory and this was the way they operated. It wasn't going to work. The crazy was setting up an impossible situation, demanding that the money be left in a McDonald's, for God's sake, an easy place to stake out. There was no chance at all that the money could be picked up. The craziness would continue.

He started the car, turned on the air conditioner, and drove down Tropicana. From the moment he neared the McDonald's, he saw the absurdity of the situation. The police could not allow children to be present in a place where an armed confrontation might take place, so they had carefully cleared all families with children out of the restaurant. A few cops sat around dressed like workmen.

Stein was sweating by the time he went inside, and the thirty-five-year-old manager of the franchise was close to losing his cool. All the time he poured Stein's coffee, he was grousing under his breath to a plainclothesman just on the other side of the order window.

"I can't afford another San Ysidro," he said. "You know what the community wanted to do down there, for God's sake? They wanted to burn it to the ground so it wouldn't be a reminder."

Nothing's going to happen here, Stein wanted to say to him but did not. Because at San Ysidro some nut had come in and opened fire and slaughtered people, all without warning, and here the crazy was setting up an exercise to make the police jump through the hoops. It was his way of feeling superior.

Stein sat down at the rear of the restaurant on a red plastic seat that did not fit him. He looked out on a deserted plastic playground with a statue of Ronald McDonald in the middle of it and slides and swings, all empty. He sipped his coffee, put the bag with the money on the seat next to him, waited. A half hour passed. Nothing.

The manager came up to the table. "There's a telephone call for you, Mr. Stein."

Stein went behind the counter and Picone materialized from the kitchen area.

"Stein here," he said into the telephone.

"You have the money?"

"Yes."

"How do I know it isn't doctored? It's easy to doctor money, fix it with powder that stains or glows in the dark."

"It's twenty thousand, small bills, rubber bands around each five hundred. It hasn't been treated."

"I know better than to trust you. What was the priest doing with you at the casino?"

You were there, then, you son of a bitch. I knew it, he thought. "The priest's in a bad position."

"He's betrayed his responsibility."

"He hasn't betrayed anything. You've been using him as a go-between. You can't damn him for that. He's concerned about the little girl. Hell, I'm getting tired of this," he said into the telephone with calculated disdain. "You and I made a deal and came to an understanding, but I'm just about to back away and let you have it. I've followed your damned instructions for a drop you never meant to pick up. If you want to talk, fine; if you want the money, fine; but don't jerk me around anymore."

"You keep forgetting. I have the little girl."

"I don't give a damn," Stein said. "How do I know you're not going to welsh on the deal we made?"

"I can do as I please."

"Right. And I don't have to do anything. I'm going to give you exactly two minutes. You either make sense to me or I hang up and go back east and leave you on your own."

There was a pause and Stein knew what the man was thinking. His mind would be muddled now. The man was an obsessive. "You can't back out," Desmond said.

"Watch me."

"You leave and I'll kill the girl."

"You do what you have to do," Stein said. "I trusted you and you're trying to make a fool of me. I've been waiting for this miracle of yours, and so far I haven't seen shit. I have the cash. It's your turn."

The man's mind was scurrying through unfamiliar territory. Stein could feel it. "You drive out to Hoover Dam tonight and go up the mountain on the other side," Desmond said. "You'll pass an Arizona information building on your left. The next turnout to the right is an unimproved rest stop. You be there at ten o'clock. You turn out your lights and you open the bag of money and you put it on the hood of your car. I want to see if it glows in the dark."

"Only if you have the girl there."

"No."

"Then I won't be there, either."

"You don't get the picture," Desmond said, his voice almost apologetic. "If I showed up with the girl, cops would come out from every rock. You'd have me and the money. You'd never find the girl. She'd live maybe twenty-four hours without my help."

"I'm tired," Stein said. "I'm tired and I don't like the deal."

"Then try this one. You give me the money and I'll take you to the girl. We'll decide where we're going to have the miracle. We'll settle it tonight."

Concessions, Stein thought. He was edging the man away from his compulsion.

"Okay," Stein said. "But this is the last time."

He hung up. The manager was fuming. "You have any idea how much money I've lost with this empty little drama?" he said.

"Would you like us to have had a shootout?" Picone said, unruffled. "Hell, just having all your windows busted by gunfire would have cost you more than this. You want me to release all this to the papers: 'Gunfight Avoided in Local McDonald's'? How many kiddie parties you think that'll bring you?" He looked to Stein. "Let's go someplace and get a beer," he said.

Stein rolled up the paper bag with the money inside. Picone drove to an area west of the interstate, a neighborhood where he parked at a sedate Yuppie tavern. The interior was cool and dark, a cave shelter against the desert sun. He ordered the beer. "I just won ten bucks," he said. "No offense, but when you first got here, the odds were two to one that you'd screw up with the first pressure. You just earned a heavy reputation for cool."

"Collect your money while you can," Stein said. "The crazy son of a bitch is getting to me." He drank the icy beer, gave Picone the details of the call.

"You think the girl is still alive?"

Stein shrugged. "I had a case once where a man kidnapped a seventy-three-year-old woman and collected on her for over a year. Every time the family began to doubt, the perp came up with a tape recording of the old woman talking about Christmas or wishing a grandchild happy birthday. But she'd been dead since the first week, right after she finished making a year's worth of tape."

"How'd you catch him?"

"We didn't. He drank too much, got into a car accident, was booked on a DWI, and then bragged about what he had done with the old woman."

"Shit," Picone said. "What odds you give the little girl?"

"Sixty-forty she's dead." Stein finished the beer. "We need to ID him. We need to know where he's keeping the girl if she's still alive, where he dumped her if she's dead."

"We've run the profile through every psychiatrist and hospital in Nevada," Picone said. "We can get past the private shrinks, but the hospitals have a list of fifty-three hundred men who could fit. There's always the chance he was never treated, never hospitalized."

"I think he was," Stein said. "I asked him if he was on medication and he said he didn't need medication anymore. I'm willing to bet he's spent time in hospitals. He knew the exact dosage of Valium to put me out. But even if I'm wrong, let's play it this way. Download the fifty-three hundred names into the computers back home and let Thatcher run matches with mental patients in public facilities in Connecticut and Southern California during the times he was there."

"We're running out of time."

"We're always running out of time. I want a deal for tonight."

"What?"

"You let me take it alone."

"Like hell. Why should I take the chance? You wouldn't have done it when you were in homicide."

"Maybe not," Stein said. "But the son of a bitch isn't afraid of getting hurt. And he wants my help with the little girl. You stash your cops around on this side of the state line and get Arizona involved on the other, and if you get lucky, you may get him, but you sure as hell won't have the Williams girl."

Picone had another drink. It was obvious he was weakening. "Shit, it's going to be my ass if you're wrong."

"I want a flat wafer homing bug. You got any patches I can stick to the bottom of this paper bag?"

"What for?"

"I'm going to go with him if I can. I'll tell him we'll have some kind of ceremony for the little girl. You stay on the west side of Hoover Dam and when you pick up the signal coming your way, tag along. I'll feel a hell of a lot more comfortable with backup."

"Okay, I'll get you one."

"Have the valet service at La Mirage put it into the pocket of a suit I'll send out for cleaning and hang it in my room."

"Will do." Picone tapped his empty glass with a silent finger. "Anything else?"

Stein shook his head slowly, negatively. "He can't have all the luck," he said. "Something has to break in our favor."

Stein did not like his room. Even with the drapes open, the room was too dark and the light bulbs were dim. The room had been built for nothing except sleep between casino runs, but at least it was quiet. He went over his notes again and once more came to nothing. He picked up the telephone and called home, needing the contact with Karen, the sense of normalcy.

She answered on the first ring. "Darling," she said cheerfully. "I was hoping you'd call. How are things going?"

"I'm still in the middle of the desert, figuratively as well as literally."

"Oh." Her disappointment was palpable. "I was hoping you were calling to say that some miracle had happened and you were on your way home."

"Soon," he said. "I just wanted to hear your voice. I miss you and Barn. Where is he?"

"Feeding Jeff's horse, I think," she said quietly. "The television says it's a hundred and twelve in Las Vegas."

"It feels like it. Is it cool back there?"

She sighed. "It's honesty time, darling," she said. "I have to know what you're thinking. Are you calling to set me up for a delay?"

"No, our deal still holds."

"You have two days left, then," she said. And then, after a silence: "Are you hooked again?"

"No, it's not that. There's a little girl's life at stake."

"And you're the only one who can save her, isn't that about it? It must be pretty strong stuff after all these years of computers and printouts."

"I won't lie to you," he said.

"I wish you didn't need to," she said wistfully. "I wish you could tell me that your ego isn't involved and that I can believe that you're perfectly happy with the life we have here."

"I can say that," he said. "I am happy there."

"But not the same way," she said. "I'm sorry, darling. But I know what this means. And you have to tell me what you're going to do. That was our deal, remember?"

"Okay, this makes me feel important," he said. "I get a rush out of it. But a deal's a deal and this is coming to an end."

"One thing," she said. "And I have to know the truth about this. Are you in physical danger?"

"I can't answer that because I don't know. I'm dealing with a psychopath who seems cool and rational at the moment. But he can blow anytime, I know that."

"I appreciate your honesty. Take care of yourself. I love you."

"Nothing's going to happen to me. I'll come home and everything will be like it was before."

"We'll have to talk about that. Call me when you're on your way." The line clicked, gave way to a dial tone. She had hung up.

His suit came back from the valet service. He found the patch inside, marveled at the ingenuity of the minuscule transmitter, then peeled back the protective paper and applied the bug to the bottom of the sack. He found an envelope in the suit pocket containing a .32-caliber Smith & Wesson and a note from Picone. "See if you can hang on to this one."

He put the pistol in his waistband. Okay, D, or whatever your real name is. You have another twenty-four hours and then I'm going home.

When the priest answered the telephone and found the man on the line, he was not only startled but frightened, and he compressed a prayer for guidance into a fraction of a second.

"I didn't think I would hear from you again," he said.

"Things have changed," Desmond said in a subdued voice. "I've made a deal with Stein."

"Oh?"

"I never really meant to hurt the little girl."

Father Rowan was silent, eyes closed, mind in turmoil, because he was not trained to know what this sudden reversal in attitude meant.

"Are you still there?" Desmond said.

"Yes."

"I want your help."

Never, he thought, but he did not say it. "What kind of help?"

"I don't trust Stein. After all is said and done, he's still a cop. But the little girl's life is what matters, and I know if we make an agreement, you'll keep it because you're a priest."

No more words. I'm going to hang up the telephone because you have already caused me great pain, and until you came along, I had always been able to think of the most miserable of men as children of God. But he did not hang up. "I have to listen to you, but don't trust me, not for one second. I'll turn you in if I get the chance."

"I can understand how you feel," Desmond said with great reasonableness. "What I propose is this. The little girl is running a fever and she needs help. You pick me up in half an hour and I'll give her to you."

"Go on."

"You'll be able to describe me to the police, so you have to agree to take the little girl to the hospital before you turn me in. That'll give me about a thirty-minute head start."

"What's brought about this sudden change of heart?" the priest asked suspiciously.

"I'm on my medicine again," Desmond said. "So I'm lucid and ashamed of myself. But I'm still not stupid enough to trust blindly. I want a little free time before the cops pick me up. So if you can't play straight, then say so."

The priest took another long moment to sort through his feelings, to balance the risk. He had lost the power to believe in instantaneous conversion and he was not sure about the medication story. But what he did now would be a test of his faith and he knew it, for the life of the little girl was at stake and he was positive he could make a difference. The moment called for boldness, the abandoning of caution, and the belief that, in this case, God would allow him to help a child in pain.

"All right," he said. "Where shall I pick you up?"

Stein called the church to talk to the priest, only to be told that he was not in. The nun said that this was Father Rowan's day to make hospital visitations.

"Shall I have him call you, Mr. Stein?"

"No, thanks. I'll get in touch with him tomorrow."

He ate a late dinner and after dark drove the Henderson highway out to the twisted road through the surrealistic rock crags down to the dam. The souvenir stands and the commercial lookouts were all closed for the night in this ninth wonder of the world, this combination of massive concrete slabs and buried turbines sending great pulses of energy through the thick, ropy cables suspended from the great metal towers marching across the mountains.

He drove up the far side of the canyon, through the service lights into the intense darkness, adrenaline flowing, nerves tingling. Traffic was sparse on the highway. A large motor home approached from the south, swept past him, left him in darkness. He saw the small white building on his left, then looked sharp and pulled off at the next turnoff to his right, a trapezoid-shaped piece of land that angled slightly upward to boulders and rough country. He was aware that by daylight he would be looking past the boulders down a sheer cliff toward the miniature Colorado River snaking through a canyon far below.

He parked and waited. He thought of Karen at home, Barn and the horse Stein would buy for him, all the ways he would reassure Karen that this situation was a freak happening and would not be repeated. He purposely kept his mind away from the matter at hand but was unable to escape the realization that this psychopath could kill him without a second thought, directed by unseen voices. A vague breeze sprang up, a fitful wind, warm from the heat retained by the rocks. He smoked a cigarette despite his best intentions, vowing to quit smoking again once he was home, then climbed out of his car and held the glowing coal next to his watch dial.

Ten thirty-seven. D was not coming. He ground the cigarette out beneath his heel. He would wait until eleven and then call it a night. He would drive back into Boulder City and wait for the police cruiser to home in on the bug. Then he would go into Vegas and have a final drink with Picone (whom he had come to like), wish the Metro team good luck, and catch the next flight home.

He walked to the high corner of the trapezoid, the clumping of rocks that separated him from the void, and he heard the murmur of the river far below. He was edgy, listening for the sounds of the car that had to come. So when the strong beam of the flashlight caught him full in the face, soundless, he jumped slightly, blinked.

The son of a bitch had parked somewhere else and walked here. For him to have been caught by surprise was unforgivable.

"Where are they?" Desmond's voice was wired up, jumpy, irritable. He's right in the middle of a psychotic episode, Stein thought, volatile, seeing things that don't exist, projecting his own world onto the black screen of the night. "I've been watching the road for the past two hours. Where are they?"

"Where are who?" Stein said coolly.

"You know what the hell I'm talking about. You're bound to have cops all over the place. They're out there in the rocks, right? You think you can get by with this, don't you?" He raised his voice. "I know you're there. You make a move and I'll send this Jew to Christian heaven."

Hallucinating. No medication to ease that wired-up mind, straighten out the cerebral kinks.

"If you think I'm setting you up, check it out," Stein said quietly. "There's nobody around, but you can waste the time if you want to. But I have the money and I'm ready to go with you, your car or mine, to hold the ceremony for the little girl."

Desmond was stalking around, a restless shadow, and Stein could tell from the position of his arms that he carried a pistol in one hand and a flashlight in the other. He was beginning to calm down now.

"I'm alone," Stein said. "You can see that. And I'm playing straight with you."

"Because you're afraid of me. You know what I can do."

"Come off it," Stein said. "We made an deal and I'm ready to honor it."

"Yeah," Desmond said. His stalking slowed down; his movements became less jerky. "Yeah." The spikes of his mind were smoothing out.

"You wanted my help. So now you have it," Stein said.

"I've been thinking about that," Desmond said. "I've given you too much credit all along, you know that? You may have the power but you're hiding who you are and that doesn't show a hell of a lot of courage, not when I'm willing to stand up and take the heat. If you had been such hot shit, then God would have picked you instead of me."

"Maybe."

"So I have every bit as much power as you do."

"We're not arm-wrestling here," Stein said. "This isn't a contest. Hell, even if you're right, you still need a witness."

"What do you mean, *even* if I'm right? You know what would happen if you were with me when the miracle happened? Who you think would get the credit? A laboring man like me? Or some guy from back east with a big reputation and lots of publicity. Hell, they'd call me 'shit' and you know it."

"Believe what you want to believe," Stein said. "Hell, I've had enough publicity to last me a lifetime. And all I care about is the little girl. I have powers, sure, I'll admit that, but I could never make a finger grow back when it's been cut off. And I'll sign a paper in advance giving you all the credit."

A match flared. Desmond lit a cigarette and Stein caught the flash of his eyes. Calculating. "No, I'm going to do it alone."

"Suit yourself," Stein said. "If you don't want my help, fine. I've got one more day here, then I'm going home." He said nothing for a moment. "I have your money. It's in the car."

"Put it on the hood where I can see it. Get it out."

Stein started toward the car, the beam from the flashlight preceding him as he opened the door, removed the paper bag. He put it on the hood.

"Open the bag," Desmond said.

Stein folded the bag open. The finger of light probed inside, showed green, then went momentarily out. The darkness was intense. The light came on again. "Now, back away from the car," Desmond said. When Stein was ten feet away, Desmond moved forward to grab up the bag and make a tight roll of it, which he tucked under his arm. "I know what you're thinking," he said. "You're wondering if you can get past me, all by yourself, and still find the girl."

"Wrong," Stein said.

"No, I'm dead center. I can hear your thoughts. I can hear clouds and fish and blood in your veins. I hear the electricity in your mind when you think. Click, click, buzz, buzz. You'd love to have the credit and cut me out altogether. I know what you're thinking."

"Then you know I'm telling the truth." Not the truth, of course, because he had just decided not to use the pistol in his waistband; a clear shot, and the shadow in front of him would drop like a rock. But that would mean the certain death of the girl, if she was not already gone. The chance of finding her would be small, even after they ID'd this man.

"Look to your left," Desmond said.

The light flicked briefly toward the far side of the turnout and Stein was given no more than a glimpse of a man crouched in the rocks fifty feet away. At first, Stein believed it was an illusion. The presence of a second man did not fit the pattern. Crazies like this invariably worked alone. Desmond's voice was smug.

"You'll wait here," Desmond said. "In five minutes, my friend will be gone as well. Then you can leave. Go back to your hotel and I'll call you there. I'm going to do the miracle tomorrow."

"That's up to you," Stein said.

"Does your watch have luminous hands?"

"I'll know when five minutes have passed."

"Sure you will."

The flashlight clicked off. Snap! Stein was plunged into darkness and silence, as if D were floating away from him, soundlessly. But he was carrying the bag and the bug with him. You're carrying the seed of your own destruction, Stein thought. And maybe you've left my destruction here. He stood perfectly still until he thought he could make out the shape of the man crouched in the rocks. Was there something in his hand? A pistol, perhaps, and Stein remembered a crazy named Edelman in the Bronx who had taken in another mental patient named Mex, a quiet little red-headed man who shot ten people dead at Edelman's direction and never came to trial because he did not have the slightest idea what he had done.

"I don't have any beef against you," Stein said. He flicked his lighter into flame, touched a cigarette. "You can leave now. I'll stay put. I'm in no hurry."

Did the man speak or was the sound he heard a sigh of wind through the deep slash of the canyon? Suddenly, he threw his lighter toward the man, the flame tumbling end over end as Stein dropped to the ground, snatched the pistol from his belt. He did not fire. The man in the rocks did not move. The lighter lay on the ground near his feet, the flame sputtering, and Stein saw the red stain, was sickened by it. He stood up, heaved an involuntary sigh. He climbed into the car, started the motor, and pulled it around to fix the man in the glare of the headlights.

The priest, his St. Justin Martyr T-shirt like a self-proclaiming description of his condition. He was wedged between two boulders, his arms spread over the rocks to either side to hold him up. His eyes were open, expressionless, and there was the familiar hole of the bullet wound in his forehead and the slashed cross on his left hand, pinkened by lipstick. Blood everywhere. Stein felt sick.

He climbed out of the car, retrieved his lighter, touched the back of his fingers against the dead cheek. Cooling. Long dead.

Stein sat down in his car again, finished smoking the cigarette. You preserved your integrity the hard way, he thought. You gave away no secrets.

It took an hour for Metro to process the crime scene, flash-bulbs popping, a purring generator flooding the turnout with light yellow Mylar tape blocking off an area where no one would have trespassed anyway. The priest was photographed more times in death than he ever had been in life, while another team combed the area, collecting beer cans and gum wrappers and cigarette butts, just in case. Another team went up the shoulder of the highway, looking for tracks from a parked vehicle, for footprints.

Always the same, Stein thought. The only difference here was the thoroughness of the coroner and the forensics team. He was always reminded of ants swarming a picnic site. Picone was on his radio at length before he came over to Stein. "He's one shrewd son of a bitch," he said. "Our radio never picked up a beep from the bug. It should have, but it didn't."

"What's your range?"

"Should be five miles. But we didn't count on all the interference from the electric lines coming out of the dam." Picone un-wrapped a stick of gum, which he doubled and put in his mouth. He was careful to tuck the wrapper in his pocket. "He sure as hell didn't drive back toward Vegas."

"He could have discarded the bag."

"We've scanned the highway on either side for ten miles down. No deal."

"He could have disabled it."

Rizzuto walked up to them, carrying Polaroids.

"Does the coroner have any idea when he was killed?" Stein asked.

"Sometime this afternoon," Rizzuto said. "He was brought out here after dark, dragged to the rocks, and wedged in. Then his hand was slashed."

"Goddamn, I hate religion," Picone said.

"What kind of cover you have on the roads?" Stein asked.

Picone shrugged. "Three theories. Either he would head straight back into Vegas, which he didn't, or we would have picked him up. We notified the Arizona state police and they set up a roadblock at Kingman, in case he went that direction, and we sent a plane down the Kingman highway in the hope of picking up his transmission. Not a sign of a vehicle. He couldn't have been on foot in the beginning because he had to get the body out here."

"So?" Stein said.

"I think we'll find the car in a canyon someplace around here in the next couple of days. He couldn't go west on foot. My God, he'd hit a straight drop onto the rocks. So my guess is he went east, over the rocks toward Mount Wilson, onto some back trail that will bring him back to the dam sometime tomorrow."

"I made the mistake," Stein said. "I thought I had him cooled out, but he's killed again and I don't think there's a chance in hell the little girl's going to be found alive. I should have dropped him while I had the chance."

"Never any guarantees," Picone said. He looked toward the boys putting the priest's body on a stretcher. "You feel up to going downtown?"

"Yeah," Stein said. "Put a switch on my room phone and transfer to a straight line downtown. Just in case he gets past your boys and calls."

"Done," Picone said.

Tranquil, Stein thought, stretching, taking the elevator downstairs in the modernistic building that housed the city offices. The sun was just coming up in the east. He had worked all night, on the other end of things this time, being debriefed. He had gone through the whole conversation again, word for word, and even as an expert witness he could not answer questions that, as a trained observer, he should have anticipated.

Q. He walked into the turnoff from which direction?
A. I don't know.
Q. Did he mention his van, any vehicle? Did he mention driving?
A. No.

Q. Did you hear the sound of an engine starting after he left?
A. No.
Q. So you heard nothing.
A. My attention was on the man he left behind.

Words, streams of words formed into questions, designed to separate what he felt from what had happened. And he had to tell them that he had thought he had detected movement in a man long dead, thought he had seen a pistol in a hand that could not have held a gun.

Q. How would you characterize the perpetrator?
A. Hyper. Really up. Manic phase.
Q. He got off on killing the priest?
A. Yeah, I think so. But he got off more on playing one-up with me. He's put himself in competition with me, and as far as he's concerned, he's already won.
Q. I don't follow.
A. He thinks I have some sort of supernatural power and that I made him immortal but that I've been keeping my real identity under wraps. It's what I call the Superman syndrome. Superman pretends to be Clark Kent until there's a reason for him to go into the phone booth and change. D believes he's Superman all the time, a real prophet of God, and he wanted me to validate his specialness, help give the world a miracle. Then he decided to do the whole thing by himself. There's only room for one Superman and that's going to be him.
Q. We have some earlier lab results. After you were abducted, the lab turned up flakes of dried blood on the edge of your left shoe sole. Was your left shoe sole resting against the bed of the van?
A. Yeah. Could you type the blood?
Q. The flakes had deteriorated. The question is, did the perpetrator make any statement that might confirm that other victims had been lured into the van and shot there?
A. He didn't say anything, but I think that's happened. We'll have to examine the van when we have a crack at it.

They had covered everything with him, not once but many times, and today teams had been dispatched to collect parish and diocesan rolls from Catholic churches to match against the names collected from hospitals. The detectives would nose around and talk to church employees, looking for a church member who might have been behaving peculiarly, who might have mentioned hearing voices.

Stein looked up from a bench as Picone sat down. "He gets all the breaks," Picone said.

"What's up?"

"Arizona has decided to do their own search for the car in the canyons, and it's going to take three days for them to move men up in enough force. And there are so goddamn many tourists at Hoover Dam, our man can lose himself in the crowds there with no trouble at all. And the Feds want all the proper paperwork before we mess around with their tourists. Any predictions?"

"He's got his money. I think his compulsions will hold. He'll have to call me."

"I've been thinking," Picone said. "Maybe his connection with you is pretty damn simple, like maybe you took down his cousin or somebody he knew and all the rest of this mumbo jumbo is bullshit. Maybe he's out for revenge."

"No, he could have killed me flat out. He's established his bona fides. He has his own itinerary and it doesn't include revenge."

Picone stood up. "Let's go get breakfast."

Stein fell in beside him as he walked down the street toward Fremont. "My ex-wife called me again early this morning," Picone said. "She makes a try every once in a while. She's bright as hell and she listens to her customers. I mean, some guys just sit there and watch her like a hawk, dead sure she's trying to cheat for the house, but she's got some guys who sit down and talk business with each other while they're putting out nickel and dime chips without even thinking about it. And so she picks up stock market tips and real estate tips and she makes ten times as much as I do. Hell, she's trying to talk me into going into hotel security and working the conventions."

"You tempted?"

"Do I look like a businessman?" Picone asked with a grin. "Hell, I'm a desert-rat cop. I like playing whodunit and hide and seek." He turned into a casino and threaded his way through the aisles of slots to a dining room where a hostess recognized him and gave him a smile and a good table. Picone unfolded his napkin, picked up where he had left off. "So what would I do with a million bucks' worth of real estate?" he asked. "If it's buildings, something always needs fixing. I tell her I'm no goddamn carpenter." He didn't open the menu. "Bring us the special, honey," he said to the waitress. He looked at Stein. "Your wife doesn't mind the business?"

"She minds," Stein said. "This is going to be my last time in the field."

"Sure it is," Picone said with a derisive grin. "You can't give this up any more than I can. You're a gut cop. You work by instinct. But something bugs me. Where's your insulation?"

"What you mean?"

"I sleep at night," Picone said. "I mean, if we picked up this crazy, I could get him by the balls with a pair of pliers and squeeze the truth out of him and my blood pressure wouldn't go up a point and then I could have a highball and drop right off and pick up again in the morning. And the priest, I'm sorry for him, sure, and I know we all buy it sooner or later, and he died hard. But I don't take it personally." The waitress brought them chips and hot sauce, coffee, and a pitcher of ice water. "I expect the worst out of people, maybe that's my insulation. So they don't get to me. But I see you reacting to what's happening. The crazy's pulling your string and you're twitching. He's jerking you around and you're feeling it, right? If I were you, I'd go home."

"And leave the little girl?"

"You see?" Picone said, as if Stein had just made the point for him. "It's a goddamn shame about the little girl, and even the boys in the joint would slice him up for that. He's real scum, sleaze, the bottom of the barrel. But I don't take it personally. I want to nail him as much as the next man, but you said it yourself, the little girl could have been killed a long time ago. You're what I call a hot cop. Anybody turns up the fire, you boil and bubble."

Right on the money, Stein thought, and as the enchiladas were served, the waitress warning about the heat of the plate, he was aware of his own craziness, his empathy for the dead priest and a small girl he had never seen and his desire to gut the man who had caused this misery. He had been kept cool only by the screen of a computer that reduced murder and evil to lines of symbols, abstractions, requiring the use of his mind and his intellect, leaving his feelings free.

"I can't go until I know what happened to the girl," he said. "And I may be the only hook you have in this guy."

"I like you, so don't get me wrong," Picone said. "I'm not putting you down, but we see it all the time out here, the bananas who get off on trying to outwit the big-time cops with all the publicity." He wolfed down the enchiladas. "Jesus, that's hot," he said. He waved the waitress down and ordered a beer. "Now, who's going to say that the second you fly out of town, he's not going to calm down? Because all of a sudden he's back in the bush leagues, no big newspaper stories anymore. He killed four people to get you here. What's to stop him from offing four more just to keep stirred up? A guy like this thinks Las Vegas is big-time, when it's really bush-league. He just doesn't know it."

"He's not in control of what he does," Stein said. He abandoned the enchiladas, ordered cereal and skim milk. "He thinks he's getting instructions straight from God, but maybe you're right. Maybe he's counting on me to get him publicity for whatever he's planning. And I sure as hell don't belong here. I'm going home on the red-eye tonight. Can you get that into the afternoon papers?"

"Sure. One last try to draw him out. You really leaving?"

"If he doesn't bite, yeah, I'm gone."

The waitress approached Picone with a cordless phone. "Call for you, Picone."

"Thank you, darling." He pulled out the antenna. "Picone here." He listened, his forehead knotted in a frown. He held the coffee cup in his other hand, midair, everything suspended. "Where'd you lose it?" He put the cup down on the table. "Okay, do it." He clicked off the telephone. "We picked up a signal from the bug, briefly, about fifteen minutes ago."

"Where?"

"Interstate Fifteen. Coming in from Baker."

"I'll be damned," Stein said. "He's sharper than I gave him credit for. He didn't head back to Vegas after all. Where could he get across the river south of here?"

"Laughlin," Picone said. "This side of Kingman. He probably came up through Searchlight and then over to the interstate. Jesus, he's been driving all night."

Stein's skin prickled. The crazy was back in town. "How far did you track the signal?"

"We tracked it up to the Strip and then it disappeared. These new goddamned high-tech bugs work like a Strip whore, on and off. But we've got cruisers out looking for the signal again." He began to work on his beer. "You still want publicity?"

"Yeah."

"You got it. We'll set you up this morning."

Desmond had driven all night, on a high, senses so alert that his head almost hurt from his heightened awareness of light and sound. Clever, yes. His conditioning had paid off, his instincts, and the protection of God Almighty. Because when he had left Stein and the dead priest in the turnout, he had broken into a dogtrot on the hard shoulder of the highway and run three miles to his Ford, where he started the engine and drove south without turning on his lights, hurtling through the darkness on the southbound lanes of the Kingman highway, listening all the time.

When he heard the drone of an aircraft, he knew exactly what it was, a cop plane, high up so it could cover a lot of territory, but they would be looking for lights and they would never spot his car because he blended in with the darkness. He even pulled over to the side of the highway and got out to watch the lights of the plane far above him as it cruised on to the south. He climbed back into his car and drove on. Twenty minutes later, he saw the lights of a car going north on the other side of the separated median, and above and behind it was the aircraft, following a false trail.

They were thinking logically, he decided, not divinely. They would figure that if he had come down this direction, he would have doubled back, thinking that the road would be clear by the time he reached Boulder City. They were wrong. He had planned his whole route to keep himself safe. He turned west on the highway just north of Kingman. He came down the long, straight scar of a road that flattened out in the valley and then climbed into the crags of rock-like jagged teeth pushing up through softer earth, and then the snaky river was spread below him, at the foot of a long incline. The light of the casinos on the west bank were reflected in the swift water of the Colorado River, the taxi boats darting like bugs back and forth between the casinos and the parking lots on the Arizona side. Yes, the mouth of God, the jagged teeth of God along the flanking ridges, as if He was ready to devour, to swallow the river and the tall lighted casinos whole.

Desmond saw the tall stick figure of a cowboy above a casino, rimmed in neon, and he remembered trying to stay at that place once, a sharp-eyed bitch of a receptionist behind the registration desk who had turned him away. "All booked up." A snappish dismissal. He willed misery to seek her out like a river, drown her in unhappiness.

He pulled into the parking lot of a casino shaped like a riverboat. He went to the men's room to wash flecks of blood from his shirt. They refused to come out, but they would pass as rust stains. Then he went into the coffee shop and had three cups of coffee to jerk himself totally awake and preserve his powers.

He wandered over to a blackjack table, where he played a hundred-dollar bill. He watched the dealer with cool eyes as with a peculiar snap her narrow hands slid cards from the shoe. She was Oriental. Her nametag said TING/CHICAGO. She was a tough-eyed woman who appeared not to notice him at all. He made a mental note to put her on the list when God came to separate the sheep and the goats. When she stood in the presence of God with desperate, frantic eyes, Desmond would remind her of this moment. She slid him two cards, two aces, and he turned them faceup and doubled his bet. She hit the first one with a seven and the second with a king and then she went bust herself without the slightest flicker of emotion. He collected his winnings and left her a fifty-dollar tip. When he reached his car, he thought about how much he would have enjoyed harvesting her and sending her spinning into eternity.

He was tempted to hang around until she got off work and do it, but he had made a schedule for himself and he headed up the desert road into Searchlight, where he gassed up at an all-night station.

Driving through the darkness, he remembered the priest's old Ford going into the industrial district near the interstate to pick him up. Desmond had waved at him to stop, displaying a fixed smile as he tossed a package into the backseat and told the priest to slide over so Desmond could drive. But he had been most aware of the priest's eyes memorizing every detail of his face while asking where they would pick up the little girl. Desmond had not even bothered to tell him what lay in store for him, the new instructions from God. The priest had been so relieved at Desmond's pleasant demeanor that when the pistol had suddenly whipped up to shoot him in the face, right on a city street, in one of those moments when there were no witnesses, the priest did not believe it was happening. People never expected murder. They explained away gunshots and described them as pops, or the sound of firecrackers. When Desmond shot the priest, Father Rowan slumped forward and to one side and Desmond grabbed the sheet from the package in the backseat. He wrapped it around the priest's head immediately to soak up the blood and then, once he reached the desert, he dragged the priest out of the car and around to the trunk, where he lay doubled up like a bag of dirty laundry. He drove to the turnout after dark, left the body of the priest wedged in the rocks, then drove three miles down the highway before he parked and walked back to meet Stein.

The priest would find no favoritism in heaven just because he was a priest. Desmond knew that much. The priest would receive special attention, however, because Desmond had harvested him.

Driving west from Searchlight, he had the time to examine the paper bag with the money. He shook the packets of bills out on the car seat, counted the bundles, knew that the money was all there. He ran his fingers over the surface of the bag, found the bug on the bottom, the thickness of the extra paper like scar tissue. He allowed the bug to work awhile, then took a magnet shaped like a smiling face from the metal front of the glove department and used it to fix the bug to the metal, hoping to cut off the signal from the patch.

When he approached Vegas, he let the bug sing for a short while, then shut it off again. He wanted them to know he was back in town. When he parked the car outside his apartment, he looked up at the sky, saw no sign of the angel, was reassured that it had not followed him during the night.

He unlocked his apartment, washed his face in the kitchen, and then went into the bedroom and stopped short. The girl lay on the cot, unmoving, a bluish cast to her flesh, eyes hollow and sunken. He touched the back of his hand to her face. Cold. She had assumed the semblance of death. The time had now come, he thought.

He was sweating. He took a cold shower and then toweled off before he put on fresh clothes and went into the room to light a cigarette and straddle a reversed chair, leaning on the latticed back while he tried to decide how to handle this. He was in a tough spot now because he could never prove a miracle unless he had a before and after and there was no way to do that with this little girl.

He looked out the window and saw a couple of bums on the sidewalk. No good. Even if he called them in to look at the girl and later they testified she had been dead when they saw her, no one would believe them. He really needed a crowd, including a doctor to examine her, and better conditions, to make his miracle. He needed to have her laid out on a perfectly rectangular flat rock, oriented east and west, head toward the sunrise, and then he could summon her spirit back from the land of the dead. It would not want to return, of course, but it would obey. Slowly, almost imperceptibly, the color would return to her flesh, and the muscles of her neck, now pale and motionless as marble, would begin to tick beneath the surface, the first indication that her heart had begun to beat again. Her eyes would flutter, the vacancy of spirit refilled. She would sit up and, in a sweet angelic voice, proclaim the glory of her maker. To cap the demonstration, she would hold aloft the mutilated hand with the bloodied stump of finger and magically the tissue would begin to form in a wavering light and the finger would become whole again.

Stein would have to be there.

Desmond was tired. He crushed out the cigarette and lay down on his bed and went blank until early afternoon. Then, being a practical man, he went across to the Convention Center and found in a refuse dumpster a large box made of waxed cardboard. He took it back to his room and laid the girl's body in it with great tenderness, then he drove out to pick up a hundred pounds of ice in plastic bags, which he used to pack the body, folding a blanket over it to keep the cold in.

He examined his face in the mirror. He had the beginnings of a beard, scraggly now, but he knew from experience that people trusted a clean-faced man, so he shaved.

At three o'clock, he drove over to the warehouse and went into the unused area, to find his throne gone, a large pile of whiskey cases stacked in its spot. His blood turned cold, icy, and he went to Swannie's office, where the old man's wheelchair sat in the midst of disorder, with Swannie himself looking scruffier than ever. He had taken his teeth out because they were uncomfortable. The pink

154

plates rested like anatomical specimens in a glass of dirty water atop a desk littered with paper.

He glanced up at Desmond with rheumy hate-filled eyes. "Where in the holy name of hell you been?" he asked. "You missed all the deliveries yesterday. You know what that cost me? I had to call Willard and he charged me seventy-six dollars and he god-damn gloated. Got that? Gloated. Because he said I was a double goddamn fool to hire you in the first place, and I sure as hell agree."

"Where's my throne?" Desmond's voice was a slicing whisper.

"Your throne?" Swannie said with a bark of a laugh. "I don't know nothing about a goddamn throne. But that ugly chair is in the old ice room. I told you to get it out, remember? I got a good buy on a hundred assorted cases."

"You replaced the throne of God with whiskey cases?"

"Oh, hell, I've had it with you. You can haul that damn chair out and park your butt in it anyplace you want to, because you are just plain fired."

Desmond took the bundles of money out of his pockets, laid them one by one on the desktop. "I own this place now. I'm taking your deal."

Swanson cocked his head, looked at him incredulously, as if he had not heard right. "You think you're buying this place? That what you think?"

"You set the terms. I just met them."

"And I just changed my mind. Shit, I got customers depend on me, can't get along without me. You showed your true colors yesterday." He lit a cigarette, held it between his lips so it bobbled as he talked, spewing ashes everywhere. "And what was worse, you made me look like an idiot to Willard and you know what that son of a bitch is going to do? He's going to blab the whole thing to Sis and Cousin Opal and they're going to chew my ass because each of them has a lousy thousand dollars in this business." His voice stopped short as he saw the switchblade emerge from Desmond's pocket. The thumb pressed the chrome button and the sliver of steel blade sprang out and glittered in the light. "Put that god-damn thing away. You ain't going to kill me."

"Get yourself a blank piece of paper out of that desk and a ballpoint pen. No pencil. Got to be a pen."

"What for?"

"I can start off by slicing me an ear. Just snick, just like that. No bones in an ear."

"Hell, you ain't going to cut me." But he pulled a piece of paper in front of him anyway, uncapped a ballpoint.

"Now, take down what I tell you," Desmond said conversationally. "Exactly what I tell you. Up in the right-hand corner, you put the date and under that you write 'Las Vegas, Nevada.'"

"I should of listened to Willard when he said you was a dumb asshole." Swanson wrote, the figures and letters shaky but legible.

"Keep writing. Drop down on the page. Write 'To Whom It May Concern.' You put capital letters on all those words. Now, drop down a line. I, George Swanson, hereby sell and convey . . ."

"Slow down."

". . . sell and convey," Desmond said, allowing the words to creep out of his mouth. ". . . the business known as G&S Wholesale Supplies . . . located at 1016 East Columbus, Las Vegas, Nevada . . ." He paused, waited for the pen to catch up. ". . . to Gordon Oliver Desmond, for the following consideration."

Swanson mumbled to himself, continuing to write while Desmond dictated, the knife still open, waving like a baton. ". . . the money to be paid as follows. Put a colon there. Twenty thousand dollars in cash and five hundred dollars a month for as long as George Swanson lives."

Swanson put down his pen. "By God, you got balls, I'll give you that. You're really out to shaft me, ain't you? But it ain't going to work."

"Finish writing." Desmond lit a cigarette for himself, suspended breathing for a moment, certain he heard the rustle of wings. He saw nothing. He started breathing again, watched the pen crawl across the paper. "In addition, it is agreed that my sister, what's her name?"

"Edna Rust."

"That my sister, Edna Rust, and my cousin, Opal . . . ?"

"Gilberts."

". . . my cousin, Opal Gilberts, can either have their thousand dollars back with ten percent interest or a guaranteed income of a hundred dollars a month."

"Boy, you sure are stupid," Swannie said. "I never pay 'em more than twenty dollars a month together."

"Write."

Swanson caught up. "Now sign it," Desmond said.

Swanson wobbled the cigarette in his toothless mouth, eyes narrowed against the smoke, a mean expression on his face. "You got your ass in a crack, Des. Because you ain't bought yourself nothing but time in jail." He watched Desmond putting the bundles of money back in his pocket, leaving only two on the table. "You just crazy as hell, Des."

"You going to show me where my throne is now."

"It's in the old ice room, I told you."

"Show me."

Swanson muttered to himself, wheeled out of the room with Desmond following. "You ain't got no right to lord it over anybody, taking up space with a goddamn chair without even asking. And you ain't bought yourself one goddamn thing. Not nothing. I was an idiot to even think about selling to a dumb asshole like you."

He wheeled up to the old ice room, a large cubicle originally designed to store blocks of ice in bulk, lined with narrow oak planks, tongue in groove, used for the walls as well as the ceiling and floor. It had not been used to cool anything in years. Desmond pulled the latch, opened the heavy door. The musty smell came out of the hot, airless room to greet him. The throne was there, as well as ten or fifteen cases of expensive liquors Swanson had bought and been unable to sell. "There's your goddamn chair," he said. "I want it out of here."

Abruptly, Desmond grabbed the handles of the wheelchair and shoved Swannie into the room, then grabbed up a broom and shoved it into the spokes of the wheels, fixing it in place. He glanced at the broken handle on the inside of the door. Swanson's face turned white as he realized what was about to happen, and he tried to back the chair toward the door, but the broomstick jammed him.

"You ain't going to do this, Des," he said in a weak and powerless voice. "I give you a break, you know that. And all the rest I said, all that was bullshit, you know me, because I got a temper. My goddamn temper gets me screwed up all the time and I was pissed off at Willard."

"You blew it," Desmond said. "God's coming in a few days and you won't see him. And I'm not even going to harvest you,

Swannie, so you ain't got a chance of sudden glory. You did it to yourself. Think about that. You'll have plenty of time."

Desmond stepped backward, out of the room, and closed the door, pulling the latch bar down, clicking the open Yale lock shut. He stood outside and he listened on two levels. The human ear could hear no sound from the room at all. The walls were thick, and even as Swanson pounded the broken latch, he was using up the limited supply of air. And Desmond's God ear could hear him screaming. Demond lit another cigarette, leaned against the door, testing, smoking. He pressed the button on his knife, pushed the blade back inside the handle, then he went back inside the office and pocketed the money he had left on the desk. He hummed to himself as he flipped through the Rolodex, found Willard's number, and dialed. When Willard answered, Desmond projected a sincere cheerfulness.

"Willard, this is Desmond," he said. "Your uncle asked me to give you a call and tell you I bought the business."

"Let me talk to him."

"He's in the toilet," Desmond said. "Now, I know you're his nephew and I wanted you to let you know that your mother and your aunt will be drawing a hundred dollars a month apiece as a part of the deal."

"A hundred?" Willard said, pleasantly startled. "Apiece?"

"That's right. They'll each get a check on the third of every month." The third, Holy Trinity, God the Father, the Son, and the Holy Ghost. "And he even made a provision for five hundred to be paid to you."

"What for?"

"For all the help you've given him from time to time, I guess. We're going to be closed for about a week, taking inventory. And Swannie's talking about going to L.A. I hope you'll talk him out of it when you see him."

"You're not kidding about the five hundred?"

"I'll send it over by messenger this evening."

"Tell him thanks."

"I will. And I hope you'll change your attitude about me. I'd like to put some business your way from time to time."

"Well, I'd appreciate that. I guess I got you wrong."

"I guess you have. Anyway, you should get your money between now and seven o'clock." That would keep Willard at home for now.

He looked out the window, saw a man refilling a news rack across the street, waited until the news truck moved on before he went out and picked up a paper. He kept it folded beneath his arm until he was back in the office. He found what he was looking for almost immediately, the murder of the priest, whose body had been found at the rest stop, and then a second paragraph, the meaning of which escaped him until he read it a second time. It said that Peter Stein, a consultant from the East Coast, was returning home sometime this week and giving up his part in the search for the Tropicana killer. He read it again to make certain he was not imagining the words. He lit another cigarette, picked up the telephone, dialed La Mirage, was aware from the clicking and the different background that the call was being shunted off from Stein's room to somewhere downtown. But Stein answered.

"Tell me the paper's wrong," Desmond said.

"No," Stein said, matter-of-factly. "I have to admit that you're smarter than I am. So I'm going home."

"It's about to happen," Desmond said. "You have to witness it. You gave me your word."

"The killing of the priest was the last straw for me."

"Just listen," Desmond said. "Stop jumping to dumb conclusions. The miracle's going to happen, starting with the little girl."

"You're going to restore her finger?"

"No, much bigger than that. And not me, God."

"I don't think I want to hear any more of this," Stein said. "If you have something to prove, take it up with the locals."

"Please listen to me. The little girl is dead but God will bring her back to life."

There was silence on the line.

"Are you listening?" Desmond said.

"Barely."

"I'll take some Polaroids of her. You can see her condition. I guarantee she's dead. And I intend to bring her back to life."

"When?"

"I see I have your interest again."

"I don't believe you."

"Seeing is believing. I'll call you tomorrow and tell you where to be."

Silence again.

"What are you going to do?" Desmond said.

"I'll have to think about it," Stein said.

Desmond could feel the jagged streaks shooting across his mind, but he kept his voice down so he would not begin screaming into the telephone. "Let me tell you what's going to happen if you don't," he said. "Now, I have harvested for God, but I can also be an avenging angel and I can make the blood flow knee-deep."

"You better hope that there's not one killing in this city tonight," Stein said. "I won't take any of your shit. I'll talk to you in the morning."

And then, like a slap in the face, the supreme insult, Stein hung up and the dial tone droned into Desmond's ear. He slammed the telephone down on the cradle with such force that the plastic base cracked, and he sat with his head in his hands, forcing deep breaths into his lungs, so angry he felt like beginning the killings he had threatened now, this moment, taking up a position out along the interstate and taking on the cars one at a time, blowing tires and watching the high-speed vehicles flipping end over end to break into flames, or killing drivers only, or an occasional passenger, and then waiting for night and with a silencer killing at random along the street, siting in on a head and pulling the trigger, watching the victim drop without a sound, the crowds around him panicking.

He gained control of himself. He's trying to rattle me, he said to himself, trying to jinx me so I can't succeed. He walked over to the window, looked out with slitted eyes, wondering if the angel was not lurking someplace close, spying on him, wondering in an inner mind—which an angel could not penetrate with its metaphysical mind—whether he could kill an angel with a pistol.

"I think he's killed the girl," Stein said. He had been walking for a long time, Picone trailing along beside him, through the bright neon of Fremont Street and then out toward the suburbs, where the darkness was broken only by streetlights.

Picone sucked quietly on a cigarette, then flipped the butt away into a shower of sparks on the street. "We covered that possibility, didn't we?' he said.

160

"Yeah, we covered it."

"So now you can turn this over to us, can't you?"

"And what will you do to him?"

"That depends on what he tries to do to us," Picone said. "This is going to be a goddamn delicate matter because we're going to have two sides all lined up. The bleeding hearts are going to say we should be out there with butterfly nets, grabbing him like a specimen, and the mother of the little girl is a real bloodthirsty killer who'd like us to castrate the son of a bitch and hang him up by his heels whether the little girl's alive or not." He fished out another cigarette. "Now, he's got to arrange a meet with you if he wants to show you a miracle and we'll be there in full force. If he decides that the meek are going to inherit the earth and puts his hands on top of his head, we'll bring him in. If he starts shooting, we'll cut him in half."

"That's my decision to make," Stein said.

Picone shook his head. "Not anymore."

"He'll be calling me."

Picone smiled wanly. "You had your way the last time."

"I honest to God don't know what I'm going to do."

Picone's beeper sounded and he looked up the street, spotted a 7-Eleven, held up a cautioning hand as if to tell Stein not to come to any decisions, and then quickened his pace toward the store and the outside telephone. He listened, nodded, came back to Stein. "There's a guy looking for you, big-time according to downtown, just flew into Vegas in his private jet. You know an Anthony Phillips?"

"Yeah."

"He wants to meet you at the Top of the Mint in thirty minutes. You want the meet?"

"Sure," Stein said.

"Before you go, old buddy, just keep in mind that you don't want a lot of hassle with the department here."

"I'll catch a cab," Stein said.

"No need," Picone said. "I told the boys to send a car."

Phillips was bronzed, Stein thought, not tanned but bronzed with the right combination of sun and exercise, saunas and hot tubs and rubdowns, a civilian athlete who probably thought positive, jogged, and put the bulk of his energy into winning gold instead of gold medals. They sat at a window in the bar on the Mint's highest floor, and Phillips appeared to be stimulated by the height and the city that stretched into the distance, the lights incredible.

Phillips specified his Scotch and a brand of mineral water, smiled out at the mountains and then at Stein, radiating confidence. "It's really fantastic, isn't it?" he said. "Life imitates art, life becomes art, and we're all a part of the action on the tube." He straightened the knot of his silk tie against the collar of his linen shirt. "I've just come from a meet on the coast. One of our subsidiaries is an advertising agency."

Stein sipped his bourbon. "I'm not sure I follow."

"You don't follow, you lead," Phillips said enigmatically. "Aren't you aware of your own publicity? It's sensational. It's a natural. A little girl in danger, kidnapped by a maniac who calls in one of the most celebrated criminologists in the world, a race against time."

"You don't know, then?"

"Know what?"

Stein told him the whole thing, straight, the craziness of the situation. "I think he's killed the girl," Stein said. "And now he wants to resurrect her to prove he's a messenger from God."

Phillips had a rapt expression on his face, a sober frown of intense concentration. "He intends to bring her back to life?"

"Yeah."

"And what are you going to do?"

"I don't know. The Metro police are running it."

"Jesus," Phillips said with a shake of the head. "You're not going to let them interfere, are you?"

"This is their ball park."

"Hell, the man called for you." He scratched his chin. "I could get a crew together by noon tomorrow. I wouldn't use locals. I'd fly them in from L.A."

"Crew?" Stein said. "What are you talking about?"

"Coverage," Phillips said solemnly. "This is the age of the media event. My God, television stopped the Vietnam War and brought down Nixon. And we couldn't buy the kind of coverage we can get with a tape of you and the psychotic on this story."

"Shit," Stein said in disgust. "No way."

"Only because it puts a commercial spin on the situation, there's a commercial angle, correct?" Phillips said, swirling the ice in his glass. "I mean, it all smacks of exploitation, right?"

"I won't do it," Stein said.

"And yet if there was a shootout on Fremont Street, you wouldn't have any objections if the media covered it. Because that's their function in society."

"Nobody's going to turn tomorrow into a spectacle," Stein said. "Nobody's going to cash in on it."

"I know you mean well," Phillips said, not a hint of patronization in his voice. "But, of course, people are going to profit from what happens. They already are. I could bring a bean-counting team into town and show you that this very odious man has been worth millions to the local economy. Television ratings are bound to be up, and that means people are going to be afraid. They're going to buy handguns to protect themselves with. They're going to vote in a larger police budget. People like to be frightened, believe it or not. It saves them from boredom. And you're going to profit from it whether you want to or not."

"No," Stein said. "I came out here on my own."

The waiter approached with a telephone. "You have a call, Mr. Phillips. You want to take it here?"

Phillips nodded, took the telephone. "Yes?" he said, and then leaned back in his chair. "Sure, Charlie," he said. He listened and took a gold ballpoint out of his pocket and clicked the point in and out as if he was ready to make a calculation on the tablecloth at any moment. "Great, great, great," he said. "We can deal with him, but not at those numbers. I'll talk with you at seven in the morning. Yeah, Charlie." He slipped the gold pen back in his pocket and then held the telephone out on extended fingers without even looking, knowing that the waiter would take it the moment he was through. He turned his attention to Stein again.

"You have a natural gift for this phase of the business," Phillips said with a smile. "And you don't even know it. You came out here on your own, no fee, and that automatically doubles your publicity value. And now you're trying to save the life of a little girl. *People* magazine wants this. I know that for a fact. *Time* and *Newsweek* always play coy on deals like this because they know I stand to make more money if the story gets a lot of play. The networks are covering. And this makes the deal between you and me worth a hell of a lot more. I was just talking to one of my VP's on the coast; he's talking franchise expansion overseas. And what you're doing here is really bumping up the price."

"We haven't signed off on any deal," Stein said.

"We will," Phillips said. "It's just a matter of the right price and the right circumstances." He sipped his drink, giving himself time. "I don't want you to think I'm hardhearted, Mr. Stein. You mind if I call you 'Pete'? And call me 'Tony.' I have two daughters, Pete, and I think the world of them. And I want them to have good schools and a decent start in life, and sometimes that makes me a little analytical, because if I don't prosper, then they sure as hell don't."

"What are getting at?"

"Look at it this way. I have two million on the table for your company. That's a good price both ways. But the more prominent you become in this case, the greater the benefits. Look at it this way. If you succeed in rescuing the little girl and nailing this son of a bitch, the value of your company to us will double."

"Maybe you didn't understand what I said. The crazy told me the little girl is dead. I believe him."

"But you can't be certain of that."

Stein shrugged. "Believe what you want," he said. "But you can't do it. The Metro police wouldn't let me make a big production out of this even if I wanted to, which I don't."

"Let's take the angle that the little girl is dead," Phillips said, not fazed for a second. "The whole country would be caught up in grief and a desire to see justice done. If you're in on the kill, that will still be worth a hell of a lot of money to us. What if I were to offer you a bonus of five hundred thousand dollars?"

"To do what?"

Phillips shifted slightly in his chair as if seeking a different vantage point. "Look, I'll drop the crews, television coverage, all of that. But when this is over, we'll have your personal story ready, everything you've gone through on this case, your feelings, the whole works, and we'll get national exposure. You won't even have to write it. Just talk to a professional we'll bring in. You can say anything you want to. If you want a national audience for anything you think is important, then you get it here. You get final approval of the piece, of course."

Stein realized how tired he was and how Phillips had reached a point where he had more money than he could use for the rest of his life. Yet the man was indefatigable in his push for more, a battering ram of an individual who was persistent rather than crude, who, when faced with an obstacle, found six ways around it. And now he had placed Stein in a position in which it was almost impossible to say no. This man was offering him half a million dollars extra to do precisely what he was going to do anyway, with the added bonus of a public forum for his beliefs.

"I know what you're feeling, of course," Phillips said with such resignation in his voice that Stein could not tell whether it was sincere or not. "You're an idealist. It would be wonderful if the whole world operated on higher principles, but of course, it doesn't. Every advance in criminology has made money for someone. And police strikes are getting more common all the time when cities can't come up with what the unions are demanding."

All perfectly clear, Stein thought with a touch of melancholy, a proposition delivered with tact and regard for his feelings, which tapped into his own greed, as well. An extra half-million, with room left for further bargaining. He could probably up the ante if he wanted to. He thought of Karen. His time was up. He wondered how firmly she would hold him to the agreed time limit in the face of all this extra money.

"I'll consider it," Stein said.

Phillips seemed to relax a notch. "I appreciate that, Pete. You call the shots. Say the word and I'll back off and the original deal holds. No more pressure from me. Or if you want to go the scenic route, everything gets loftier."

"Where are you staying?

"The Bally Grand."

"I'll call you."

At La Mirage, the desk clerk had a package for him, an over-sized envelope. His heart sank and he knew he should call Picone even before he opened it, but he had too much to think about. He went out of the Casino and started walking in the warm night, on a street parallel to the Strip. The crowds were in the casinos and the street was almost deserted, a few cars, yeah, practically no one on foot except for an old man walking his dogs.

Finally, Stein stopped at an all-night coffee shop and picked a well-lighted booth at the back. He ordered coffee from a young waitress and carefully opened the package, using the tweezers from his Swiss army knife to extract the photographs. Sad they were, heartbreaking, the little girl on a bed that looked like it had not been made for days. Her flesh was blue, her body wasted, no expression in her eyes.

Just as D had promised.

Dead.

He unfolded the single sheet of notepaper and saw D's handwriting this time, a rather surprising cursive, reflecting practice and basic education, as if D had reached the point where he no longer needed the anonymity of block letters.

Dear Mr. Stein,

I think you can believe from the pictures that the little girl is dead. I have also taken her pulse and found there is none, and, likewise, I have held a mirror to her mouth and nose and found no evidence of respiration. I also shined a flashlight into her eyes and there was no responsive contraction of the irises. As one further indication, picture number five is of the hand from which I cut off a finger, with the bandages removed, and I also made a fresh incision into the flesh and you will notice that there is no bleeding.

Now, you will also have a chance to examine the body tomorrow before the miracle. I will warn you ahead of time that if you mess this up by not following my directions in every detail, then I will not risk my neck to engage in bringing her back to life.

I have a very short fuse and a violent temper. I used to take medications to control that, but since I have become a messenger of God, I have given all those medications up. But God has also given me permission, no, he has urged me to take any steps necessary to prepare for His Coming, and if that involves killing a lot of people to convince you I mean what I say, then all their blood is on your head. And the first thing I'm telling you to do is to call off your creature that has assumed the form of an angel. If you choose to engage in a power struggle with me, you will find that my powers are greater than yours and I don't owe you anything from the past anymore. After all, I realize now that it was really God who brought me back to life and you only helped. I know all your tricks! Don't try anything!

He stopped reading as the blond waitress came back to fill his cup. "You like anything else?" she asked. "We have a special lemon pie tonight. Either meringue or whipped cream."

"No, thanks," he said.

"I'll just leave your ticket, then," she said. "I'm going on my break and if you need anything else, Kathy will be your waitress."

He smiled, nodded, everything ordinary, a quiet summer night, and his waitress pointed out Kathy, a dark-haired girl currently putting in orders at the window beyond which he saw two young Iranians wearing chef's hats. He sipped his coffee and wondered what Karen was doing at exactly this minute. It was three hours later on the East Coast, so she had probably put Barn to bed by now and was sitting and watching the Johnny Carson show until she got sleepy enough to go to bed. Everything normal, and yet in his hand he had a letter from a delusional man who was not only seeing angels but imagining that Stein was contesting his power by stealing one of his winged creatures. He was demanding cooperation from Stein, even as he himself was preparing to perform a miracle tomorrow; And in the envelope were pictures of a dead little girl whose only mistake was to have been in the wrong place at the wrong time.

Stein sipped the black and bitter coffee, went back to the letter.

Now here's what I want you to do, what you HAVE TO DO!!! You go out on the same road where the salesman's body was found and you turn off, because that's as far as you need to go before you can't see the highway anymore. But first, you go to a rental agency at the airport and you rent a white car (I don't care what kind of white car it is as long as it's white), because that way I will know what to look for. And you be at that spot at ten o'clock. If you don't do as I ask, then you know what the consequences will be!

At the bottom of the letter, almost as if it had been copied from an exercise book, was the word *Sincerely,* and lined up below that, the initial *D.*

He slid the sheet back in the envelope, careful not to touch the surface of the paper. He left a dollar tip, paid for the coffee, and was directed by the cashier to the public telephones, where he put through a credit-card call to Karen. He visualized her stirring on the couch, turning down Johnny Carson with her remote-control unit before she picked up the telephone.

"Hi," he said, trying to be cheerful. "I hope I caught you before you went to bed."

"I expected you home tonight," she said. "Barn and I went up to meet the plane."

"I want to talk to you about that," he said. "Are you okay?"

"No," she said. "All the papers I see are full of the little girl's picture. And I'm getting calls from the news services asking me if this has become a personal matter between you and the killer. I even got one paper with a picture of you from the old days at the NYPD, next to a picture of the little girl and a headline reading MONSTER CATCHER AT WORK."

"This is pretty hard on you, isn't it?" he said.

"That's the understatement of the year. I'm having trouble sleeping."

"History doesn't repeat itself."

"Get that message to my subconscious," she said. "I've had a couple of sessions with Dr. Chambers."

"And?"

"She thinks I'm angry as hell because I've counted on you to protect me and I feel betrayed."

"Is she right?"

"On the nose," Karen said. "I don't think you can resist the limelight and the publicity. And I think you'll end up dead and I'll end up abandoned. Damn it, you can't do this to me, Pete. As much as I love you, I simply can't take this."

"I have some things I want to talk to you about," he said. "You feel like listening?"

"All right," she said.

And he told her about the little girl, dead, and the killer's intention to create a miracle, and the letter he had just read. And then he told her about dinner with Phillips and the offer and he realized he was not relaying information as much as he was using her as a sounding board while he thought things through.

"Five hundred thousand?" she said.

"He'll go higher. Maybe up to a million more."

"I see," she said. "And what do you want to do?"

"He touched my greedy spot," he said. "And he sure as hell quickened my vanity. National celebrity, that's what he's offering, and I believe him. But then I get to thinking of the money he's already going to pay for the business. If that's not enough money for us, then two million wouldn't be, either. Do you agree?"

"Go on."

"So I'm going to turn him down and I'm going to turn the case over to the Metro out here. I'll go out in the morning, just like I've been instructed to do, but there's no danger. I'll be covered from here to Christmas. Then there's a one-o'clock flight from here to Charleston, through Chicago, I think. So I'll be home tomorrow evening."

"You really mean it this time?" she asked. "I don't think I could take another delay. I'm sorry." She was quiet a moment. He realized she was crying. "I've missed you," she said finally, her voice teary. "And Barn has missed you, too."

"Tell him to shoot a few practice hoops in the morning. It's going to be one-on-one when I get home. And the schedule's definite. No more putting it off."

"Thank you, darling. Let me know your flight number."

"I will. I love you."

"I believe you now."

He put in another call to Picone at home. "You tied up?" he asked.

"I never go in for the kinky stuff," Picone said. "What's on your mind?"

"We need to get together," Stein said. "I think we can get our man tomorrow."

"He's been in touch?"

"Yeah."

"I'll pick you up in twenty minutes," Picone said.

They went down to the crime lab and sat down to look at the Polaroids together. Picone put a shot of the bed and the body under a magnifier. The picture included a shot of the window, really washed-out because the exposure had been set for the body, but Stein could see boxy shapes through the window, although he could not be sure whether they represented trucks or buildings. He called a technician, asked him to do what he could to enhance the window section of the photograph and to lift whatever prints he could from the surface of the emulsion.

"Interesting," Picone said of the letter. "He's turning into a real pen pal. What do you make of it?"

"He's giving himself away now in large chunks," Stein said. "He's telling us more about himself than I think he knows, but it all makes him more formidable."

"How?"

"I've been looking at him as a slightly subnormal intelligence, street-smart maybe, but not very bright otherwise. I've been stereotyping him as a disgruntled, insecure religious freak with a strong streak of inferiority, and he's a hell of a lot more than that."

"Says who?'"

"Handwriting. Pencil before. Unsharpened pencil, stabs at the paper to make a line, the equivalent of a written grunt. Bad grammar on the telephone. But his handwriting is perfect here, the paper a good grade, the writing done with a fountain pen or a nibbed pen, pretty good grammar. I think he's a linguistic comedian. There have been intelligent people in his background. We have to get him tomorrow."

"I agree with that," Picone said. "But I don't see your concern."

"I've dealt with straight religious fanatics," Stein said. "People who've murdered their children because they thought God demanded a sacrifice, men who became sociopaths because they felt God had given them a mandate and a special reprieve from the law, but none of them was particularly bright or educated. I've been sure this crazy would be easier to handle because once I could get inside him, once I could break his particular code of behavior, then I'd have him cold. Now he's showing a new side, still paranoid as hell but revealing something different. That changes the range of places where he'd be able to fit in."

"You're not giving me the multiple-personality shit?"

"It's no shit. We already have that. We already have one man called D who leads a normal life, works, eats, talks with people, gets constipated, makes enough money to eat, but inside he's a messenger from God and he hears voices and he harvests people, not kills, harvests, with no sense of guilt, because that's what he's supposed to do. That may not be two distinct personalities, but the split is certainly there."

"So we'll get him tomorrow and sort him out."

"Maybe," Stein said. "But not unless I'm a part of it. Is the department going to permit that?"

Picone grinned. "I'm going to be running this operation."

"With help. You got a map of the area?"

"Sure," Picone said as he led him into a room with a chart cabinet against one wall. He slid open a drawer and thumbed through the maps until he found the one he was looking for, then flipped it free from the rest and laid it out on a flat table and flipped on a strong overhead light. "United States Geological Survey," he said. He examined the contours and the roads.

"How current is this?" Stein said.

"Updated every six months if they need it," he said. He was tracing a highway from Henderson with an index finger. "Okay, here," he said. "This was the spot where he snuffed the guy from Iowa." He traced the trail with the tip of his index finger. "He picked a good spot. No view of the highway. There's a wash here, widens out to maybe fifty feet, fair-sized bluffs on all sides. A logical spot. Protected."

Stein followed the road with his eyes, looking for the rise in the contour markings on the map. The crazy had finally boxed himself in, but catching him was still going to be tricky. "There's only one road he can use to get here," he said. "He's got to use the Overton highway, whether he comes in from the north or the south. We can seal him off, but we've got to be careful. If he gets one whiff he's being covered, he'll fade. Now, since he's going to do his bit out in this wash, he'll scout it before dawn. He may come in on foot from any direction. Only when he's positive it's clean will he bring in a vehicle."

"Easy enough," Picone said. "We'll put one lookout up here." He tapped the map along the road north of the site. "We'll set up home base in this wash. He can't spot us from the road and he sure as hell won't be on foot this far north. When he gets into position, we'll seal off the highway."

Stein put an X on the first intersection to the south. "What have we got on this corner?" he asked.

"An RV repair shop."

"Fine. We'll put a stakeout there. Make it a dirty-looking Winnebago with out-of-state plates, and you use the fattest detective you have and the most unattractive woman on the force with her hair in curlers. Hood up, mechanic working on the engine, the couple sitting outside the door eating cereal. You give him any normal kind of logical stakeout and he'll smell it. Their radio will be in the RV. And we'll use a different frequency for communications, just in case he has a scanner."

"You got the instinct," Picone said. "How big a force you suggest?"

"Two dozen men," Stein said. "I want fifteen men to seal off the area, no one comes in, and I want nine to catch him. If you've got a couple of helicopters, we can use them."

"We aren't going into battle, buddy," Picone said with a smile. "Wouldn't you call this overkill?"

"Maybe so," Stein said. "But I want him tomorrow. I don't want to give him a chance."

"And you're going to go driving in there in a white rental car?"

"Right."

"You might as well take my Chevy out to the airport. I'll make arrangements to pick it up."

"Thanks, but I'm playing this his way. I'll catch a cab out to airport rental. He'll be watching for that. Where's the nearest place I can get a police radio installed?"

"I'll have a mechanic in the parking garage under city hall."

"He'll have fifteen minutes to do the job. No antenna showing." Then I go straight back to La Mirage, where I'm going to stay put until morning."

"Fifteen minutes?" Picone said. "Hell, it takes three weeks just to get a tune-up."

"You can't do it?"

"I'll get it done."

He left a wake-up call for seven o'clock, but he did not get much sleep, and in the middle of the night he clicked on the droplight over the table in the room and sat down with a pencil and paper to make a chronology to prompt his memory. D had not been a bystander or a relative; neither had he been an onlooker. He had made too many references to a personal contact in which Stein had brought him back from the dead, physically, not metaphorically, not some spiritual awakening. It had happened in such a way that D could have assigned supernatural powers to Stein in the process.

He worked his way backward, eliminating anything that had happened while he ran the small-town department in Pennsylvania, and came up with nothing. Now New York and fertile ground for perceived miracles, with flashing lights and paramedics grabbing their share of people back from the brink. A case came back to him, a wild man named Owenby, tall, rangy, wild-eyed, who had believed he was Davy Crockett battling Mexicans at the Alamo. He had shot three and knifed four before Stein took him out in a Times Square bar. There had been another man seriously injured, lying half beneath a table, his throat cut, and Stein had been sure he was dead, but the paramedics grabbed him up, applied compresses, got him to the hospital, where his throat had been repaired, blood transfused. Certainly a miracle and it was possible he could have believed Stein responsible. Stein rubbed his forehead.

Impossible.

That man had been black.

He pushed his memory back further, to the time when he had first gone through the police academy and was gung ho with the headiness of being a new cop. And on his first vacation, he had volunteered to work as a counselor at an experimental summer camp up at Saranac Lake, where mentally disturbed kids came for a couple of weeks in the great outdoors.

Stein had taught swimming and worked as a lifeguard and he had hauled more than one of the boys out of the water and pushed the lungs clear until he got them sputtering and breathing.

A clue, yes, a memory so vague as to be almost nonexistent, one oversized guy who had been under so long before the whistles started bleating that by the time Stein fished him out, he was sure the boy was a goner. But he flopped him over on his stomach, started the drill, hands pushing up beneath the rib cage. It was all like a dream from this distance, but it seemed that the boy had come around later to thank Stein for bringing him back from the dead, but Stein was playing cards at the time and paid little attention. He had no memory of what the boy looked like.

Despite the lateness of the hour, he put in a call to the NYPD, One Police Plaza, and a girl he had known at that camp, a pretty North Carolina girl named Powell, who was a lieutenant now, and still a night owl. The impossible odds paid off. She was not only still on the force but on duty as well, and he felt as if things were finally going to break for him when her marvelous drawl came on the line.

"I didn't think they let Crackers rise in the ranks," he said.

"You never could get it straight, Stein," she said, as if they they had just spoken yesterday. "North Carolinians are Tarheels. Crackers come from Georgia or Nabisco. I've been reading about you and your latest. What's up?"

"A hunch," he said. "You remember the summer camp we worked just after the academy?"

"Sunshine for the psychos," she said irreverently. "You're talking Paleolithic now."

"You think you could find me a roster of that camp?"

"Us or them?"

"Them."

"Oh, I'd say the odds are a hundred to one against. But I'll give it a try."

"I'll owe you one."

"Considering your hobbies, you probably won't survive long enough to honor a promise."

He gave her his number in Vegas as well as West Virginia.

A waste of time, he thought, really reaching for it. But he had exhausted the possibilities.

He went back to bed, clicked on the television set, and watched a mindless rerun of an ancient sitcom. He dozed through it until six o'clock, when he came slowly awake, to see a cheerful young woman with a fantastic body and boundless energy coaxing her television audience into aerobics. He turned off the television, took a shower, and shaved. He could not make any mistakes today. The biggest error he could make would be to underestimate the man who was supposed to meet him in the desert.

He went into the windowless casino coffee shop and ate ham and eggs without tasting them. He drank four cups of coffee while he tried to project himself into D's mind, to guess how he would carry out his plan. In the first place, D would have to take the girl's body, either by van or by car, out into the desert and he would be spooky as hell in the process, alert for any sign of a trap. He would have to abandon his vehicle long enough to walk to the top of one of those contoured hummocks to spot the white car Stein would be driving.

Nope, something wrong with that arrangement. D was too canny to let himself be boxed in. He wasn't going to sit on his ass in that arroyo and wait around to be trapped. D was much too smart for that.

He paid for breakfast and climbed into the white Chevrolet. He headed toward the Strip, taking nothing for granted. It was possible that D had never intended to meet him in the desert but would intercept him someplace along the Henderson highway and lead him in a different direction. This ceremony of his could be performed anywhere.

To make sure he was not followed, he turned into the street approaching the immense shopping mall on the Strip, the Fashion Show. He ignored the valet parking and headed down the ramp into the vast underground parking area, color-coded according to escalators and department stores. He parked his car in the middle of the Orange Zone and sat there a long time. The stores would not be open for another couple of hours yet but the food stalls would be operating. When he was sure that D was not following him, he locked the Chevrolet and took the escalator up to the first level, where he found a bank of public telephones close to the food stalls. He dialed the detective squad room. Rizzuto answered.

"I need to talk with Detective Picone," Stein said. "Can you patch me through?"

"They're setting up communications," Rizzuto said. "But the goddamned mobile command post has gone on the fritz. They should have everything working inside an hour. All I know is that we got a regular army in the field."

"How come you've been left behind?"

"You won't believe this," Rizzuto said. 'Hemorrhoids. I go into the hospital this afternoon to have them taken care of."

"Bad news."

"You're telling me. You want to leave a message for Picone? Or you can get in touch with him as soon as the command post gets going."

"I'll talk to him later," he said.

"Yeah."

"And good luck with the hemorrhoids."

It was now eight-thirty and he went back to the car, knowing he should have Xeroxed a map of the terrain around the meeting spot. Shit, he thought, maybe I'm being too careful. If D really intended to meet him in that arroyo, he'd have to use the open highway or cross some very rough terrain. He wasn't going to be able to move with any speed. With helicopters covering the territory, the son of a bitch wasn't going to get away.

He drove down Tropicana, clicked on the air conditioner and rolled the windows up, then tried the police radio, only to find he still couldn't get through to the field team. He turned off the Henderson highway at nine-thirty, onto Lake Mead Road, pacing himself, still plenty of time. He crawled along through a business district, residences off to the right. The buildings began to thin out. He saw the RV shop and his heart sank.

The Winnebago was there all right, but it should have been closer in to the garage, more tools and parts around the open engine cover. The couple was at a card table in the shade of their motor home, having breakfast. The woman was in her twenties and the man in his forties, hardly retirement types. Well, hell, maybe they would pass D's scrutiny. There was no way to make everything perfect.

There was a few cars on the Lake Road, but once he followed the Overton cutoff, there was no traffic at all. He turned off on the dirt road, his car crawling through the sand. The midmorning heat was rising from the desert by the time he reached the wash. When he killed the engine, the silence of the desert was overpowering and the heat relentless. He sat in the car, rolled the windows down. He checked his watch as the minutes crept by. Ten o'clock, then ten-fifteen, and still no sign of D. He got out of the car and walked around. He checked the sandy areas of the arroyo for any tracks but found nothing, not even a gum wrapper or an old beer can. He lit a cigarette, walked back to the high ground where he could see the highway, but he saw no cars or trucks, nothing. He sat there until he had smoked the cigarette and then stubbed it out and field-stripped it with his thumbnail, dispersing the tobacco, rolling the fragment of paper into a ball between thumb and forefinger, and flipping it away.

He walked back to the car, sweating, started the engine, and turned on the air conditioner. He was relieved by the cool stream of air, but he was aware that the engine heat was slowly climbing. He turned off the engine.

Eleven o'clock. He was sure that something had gone awry because there was no sign of D. He used the radio again and this time he got through to Picone, who was equally frustrated. "Goddamn," Picone said. "Where is he?"

"I don't think he's coming," Stein said.

"Look, I'm going to send one of the helicopters on a routine surveillance. If our crazy is anyplace within twenty miles of here, we'll spot him."

But suddenly there was no need to look. They both heard the explosion at the same time, felt the concussion, and off to the south and east, a column of smoke was pushed up into the still sky.

"Jesus Christ," Picone said. "Can you give me a location on that?"

"No," Stein said. "But it's our man."

"I'll get the copters up."

Stein jumped into his car, backed around, made it out to the highway, the black smoke still rising straight up like a beacon, no crosswind to spread it. Driving the highway back toward Henderson, he saw the helicopters converging, one from the south, another from the northeast, and as he turned on to Warm Springs Road he found himself behind a local fire department brush pumper, siren wailing to clear a path through the cars streaming up from the residential districts to see what was happening over a desert rise to the north. The police cars had already put a roadblock on the northbound turnoff. Stein followed the pumper. Less than a mile north, just beyond the rise, was the burning van, which was so completely ablaze that the fire belched from the open sockets of the windows, and the exploded tires were still burning, rings of flame. The firemen drilled off the pumper in seconds to set up a stream of water. One helicopter had already settled a hundred yards away and the second was raising sand as it settled down and cut its engine, the blades still turning. A crew leaped out and went to work, stringing Mylar to set up a perimeter. Picone was last out with a radio man, establishing temporary communications until the command center could be moved in. Picone was directing the search teams, glowering at Stein, the sweat rolling down his face.

"The son of a bitch couldn't have gotten very far."

"I wouldn't bet on it," Stein said. "He would have put a delay on whatever explosive he used in the van. He's not going to let himself be caught so easily."

They both spotted the body of the girl about the same time.

She lay twenty feet from the burning van and she resembled a waxy doll except for the contorted expression on her face. Stein moved past his desire to be sick. The death of an adult was one thing and even the death of a child in an accident evoked in him a terrible sense of sadness. But this was no accident. The son of a bitch had killed this child certainly enough, starved her to death from the look of it, and yet so compulsive was his sickness that he had laid her out in the sand, even brushed her hair so the straight yellow locks fanned out against a dune. Her legs were straight, shoes shined, toes pointed upward.

The crosscut had been made in her left hand and the lipstick that covered the wound had begun to melt and run in the heat of the direct sunlight. She did not look as if she were asleep; in all of his time as a cop, he had never seen a death that resembled sleep in any way.

The cop cars began to pour in now, everything getting organized, the forensics people arriving. Stein was aware of short bursts of talk, Picone gathering information from a short sandy-headed man whose voice was pessimistically shrill. "I don't think we're going to get a goddamn thing from the van," he said. "He doused it in gasoline. I'm betting two to one the son of a bitch filed off the serial numbers."

"When it cools down, I want every fucking square centimeter of the interior checked. If he did his shootings in the van, he had to leave marks."

Techniques, Stein thought, game and countergame. A debriefing would follow this operation, to determine where it went wrong. An officer took a piece of paper in a glassine envelope to Picone, who grimaced at it and then handed it to Stein without a word.

It was another note from D, again in handwriting.

Dear Mr. Stein,

I'm very disappointed in you because you broke faith and lied to me, making it impossible for this little girl to be revived. HER BLOOD IS ON YOUR HEAD AND GOD IS NOT GOING TO FORGIVE YOU!!!

So now I am going to set an example. I am not a harvester but, instead, I am an avenger, so you will play closer attention next time. You should have known that I would spend the night out here, so when the police moved in, I SAW THEM. Now I am going to send one life spinning into hell without hope of heaven—for each letter of your name. S-T-E-I-N. That's five. THIS WILL SHOW YOU THAT I MEAN BUSINESS!!!

Sincerely,
D—

"What you think?" Picone said, chewing on a toothpick, shaking his head at the impossibility of the crime scene.

"I have no doubt he'll do it," Stein said.

"Where? When?"

"The where's in doubt," Stein said. "But I think we'd better figure out what kind of transportation got him out of here when he left the van. And as to the when, I'd say as soon as he can swing it. He's one angry son of a bitch. We've lit his fuse now."

No sign of the angel now, none. As he drove down the interstate, the air conditioning purring in his Ford, he occasionally leaned forward to glance upward into the cloudless sky. Much too hot for an angel to be flying today. He would bake up there, no shade. Desmond was feeling good because he had specific work to do, a list. He had enjoyed working for Swanson because there was always a list of things to be done. He passed one casino on the interstate, waiting for the larger one beyond the town of Jean, where there was a corrections facility and which was bound to have a police unit. The casinos would also have security forces, but out here in the desert, they would not be nearly as sophisticated as they were in Vegas.

He cruised into the parking lot of a large new casino-hotel complex near the state line. He went into the main casino and sat down at the slots. He played quarters and ordered a drink from the roving waitress while he had a look around. Lots of senior citizens here, dressed in silly-looking caps and hats. Desmond was sure that most of these old folks, foolish as they were at the moment, whooping it up at the blackjack tables and the slot machines, were indeed close to heaven, and Desmond was going to deprive some of them of that chance of glory. It would be Stein's fault.

He just needed five people and then he needed to be out and away. He had to accomplish his task quietly. The slots were a lot tighter here and he did not invoke his special powers to change things. He did not want the attention of a jackpot, no bells or whistles or showers of noisy coins. When the waitress brought him his drink, he tipped her fifty cents and then sat feeding the machine while he thought things through.

Should he kill men or women? Women, probably. Stein could turn off his feelings, but Desmond was tempted to believe that Stein would suffer from the death of a woman more than from the death of a man. On the other hand, Stein was a cop, a team player in the company of men. Well, Desmond wouldn't really make his own choice. He would drift around like a shark, just swim around with his mouth open and take whatever came. He walked down one of the halls and followed two elderly couples who were laughing a lot. He gathered that the two women were sisters who had married men from different states and they had gotten together in Southern California and were on their way to Las Vegas. Four, Desmond thought. Not quite right. They stopped at a door to a suite where a Mexican maid was just finishing their room. One of the old men was flirting with her in pidgin Spanish while the women laughed. They all went in and Desmond knew this was the place.

Introducing himself as the manager, he followed them in, and when they turned blank faces toward him, he gave them a courteous smile, knowing that the Mexican maid wasn't going to be able to understand enough English to contradict.

"Sorry to disturb you," Desmond said, "But Conchita here has been stealing towels."

"Goodness," one of the women said.

"You say she's stealing towels?" asked one of the men, the one in a flowered shirt.

"I just need to talk to her momentarily," Desmond said, and then he turned to the Mexican girl, who could have been no more than eighteen. *"Vaya conmigo momentito, por favor."* He led the way through the small dressing room into the bathroom. He picked up a towel and at the same moment clicked open his knife and, with one deft twist of his hand, stabbed her in the chest, using the towel to staunch the flow of blood. She went into shock instantly, dropped on the tile floor. He wiped off the blade and picked up a stack of fresh towels and then went back into the sitting room, where one of the ladies was just pouring cold drinks and dropping ice into the glasses.

"Well," the man in the flowered shirt said to Desmond. "You get Conchita straightened out?"

"As straight as you can ever get immigrant labor," Desmond said. The smile was still on his face as he hit the man with his fist and knocked him backward. At the same time, he stabbed one of the women in the neck. He was surprised that there was no outcry, but then he was working quickly and effortlessly. He killed the second woman where she sat and then, with a backhand slash, cut the throat of the second man, who raised a fist against him. He kicked the man in the flowered shirt in the stomach, stunned him before he stabbed him as well.

Desmond danced back, breathing heavily, looked over the room for any sign of movement, the smile still clinging to his face. Blood everywhere. He had never seen so much blood, and yet none of it was on him except for one speck on the side of his knife and he wiped that off with a towel. Then he picked up a travel brochure, dipped it in the blood, and wrote a name on the wall: STEIN!

He went back into the corridor and closed the door to the suite. He pushed the maid's cart three doors down the hallway before he left it.

Back in the casino, he made his way toward the exit very slowly. He dropped a quarter into a machine here and another there, and finally emerged into the blinding sunlight again. No cry followed him. There were no sirens, no furor of any kind. He opened the door to his Ford, turned on the air conditioner, and let the car cool off somewhat before he climbed in and drove away.

He began looking for some direction from God again. He felt peaceful, calm, purged of his anger. He had not harvested these people, no, he had exacted retribution, and on the Day of Judgment, Stein would be called to answer for their deaths.

It was obvious now that God could not descend here into this unfavorable climate, and Desmond would have to move elsewhere. He saw a billboard, a smiling stewardess with blond hair standing next to a paternal gray-haired man in a pilot's uniform who had his right hand outstretched in invitation. In the background was a jet with silver wings. COME FLY WITH US! the sign announced soothingly, and Desmond blinked and looked again to make sure he was not hallucinating, and when he saw that the sign was really there, he took it as a message from God.

Desmond was ready to go.

Stein had seen pandemonium before but never anything like this. There was a monumental traffic jam on the Henderson highway as tourists slowed down to see what was going on, and television helicopters hovered within camera range.

He went back into town in one of the police choppers, Picone in a black mood, almost unapproachable, stalking around the squad room as if he held himself responsible for what had happened. And Rizzuto, having known him for years, simply ignored him and settled down to have a cup of coffee with Stein while he thumbed through a stack of calls.

"I thought you were going to the hospital," Stein said.

"Piles can wait. This can't," Rizzuto said. He glanced toward his partner. "Picone was sure he was going to win this one. I keep telling him he's a dumb shit to expect to break thirty percent. And he's going to be like this for days. Shit, I don't know how it is with you, but besides having to cope with everything gone sour, he's going to have paperwork coming out his asshole."

"Have the leads developed?" Stein asked, trying to erase his mental picture of the girl's body.

"In all directions except the right ones," Rizzuto said. "We've made all the first victims and have witnesses who saw them talking separately to a man who seems like the same guy in all the cases. Ballistics has matched enough grooves and dents in the burnt-out van chassis to prove he used it like a shooting gallery. So we know where he executed his Tropicana victims. All we need is just one little break and we're going to have him cold, strung up by the balls." He examined a piece of paper. "Leads," he said. "We got a monsignor wants to talk to our group leader, but we all know exactly what he's going to do. He'll sympathize like hell and make some fine public statements, but he still won't turn over his church rolls."

"Let me have that one," Stein said. "You mind?"

"Be my guest," Rizzuto said, handing him the slip. "We always like to share the real bullshit with visitors."

He met the monsignor at the Desert Inn Country Club dining room, where the monsignor made his appearance in pale blue golfing pants and a turquoise shirt. From the first moment he saw the monsignor, Stein was sure that he would have gotten along very well with Phillips because they both had the same physical sleekness, evidencing steam baths and massages and a comfortable familiarity with people of wealth.

The monsignor shook his hand and then sat at his regular table near the wall of windows, making small talk, examining the menu, smiling, joking with other members who drifted by his table and kidded him about heavenly influences that improved his game.

He was a smiling, gracious man, but Stein could no more connect him with heavenly influences than he could with the mysticism of the mass. The monsignor may have been a man of the cloth, but he was certainly more of a businessman than a priest. He had a precise quality about him as well; he carefully realigned his silverware as if he had little tolerance for anything irregular.

"This is my parish," the monsignor said. "You'd be surprised how much of my ministry is spent on the golf course. I get kidded about divine help with my game, but lots of people want to believe in some tangible benefit of the supernatural." He glanced at the menu. "I recommend the Cobb salad and the house dressing," he said. "And feel free to drink anything you wish."

"The salad is fine," Stein said. "And black coffee."

The monsignor relayed the order to the waitress, making a joke about his weight and the fact that she was taking too good care of him. She departed the table, beaming, and the monsignor bit into a bread stick and turned back to Stein. "I'm very pleased that you came," he said. "I hoped to get a chance to meet you. I've read a good bit about your work."

"Then maybe we can get right down to it," Stein said.

"Straight to the heart of things."

"Yes. You lost one of your priests to a psychopath unnecessarily. With a little help from your church, we could have caught him."

The monsignor had ordered white wine. He accepted the glass from the waitress with a smile. "You're very blunt, Mr. Stein."

"I see no sense in being otherwise."

"Of course not." He paused to sip his wine. "Johnny was an excellent priest and I feel his loss personally. You don't find a man like him very often. But suppose that he had been a doctor in a hospital and had caught an especially virulent disease from one of the patients he was trying to help, and then died because of it. The grief would have been the same, the sense of loss, but no one would have blamed the hospital."

"The priest wasn't a doctor. He wasn't killed by a disease."

"My metaphor wasn't a good one. I'm trying to convey a sense of inevitability, of natural laws, of cause and effect. I wouldn't expect you to believe it, but the laws of the Church are such that to have broken his vows, to have profaned a sacrament of the Church, would have been worse than death to Johnny."

The salads were served. "I'm a believer in life," Stein said.

"You'll get no argument from me there."

"I wonder how God would balance the equation," Stein said. "Whether he would consider the life of one dead little girl as being worth the bending of a Church rule."

"We believe in different values," the monsignor said. "I really don't see any point in argument."

"Good enough," Stein said. He drank his coffee, watched a foursome on a green just outside the window, two men, two women, silver-headed, laughing, affluent, enjoying. "We want a copy of your church rolls," he said.

"You don't need them," the monsignor said, again with a smile meant to disarm. He began to eat his salad. "I'll tell you what I've done, Mr. Stein. I have gone over the parish rolls, personally, the members as well as registered visitors. I've discussed the possibilities with members of my staff, and I can guarantee you that the man you're looking for does not appear on any of those lists."

"Unfortunately, you're not in a position to make that judgment," Stein said. "There are other ways the police can get ahold of your rolls."

"Probably so," the monsignor replied. "But we have ways to delay legal actions that are not to the benefit of the Church. This is a matter of Church versus state, after all. So by the time you can get the rolls, they won't help you."

Impasse, Stein thought. He toyed with his salad. This was incongruous, that a moral tug-of-war would be taking place in such a pleasant setting.

The monsignor held his water glass in such a way that it caught the light, refracted colors onto the linen tablecloth. "Tell me something," he said. "I'm a great admirer of detective novels, movies as well. If there's anything to this deduction business, how could a criminal do so many terrible things and leave you with so little to go on?"

"Random acts," Stein said. "Take for example that man standing out there on the green, the one in the lavender shirt. Now, if he was killed tonight, the odds would be ten to one that his killer would be somebody he knew, probably a family member. Or it might be a killing for profit or revenge. His case probably would be a fairly simple one. Even if he was killed by a stranger who wanted to steal his car, there would still be a connecting link.

"But suppose he was killed by someone who had never seen him before, for reasons we would never be allowed to know, so that we had no connections." He drank the rest of his coffee. "I had a killer once named Ernest Sweetfellow, well-educated man, graduate of Columbia, a respected lawyer who snapped one night in Greenwich Village. He picked up an iron bar, crushed the skull of a man he had never seen before, unobserved, mind you, because voices had told him to do it. He was immediately aghast, called the police and the paramedics. But if he had walked away, he would never have been caught. He acted on a temporary aberrational compulsion. Nothing to tie him to the man he killed. And that's the only way we can work, through connections."

"I guarantee you there's no connection between this killer and my church."

"Maybe not. But you can't be sure any more than I can. Talking with members of your parish doesn't cut it. This killer thinks he's a messenger of God. He had multiple contacts with your associate priest. So I'm asking you for your church rolls. If there's a connection, we'll make it. If not, you'll have the satisfaction of knowing for sure."

He was interrupted. A burly man in a pink sweater, gold chains around a tree trunk of a neck, came up to joke with the monsignor. Scores. A miraculous shot on the ninth hole. A whoof of wind out of nowhere. Introductions, with Stein shaking the engulfing spatulate paw of a former linebacker turned airline pilot, keen brown eyes that x-rayed him for importance and politely discarded him.

The waitress came up to ask him whether he was Mr. Stein and to tell him there was a call for him at the bar. Stein excused himself and took it. From the moment he heard the agitation in Picone's voice, he forgot the monsignor and the tug-of-war.

Murder. Five people slaughtered like animals near the California line.

And on the wall of a hotel room, Stein's name written in blood.

The casino had contained the multiple murders very well. By the time Stein arrived with Picone, it was early evening and the night crowds driving up from California had filled the place. From the moment Stein and Picone hit the inside of the casino, the head of security had picked them out and was drifting alongside them. Alonzo Highsmith was smooth, one of the few casino security people who were not former cops. He had been a professional dancer who had gone back to the university to study criminology and was very good at his trade. He was a tall, willowy man in a conservative suit. He introduced himself to Picone first and reminded him of their having met before, and then shook hands with Stein. He led the way down a corridor past a door that was labeled with a red sticker reading CRIME SCENE. DO NOT ENTER.

"It was bedlam earlier," Highsmith said, "but we controlled it pretty well, I think. We closed off this corridor for an hour while your forensics people were in and the bodies were taken out the back to the ambulances. We told everybody that a motion picture company was on location here." He displayed an ironic smile. "We even had some guests who swore they saw Burt Reynolds." He took a sheet of paper from his pocket, unfolded it, handed it to Picone. "These are the victims," he said. "Two couples who drove up from Anaheim, plus one Mexican maid. As a favor, I ask you to treat her death the same way you treat the others. Frankly, I think she's an illegal. Management took a chance on her, never considering anything like this."

"We're Homicide, not Immigration," Picone said.

"I appreciate it. I'd like to make comps available to any of your men who might want to get away from Vegas for a while, but I can't imagine why anybody would trade there for here." He unlocked the door, let Picone and Stein in, and locked the door from the inside. The bodies had been removed but the blood was still there, stinking despite the coldness of the air conditioning. "I've got a fumigating and cleaning crew standing by," Highsmith said.

"Can you get rid of this smell?" Stein asked.

"We have experts who can get rid of any smell and any substance known to man," Highsmith said. "You'd be surprised at what people have done to these rooms, as well as *in* these rooms."

"What about chronology?" Picone said. He lit a cigarette against the sweetish odor.

"We can make the time almost exactly. Noon, plus or minus five minutes," Highsmith said. "In the first place, the casino is owned by a California firm that believes in cost efficiency and the Mexican maid, Consuelo Rodríguez, would have been in this suite sometime between eleven fifty-three and twelve-ten unless there had been a 'Do Not Disturb' sign. But the two couples had been playing blackjack and had gone back to clean up before lunch. That time is established by the blackjack dealer on duty at the time. The seniors evidently reached here just as the maid was finishing up, because she was resupplying the bathroom. And the killer moved in on them."

"Yeah," Picone said. He went into the bathroom, came out again. "He must have taken the maid out first thing."

Highsmith shook his head. "I can't figure why there wasn't a struggle. I mean, from the time the first of the four was killed, some time had to elapse, maybe not a hell of a lot, but time enough to try to run, to yell, something."

"It's the unexpected," Stein said. "Even when somebody witnesses a killing, the mind tries to deny it." He looked at his name on the wall, letters formed with a rolled-up piece of paper. "When was the crime discovered?"

"Three o'clock," Highsmith said without hesitation. "The

head housekeeper runs a check of all the rooms remaining to be done. She worked her way back from the cart, found three rooms undone, then she hit the jackpot. She called the sheriff's office and Metro was here within a half hour.''

"Then the killer had a three-hour lead time," Picone said.

"Interviews?" Stein said.

"Complete statements from everybody in the casino at three who had been here before twelve," Highsmith said. "Plus all the dealers, pit personnel, waitresses. They're pretty sharp observers because they've been trained to see trouble before it happens. We have a couple of leads, men who acted in some peculiar manner to call attention to themselves. Or I should say your boys have the leads."

"Do you have a security crew covering the parking lot?" Stein said.

"Against break-in, theft, accident, vandalism," Highsmith said. "We have a pull-in traffic of five hundred cars an hour."

"Check with them anyway."

"Looking for what?"

"A man alone, about six feet, one hundred and eighty pounds, thirty to thirty-five years old. Maybe he talked to himself, maybe did something out of the ordinary before he got into his car."

"Sure," Highsmith said, but Stein could read the doubtful tone in which he said it. There were probably a hundred such men floating through here on any given morning. His beeper sounded and he picked up the telephone. "Highsmith," he said.

He listened. "Tell them there was an incident here and we don't have all the details, but there will be a release from Metro in Las Vegas in the morning." He scratched his nose. "No, we can't confirm anything. That's right." He put the telephone down, looked at Picone. "If there's any way that this can be played down, we'll be grateful," he said.

"You're going to catch some of it, Lon," Picone said. "But the big story's going to be the little girl."

"I was sorry to hear about that," Highsmith said genuinely. "A goddamn shame. Now, in any release you put out, I know you'll have to use the name of the casino, but I'd appreciate it if you'd use the suite number 1104 if you have to get that specific."

"I don't get it," Stein said. "This is 206."

"We'd have a hard time renting a room with bad vibes to it," Highsmith said. "There isn't an 1104."

Stein sat in a chair in the squad room, watching Picone filling in information on a wall chart, and it occurred to him that there were always loose ends that were never tied up, a veritable bog of information to be processed, which had little to do with what was happening now. My God, there had been a bloodbath at the state line today and yet the final information had just come through on the Japanese victim in the Tropicana field, Yatsui Ichihara. The identification of his body had now been made and all the forms were being filled out to ship his mortal remains back to Kobe, Japan.

A grid search had been made of the desert area where the little girl's body had been found. Twenty-seven Field Interviews had come in from people in businesses along the highway. It was believed that D had left the van and the body in the field, walked back to the highway, and hitched a ride back to Vegas, where he had picked up his car and immediately driven down to the state line to kill his handful of strangers.

The requiem mass for the priest would be held tomorrow, the body to be flown back to D.C. for burial. And even as Picone stood filling in his latest information, Detective Rizzuto was at the weekly meeting of the casino security chiefs. Another team had managed through a subpoena to get ahold of the church records while the monsignor was out. The names had been copied and the files returned before the monsignor could make a complaint.

A computer technician brought in a stack of printouts and put them on Picone's desk. Stein picked them up, a demographic study of all the members of the St. Justin Martyr Parish. He flipped through to the conclusions.

"Let me guess," Picone said, sitting down with a lukewarm cup of coffee. "We got us total demographics and a mini-essay on the gradual aging of church populations. And after all the goddamn trouble we've had getting the names, we got absolutely nothing useful. Zip. *Nada. Rien.*"

"Only three single male members who even vaguely match," Stein said. "One widowed. One paraplegic. The third a black."

189

"Luck of the draw," Picone said. He lit a cigarette. "Is our crazy through for the day?" he asked. "Or are we going to have another eruption on our hands?"

"I think he'll cool it for a while," Stein said. "He thinks I betrayed him by not playing along with him and now he's paid me back for the moment."

"And what's your next move?"

"I'm going home," Stein said. "I've overstayed as is." He picked up the telephone, dialed his home number back in West Virginia. He let it ring fifteen times before he severed the connection. He dialed the office and was slightly surprised to find that Thatcher was still there. The connection was scratchy with static. "You want me to try another line?" Stein asked.

"Won't do any good. Electrical storm," Thatcher said. "I switched the computers to the auxiliary generator a couple hours ago. I hear that everything out there has gone into the crapper."

"How'd you know?"

"Network news, CNN, all the papers. You name the media and you're covered. Damn terrible about the little girl."

"Yeah, it is."

"And the murders at the casino."

"Has my name been mentioned?"

"Yeah," Thatcher said. "There was even an interview with Phillips, who said that since we were merging with his company, he had all the latest information and you were on top of the situation."

"Shit," Stein said. "I needed that. I've been trying to get in touch with Karen. She's not answering the phone."

"She's steaming," Thatcher said. "She spent the afternoon with Alice and she's pretty pissed with you, buddy. She says you broke a promise to her. She's threatening to take Barn back to New York for a while and see how you like living alone."

"I wouldn't like it a bit," Stein said. "Will she listen to you?"

"Nope. I'm your partner and tarred with the same brush. But she'll listen to Alice."

"I'll catch a plane out of here in the morning," Stein said. "There's a layover in Denver and Chicago and I should get into Charleston about eight o'clock, your time."

"I'll check the schedules and pick you up."

"You think you can get Alice to talk to Karen?"

Thatcher chuckled softly as if he couldn't take this too seriously. "Alice isn't on your side."

"I don't expect her to be. But if she can just delay the departure for twenty-four hours, I think I can get Karen to understand."

"I'll give it a try."

"I'll see you tomorrow, buddy. And thanks."

"No sweat."

Picone grimaced across the table at him. "I hate these fucking dead-end cases," he said. "I have the most terrible feeling that this son of a bitch will have gotten off on this bloodbath of his and he'll just evaporate and get away with it."

"Possible," Stein said.

"And you're really leaving us tomorrow?"

"First thing."

"You want a final night on the town? This is one hell of a place for a final night. I can get comps for everybody from Frank Sinatra to Wayne Newton."

"I'm flat out beat," Stein said.

"I'll miss the way you think," Picone said. "I always meant to get you out to a poker parlor. I think you'd really clean up. It takes a particular way of thinking to play good poker."

"Next time," Stein said.

"Yeah. Next time."

Picone was driving to work the next morning when he saw the passing shadow on the street ahead and shaded his eyes to glance upward at the silver jet in the sky. Stein's plane, he thought, and for a moment was envious because Stein was going home to a temporary domestic problem but he was stuck here with a situation that was not going to go away.

He was tempted to take an hour and go by Mimi's place, just to talk, but they would end up playing another round of the problem that had no solution. And he would be pretty damn vulnerable to her arguments today. His town had been violated and the whole damned department rendered helpless by this crazy shit who would probably get away with it.

He parked in the basement, went up to three, to find a note on his desk to call Detective Clymer, who handled complaints at the outer reception area. He picked up the phone and Clymer was downright good-natured with the news that there were two people waiting to see him.

"Hold on," Picone said. He left his desk to look through the door to the waiting area at a scroungy-looking couple standing by the counter. The man was youngish, thirty-five maybe, polyester suit, hair dyed jet black, nylon shirt and socks, and Kinney shoes. The woman was obviously a much older relative, the same prominent nose, owlish eyes, in her sixties, slacks and plastic sandals, thrust-out chin, green eyeshade over rimmed glasses.

He went back to the telephone. "What do they want?" he asked.

"Won't say. But they won't talk to anybody except you. They're sure there's been a homicide, but that's as far as they'll go."

"Okay. Interrogation room," Picone said, and he poured himself a fresh cup of coffee and braced himself as he went into the small room. The couple was ushered in and Picone was handed a sheet of paper on which their names were written. Picone asked them to have a seat and then sat down himself with a freshly sharpened pencil. He glanced at their names. "What can I do for you, Mr. Swanson, is it? And Mrs. Rust. That's correct, isn't it?"

"You tell him, Willard," the woman said, adjusting her eyeshade. "But keep to the point."

"I never trusted the man," Willard said. "And I should have known he was lying in his teeth when he said he would pay more than we were owed."

"It wasn't him," the woman corrected.

"I didn't say it was Swannie, Aunt Edna," Willard said crisply. "I was referring to Des."

"I never trusted him," Edna said to Picone.

"I really think you have the wrong department," Picone said. "You should give a statement to the officer downstairs and then we'll get things all sorted out. What you say?" And with a professional smile, he put the pencil down and prepared to stand up, when Willard stopped him.

"It's murder," Willard said. "Des killed my uncle. And I think you want Des anyway."

Picone's interest picked up. He wrote the word *Des* on the

paper in front of him. "Now, what makes you think we want this man named Des?"

"I never trusted him," Edna said.

"I'll handle this," Willard said firmly. He looked at Picone. "My uncle supposedly sold G & S Wholesale Supplies to the only employee he had, Gordon Desmond. But then some mighty strange things happened. My uncle's in a wheelchair and he has a regular doctor's appointment once a week. But he hasn't shown up for two days and he hasn't been near his apartment. And Desmond has disappeared, as well. He said they were going to close down a week for inventory. The place was locked up and nobody went near it the first day and the postman says the mail is piling up on the floor inside the door with the mail slot. There's a mail slot, you see, and the postman just looks through the venetian blinds."

"And we never got the bonus money we were promised. We never even got the regular payment," Edna said.

"The detective doesn't give a damn about the money, Aunt Edna."

"Don't curse. I don't like cursing."

Picone doodled an oval around the name *Des.* "Go on, Mr. Swanson."

"I wouldn't have made any connection except that Des and my uncle had a fight once. Des had been driving and there was this cement-filled iron post next to a fireplug and Des got too close to it and it made a crease right across the hubcap. Really odd because the hubcap got creased and jammed onto the wheel instead of falling off. Now, I didn't think anything about it until I saw the picture in the paper and then I went back down to the company and looked in the garage and it was gone and it occurred to me that it must be the same, the crease in the hubcap."

Picone felt a prickling sensation in his scalp, as he often did when a case was on the edge of breaking open. "What kind of vehicle are you talking about, Willard? And what picture?"

"The story said that all the serial numbers had been filed off. But that crease is a dead giveaway, isn't it?"

Picone blocked in the three letters on the paper, each letter separated by a dash. "You're talking about the van, aren't you?" he asked quietly.

"Yes," Willard said. "The one that was out there in the desert with the little girl."

Picone leaned back, lit a cigarette, his mind leapfrogging ahead. The break was here. He needed to get organized.

"If it's the same van," Edna said to Picone, "I want you to sign a paper. Swannie paid insurance on it for years and I'm sure it was covered against fire."

Streaks, Picone thought as he got out of the car at the building labeled G & S in faded red paint on beige stucco, looking flat in the relentless desert light. Streaks and lucky rolls and he was on one now, and playing it cautiously lest his confidence should cause him to miss something. He approached a deserted hulk of stucco and stone and the cracked asphalt parking lot behind a warped chain-link fence held erect by banged-up metal posts. The whole thing resembled an archaeological dig.

He had Wilson and Rizzuto with him. Wilson was a young man with cherubic features, round dumpling cheeks, and the softest touch with locks and physical evidence Picone had ever seen, a perfect combination of circumstances, because Wilson had been a locksmith before he went through the police academy.

He had the lock off the gate in a moment, the front door opened without ever compromising the integrity of the push-down latch that might be holding a thumbprint. Picone called out, more from routine than from a hope of being answered.

"Police! Anybody here?"

The building was stuffy, unmercifully hot, electricity shut off, windows battened down. Picone moved carefully through the interior, would have floated through it, touching nothing, had that been possible. He was reverential about evidence. He had an instinct for significance, a sixth sense that told him he had much more here than a complaint from two rather ridiculous locals.

He paused at the doorway of an office, a room with multiple wood-framed windows, all closed, and a decrepit air-conditioning unit set in one of them. The desk was pine with an ancient yellow varnish, a stack of "in" and "out" wire baskets, telephone, dented metal filing cases, a stack of paper next to the blotter. Rizzuto was about to go in when Picone's extended arm stopped him.

"You smell it?" Picone asked.

"Yeah," Wilson said, head raised as if testing the air.

194

"What the fuck you talking about?" Rizzuto said.

You could either smell it or you couldn't, Picone thought, that subtle brackish, sweetish, terrifying odor, but it was here in this stuffy building, accentuated by the terrible trapped heat. He went on down the corridor, wood underfoot, no carpets to interfere with a wheelchair, and he opened doors with the flat back of his hand, storage rooms, cases of whiskey stacked up, boxes of cigarettes, abandoned, a metal dolly propped against a wall in a larger room.

"Looks like he just walked out," Rizzuto said. "Why didn't he cash this shit in?"

"He must have been in a hurry," Picone said. "Besides, he was carrying twenty thou."

Picone stopped in front of the heavy door to an old cold-storage chamber. The smell was strongest here. He nodded to Wilson, who jimmied the lock and caught the iron crossbar low, where he would not interfere with fingerprints. The door opened reluctantly and the smell flashed out with a burst of putrescent gases. Rizzuto said, "Jesus Christ" in a gagged voice and went down the corridor to open a back door and let some fresh air into the building.

Picone covered his mouth and nose with a fresh handkerchief. Wilson's face took on a quizzical expression. The crippled man was kneeling on the floor, head pressed against concrete, palms extended, like an Arab facing Mecca. Swanson, all right. Putrefying, stinking, his wheelchair folded against the wall, the dead man paying obeisance to an empty red velvet throne. On the wall to the left of it, drawn in yellow with a spray can, was an eye, like the CBS logo, with jagged sprayed letters—I AM.

Wilson stirred. "I'll roust out Forensics and the coroner," he said.

"Yeah, do that," Picone said. Carefully, he edged the door shut with his foot. Shit, Stein, he thought. You left too soon. Our crazy has broken into the open and there's no way he can avoid being known now. You just left a day too soon.

CHARLESTON, WEST VIRGINIA

Thatcher's eyes were hurting him. He held his head back and put in a couple of drops of Murine and then took two aspirin and a glass of water, but he knew none of this was going to do him any good. He had been here since midnight, moving from one seeming crisis to another, and all of the PD's wanted their material now, and he finally put the telephone on the answering service and spent hours just routing results of matches and sorts to a dozen different police departments. He had learned one thing for certain. Two men could scarcely handle the load here, even with occasional temporary help, and with one man gone, it was impossible.

At ten in the morning, he had reached a point where he was caught up with all the actives for the moment. He left the computers for a while and poured himself a cup of strong coffee and went downstairs, where he could look out the window at the boats on the river and try to relax. There was still a hell of a lot of work to be done, all of it routine at this point. The government paperwork had certainly suffered during Stein's absence, but Stein would be on the evening plane from Chicago and some sense of normalcy was bound to return.

He was startled by the rare sound of the buzzer at the front door and he left his coffee behind and went into the anteroom. He opened the door to admit a pudgy-faced man in a rumpled but expensive Italian suit, and his first thought was insurance salesman because the man seemed to exude a placid, easygoing demeanor that Thatcher felt could become hard-sell in the flicker of an eyelid. He had a clipboard under his arm.

"My name is J. B. Agnew," the man said, extending his hand. "And if I'm not mistaken, you would be Mr. Thatcher."

"How can I help you?" Thatcher said.

"I don't like to inconvenience you," Agnew said, his smile undiminished. "But I'm personal assistant to Mr. Phillips. I'll be in charge of the actual physical move and I need to get some idea of what's involved. If you could spare ten minutes to show me around, I'd much appreciate it. Or if it's inconvenient now, I can always . . ."

"No, it's fine," Thatcher said. "But you may be wasting your time. As far as I know, the contracts haven't been signed yet."

Agnew's eyes were already roving, taking inventory, as if filing in his mind the physical shape of the desks and chairs and filing cases in this office. He took out a ballpoint and began to record figures on his clipboard. "Mr. Phillips moves around so much I never know exactly where any of his deals are at any given moment. But I do know he likes to be prepared for any eventuality," he said. "I'd hate to have to guess how many times I've done this, but I can tell you that it has yet to be in vain." He glanced toward a closet door. "What's in there?"

"Filing boxes."

"Full or empty."

"All full. We keep a hard copy of everything. So we have printouts coming out of our collective ears."

Agnew followed him on his tour of the computer rooms, overlooking nothing, spending as much time on the little stuff, the chairs and the computer work stations, as he did on the jukeboxes, making long lines of figures and diagrammatic drawings. "Your Mr. Stein is in Las Vegas?"

"He's due in this evening."

"Maybe I can make an appointment to talk with him in the morning."

"I'd make it fairly late. He hates flying and he probably won't come in tomorrow until noon."

Agnew nodded and Thatcher got the impression that Agnew was only making conversation, that he was primarily interested in weights and sizes of things to be moved. Any call he would make tomorrow would be from courtesy only.

"When is Phillips planning the move?" Thatcher asked.

"*Mr.* Phillips will want to set this in about a month, I imagine, and moving the computers is going to take a good-sized technical team. You don't move machines like this with a van line."

"You don't need to tell me about my computers," Thatcher said, bristling slightly. "And you'll sure as hell have to clear any date with me, because we have ongoing cases I don't intend to stall for any move."

"I didn't mean to upset you," Agnew said in a placating voice. "And I'm sure Mr. Phillips will want to make this move as convenient as possible for you."

Thatcher shrugged, took him through the rest of the building, feeling slightly ashamed of himself for flaring. None of this was Agnew's fault. He was no more than a flunky, a errand boy carrying out what he was supposed to do. He concentrated on his clipboard and Thatcher's mind wandered, seeing this building emptied out, and it occurred to him that very soon he might not be coming to work here anymore. It's a damn shame, he thought, that something he had enjoyed so much was coming to an end, but Pete was in the process of losing a hell of a lot more than he was. And picking up the pieces would be Phillips and his myrmidons like Agnew, who nodded as they came full circle to the downstairs office.

"I appreciate your showing me around," he said. He snapped the cap on his ballpoint, smoothed the paper on his clipboard. "Please give my regards to Mr. Stein and tell him I'll try to stop by tomorrow."

Thatcher saw him to the door, watched him climb into his Lincoln and ease off down the hill, then he went back to finish his coffee. It was cold.

Karen picked up the telephone and punched in the numbers of the airline, looking around the front room while she waited with a faint despair, half-hoping that the clerk who answered would tell her that the flight had been canceled, that she would have to book another day. But the cheerful voice confirmed her flight number, and she put the telephone down just as the doorbell chimed. She peeked out through the clear section of the leaded glass to see a tall blocky man in an expensive Italian suit, a new Lincoln at the curb, a polished attaché case in hand, a presidential Rolex glinting wealth on his left wrist, and the most even white teeth she had ever seen.

"I'm sorry to disturb you, Mrs. Stein," he said. "I would have called first, but Mr. Phillips asked me to stop by and see if there's anything I can do to facilitate your move. My name is J. B. Agnew."

She shook his hand, a little flustered, not wanting to have to deal with him on this of all mornings. "My husband went through with it, then," she said.

"I would suppose so," Agnew said pleasantly. "I've just come from surveying the computer equipment for the move. I'm sorry to say so, but I think Mr. Thatcher is very upset with me. I hope you'll assure him that I'm just doing my job."

She shrugged. "Come in and please overlook the clutter." And then, in a louder voice toward the kitchen: "Barn! You're going to miss your bus."

"I'm ready, Mama," Barn said, dashing out of the kitchen, doughnut in hand. He paused long enough to be introduced to the beaming Mr. Agnew.

"And you come straight home," she said. "We'll be catching a six-o'clock flight to Washington."

"Will Daddy be home by then?"

"We'll talk about that later. Now scoot."

And he was out the door with an energy and an acceptance she envied.

"He's got a canoeing class at the Y," Karen said, taking some of her canvases off the furniture, making space for Agnew to sit down. He sat in a straight-backed chair, picked up a small painting of an autumn tree, white bark, a spray of yellow leaves in bright sunlight.

"Gorgeous," he said. "I had no idea you were such a splendid artist."

"Thank you," she said. "I work at it."

"Beautiful," he said, his eyes focused on the leaves. "I would like to buy this one myself. But we can talk about that later. First things first. I take it you're going to Washington this evening."

"Yes."

"That should work very well. I've located five possible houses for your stay in Washington, but as I see your taste in this house, I'd have to eliminate two of them. However, there's one in Virginia that's within commuting distance. It was the former residence of a painter named Powell—maybe you've heard of her?—and it has a studio that would be ideal, northern skylights."

She made a sudden decision. Mr. Agnew might turn out to be a godsend after all. "Since I'm going up this evening, is there any chance I could look at the houses tomorrow?"

Agnew was obviously startled but pleased. "Certainly," he said. "And I don't want to be presumptuous, but I can shift things around and go back this evening and I would be delighted to offer you a ride."

"That's very nice of you, but I already have reservations."

"I'd truly enjoy the company," he said. "And we can carry a lot more luggage in the car than they would allow you on the plane."

"I don't want to impose," she said.

"It would work out very well for me," he said. "I really don't enjoy driving by myself. And if you and your son would like to stay in the company's guest apartment in Tyson's Corners, I'd be glad to arrange it. I happen to know it's unoccupied at the moment. And I can set the appointments to see the houses for tomorrow."

Unfair, she thought. I'm not acting in good faith. She had an old school friend named Patricia Bennington living in Washington. Once she was in D.C., she would take Barn to Patricia's house until she decided what she wanted to do.

Riding up with Mr. Agnew would save her a good bit of money. She could leave the car in the garage here for Pete, when he got home, instead of parking it at the airport.

"Look," she said finally. "We'll ride up to Washington with you, Mr. Agnew, but my son and I will be staying with friends."

"Fine. What time you want me to pick you up?"

"Five," she said. "Barn gets home at four. That'll give me an extra hour."

"That'll work out fine," he said. "It's a long drive and we'll stop for dinner along the way."

She took the time to drive to Alice's house, and no sooner had she entered Alice's kitchen than she began to weep, trembling with sadness and rage and a feeling that she was about to commit an irrevocable act. Alice held her in skinny arms and rocked her slightly, maternally, a low comforting sound coming out of her throat until Karen's crying subsided. She blew her nose into a Kleenex and sat down at the bleached pine table, a cup of black coffee in front of her, Alice across from her.

"I've decided to leave Pete," Karen said. "Barn and I are going to Washington this afternoon."

Alice stirred her coffee. She was a plain woman, pencil-thin, self-conscious about her lack of formal education beyond high school, but she lacked pretense and her face reflected sadness and concern.

"You have your artwork to fall back on, at least," she said, dipping a teaspoonful of sugar into her cup and then stirring with a slow circular motion. "I never told anybody, but there were a lot of years when I would have left Thatch if I could have, when he was a cop. I remember one night, somebody called me, a practical joke, and said Thatch had been shot and was in the hospital. I rushed right down there—two in the morning—and when a nurse told me he wasn't there, I started crying because I was sure she was saying he was dead. And when I got home and found him there, safe, I could have killed him."

"Then you understand how I feel."

"Not exactly."

"But you just said it."

"That was then. Now is now. They're selling the business."

"He'll never quit," Karen said. "Sometimes I think he doesn't have any control. He takes a case personally and he'll leave Barn and me anytime as long as the challenge is there. He made me a promise and he didn't keep it."

The spoon kept making its rounds, clinking against the cup. "I think if you hold on, it will come to an end."

"How?"

"Thatch is already thinking about other things he can do. The state police have a first-class crime lab with top people. He's prepared to go with them."

"Pete's made promises but I don't believe he'll keep them. The first chance he gets, he'll be off and running."

"Then I'd issue a final ultimatum," Alice said, tasting the coffee. "Give him time to make the change. Then no more cop work, and I mean absolutely none."

"The past few nights . . ." Karen said.

"The nightmares are back?"

"Yes. The man with the ax is in the kitchen and he's ready to split Pete's skull."

"That's enough to . . ."

"I never told you the rest," Karen said, fishing for a cigarette, using the saucer as an ashtray. "I didn't even talk about it with the therapist."

"Are you sure you want to talk about it now?"

"The man had terrified me, truly frightened me, and when he was in the house, my first thought was that he would kill Pete, and he almost did. And when the police came and Pete was standing there, injured, covered with blood and the crazy was still alive, I was stunned. Pete could have killed him but he didn't. For years after that, there were times when I had an absolute black fury. I thought it was PMS and the therapist kept relating it to my father or male authority figures, but that wasn't it at all." She took a drag on the cigarette, fingers trembling. "When the truth came out, when I could put a name to my feelings, they were irrational as hell, but I felt them just the same. I had an enemy who had caused me great fear and pain and even after Pete had damn near been killed, he let him live. There's no logical reason for my feeling like that."

"Feelings aren't logical," Alice said.

"Jesus, everybody was so complimentary at the sanity hearing, in the press, and they made Pete out to be some sort of sainted liberal hero who let this pervert stay alive, this son of a bitch, because he was mentally off. The reasonable part of me said that's the way it should have been, old good-hearted Peter Stein, but deep down I resented the hell out of it because he didn't care enough about me to take revenge. He's always had to be some sort of good-guy cop, a gladiator who could vanquish and then spare. And now he's off and running again and I feel abandoned. He doesn't have to stay in Las Vegas, except that he wants to and he can justify it. He's willing to sacrifice how I feel to make another score."

Alice reached across the table, covered Karen's hand with her own. "I'm sorry, kid."

"I'm sorry, too," Karen said. She crushed out her cigarette. "Barn and I are riding up to Washington this evening with Mr. Agnew."

"Who's Agnew?"

"He works for Phillips. He's supposed to make all the arrangements to move the business to Washington."

"Is there anything at all that I can do?"

"Just understand."

"Oh, I understand. In spades."

"I'll leave a note for Pete. I'll be talking to him in a few days. See that he takes time to eat dinner, will you? Sometimes he gets so caught up in things, he forgets."

"I will."

And then they hugged again and Karen went back to the house to pack what she needed for the time being.

She was not surprised when Agnew's car pulled into the driveway at exactly five o'clock. The punctuality was a forerunner of things to come, the first wave of the new organization, everything so damned precise. Agnew rang the doorbell with authority, and when she let him in, he smiled pleasantly and looked around for her luggage. The two big leather suitcases she had brought to the marriage were sitting next to the door with a half-dozen of her smaller canvases. "Is this all you're taking?" he said.

"For the time being," she said.

"I'll put them in the trunk."

Barn came down the stairs with a small canvas bag in one hand and a stuffed teddy bear under the other arm.

"You want your bag in the trunk?" she said.

"No, thanks," he said. "Backseat." He went on out the door while Agnew picked up the two bags and followed him down the porch steps, making a second trip for the canvases. She stood in the living room, reluctant to leave now that the time had come. She had been truly happy here, and for one brief second, she considered reversing herself and staying, trusting that she could resolve the problem with Pete. But she knew even as she considered it that such a revolution was impossible. He would return, contrite, swearing that he would never get caught up in a case again, and life would be peaceful with him for a while, but sooner or later it would happen all over again, after the pain had faded and she had come to trust again. She picked up her drawing case and left the house, pulling the door shut behind her, trying the knob to make sure it had locked.

Agnew opened the door for her and then went around to the driver's side. The engine purred and the car moved away from the curb. "Hell," she said abruptly as a thought occurred to her. "I need to go by my husband's office."

"Fine," Agnew said. "Would you do me a favor? Tell Mr. Thatcher I'll be in touch with him later. He's expecting me tomorrow."

"Sure," she said.

Barn had just discovered a Styrofoam cooler in the backseat, filled with ice and cans of soda. "Hey," he said. "This is great. Can I have one?"

"That's what they're for," Agnew said with a smile. "Help yourself."

"Wait until we're on the interstate," Karen said.

"How come?"

"Because I'm mean and cruel and like to see little boys suffer," she said. She looked out the window as if this were the last time she would ever see this green city and the blueness of the river rolling through it, and the shady street that led up the hill to the office building. Thatcher's car was still in the lot, a perfectly polished vintage Mustang. I will miss all this, she thought.

Agnew pulled up to the curb and she went into the building and up the stairs to the second floor, where Thatcher was on the telephone in his office. He motioned to her not to run off and she listened to him trying to cut the call short while she took out her checkbook and wrote a check to cash for a hundred dollars. He finally terminated the call and she could tell from the stricken expression on his face that he had talked to Alice and knew that she was leaving.

"I forgot to go to the bank," she said. "Do you have a hundred in petty cash? I've written a check for it."

"You don't need to do that," he said. "We always have a couple hundred around here. You can have it all."

"A hundred will do," she said. "You can tell Pete the check's on my personal art account."

"He wouldn't give a damn about that."

"I want to do it this way."

He got the money from a filing case, counted out a hundred, and handed the bills to her, letting her check lie on the desk. "We need to talk, Karen," he said. "This isn't right."

"Mr. Agnew's waiting for me outside. We're all packed and ready to go. He asked me to tell you he'll be in touch."

He looked out the window at the Lincoln on the street below, shrugged. "Look," he said. "We've all been close friends for a long time. So do me this one favor. No manipulation. Just stay until Pete gets back and you can talk to him. Listen to what he has to say and then, if you still want to go, I'll drive you and Barn up to Washington myself."

"I don't want to see Pete right now," she said. "I don't want to take the chance of being talked into anything." And now she realized why she had stopped here, not for the cash, no, because Patricia would be more than happy to cash a check for her in Washington. She was stalling, putting off her departure until she could look at this office again, and even now she could hear the electronic hum of the big computers deep in the building and a printer chattering in another office. This was the center of Pete's universe and she could almost feel the sense of excitement here as he must experience it working here, at the center of everything, nothing passing him by, his move to the country an illusion. Through electronics, he had brought a sophistication to West Virginia with him in a form a thousand times more powerful than he ever had in Manhattan. "Tell me something, Thatch," she said. "Do you really want to sell the business?"

"No," he said. "But you can trust Pete when he says he's going to sell. He's got a deal or Agnew wouldn't be here."

"You like the work that much, then?"

"Not a day passes that I don't cuss it all to hell and back. And not a day passes that I don't thank God that I have this place to look forward to."

"And what happens to you when it sells?"

He shrugged. "I'll get a job in the crime lab here."

"He's selling the business because of me, isn't he?"

"Partly," Thatcher said. "But it just makes sense to do it. If we don't sell to Phillips, he's going to put up such a hell of a lot of competition that we could end up with nothing."

"You don't believe you and Pete would lose, do you?"

"Not really," he said with a half-smile.

"The two of you are just too damn good at what you do."

"Pete is."

"But you can turn the business off when you go home, can't you?" she said. "You can set limits."

"You think Pete can't?"

"I know he can't."

"I'll tell you the truth," he said. "I'd give half a year's pay to have traded places with him and gone to Las Vegas while he stayed here. But it's not every man who has the gift he does."

Not a gift, she thought. A curse. She leaned up, kissed him on the cheek. "Take care of yourself, Thatch. And take care of him."

"Just don't write him off," Thatcher said. "Leave it open."

In the car, Barn was ready to go. "Is Dad going to come up to Washington?"

"We'll talk about that later."

They hit the interchange, headed north. "This is beautiful country," Agnew said.

"You've never been to Charleston before?"

"No."

"Can I have a soda now?"

"It's *may*," Karen said. "And you've been such a patient kid, how could I turn you down? Go ahead."

"There are diet drinks as well," Agnew said. "If you'd care for one."

"That's very thoughtful of you, Mr. Agnew. But not right now."

"My mission in life is to be helpful," Agnew said with a smile. "Excuse my butting in, Mrs. Stein, but I pick up the feeling that you're not entirely happy about what's going on."

"How long have you worked with the Phillips organization?" she asked, changing the subject.

Agnew shrugged. "Forever," he said.

"Do you have a family?"

"Grown children," he said. "No wife."

"Have you ever been in the law-enforcement end of the business?"

"Yes."

"Tell me something, Mr. Agnew. What's the fascination in this business that turns a grown man into an irresponsible teenager? Is it the chase, cops and robbers, cowboys and Indians?"

"With me, it's the upholding of the law," he said dryly. "I can't say what it is with other men."

She sighed soundlessly, glanced at Agnew and then out at the countryside, typing him in an instant as one of those stolid, humorless black-and-whiters she had seen so often in Pete's business. There would be no real conversation with him, no exchange of ideas.

She looked into the backseat, where Barn was sound asleep, sprawled over the pull-down center armrest, out to the world, an aluminum cola can ready to drop from his fingers onto the leather upholstery. She reached back and took it from him. "He's out like a light," she said. She worked the loose tab back and forth on top of the can, absently, and she detected a faint bitter odor, as if the cola had gone bad in some way. "Smell this," she said to Agnew. "Doesn't that smell peculiar to you?"

He took the can, held it beneath his nose, then shook his head slightly. "All these synthetic drinks smell alike to me," he said. "Taste one of the other cans."

She fished a can of diet cola from the ice, examined the top of it. Nothing wrong with it, she thought at first, running her fingertips across the smooth aluminum, and then she felt a slight burr of rough metal near the edge of the opening tab. She examined it closely, squinting. At the edge of the tab, there appeared to be a perforation, the tiniest of holes. She put the can back, grabbed up another. It too had a puncture mark.

"Where did you get these?" she said. "They've been tampered with." She reached back, shook Barn's arm, tried to awaken him. "Okay, chief, time to wake up." He did not stir. Doped, yes, and her mind seemed to flutter with the insanity of the moment, the craziness. "We have to find a doctor," she said. "There's something wrong with Barn."

Agnew smiled a slow, benevolent smile. "It's harmless, just something to help him sleep. And you'll be better off if you have one yourself. It will make everything much easier, believe me."

Slowly, with rising terror, she began to realize the truth. For a moment, she felt crazy and disoriented, as if she were caught in a trap she should have seen sooner.

Jesus.

Him!

Dozens of cars were going past them on the interstate and none of the drivers could know what was happening here. She was tempted to grab the wheel and yank it sharply to the right and send the Lincoln into a guardrail, onto the shoulder. She knew who he was. No doubts. She should have seen the madness beneath the veneer of normalcy, the shining glint in the eyes, the smile that was too fixed in place. She took a deep breath. "I want you to stop the car right now, Mr. Agnew. Right now and right here."

"You'll do better to relax," he said. "You *have* to relax." And casually, with a deft sweep of his left hand, he reached across his own chest and she caught a glimpse of the hypodermic syringe just before the needle hit her arm, the sting of an insect, the drug emptied into her before she could resist it. She yanked away, reflexively, but the buzzing sound had already invaded her head, her vision blurring, and she meant to reach back and touch Barn, but her arm had no strength and raised slightly, only to flop down powerlessly at her side. The blackness was rushing in now, quietly. She screamed without a sound.

Pete!

And then she was swallowed up by the darkness.

Stein was tired. The flight had been a long one with the two layovers and it was well after dark by the time he landed in Charleston. Thatcher was waiting to pick him up.

"We have a lot of catching up to do," Thatcher said, and even though he was trying to be upbeat, Stein could hear the doubt in his voice. He loaded the luggage into the backseat of the car and drove down the winding wooded road toward the city. "Maybe we could stop someplace and have a drink."

Stein picked up the scent of the trees in the darkness and something within him relaxed at being home. "I don't need a drink," he said. "I just want to go home."

"I hate like hell to have to be the one to tell you, Pete," Thatcher said. "But Karen's gone."

"Gone? Gone where?"

"She went to Washington. I tried to persuade her to wait around, but Agnew was here and he offered her a lift."

"Agnew? Who in the hell is Agnew?"

"Phillips's second in command."

"What's he doing here? And why's she going to Washington?"

"Agnew was here to make prearrangements on the move. He took measurements on the jukes, all the equipment. Have you signed a contract?"

"No," Stein said. "I think Phillips is a son of a bitch. I don't like him. But he keeps upping the ante, another half-million, maybe double that. I hate to believe I have a price, that I can't tell him to go to hell and walk away. But I keep thinking that he can put us out of business in five years and we'd end up with nothing."

Thatcher kept his eyes on the winding highway. "I think a lot about that. And I guess Alice deserves to be rich and I'm sorry as hell about Karen. Maybe all that's going to work out, too. She needs reassurance, Pete."

Stein felt deflated, emptied, as if his prime reason for coming home had been removed. "We might as well have a drink after all," he said. "I'm not that anxious to go home to an empty house."

Thatcher pulled into a bar off the expressway on the edge of Charleston, smoky with unvented fumes from fifty years of cigarettes. They settled down in a dark booth with beers while Thatcher brought him up to date on the business.

The publicity about the impending sale had shaken up a number of client departments that wanted to know if all the current projects would be finished on budget. Thatcher assured them they would be. "The newspaper stories imply we're going full-time on the Las Vegas killer," Thatcher said. "If that's true, we're going to have to add extra staff."

"That's all public relations," Stein said. "Phillips tied me to the Las Vegas extravaganza in the press to make his company look good. The whole damn thing got out of hand."

"How soon is all this going to happen?" Thatcher said. "The sale, the move."

"We'll probably finalize in the next thirty days. Then another month to move."

"So what it boils down to is that I have a month left here, no more than that," Thatcher said, running his fingers over the rim of the frosted glass. "He knows I'm not going with the new company, right?"

"I don't think he really wants either one of us," Stein said.

"And he'll dump me as soon as the transition can be made. He's a buzz saw, a whirling dervish, and he'd like to turn what we have into a high-profit money machine. He's all glitz, high tech, and bullshit."

"Yeah, well," Thatcher said. "It's good to have you back. I'm just sorry you couldn't come home to sweetness and light."

"It'll work out," Stein said.

Once they had pulled up in front of Stein's darkened house, Thatcher helped him with the suitcases. Stein clicked on the light in the living room, miserable, half-expecting Karen to pop out of the dining room with a happy surprise written on her face, but she would not, of course, and there would be no Barn bursting down the staircase to see what his father had brought him from Las Vegas. He put the suitcases out of the way. "Well," he said with a wry smile. "Pretty damn bleak, right?"

"Yeah," Thatcher said. "Your dog's over at our place."

"I appreciate your taking him."

"And I almost forgot, you're supposed to call Picone in Las Vegas."

"Did he mention what's up?"

"Nope. He said it was urgent, though."

"I'll give him a ring. And thanks for picking me up."

"I'm sorry you're having such a hard time," Thatcher said. "I'll talk to you in the morning."

When Thatcher was gone, Stein prowled the empty house. Karen would not have gone without leaving him a note, and, sure enough, he found the sealed envelope on the kitchen counter, his name in her distinctive cursive on the front. He picked up it, tapped the edge against the palm of his left hand as he looked into the closet, found both her big suitcases gone. He was depressed by the implication that she was prepared to be away for a long time. A number of her canvases were missing, her painting box as well. Barn's bedroom had been left tidy, only the teddy bear gone from the pillows. He went downstairs, mixed a bourbon and water in the kitchen before he settled on the couch and opened the letter from Karen.

"Peter—" it began, no endearing adjective, and she set the tone of her stern resolve in the name followed by a dash.

Barn and I are going up to Washington for a while. I have to be honest with you and not hold out any false hopes by implying that this isn't serious, because it is. What's happened is not really your fault, I know that, because we just happen to need different things out of life, but I do blame you for not leveling with me sooner. I'm going to find an apartment, and until then we'll be staying with Patricia in Georgetown. Her number's in the book but please, please don't call unless there's an extreme emergency, because I don't want to discuss this, not yet. Barn's just fine. He has a rash on his left arm and I thought it might have been poison ivy but it wasn't. I'll call you in a few days when I know exactly what I want. I suggest you think things through as well.

No signature. Not even an initial. He would have to wait it out and give her time and plenty of freedom, because this time he had made a terrible mistake. He had allowed her worst fears to be realized, permitting himself to be seduced by pride and pushed by boredom into believing that he was the sole person who could have made a difference in this case. From his long years as a cop, he knew that kind of hubris inevitably led to trouble, but it was easy to be hooked by a desire for self-importance.

He lifted the telephone and called Las Vegas. The moment Picone came onto the line, Stein could feel his jubilance.

"The case has broken wide open," he said. "Hell, you just left too early." And Picone gave him an abbreviated version of Swanson's relatives and the subsequent visit to the building, the kneeling body of the crippled man, and enough fingerprints and papers and assorted evidence to make the crazy once and for all. "His name is Gordon Oliver Desmond. We've got institutional records, pictures, everything."

"Have you picked him up?"

"Just a matter of time. We found his apartment. Jesus, it was like something out of tobacco road, filthy. He kept the girl there, doped her, fed her out of cans from the grocery store that he threw in trash bags when they were empty. It was a miracle she didn't die of food poisoning. And there was a bunch of stuff about you."

"What kind of stuff?"

"You name it. He subscribed to a clipping service for years, tacked everything he got on you to his closet wall. Stein the cop, Stein the computer expert, Stein the family man. There's even an early eight-by-ten glossy of you at some camp in New York, I'd say, maybe twenty years back or better. You have white marks on your nose and below the eyes. He's circled your head with a red Crayola and a teenager's head, probably Desmond himself, with a blue circle. Then he's got arrows running between you."

"Send me a copy."

"Will do."

"He also wrote a poem to you. I think it's to you. Anyway, I'll send it along, too. I take it you haven't been to your office yet?"

"No."

"We've been sending what we have to your FAX machine for the past hour. You'll have it all by now."

"Where is he?"

"Maybe you can give us an educated guess after you see the material," Picone said. "Hell, we talked to his former shrink here, who treats one hundred and fifty welfare crazies a week and gives everybody Thorazine and Valium and works as an adviser on movies shot in Las Vegas and doesn't know shit. He's so goddamn money-hungry, he doesn't really have time to treat his patients, much less understand them. You have a good flight?"

"There's no such thing as a good flight anymore."

Picone laughed. "I'm with you. At least there's a chance to stay alive on the streets. I'd appreciate an opinion as soon as possible. You want to call or send it by FAX, fine. Hang loose."

Stein hung up the telephone, filled with a weary depression at how easily everything could go awry, at the basic disorder in life that could never be tidied up or straightened out. There was nothing to be done at the moment except to cast that great, broad net out across the country and hope that Desmond would eventually be caught up in it.

He carried the bottle with him and escaped the loneliness of the house. As he drove through the quiet city, he envied the men who owned the now-deserted shops and stores, who could close down at six and carry no emotional or mental baggage home with them.

He opened up his building, and as he flipped on the light in his office he saw the fresh sheets in the tray of the FAX machine. He put on a pot of coffee automatically, as he always did when he was going to put in a long night. He poured himself a fairly stiff drink and sat down with the FAX sheets, to be immersed in the crazy life of Gordon Oliver Desmond.

On the top of the FAX pile was a photograph, in black and white, and Stein spotted himself on the top row of the group portrait, standing next to Lieutenant Powell. The white streaks on his nose and forehead were sunburn lotion (God, he had burned to a crisp that summer, anyway). And down in the second row of kids, Desmond had circled his own head. Stein examined it under a magnifying glass. There was no expression at all on that broad face, no glower, not a trace of defiance or joy, as if the mind had been blown away by medication and all that remained was a body to obey orders, to move where he was told for the group picture. Stein looked at the face a long time, finally shook his head in dismay. He had no memory of this particular face at all. But Desmond obviously remembered that time at camp because the two heads were circled, connected by arrows.

He picked up the poem Picone had mentioned. It was written in the strangest handwriting Stein had seen, the tops of the cursive flattened out as if there were an invisible lid on each line beyond which the ballpoint pen could not go. He would send a copy of this to Documents in the local crime lab, where they had an expert graphologist.

The text was not quite a poem in that there was no rhyme, no pattern to the words that crawled from the left edge of the paper to the extreme right-hand side and then, out of space, dropped down to begin again on the next line.

Shaman there were two lines of buoys in the lake water one white for those who could not swim and red farther out for those who could swim and D went past the white because god whispered in his ear and pulled him there and then let him sink until he couldn't breathe anymore and he died and was on the edge of heaven and then blinked three times at bright sunshine not in heaven but on the lake bank and you sat on D and pumped the water out of his lungs and turned him from dead fish to live ? and whispered all round hes dead dont work on him until he opened his eyes and saw your marked face and he knew you had brought him back from death so god allowed it and why

The writing ended abruptly. The sheet was undated. Stein was curious to know whether it had been written by boy or man, but it confirmed his own vague memory and the only positive connection he had been able to dredge up between them.

Desmond was not dumb, no, not according to the transcripts of the earliest tapes from a Connecticut institution. The transcripts were fully developed in the beginning and then tapered off as the institution became so crowded that the psychiatrists were swamped. Gordie, as he had been called as a boy, had been born in a small town near New Haven. His father had been a religious scholar on the fringe of the Yale faculty, where his being far-out was not acceptable. He had not had tenure at the university, but after Yale, he was bright enough and possessed of sufficient academic credentials to teach philosophy in a small religious college. He had run quasireligious groups in the house, groups that tracked through every fad, every change of approach to things religious, from rebirthing and mass anointing with olive oil to primal screaming and variations of EST.

Gordie's mother had been an uptight woman with a history of mental troubles, who occasionally had been institutionalized and eternally medicated. She had spent most of her time reading her Bible and various commentaries on the Scriptures, watched all the television evangelists who were climbing toward riches at that time, and spent the rest of her hours in meditation or sleep.

The transcript provided an incident and Stein's interest quickened. There was a police report on Gordie's mother; the charge was "child abuse," at a time when there was no great censure of the way a mother treated her child. But his mother's crime had been so outrageous that had it not been for her mental state, she would have been formally charged.

Gordie had been six years old at the time, and she had gone into his bedroom, to discover him fondling his genitals with his left hand. Quite lovingly, in a soft voice, she had chanted a couplet of her own creation.

Alas, the sin of Adam's fall,
The serpent's mark has touched us all.

She took him into the kitchen and calmly explained the concept of original sin to him while she put a carving knife on the stove, with the blade resting over the gas flames. Then she fed him a cookie and asked him for his left hand, which he willingly gave her. "God wants you to have the serpent's mark on you so you will never forget," she said.

She took the white-hot knife blade and dug a searing line into the palm of his left hand, while Gordie screamed but did not run, for he had been taught obedience. She went to the refrigerator to get butter to put on the burn while Gordie sat sobbing. There was no butter, so she used her lipstick and with a smile covered the deep cut of the burn with pink cosmetic. Later, psychiatrists were to discover that Gordie never held that punishment against his mother. He came, in his own dementia, to regard the scar as a purifying sign of faith.

Ah, I am beginning to see you, Desmond, Stein thought, beginning to know your mind and feelings, trapped between rage and guilt. The logic was now plain, the serpent's mark converted into a cross to attract Stein to Desmond's magic powers, salvation and murder in the tortured adult grown from the confused and crazy child.

His mother had been committed for six months' observation. When she went home, she picked up her life as it had been before. Gordie maintained a low profile. He drifted through grade school, quiet, studious, unremarkable, a low-B student, occasionally delusional in that he sometimes signed a classmate's name to his own work, even when that work was inferior to his own.

He went home each evening to a frame house, where he poured himself a glass of goat's milk and watched his mother sitting in silence. When she talked to Gordie, it was to tell him of the miracles God demanded from those who believed in Him and were thereby a part of Him. Gordie had been trained to measure out the pills his mother was to take, to provide them at specific hours with half a glass of water.

No one gave a great deal of thought to Gordie until the November day, shortly after his ninth birthday, when the maid, named Adrienne, a student from the college, put together the laundry and found Gordie's T-shirt covered with blood. Alarmed, she had

216

called Gordie's father, who canceled a religious seminar to hurry home even before Gordie arrived on the school bus. She also had discovered in Gordie's room a notebook with dates and times and a strange coding.

Then Gordie's father sent Adrienne home and had a conversation with his wife, urging her to retire to her room to preserve any shock to her nerves (which she did), and then he took his place in a large carved Jacobean chair in the parlor, facing the door through which Gordie always came on his return from school. Gordie's expression did not change when he saw the notebook in his father's hand, his father's face a combination of pain and befuddlement, as if he knew something was terribly wrong.

He asked Gordie about the notebook and Gordie smiled benevolently and explained that the code was mirror writing for GTG, which was short for "Gone to God." He poured himself a glass of milk and explained that he had been hearing voices that told him what to do, voices that he was sure came to him from heaven. Occasionally, they directed him to use the name of a classmate in his work. And, as it was his father's mission to cure human frailties, Gordie had been called to the world of animals.

He led his father to a small storage room behind the garage, which contained old cartons of clothing destined eventually for the Mexican poor. As he opened the door, the stink was overpowering. On every exposed stud and rafter were the bodies of birds and lizards, dogs and cats, all shot with Gordie's air gun and then attached to the wood with long spike nails and a small cross carved in each animal. Gordie had fastened little scraps of paper to each of the specimens to mark the date and a name, for he had not dispatched these creatures nameless into the next world. The names were all nonsense, all vowels or consonants, XYBPT or EEUAO, with occasional numbers thrown in, so that God would know that Gordie had been following orders.

All the blood the student maid had found had come from a large stray dog that Gordie had shot with the air gun, but the dog had not even been wounded. Gordie had finally caught him beneath an oak tree and stabbed him to death with a Boy Scout knife. As he told his father about it, he pulled a cardboard box from beneath a table, opened the flap to show him the dog's bloody fur. This time, Gordie had punctured the animal's eyes, because no creature was good enough to look at God's countenance in the next world. There was not enough space left for Gordie to nail the dog to the wall.

Gordie's father threw up.

The next day, Gordie was sent to a psychiatric ward at a local hospital, where the shrinks pronounced him delusional and schizophrenic. Gordie enjoyed being confined to a small room with a barred window, where he could read his Bible and not have to go to school.

When Gordie's condition stabilized, his father moved the family to Southern California. Stein paused to check the dates of the murders, the cut hands. Yes, the first series in Connecticut before the move and the next series in California after they had arrived. Gordie had been a precocious killer. Unsuspected.

In and out of hospitals. Drugs, electric shock, insulin therapy, counseling. Gordie had occasional months of lucidity. He actually enrolled in some college courses, doing quite well in drama, prompting an instructor's written commendation: "Desmond knows how to stay in character."

His father died. His mother was confined and passed away some months later. Gordie had an occasional job but never stayed at one thing for very long. In and out of institutions, "condition stabilized," "delusions lessened." He was temporarily out of the hospital when he was exposed as the author of a series of letters to the Pope in mirror writing, threatening his life and advising him that his "impostiture" (Gordie's word) had gone on long enough.

When the federal officer went to talk to Gordie about these threats, he found a very pleased young man who had draped an old armchair in red velvet and offered his guest wine in an ersatz silver goblet. Yes, Gordie had sent a number of letters to the Pope, demanding that the Pope authenticate Gordie as a "messenger of God to earth." Gordie had discovered the power of his own initials—G.O.D., and from there to G!O!D!—which meant that he had been selected for special missions by the Almighty but had only recently discovered it. When the Pope did not answer the letters at all, much less acknowledge Gordie's specialness, the threatening letters began, in which Gordie promised to dispatch the Pope straight to heaven, where he could speak to God personally.

In a private institution financed by a meager inheritance from his father, he was cured again and put back on the streets. He took vocational training as a truck driver until the day came when a workman fell off a loading dock at a warehouse and broke his leg and lay on the concrete writhing in pain. Gordie and the workman were alone together at the time. Help arrived within minutes and Gordie was involved with the law again.

The medical examiner determined that the workman had died from a blow to the temple that had been inflicted by a ball-peen hammer belonging to Gordie. There was also a small cut in the man's palm, which a witness testified would probably have been more extensive except that when he had arrived on the scene, Gordie put his knife away.

Gordie admitted everything. His delusion was by now full-blown and relentless. The workman's name was Frank Jones, and when he fell Gordie interpreted the action as a literal fall from grace. He sank down beside the hurting Jones and asked him to accept God, and Jones told him to go fuck himself and demanded an ambulance. Gordie claimed him for heaven and sent him to paradise with a ball-peen hammer.

The police had underestimated him. Gordie heard them talking about "the loony." They left him alone in a hospital waiting room for five minutes. No one was paying attention as Gordie drifted out of the hospital and, with a screwdriver, stabbed a businessman named Arthur J. Croce in the chest and wrote a note in a tidy script that said, "Gone to God." He took Croce's identity and his Ford Ventura, which was found abandoned in Texas a week later.

Ah, Christ, Stein thought, eyes hurting from too much reading, stomach soured from too much bourbon, and saddened by what he had read. He could see the rest of Desmond's history coming and they should have, too, these psychiatrists and psychologists and social workers. Someplace along the line, Desmond should have been stopped. But the system was defective and overloaded, and when Desmond showed up in Las Vegas and was dragged in as a loony-tune, no one really had the time to check him out. He seemed to be under control as long as he took his drugs. His delusions seemed to spiral inward and were not considered threatening.

Under these circumstances, Stein wondered, thumbing through the sheaves of paper, who would have taken Gordon Desmond seriously and really checked him out? After all, he had a job and seemed to be a responsible member of society when there were too many people literally banging their heads against the wall, or slashing their wrists. And something had sent Gordie off again on his crazy spiral, mind flashing back. What a heavy emphasis he must have put on an act that Stein had considered routine. Stein had dragged a boy from the water, one of dozens; Desmond had died and been brought back from a baptism of death by a shaman, a miracle worker endowing him with the very same power of pulling life from death.

It all fit: Stein as a substitute father, and God as the real omnipotent father, soon to return.

It was over now; Stein's part in the case was down to words, and he was supposed to take everything into consideration and predict. He poured himself one more drink, despaired of getting sufficiently drunk to sleep. He sat down at a work station and addressed his data base under DELUSIONS—RELIGIOUS and then under JESUS CHRIST and GOD. A dozen diverse cases popped onto the screen, names of individuals followed by coded categories. With a sigh, he punched in JC and read through the précis of the criminally insane who had believed themselves to be Jesus Christ or heavenly emissaries. There were some dangerous ones indeed: H. P. King, Anaheim, California, who called himself "The King of Peace" and in 1984, dressed in a pure white robe, entered the First National Bank of Anaheim, yelling gibberish. He had sprayed personnel and customers alike with a semiautomatic Ruger .22, killing two tellers, injuring six customers before a bank guard shot him in the leg and downed him. The King had been chasing money changers from an imaginary temple. In 1985—New York City—another Jesus, killer of prostitutes, who demanded to be stoned to death. Another more malevolent Jesus in Philadelphia last year, who tortured bums and shoplifted to support his deadly ministry.

But there was a difference here. Desmond was one of the crazies with long periods of lucidity in which he could pass for sane. Only a functional man could have operated the whole Swanson swindle, getting the old man to sign a bill of sale before shoving him into an airtight locker. When he returned later, he did not even bother to clear out the storage rooms or to try to sell the stacked cases of whiskey still in stock. He had plenty of money. He came back to arrange the grisly *tableau mort* with the crippled man, dead of asphyxiation, posed before the empty throne and the hurried symbol on the wall (shades of the velvet-covered chair from which Desmond had talked to the detective so many years ago).

From Stein's personal observations, the man was suffering from massive self-doubt, among his more lethal delusions, and had wanted Stein to validate him, but all of that was now past. It was highly likely Desmond would head for someplace where neither his eccentricity nor his new affluence would be questioned. He would be smart enough to know the police were after him and he would certainly change his name.

San Francisco was Stein's first pick for Desmond's new location, home of more cults than showed up on any lists. Only a hunch. Maybe not San Francisco. There was too much of the desert in the Bible and there was a more logical place for Desmond. Los Angeles. Literally, "The Angels." Not the city proper but out on the fringes, the poorer sections, Hemet or Lake Elsinore.

He sipped the bourbon. A cycle here . . . sporadic violence and enough blood to last awhile. He uncapped his pen, wrote his conclusions and put the sheet on his facsimile machine and dispatched it to Las Vegas Metro, attention Picone. Then he walked around the building, checked the computer rooms, found an accumulation of mail on his desk, a letter from Teddy, which he would put off until morning, some printouts of electronic mail, most of them from police departments wanting to know what was going on.

He took the bottle with him and lay down on the daybed in the lounge. Easier to sleep here in the office than to go home to an empty house. Tomorrow he would call Washington and make things right with Karen. Maybe take a vacation to Disneyworld for Barn and then a condo on Myrtle Beach for a while. He closed his eyes.

Morning.

He had been sleeping but he came instantly awake, wondering how he was ever going to quell the instinct for the chase that burned within him, the sharp jolt of adrenaline that was like an addictive drug to him. Zap! Standing in the dark, a disembodied, crazy voice washing over him, the silhouette of a dead priest squeezed in the rocks. Zip! The electricity singing through him with all the intensity of sex.

He heard the door open and Thatcher banged into the office. "You been here all night?"

"I didn't want to go home."

"There's coffee but it's strong enough to walk by itself."

"I can use it," Stein said.

The coffee was strong enough to jolt him awake. Stein stood up. The FAX light was on; the machine whirred with an incoming. He knew it was Vegas and he read the sheet as it came off the roller. Picone was a lousy speller but he was right to the point. He thanked Stein for the poop, said it made *beaucoup* sense, and they were checking flights out, buses, new- and used-car purchases, hitchhikers, any way Desmond could have left the city. Desmond's car had been found deserted in the Circus Circus parking lot.

He also sent one picture from the mental hospital, and Stein was aware that Thatcher was standing behind him and looking over his shoulder at the full face of a man with a shaved head and a thin scar right down the center of the skull, a self-inflicted wound with a single-edged razor blade, and a square, strangely plump-cheeked face with a screwy self-satisfied expression, as if the hospital photographer had said, "Gimme a smile, Des, bigger now, say cheese." The delusional son of a bitch had really turned it on like a door-to-door salesman who had just sold a set of Britannica, not a care in the world.

"He looks familiar," Thatcher said. "I've seen that picture someplace."

"Where?" Stein asked. He took the picture from the machine and examined it in a good light. "He looks so damn normal. My God, there should be something crazy in the eyes, or a twist at the corners of the mouth. Yeah, something to warn the world and say, 'Look, this guy can put a bullet through your head or cut your throat without a change of expression, no advance warning.'"

Thatcher shook his head. "Maybe he just reminds me of somebody. There was a guy ran the drugstore in the town where I grew up looked something like that. He's not even weird-looking. Hell, put my picture against his, except for that scar, and nine out of ten people would make me for the loony."

The dangerous ones should be marked, Stein thought, as in

primitive societies, some brand on the forehead to cancel out the benign demeanor, to serve as a warning to the unwary. Beware!

"Let's go get some breakfast," Thatcher said. "You look like the wrath of God."

"I'm not hungry."

"Let me heat you a cheese Danish in the microwave. It'll help, believe me."

"Okay," Stein said. He took his coffee and sat down at the desk with Teddy's letter. Teddy was grim as usual, but Teddy would be grim even if he were having fun, as if it were his duty to turn over every rock and examine the underside. Teddy had heard that Stein was selling out to Phillips and he wanted to fly down and do a story if the publicity was true.

Stein smiled despite himself. Teddy would have made a first-class homicide cop, with his attitude of looking at even the most commonplace event and asking, "What does it mean?" Stein examined the postmark, the date on the letter. It had arrived last week. He'd give Teddy a ring later.

The telephone rang. He picked it up, to find Phillips on the line, voice hollow, as if he were in a tunnel. No, on a car phone, of course, high tech at a buck-a-minute minimum, except that Phillips was calling from Seattle.

"Beautiful," Phillips was effusing. "All the papers have it on the West Coast. Big, big write-up in the *L.A. Times,* perfect PR, how you flushed the guy out, all the right touches and now the acquisition of your company. So now we follow up, right, friend? Good, strong push. I've put out a release that we're going all the way, no limit, and I'll cover everything, plus the bonuses we were talking about." A truck drowned him out momentarily. "So what's your next step?"

"I'm not making any next step," Stein said. "I'm out of it. It belongs to the LVPD now."

"But they're still consulting you."

"I'm not on the case anymore."

But Phillips was not about to be overwhelmed by facts. "That makes for a perfect reverse image," he said. "You're not only the best in your field but you're modest and you're going to let them have the glory of catching this guy. So you say anything you want to and we'll put a spin on it from our end and keep you looking good. The company's setting up a big funeral for the little girl, college scholarships for her brothers."

"Look," Stein said, his stomach threatening to turn over again. "I appreciate what you're trying to do and I'm sure the little girl's family is grateful, but frankly, I'm having second thoughts about the whole deal."

"I can see how you feel," Phillips said.

"I don't think you can. I'm not sure I want any part of your version of the big time."

The wind whistled through the telephone, the deep purr of the Mercedes engine. Phillips made a mental spin on a dime, a regular gyroscope of a man. "Of course, you're right," he said. "I apologize. Sometimes I push too hard because I'm too aware of the media. But something else has come up you might be interested in. It's up to you, of course, but you can be thinking about it. I have a friend at Lorimar and he approached me . . . well, a tasteful miniseries . . . and a hundred grand to you personally for consultation . . . but we need to discuss it pretty soon." More wind. "Look, I'm going out of range. If you want anything, just talk to—"

"Agnew. I know. He was here."

Static now, the car between pickup points, just enough power to send the one terrible word coursing through the line. "Agnew?" And then nothing except the cold chill Stein felt in the way Phillips had said the name—"Ag-new?"

Unfamiliar.

Stein went numb, hand on the telephone. He severed the connection, then jabbed the buttons, 202 for Washington first, Patricia's number. Five rings and the goddamn caution of an answering machine. Pat's number, revealing nothing.

"We can't come to the telephone now, but . . ." He put the telephone back in the cradle just as Thatcher came into the office with the hot Danish on a paper plate. "Let it cool," he said. "I got the settings wrong."

Stein picked up the photograph of Desmond between thumb and forefinger, turned it slowly so Thatcher could look at it again. "Agnew?" he asked quietly.

Thatcher's face drained of color. He scratched the side of his cheek. "God," he said. "Yeah. With hair, thick brown hair, combed straight back. Glasses. Cheeks not quite this pudgy."

"The picture's three years old."

Thatcher sat down heavily. "Shit," he said.

"You couldn't know," Stein said. "What kind of car was he driving?"

Thatcher shook his head slowly from side to side. "A Lincoln Town Car."

"What kind of accent did Agnew have?"

"Hell, nothing really distinct, soft-voiced. Southern California, maybe. I'll put hair on the goddamned picture and send out an APB," Thatcher said.

Stein drummed his fingers on the desk, his mind speeding up as if he had taken a Benzedrine. The chase again. "No," Stein said. "You fill in the hair on the picture and get things ready, but don't make a move. He'll be calling me. Again. That was the one thing I didn't consider. I thought he'd given up on me."

"What you want to do?"

"There's nothing we can do until he calls except get ready for him." He stopped, thinking it through. Shit, all guesswork now, all hunches. "I don't want to involve the locals or the FBI unless we have to." He picked up the telephone, called Picone in Las Vegas. "Can you catch the first flight back here?" he asked.

"What's happening?"

"A personal favor to me. Desmond's in town. He has my wife and son."

"Holy Jesus."

"I want to work this quietly, just the three of us, you, me, and Thatcher."

"Is there anything you want me to follow through on out here?"

"Everything's got to look normal. If your coming's a matter of money, I'll cover it."

"No problem," Picone said. "There are more private jets here than in Saudi Arabia. I'll call in a favor and be there in four, maybe five hours. I'll call you when we're a half hour out of Charleston."

"I owe you one," Stein said. As he put the telephone down, Thatcher shook his head doubtfully. "You sure you don't want a team from the West Virginia police?"

"Not now," Stein said. "I'm not going to give the son of a bitch any reason to blow. We're going to play everything so goddamned cool that it will seem perfectly normal when I work out a trade."

"Sure," Thatcher said. "I understand." But there was no conviction in his voice.

Stein was concentrating now, determined to miss nothing. "Desmond was completely lucid?"

"Yeah. I would have sworn he was exactly who he said he was. Good grammar, a real company man. Why?"

"That gives us a better chance, then. He'll follow a pattern," Stein said, once again distancing himself from the terrible fear that could only get in his way. "He's determined to get my cooperation. So he won't kill either of them, not yet." He fumbled around in a desk drawer for a stale pack of cigarettes he kept to demonstrate his willpower. He shook one from the pack, lit it. His hand was trembling. He looked at Desmond's picture again. You cause them even the slightest harm and I'll rip your tongue out before I kill you. He inhaled the smoke, steadied himself.

"I want you to access all the hotel, motel, and motor-lodge chains in West Virginia, Maryland, southern Pennsylvania, Kentucky, and the District of Columbia. I want a sort of all their check-ins last night," he said.

"He won't have used his real name."

"No. But he'll have to register his car. So key on the Lincoln. If it's rented, it will be a new one. What color was it?"

"Tan, beige, something like that. You think he's holed up?"

"Yes," Stein said, the smoke stinging his eyes. "He'll get in touch sooner or later, but if I can get the jump on him, I want it."

"I'll get on it," Thatcher said, heading for his office.

Stein looked at a map of West Virginia, the hundreds of small towns tucked away in the hollows of Appalachia, mining towns, river towns, bigger commercial centers along the interstates, and he knew that he could lift the telephone and call any one of a dozen officers in the state police headquarters, and every goddamned motel or boardinghouse in any part of the state would be swept by troopers within the hour. He visualized Desmond caught unaware, blinking in the glare of police headlights, raising his pistol to fire just as the police cut the son of a bitch in two. . . .

He wanted it but he could not have it. For all police work was based on certain mental standards, that the criminal's first instinct would be to ensure his own safety, his own life, and with people like Desmond, this simply was not true. He had no normalcy, nothing that could be predicted. He had written his history in blood, enjoyed killing, accepted it as his right, and it would take no more than the thought that he had been betrayed to make him . . .

Stein moved away from the thought. No police. Absolutely not. Stein turned to his own terminal keyboard and his telephone, stubbing out the cigarette, taking a sip of the coffee as he looked through his Rolodex. He made his computer search methodically, aware of the limitations, for first he had to get permissions. He called his contacts at the national headquarters of the car rental companies, and it took time for his messages to get through and his calls to be returned. Eventually, he had the access codes, which he fed into his machine, then he punched in the parameters of his search. He wanted a sort of all Lincolns rented out of airports within a five-hundred-mile radius of Charleston within the past forty-eight hours. Desmond might have been able to fly out of Vegas, paying cash and using a phony name, but a car rental required a driver's license. He made his first search keyed on the initials G, O, and D.

The screen displayed a single word: WAIT.

He took the time to examine a FAX coming in from the NYPD, from Lieutenant Powell.

"Nobody kept any lists of the campers that far back. Sorry for the negative. Try me again sometime. Nice to hear from you."

She signed it "Tarheel."

He drummed his fingers on the desk and within minutes the response came back. A Lincoln rented out of National Airport in Washington the day before yesterday. The individual's initials: G.O.D.

He waited another moment, which seemed like minutes.

GEORGIA OLIVE DODD, DALLAS, TEXAS.

He had tried to make it too simple. He keyed the search this time on any two of the three initials, G, O, and D, in any order, then poured himself a fresh cup of coffee. He waited while thousands of names went through the electronic sieve, and suddenly, bang, the names came on to the screen. One leaped out at him and he was suddenly alive with hope.

Bingo! All right, you son of a bitch, I'm on your wavelength now.

A Hertz transaction out of Richmond, a Lincoln Town Car, Signature series, light sandalwood with matching leather, carrying the Florida plates usually found on rental cars in this part of the country, Number CYX 82F. Name of customer: Desmond Gordon.

Nevada driver's license. He was about to print out when the telephone rang.

Desmond's words were crisp, clear, positive. You're still off medication, Stein thought. The manic roller coaster was on high.

"Well, hello again," Desmond said.

"You have my wife and son."

"Very nice people," Desmond said. "You really should have played straight with me in Las Vegas, you know. The little girl would be alive now if you had done what I'd asked, if you hadn't involved the police. And I wouldn't have had to kill all those people at the state line."

"What do you want from me, Desmond?" Stein asked.

"You know my name now," Desmond said brightly. "Good for you. And I bet you have one of my old hospital pictures. Terrible, isn't it? Are you ready to admit you remember me?"

It's time to take a chance, Stein thought. "Of course," he said. "I brought you back. I wouldn't forget that."

"Then you admit it," Desmond said with great relief.

"It was a hell of a mistake," Stein said. "I should have left you on the other side."

Desmond barked a spontaneous laugh. "You didn't know I was going to turn out to be competition, did you? You didn't know God would select me over you."

"Let's cut the shit," Stein said. "You obviously want a trade or you wouldn't have snatched my family. What do you want?"

Desmond chuckled. "I actually came back here to see you once," he said. "I caught the bus all the way from Las Vegas. It was right after you went into business. Your son was a baby then. I watched you and your wife having dinner at some Italian place."

"Why didn't you let me know you were here?"

"God didn't want me to. I had no idea that sooner or later he would pit me against you." Had he sighed? Stein could not be sure. "Now, there are a number of ways I can demonstrate my superiority. So you can choose. If you don't do what I say, I can harvest your wife and son. That would be simplest. But I really don't want to do it that way."

"How do you want to do it?" He looked up. Thatcher was standing in the doorway, a grave expression on his face as he listened to Stein's end of the conversation.

"Something big is going to happen here. So I want you to call somebody at *The New York Times* and get them down here to cover it. I also want a representative from the Vatican here."

Stein listened, mind racing, knowing he was following a dangerous direction. He had faced this kind of situation before, a paranoid killer who had held four hostages in Queens until he had a letter from the President himself, apologizing for Vietnam. Stein had solved that by printing up a piece of ersatz White House stationery, dictating the text and forging the President's signature. The paranoid had released his hostages.

"I can arrange that," Stein said. "I want to speak to my wife."

"She's sleeping peacefully. You don't have any other choice except to trust me, you know. You'll be tempted to try to double-cross me. You have so much information. Thatcher saw the Lincoln, so that's no secret. But you won't try to use it. You'll think about that room in Nevada with the four old people in it."

"Then meet me face-to-face, just the two of us."

"If God wants that to happen, he will arrange it."

"The reporter, the man from the Vatican," Stein said. "Who else?"

"An M.D. and a good photographer. I mean a really good one."

"Where do you want these people to be? When?"

"I'll call you tonight. You have everything ready."

"Yes."

"The old refrain. I spot any cops and I take the easy victory. Your default."

The line went dead.

Stein leaned back in his chair, told Thatcher the conversation. "I want you to line up a Catholic priest, as prominent a man as you can find. I want the use of his name, the possibility of his being available this evening. I'll get ahold of Teddy in New York."

"No luck on any of the hotels, by the way," Thatcher said.

"I didn't think there would be." He picked up his telephone. "Let's put our package together," he said.

"And then what?"

"We'll see," Stein said.

Desmond was on a high, giddy with the ability to be someone else besides himself, for by being two people, he doubled his powers. He had played this perfectly, relying on God's guidance, and once Mrs. Stein had been out cold, he had been prepared to leave the interstate at the next exit, but he had seen a billboard with a large message written in Day-Glo orange letters: DRIVE WITH CONFIDENCE. So he had kept going until quite late. Then on the side of a mountain another sign appeared, ostensibly referring to a gas station: TURN BACK AT THE NEXT EXIT FOR THE FRIENDLIEST PLACE IN WEST VIRGINIA. He took the next overpass and reversed his direction, driving back toward Charleston until a final sign caught his eye: THE CHURCHES OF CHRIST WELCOME YOU.

He picked an older section of town and a decrepit motel. He rang the night bell and smiled at the henna-haired lady who came through a door behind the desk. In a weary voice, he explained that his wife and son were asleep in the car. "We drove all the way from Atlanta today," he said.

He signed as Mr. and Mrs. Grant Divine, 6267 N. Peachtree, Atlanta, Georgia, and handed her a fifty-dollar bill, taking the change without counting it. He told her he wanted no maid service the next day so his family could sleep, and wished her a good evening. He observed that she was watching a middle-of-the-night cop-show rerun on a small black-and-white TV in a parlor off the registration desk while waiting for the bell to announce her next customer.

He took his key and drove to the back of the old motel, where he unlocked the door to the room and turned on an air conditioner to lessen the smell of pine oil disinfectant. He left the room door open, pulled Karen from the car, and hoisted her in his arms. He was amazed at how light she was. He carried her limp body into the room and laid her on the bed. Then he took in the boy and put him on the bed beside his mother. The room was old but basically clean. He pulled the drapes shut, locked the door behind him, then sat at the window, watching the neon motel sign blink off and on.

He dozed fitfully, awoke at dawn, fully refreshed. He examined mother and child, gave them another shot that would keep them asleep all day. After he shaved, he drove back into Charleston, stopped for coffee, his mind whirring with excitement, knowing exactly what he was going to do, only needing time to think it through.

He drove the new Lincoln to the capitol grounds and parked in a VISITOR slot, then took off his coat and went out to sit on a park bench, head lolled back against the roll of the top wooden slat so he was peering upward into the foliage of an oak tree.

He pulled his mind away from the distracting crowds of tourists and the security police, concentrated on the dark form hidden high in the convolution of the branches, the thickness of the leaves. The angel was there, trying to hide from him, each feather in the dark wings ruffled to resemble a leaf, but at the same time the creature was almost transparent, and Desmond had difficulty seeing the hood that concealed the face.

Desmond felt like laughing aloud because the angel had put himself in such a quandary, here to watch him on Stein's behalf and yet disturbed by the fact that Desmond had all the power. Or maybe the angel was just playing it safe, waiting to see who prevailed.

I can kill you anytime I like, Desmond thought, knowing that the angel could read his mind. The feathers quivered slightly from the impact of the threat. When the time comes, I may nail you to the wall like all the birds when I was a kid. I may dissolve you in a great ball of fire.

He blinked. The angel had disappeared.

Desmond looked at his watch. Things to do, yes, and he could not afford to miss any item on his list for fear that the rest would go awry. In this time of extravagant thinking, God could no longer make himself known through small miracles. He remembered the time at the hospital when one of the patients had strangled a cat while the claws inflicted parallel bloody scratches on a dough-colored face. Then the patient had thrown the cat into the corner of the room, neck broken, obviously dead.

Desmond had sat perfectly motionless, made not a move as the black attendant entered the ward. Only when the man bent over the dead cat had Desmond, through a flicker of his eyelids, willed that life should return to the animal, and as the bastard of an attendant reached out to touch the dead cat, the cat had sprung to life and raked him with its claws as the attendant yelled, "God-damn sumbitch."

Desmond had told the shrink at their next meeting about bringing the cat back to life, and the shrink had looked at him with passive eyes and said, "I'm sure you believe that's what happened." Desmond had made sure the shrink had a stroke and died two weeks later for his lack of belief. Nevertheless, it was going to take more than a small ambiguous miracle for Desmond to be recognized as God's messenger.

On impulse, he drove to a telephone booth outside a convenience store and called Stein, his extra senses alert, aware that Stein was scared shitless for his family, not likely to cause trouble, ready to capitulate in the face of a superior power. Oh, he would put Stein down before he was through.

Desmond sighed, went back to his car. He stopped at a hardware store, put the things he needed in the trunk, and then drove to a drugstore, where he used some of the prescription blanks he had picked up in the hospital. He stopped at a gas station and paid for full service to get all his windows sparkling, then he went back to the motel to wait for evening.

The telephone rang and Stein picked it up. "This is Stein."

"Sorry I couldn't alert you from the jet," Picone said, his voice tired. "I'm out at the airport."

"We'll come and get you. Twenty minutes."

He had the telephone number switched to the car, picked up Thatcher, and drove out to the airport, to find Picone waiting outside the modern terminal. He threw his bags into the trunk, looked up at the cloud bank to the west. "I can give you an accurate weather forecast," he said. "We flew around a squall line west of here with tops at fifty thousand feet. We're going to get wet as hell here tonight."

Stein introduced him to Thatcher and Thatcher took the backseat this time. Picone was bedraggled, but when he heard there was a vehicle description and a plate number, he brightened considerably. "You put out an APB?" he asked.

"Not yet," Stein said.

"It wouldn't hurt to locate the vehicle, Pete," Thatcher said. "And it gives us another option."

"What are the odds that Desmond would spot the cops looking for him?" Stein asked.

"Considering our psycho, better than normal," Picone said. "But I'd take the chance."

"I won't," Stein said. "He thinks he's immune to death and can simply transport himself to heaven if he gets pushed. There's no way to leverage him. No, we'll play it his way. His call was local. He wants the writer, the doctor, the photographer, the Catholic representative here, in Charleston. So that means Karen and Barn are still alive, stashed away."

"I hope to hell you're right," Picone said. "What's the game plan?"

"There's a chance," Stein said. "You take the motels, rooming houses upriver between here and the toll road. No contacts with anybody, strictly observation, on the chance you can make his car. And Thatcher takes Charleston and South Charleston, as many motels as he can cover in a ten-mile radius. Desmond's dug in someplace, but he may not have Karen and Barn with him. If either of you spot his car, you call in and we take it from there. But for God's sake, no contact."

"The West Virginia troopers are going to be pretty damn sore," Thatcher said.

"No troopers. I won't take the risk," Stein said.

"Okay, I'll go with it," Thatcher said.

"Picone?"

"How much time we have?"

"I don't know. Maybe not much. But it beats hell out of doing nothing."

"Hell, why not?" Picone said. "Give me a car with a telephone, a map, compass, and addresses and I'll give it a shot. But I want dibs on this one if we get him alive. He left blood all over my town, so I want first crack at him."

"We'll see," Stein said.

Teddy flew in by private jet at five-thirty. He landed in the rain and was helped down the short flight of boarding steps by a young man named Adams, who had bright red hair, a very pale complexion, and an easy confidence about him. Teddy stood on the tarmac, balancing on his cane, the rain dripping from the broad, flat brim of his hat. Adams lugged the camera cases out of the jet and shook hands with Stein, openly curious about what kind of pictures they were to be shooting.

"I can't tell you that," Stein said. "I don't know."

Adams squinted at the rain as if taking a light reading. "If there's time, I'd like to get some shots of the river. I've got an Appalachia assignment coming up."

"There isn't any time," Teddy said. "Check us in at the hotel and wait for my call."

They dropped him at the hotel and Stein drove through the rain to his office. Teddy studied him with large bulldog eyes.

"I'm sorry about Karen and Barn. What have you heard?" Teddy asked.

"Nothing."

"How can you do this? Are you as cool as you seem to be?"

"No," Stein said. "Give me the chance and I'd rip the son of a bitch apart with my bare hands. But I know what has to be done. I really appreciate your flying down."

"I want the story."

"I sure hope to hell that it's a simple one. I get my family back and he gets blown away or locked up."

"That's devoutly to be wished," Teddy said. "What do you have in mind?"

"We'll go along with him," Stein said. "You write whatever he wants written and your photographer takes any pictures he wants. I've made arrangements to give him a bogus newspaper page by morning, if that seems to be appropriate."

"Will that do it?"

"I don't know. That depends on what he's planning."

At the office, Teddy shed his rumpled raincoat, propped his dripping hat on a rack, and settled down with a pot of black coffee and the background printouts. Stein had the telephone switched back from the car to the office. The moment the switch had been made, the telephone rang. Phillips was on the line.

"What's going on?" Phillips asked. "I thought you were supposed to call me and keep me up-to-date."

"I don't have time to talk now."

"Desmond's there, isn't he?" Phillips asked. "I do have contacts, you know. My Las Vegas people told me Picone flew back east. So I already have background."

"Desmond has my wife and son," Stein said. "He pretended to be a representative of your company."

"My God," Phillips said. "I'm sorry."

"We're on top of the situation."

"I hope you won't take offense at this, but I'd prefer that Desmond's pretending to be with the company doesn't come out."

"I don't give a shit about that," Stein said. "This is a critical night. I'm waiting for a call. We'll have to talk later." He severed the connection.

Teddy ran his stubby fingers through his rumpled thatch of gray hair, eyes narrowed behind thick owlish glasses against the sting of cigarette smoke.

"You know the general opinion of Phillips and his companies, don't you?" he asked.

"At this moment, it doesn't make a hell of a lot of difference, but he can make me rich," Stein said.

"He has the scruples of a viper," Teddy said. "If he has his way, his companies will take over corrections in all the states, establish corporate police forces in all the major American cities, do it all with chilling efficiency at less than current cost and make himself even richer in the process."

"If he's that good, why are you against him?"

"Because he doesn't really give a damn about anything except money," Teddy said. "You have a psychopath here who's slaughtered a lot of innocent people and is holding your family hostage, and I suspect Phillips doesn't give a damn about what's happening except how it affects his bottom line. I don't care whether he can warehouse prisoners more efficiently or run police departments that are more cosmetically perfect than their public counterparts. Somebody has to care about what's happening. He makes it too easy to sweep any social concerns under the carpet." His cigarette was a short stub; he lit a fresh one from the coal.

"He can have it," Stein said. "I'm going to get my family back and take the money and leave it to him."

Teddy shrugged. "I can't blame you," he said. "If I were in your place, I'd probably feel the same way."

Stein glanced up at the clock. "What the hell's going on with Desmond? Why hasn't he called?"

"If he's trying to rattle your cage, it's working," Teddy said.

The phone rang and Stein snatched it up, but it was Picone. He had just compared notes with Thatcher. "We made our first sweep and we got nothing," Picone said. "*Nada.* You heard from him?"

"Not yet."

"It's possible he could have gone on up the interstate aways before he peeled off. You want us to cover?"

"No. Get something to eat and come back to the office."

"Yeah," Picone said. "And hang loose. You can't afford to stay uptight. So hang in there."

"Yeah," Stein said.

The first line of thunderstorms had passed and the next line was flickering lightning in the west by the time Desmond parked on the street and went into the Brass Nickel Bar, a seedy little place in the Washington-Bigby District of Charleston. It was full of migrant workers, Latinos, grimy men with muscled brown arms and tattoos that appeared to be crudely self-inflicted. The bar stank of sweat and beer and there was a single undernourished stripper dancing on a mirrored platform in the corner of the room.

Desmond felt one of his spells coming on. The pressure was mounting in his head, as if God were telling him that more people needed to be harvested here to make room for the rest of the migrants who would be coming in. He wanted this to be true, but he could not be sure the urge didn't come from the devil, who would try to distract him from his true purpose tonight.

He had to keep looking around the room. His head was so full of energy that the power of his eyes would focus into an intense beam and explode the glass shelves loaded with bottles over the bar; the mirror would crack into a million glittering fragments; the heavy Anglo bartender with a beer belly drooping over his belt would suffer a heart attack and die.

Desmond tapped a half-dollar on the polished wood of the bar. Thunk, thunk, thunk. The bartender replaced his empty longneck Bud with a fresh one.

"You speak Spanish?" Desmond asked him.

"I'd be pretty dumb to run a bar for Latinos if I didn't."

"I'm looking for somebody to do a job for me," Desmond said. "It's going to take a couple hours and I'll pay a hundred dollars for it."

"A hundred dollars? What are you, a queer or a process server?" the bartender said.

"Nothing like that," Desmond said. He paused to drink from

the bottle, closed his eyes against the cold kick of the beer. "I want him to repossess a car for me. He needs to be Mexican, Puerto Rican, because the car belongs to a Latino. And he's going to need to have a valid driver's license."

"Hell, I know a guy got shot repossessing a car," the bartender said. "I don't know if I want anything to do with that."

You don't know who you're messing with. If I wanted it to happen, your lungs would explode like balloons, he thought. "I've got a twenty-dollar bill right here in my pocket," Desmond said. "You get me five possibles to show me their driver's licenses and you get the twenty."

The man had a narrow face, and now it was all screwed up in a sharp expression of suspicion. "I'm giving you a friendly word, man. If you're from Immigration, I'd suggest you have a quick beer and split this place."

Desmond's smile did not change. You give me one more smartass remark and you're dead. "I told you what I want. If you don't want the twenty, say so."

The bartender raised bony shoulders in a shrug. "You got it," he said, thereby saving his life. He went down the bar to a group of Mexicans, talked to them in a low voice, and Desmond felt the strength of their dark, appraising eyes. He felt the excitement now. They were all in the hands of God, who would pick one to become famous and glorify His holy name and Desmond's, as well. Desmond looked directly at the men as calloused hands began to dig thin wallets out of worn pockets, the plastic cards clicking on the counter. The bartender gathered them up in a neat pile, came back down the bar to Desmond.

The bartender made a sputtering sound, exhaling air through thick lips, a horselike whinny. "Okay," he said. "Let me see your twenty."

Desmond handed him the money, took the licenses, looked no further than the second one before he knew he had his man. Jesus Maria Angel Rodriguez. Was such a name possible? He squinted at the picture, the young man looking positively jaunty as he grinned into the camera. Age: 27. Height: 5'5". Weight: 146 pounds. Everything fine, the body weight just fine for the dose in the syringe. He flipped the single license onto the counter, aside from the rest.

"This is the man I want."

"Good choice," the bartender said. He called out in Spanish and Desmond could make out the name Hay-soos in the rapid chatter of words. A short man with intense black eyes and the clothes of a laborer came down the side of the bar with the springy step of a prizefighter. He had the single word MAMA tattooed on his biceps. Desmond did not look at him directly, just one quick glance and away.

"You speak English, Hay-soos?" Desmond asked.

"Some English."

"Did the bartender explain the job to you?"

"Sure. I can do that."

"Fine." Desmond took a fifty-dollar bill out of his pocket, handed it to Hay-soos. "This is up-front money. You understand up-front?"

"Yeah, sure."

Desmond closed his eyes and tried to turn down the intensity he felt. Because if he looked at the Mexican full face, eyes boring in, the man's blood would boil in his veins and his eyes would pop out before his heart exploded. He had to take the chance. He opened his eyes, glanced at the man and then away before he returned his eyes for a longer look. Hay-soos's face was square, *mestizo,* peasant, with a large nose and high cheekbones and bushy eyebrows over intense brown-black eyes that were wary, cunning, hopeful, avaricious. He bore Desmond's full gaze without difficulty. No distress. Perfect. He has it, Desmond thought. The Mexican had passed the test.

"You want a beer, Hay-soos?" Desmond asked, and then to the bartender: "Give him what he wants, anything." The bartender served the beers.

Desmond raised his bottle. "Cheers," he said, grinning.

"*Salud.*"

They both drank. Hay-soos emptied his bottle. "We might as well get going," Desmond said. "It's really not very far from here. You can drive a Camaro, can't you?"

"Sure," Hay-soos said. "Camaro, sure."

Hay-soos only partially understood—Desmond could see that—but the business about the money had gotten through to him all right. He was trying to act cool, figure a way to squeeze more money out of this *gringo*. His eyes gave him away, shining with cupidity. He was awed by the prospect of such easy money.

When they left the bar, Desmond felt the electricity in the air. Somewhere off to the south and west was a storm, a low and visceral rumbling of thunder, echoes from multiple valleys, jagged forks of lightning splitting the sky. He would hold off the storm until a more appropriate time.

The electricity surged through him, a jolt down the veins, and the tingle hummed along the surface of his skin. Once Hay-soos was in the car, the passenger door thunking solidly shut behind him, Desmond paused before he got into the driver's side. He looked for the winged shape that might be there in the high darkness, the black feathers catching brief reflections from the distant lightning. He could not see it.

He was certain the angel was against him now. He would kill the creature when he had the chance, blast it out of the sky.

Desmond started the car, excitement rising, almost sexual. The time had come and his mind moved beyond language. The Mexican was trying to make conversation, totally unaware of the nature of this night and the fantastic part he was to play in it. Desmond's hands sweated against the steering wheel; he drew the storm closer. He drove out into the country, close now to his destination, and with a practiced smoothness, he swept the needle from his pocket and plunged it into the Mexican's arm. He was not prepared for the response now, for Hay-soos, startled, uncomprehending, took a wild swing at him with his left hand, an awkward and backward flailing of his arm that hit nothing, and, at the same moment, Hay-soos opened the door and bolted through it. He took no more than a single staggered step before the drug dropped him. He just lay there, not all the way out, no, mumbling, trying to move his arms and legs, which twitched helplessly.

Desmond left the car, glanced up toward the three crosses he had examined earlier. The lightning flickered down a far hollow. He hummed him to himself as he opened the trunk of the Lincoln, took out his gear, the ropes and the short stepladder, the bucketful of tools. He carried them all to the foot of the center cross, then climbed up on the stepladder and rigged a pulley, getting everything ready before he went back for Hay-soos.

He lifted the Mexican as easily as a crate of cigarettes, lugged him up the slight incline and set him down at the foot of the cross while he looped the sling under his arms. He pulled the rope, watched the Mexican rise into position, mumbling incoherently.

"You're going to be famous," Desmond said. *"Famoso."* He steadied the swinging body against the upright timber, climbed the ladder to stretch the man's left arm along the crossbeam. It fell away once, completely limp, no power in the muscle. Desmond grabbed it again. He took a short length of rope and swiftly tied a slipknot around the wrist and then looped the rope over the wood. He continued to wrap until the arm was tightly fixed.

Desmond moved the ladder, tied the other arm to the cross-bar. He allowed the storm to come closer now, the wind freshening with the smell of rain, the lightning and the sound of thunder closer together. He stood back, cocked his head to one side, and studied the effect.

"You're going to be perfect." He approached the feet on the top of the stepladder, old shoes, cracked leather, no socks, ankles bony. He wrapped a rope around the legs and the post, pulled it tight. "You're going to be famous, Hay-soos," he said, heart pounding.

He could feel the panic in the inert man. He climbed the ladder and cut the sling, allowing the full weight of the man to catch on the bound arms. The ropes creaked against the strain.

Desmond looked up. The damned angel was there, making great slow circles against the approaching lightning. Desmond was rapturous. He went to the car, allowing time to pass. The drug began to wear off; Hay-soos's voice was louder, yelling, cursing. Good. You should be aware to truly know the glory, Desmond thought. He came back from the car, behind the Mexican, so Hay-soos could not see what was happening until Desmond mounted the ladder. The Mexican's head rolled to the right, eyes bulging, mouth gaping and slack. He shook his head in disbelief at the sight of the spike, the point of which was poised at the palm of his hand, the small sledge beginning the slow arc of a swing. Metal whanged against metal; the Mexican screamed against the thunder. His head flailed back and forth, fingers wriggling as the hand was nailed to the wood. Desmond swung the sledge again. Blood ran down from the calloused palm.

With Desmond singing, the metal biting through flesh and wood, the angel wheeled overhead. The storm broke and the rain descended with the wallop of a wind-whipped sheet of water. The Mexican screamed once more and passed out.

The call came shortly after the rain stopped. Stein let the telephone ring twice before he picked it up. "Stein," he said.

"I want him out of here," Desmond said, voice irritated, strung out.

"Who?"

"You know who. You must think you're pretty goddamn clever having him tail me around."

"There's nobody following you around," Stein said. "You know damn well I've followed your instructions."

"You're lying. I know he reports to you."

"Who are you talking about? Shit, if I had somebody that close to you, I would have taken you long before now."

Desmond was silent. "Maybe," he said, but the conviction was gone from his voice. "I want you to follow my instructions. I want you to take the writer, photographer, and doctor ten miles east. There's a sign for Esterhazy Road, and then turn right at the forks. You'll see it there."

"See what?"

"The only true miracle."

Stein felt a sinking sensation in his stomach. He kept his voice even. "And what then?"

"I'll be watching the eleven-o'clock news, Channel Three. I want to see an interview with the man you find out there. I want you and the doctor to talk with him on television and certify the miracle. When I see the pictures, I'll release your wife and your kid. Tomorrow morning, I want to meet the guy from *The New York Times* and his photographer. I want the Vatican representative there because I'm going to make a statement."

"Where can I get in touch with you?"

"I'll call you. Ten-thirty in the morning."

Stein's hand was sweating as he put down the telephone. "He

wants television coverage," he said to Teddy. "Channel Three, eleven-o'clock news."

"They always up the ante, don't they? How will you handle it?"

"He wants to believe," Stein said. "That's in our favor."

He did not want to open things up at this point or include another person, but he had no choice. He had met the news director at Channel 3, a gray-haired retired network executive who loved fly-fishing and hard news. His name was Oxford and in his New York days he had been considered totally uncompromising. There was no chance at all he would go along with a scheme to become a part of a story that was not true or to shape the news. But Stein remembered a young man named Richards who operated a minicam for the news department. Stein gave him a ring. "I may have a story for you," Stein said, and arranged to pick him up in a half hour.

Adams and Richards did not get along well together, Stein noticed. After the ritual of meeting, it was apparent that Adams considered himself superior to his country cousin whose living depended on sufficient brawn to carry the heavy minicam equipment around. They shared the backseat of Stein's station wagon in silence, while Teddy frowned into the darkness of the hill roads and smoked one cigarette after another.

"How does he know this country?" Teddy asked.

"He came here to see me once, probably in the middle of a psychotic episode. He never got up enough nerve to meet me, but he had plenty of time to prowl the hills." Stein's premonition became stronger than ever.

"Do you know what we're going to find?" Teddy asked, as if reading his mind.

"I think so, yes." Stein peered at the road ahead, and as the car started up a rocky slope, the headlights caught on three crosses. This time the center one was not empty.

The man who hung there was naked except for his boxer shorts. His nut-brown skin shone in the car lights and the mistlike rain. Adams was out of the car in an instant, flash popping, with Richards close behind.

"No pictures yet," Stein yelled. "Stay back ten feet."

And then, against all the forensic training that had been drilled into him over the years, he moved into the crime scene toward the hanging body, the grotesque religious tableau. The Mexican was hanging from the spikes driven into the palms of his hands and his fixed feet. Desmond had botched an attempt to nail through the ankles. They were too thick for the spikes, so he had pressed each foot as close as possible to the support post and put a spike through the top of each arch in turn, breaking enough bones to flatten the feet against the post.

The face itself was blank, with a distant expression of fixed flesh from which all life had departed. The slack jaw hung open, the eyes were glazed, the hair drenched by rain so it draped like seaweed from the crown of the head. There was blood everywhere, from the pierced extremities and a stream of clotted blood from a puncture in the left side of the chest.

The clothes were folded in a neat pile at the foot of the cross, showing slits where Desmond had cut them away from the body. The laminated driver's license sat atop the clothes and reflected the light, with the picture of the man on it, a forced and self-conscious expression on his face.

"Look at the name," Stein said, picking up the driver's license by the edges, allowing Teddy to see it.

"Jesus Rodriguez," Teddy said, and Stein knew what Desmond wanted, the proof of a miracle. By God, he would have it.

"I want a particular set of pictures," he said to Adams and Richards. "The pile of clothes at the bottom, the bare cross as soon as I can get the body down."

He went back to the car for a pry bar and came back to work the spikes loose from the feet. He had Richards boost him up enough to free the right hand. And when the spike was removed, the weight of the body pulling against the sole remaining spike ripped through the flesh. The body that had been a wetback named Jesus Rodriguez collapsed in a heap on the damp ground.

"Christ," Adams said, all feelings of superiority driven out by the presence of violent death.

"I need the facts," Richards said, a little green around the gills. "I'll be frank with you, Mr. Stein. I don't know whether my station is going to go along with this."

"Your station will get a public-service award out of this," Stein said. He lit a cigarette, extemporizing. "Now, get tape of the empty cross, the pile of clothes, a close-up of the driver's license. And then I want an on-air interview with your anchor and Mr. Fleishman."

"On what subject?" Richards asked, sweating. "You going to talk about the murder?"

"As far the story is concerned, there hasn't been a murder. We're going to testify to the presence of blood here and a story given to us by an unnamed source that a supposed miracle took place here tonight, that a Mexican national was allegedly crucified by unknown assailants and somehow managed to come down from the cross and was revived from what we can call a slow and certain death."

"Nobody's going to buy that," Richards said. "We have pretty conservative viewers. They'll light up the switchboard."

"We're only after *one* viewer. We have to convince him and him only."

"And when it's all over, you give us the whole story, an exclusive?"

"Yes."

Richards looked toward the body. "If he's supposed to be alive," he said, "then why aren't we interviewing him?"

"We'll work out the details of the story. But you're right. We have to explain his absence. Perhaps he walked out of here, refused to be interviewed because he's afraid."

"I still don't know," Richards said.

"I guarantee you won't get into trouble," Teddy said to Richards. "This is going to bring a bona fide psychotic killer out of the bushes. And your station can break the story when the time comes. The *Times* will hold off until you run it."

"I don't know," Richards said like a litany.

He did not have the chance to pursue his dilemma. Stein felt the concussive shock waves of the rotor blades beating the air as a roar swept over the ridge and the helicopter appeared, running lights flashing in the darkness, a spotlight flooding the crosses in a large circle of light in which the waxy body of the Mexican on the ground seemed to shine with an obscene glow. "This is the police," came the amplified voice from the helicopter. "Stay were you are. Do not attempt to run. This is the police."

The police cars came up the rocky slope, three of them. The

state troopers spilled over the area and Stein recognized Lieutenant Andrews, a tall, tanned hunter of a man who might be counted on to understand what was happening here and cooperate. Stein looked toward the helicopter settling down and the police photographer who was taking pictures of the corpse and the cross while another officer taped off the crime scene. Andrews approached Stein with a disappointed expression on his face.

"You know better than this, Pete."

"How'd you know we were here?"

"A farmer over on the next ridge spotted lights. I know you've destroyed evidence and in general violated the agreement that you've had with the department a long time now."

"This crazy has my family," Stein said. "What I've done here isn't going to jeopardize your case. I need your cooperation, George, at least until after the eleven-o'clock news."

"You should have come to us first," Andrews said. "We might have been able to help. But as it is, you've loused it up. Shit, you know better than this."

Stein lit a cigarette. He tried to stay calm, aware that the situation was close to getting out of hand. Quietly, he explained what was happening and what he needed. Andrews grimaced slightly but he was sympathetic. He looked at Stein and then shrugged, looked to Richards. "You can run whatever Mr. Stein wants you to run on the eleven-o'clock news."

"I appreciate this, George."

"Hell, you're not out of the woods officially," Andrews said. "I can give you some leeway here but the department's going to have your ass."

Stein was sweating, aware that Karen and Barn were somewhere out there in the darkness, probably within miles of where he stood. At this point, he could only imagine what Desmond wanted to hear, the kind of illusion he would accept. It would have to be outrageous. As he looked at Andrews on the car radio, undoubtedly urging the medical examiner's office to get their collective asses in gear, he could only think of a way to handle this that would bring them all down if he wasn't careful.

"Talk to the television cameraman," he said to Teddy. "Tell him to get a remote crew out here on the double. And keep him diverted for a couple of minutes."

"What are you going to do?"

"Take a long shot," Stein said. He approached the body of the Mexican. The cameramen were standing under a tree exchanging information as Teddy approached to engage them in conversation. The cops were gathered around Andrews and the car radio.

It was now or never. Stein grabbed the cold flesh of the Mexican's shoulder, turned him over on his back. He drew his pistol, then stood over the body and, with both hands leveling the Smith & Wesson, shot the dead body of the Mexican in the heart.

After finishing with the Mexican, Desmond spent an hour in the rain taking care of a very small detail, but one that might rise to haunt him. With a razor blade, he scraped the rental sticker off the back bumper of the Lincoln. He drove up to the Charleston airport, parked in the short-term lot, and, making sure he was unobserved, took the Florida plate off his car and walked into the long-term parking lot, where he switched plates with a Dodge. The Lincoln was now a local car.

The rain let up, stopped. Desmond glanced up at the sky, scowled at the figure he saw wheeling above the scudding clouds. He stopped at a public phone outside a service station where there was no one to see him and made the call to Stein.

Then he drove back to the motel, dried off, changed his clothes. Now, with everything current taken care of, Desmond sat in front of the TV and he made his lists. He squinted at the white paper and wrote with ink as black as the devil's heart. He glanced at the woman sleeping on the bed, her son by her side. They were both drugged to stupefaction. He looked back to the television and he wondered why they didn't abandon normal programming with a burst of trumpets preceding the announcement. Perhaps they were gathering more information for the news that would be on pretty soon. Then they would be seeking him out and he had to decide when to make himself available.

He poured a little peppermint schnapps into a glass, inhaled the fumes, smiled to himself, felt the hum of blood through his veins. The time was here, and shortly he would come into full power. He would summon his father from the grave, the blinking patriarch, force him to witness miracles the old man had never even dreamed about. Then he would bring back his mother and restore her mind and allow her to show him proper respect for the first time in his life.

Ten fifty-five now. Almost time. Desmond settled back in the leatherette chair, sipped the schnapps, watched the images on the screen. A wine ad now, two men enticing people to seek happiness and eternal youth from a bottle. Then the blaring music that preceded the news, a helicopter rising from the skyline of a city, three smiling young people behind a desk.

He waited.

A story about the President. A story about a coal-mine dispute. A story about a school upstate where a gymnasium roof had collapsed.

Why are they putting it off?

Another pair of commercials. A laxative. A douche product. Significant. Emphasis on the corporeal. Back to the woman anchor. Now.

"Authorities are investigating a bizarre happening out near Esterhazy Road tonight. Our reporter, Jeff Stevens, is out there with a live report. Jeff?"

And there he was, a blond young man in a sport shirt, his face flattened by a battery of lights, with the empty crosses in the background. Desmond leaned forward, waiting, scarcely breathing.

"What's happening here is bizarre, to say the least, Sheila, and anyone who is easily offended by explicit footage should look the other way for the next thirty seconds." There was a camera shot of the body on the ground, the Mexican certainly. Desmond blinked. A gunshot wound, right in the middle of his chest. A goddamn bullet hole.

"This is Lieutenant George Andrews," Jeff said, the camera in a two-shot now. "Can you tell us what happened here, Lieutenant Andrews?"

"I'm afraid I can't make any comment at this time, Jeff, since the matter is currently in the hands of Internal Affairs."

Then Stein's face was on-camera, a serious expression. "This is ex–police officer Peter Stein, Shiela," Jeff said. "As our viewers may know, Mr. Stein is a national consultant in police matters, with offices here in Charleston. Can you tell us what happened here, Mr. Stein?"

"I can tell you only what I observed," Stein said. "I received a report that a man had been crucified at this spot and was instructed by my source to bring a doctor out here, as well. When I arrived, there was a man hanging on that cross, obviously dead, and our doctor examined him just as the police arrived and certified that he was dead. He removed the spikes from the hands and feet and put him on the ground, where he was also examined by the police, and it was determined he had been killed by a knife wound immediately below the rib cage." Stein paused briefly, as if to get his breath. "Anyway, the man who had been certified dead suddenly stood up. When he saw the police, he appeared to mistake them for immigration officials. He grabbed a pistol belonging to Trooper Randy Michaels and fired one shot before another officer shot him."

"Are you saying the doctor who pronounced the victim dead made a mistake?"

"No, I don't believe he did."

"Then you think there's a possibility this man was resurrected?" the reporter asked skeptically.

"I'm not here to guess about anything," Stein said. "Only a postmortem can determine the exact condition of the victim when he was shot."

The camera tightened on the reporter's face again. "There are at least thirty officers on the scene now, Sheila, and neither the name of the foreign national who died here nor the police officer who fired the shot will be revealed until tomorrow at the earliest. In the meantime, we're left with a happening that may represent a renewal of cult activity in this part of the country and a mystery that may well contain a miracle."

And the anchorwoman was there again, a pretty girl, smiling. "Thanks, Jeff. We'll follow up this story tomorrow on our morning edition." She moved on to another story and Desmond clicked off the set, the storm of a migraine passing across his field of vision. Jagged streaks of light. Success, yes, the miracle of resurrection, and somebody had fucked it up. Nothing clear-cut.

There was nothing for the Vatican representative to authenticate. Move and countermove, Desmond thought slyly. He had created the miracle and Stein had clouded the issue, anxious to preserve his power. He sipped the schnapps, thought it through. Stein would be organized now. With the picture, he would find a way to circulate it to motel clerks. How many people will remember my being here?

One.

She, he thought. Her. He thought of the lady in the motel office who was watching the small television set behind the counter, henna-haired, middle-aged, eyebrows penciled in, thin black arches. She had glanced at him when he signed the registration card and had captured his face in her memory. She would not forget what he looked like.

She will know.

He heard the voice as clearly as if it had been whispered in his ear, a hollow, sepulchral voice. He stood at the window, turned out the lights, and slowly edged back a corner of the lightproof drape, looking into the shadows beyond the night-light that burned beside the motel-room door. There was a slight movement from the roof down the way, a shifting of shadows. The angel. On his side now.

You witnessed my miracle, Desmond said without speaking.

She knows, the angel said again.

Desmond pulled the curtain shut against the leakage of the light. He clicked on the lamp. He could not be absolutely sure of the angel, no, because creatures of the other world were capable of lies. He tended to believe the angel's warning. But he would cover himself anyway.

He reached into the pocket of his suitcase, where he kept his switchblade knife. He pressed the button, allowed the thin stiletto blade to leap out. He tested both edges with the calloused pad of his thumb. He pressed the blade back into the handle until it clicked securely shut.

He checked the sleeping woman and the boy. He put on a hat that came down over his blocky skull and changed the distinctive silhouette of his ears. With his fingers wrapped around the knife in his pocket, he headed toward the lobby to give the lady one more chance. The lobby door jangled as he entered. He heard the exuberant voice of a sports announcer on her television set. She had watched the news, was still watching the news. He wondered whether she had seen the miracle. She poked her head around the partition of mail slots and the keyboard. "You need something?"

"We all need something," he said. "Yeah, I'd like to ask you a question."

She approached the registration desk. He was aware that she was lame in one leg and her walk was uneven.

"I was watching the news on my TV," he said. "There was something about a killing, something like that, east of the city. But my TV went black."

She shrugged. "We can't get anybody to fix it until tomorrow."

"Do you remember anything about the story?"

"I don't pay any attention to the television," she said. "I like the game shows sometimes, like "Wheel of Fortune." But I've been on the phone."

The voice was in his ear again, a hoarse whisper: She will identify you. Do it.

"There's nothing personal in this," Desmond said. "God has nothing against you."

She gave him an exasperated look. "If you think I'm—"

She did not finish the sentence. With casual swiftness, he pulled the knife from his pocket, pressed the button with his thumb as it cleared the cloth. The blade popped out on the rise, glittered in the fluorescent light for a fraction of a second before he swept it across the counter. She had no chance to realize what he was doing before the razor tip slashed the folds of flesh across her throat and she dropped like a stone, leaving not a trace of blood on the counter. He felt the glorious rush of feeling while the sportscaster continued his eloquent nonsense.

The angel's voice hissed in his ear: Yes! Yes! Yes!

He took deep breaths. He felt cleansed and refreshed, renewed. This woman would not be swept into the presence of God, because she had died in the midst of a lie. He went over to the pay phone on the wall and carefully pressed the pristine blade back into the handle. He was aware that a call from a long-distance telephone could be traced, but it no longer mattered. He dialed long-distance, asked the operator to dial Stein's number, then fed coins into the slot until the call went through and Stein was on the telephone.

"You know who this is?"

"Yes," Stein said.

"So a cop killed the Mexican, did he?"

"Unfortunately," Stein said.

"He has to be punished for what he did."

"I'll take care of that," Stein said. "And the miracle will be confirmed by the autopsy. The police are ready to testify that he came back to life, and so am I. But we're going to change the deal. You let my family go and you take me as hostage. I can do you a hell of a lot more good than holding them will."

"They're really no trouble," Desmond said. "But I'll think about it."

"You're going to need help," Stein said.

"I'll be back in touch." Desmond hung up the telephone.

A stubbly-faced man came into the lobby, smelling of beer, a truck driver type in a T-shirt, with an eagle tattooed on his left biceps. He banged the punch bell on the counter, looked toward the television set playing behind the counter. "Georgie?" he yelled out playfully. "Get your goddamned nose out of the television."

Desmond forced a smile. "She'll be back in a minute."

The truck driver turned toward him. "What?"

"Georgie went out. She said she'd be right back."

"Where'd she go?"

"Something about an ice machine on the fritz."

The truck driver grunted, nodded, left, and Desmond released his grip on the knife, amazed that the man had not seen the bleeding body, thereby saving his own life. Desmond went out into the warm night air. A shadow passed across the moon. He squinted upward. He could not be sure but thought it was the angel circling.

The truck driver had left his eighteen-wheeler running and was heading toward the back of the motel on foot as Desmond pulled himself up on the running board and looked into the high cab. Empty. He opened the door, closed it slightly without latching, then punched his foot against the clutch, pulled the gear into a compound low, then eased off the clutch and felt the truck inching forward. He pulled the wheel around, aimed it toward the office, and dropped to the ground. The tractor-trailer moved with excruciating slowness toward the lobby with its large expanse of plate-glass windows.

Desmond went back to his room. He paused to unlock the car door. He took his time, helped the out-of-it woman from the bed to the backseat, then carried the child. He closed the door and put the suitcase in the trunk.

He started the Lincoln, backed out, and edged toward the street, watching as the truck crawled with a relentless crunching force into the side of the lobby, wood splintering, bricks toppling, glass popping into glittering shards while the structure disintegrated. The driver came running from the back of the motel, screaming at the top of his voice.

Desmond moved out onto the highway and picked up speed in the darkness.

"We have a positive ID," Andrews was saying on the telephone. "The truck driver at the motel picked out Desmond's photograph. And the call to you was placed from the motel."

"Desmond's over the edge," Stein said. "He really believes he crucified the Mexican and raised him from the dead."

"The Mex is not the only one who's going to get crucified," Andrews said. "The governor called the D.A., who called the head of the state police, who's chewing out the local commandant, who wants my ass. He'd have me for breakfast if he knew I was even talking to you. They're thinking about filing charges against you, Pete."

"I appreciate your putting your ass on the line."

"I can only go so far," Andrews said.

"I owe you one."

Picone came wandering in from the office, carrying a pint of brandy. He flopped down in a chair by Stein's desk. He looked at the blinking cursor on the computer screen. He passed the bottle to Stein, who drank and handed it back. "There should be a law that cops can't marry and have families," Picone said. "I feel for you, buddy. And the hell of it is, she never would have left if you hadn't been a cop. Hell, maybe Mimi's right. Maybe we'd all be better off selling insurance and real estate."

"And who would take out the Desmonds?"

"Fuck them," Picone said, and Stein could see that he was more than mellow from the brandy. He waved the bottle in the air. "Let the people who bad-mouth us deal with the creeps for a while." He drank again. "How come you asked me to come back here and chase this nut?" he asked.

"Because you care what happens," Stein said. "Or maybe because you're a good cop. Hell, I don't know."

"It's because we're *simpático,*" Picone said. "You know goddamn well that when the crunch comes, I'm going to throw the goddamn book in the toilet and go out for blood."

The brandy burned in Stein's stomach and he remembered all the crap he had given Teddy about unbalanced criminals and remedial drugs. Now, when he was strung out with the realization that Karen and Barn could be dead, the intellectual bullshit went straight out the window. If he had the chance, he would blow this motherfucker away.

"Out for blood," Stein said, echoing. "I want the chance. Goddamn, how I want it."

She existed in a dream, as if she were in total darkness, where she could hear nothing, see nothing, experience no feelings beyond a clammy cold. Then she began to drift toward the surface and the light and a dull awareness in which there was no panic. She knew she was lying on a bed next to Barn, a strange bed, not the same motel where they had been before, and Barn was whimpering slightly as he sometimes did when he was caught in a bad dream. She was aware of how thin he was becoming, those dear, knobby knees, the pale, drawn face, and then the man would approach with the syringe and the needle, putting Barn out first before he turned to her, a dull expression in his eyes.

And on this one gray morning, she knew that to go into the darkness again would mean that she would never come out, and although it did not seem to matter to her for her own sake, she knew she had to protect her son. As the needle approached her arm, she looked pleadingly into the man's eyes and managed one word, followed shortly by others.

"Please," she said, an exhalation of air. "For the love of God. Wait."

Desmond cocked his head to one side, fixed her with a birdlike stare. "Do you love God?"

"Yes," she said. She would say anything now to stay his hand. He had the power of life and death over them both and he was permitting her to stay alive for this moment.

"That's good," he said. "There aren't many people who truly love God anymore, not really, not people who would do anything for him. I have been persecuted for his name's sake, but he has seen fit to reward me beyond measure. I was his harvester for a long time, sending people straight to heaven, until I proved my loyalty, and then he made me a messenger. But most people won't believe, you know."

"It must be hard," she said. She struggled to clear her throat. "Coffee," she said, aware that she needed to rise above the drug-induced level of slow awareness, and quickly. "Please, if it's convenient."

He smiled. "Good manners are rare nowadays," he said. "You have good manners." He brought her a cup of coffee from an automatic pot, helped her sit up enough to drink the bitter liquid. The coffee nauseated her even as it helped clear her mind. "Your husband wants to trade himself for you and the boy," Desmond said. "What do you think of that?"

Everything began to come back to her as her senses cleared, relationships and exactly who this man was, crazy as hell, volatile. She was in a verbal mine field, picking her way across explosive words. She was so weak, she could hardly support the weight of the cup in her hand. "I don't know," she said in answer to his question. "What do you think?"

"Advantages and disadvantages," Desmond said. "What's the boy's name?"

"Barney," she said.

"Yes, I know it," he said. "Bar-nasha. Son of man."

"Yes." She swallowed as much of the coffee as she could, as quickly as possible. She welcomed the fire in her throat, any feeling at all to affirm the life within her. Her power to reason was coming back. When she finished the cup, she tested her strength. She stood up and walked to the hot plate, where she poured the cup half-full again. She held the cup beneath the water tap to cool it down, then approached the bed.

She raised Barn's head, upset by the dark depression of the eye sockets, the lack of rapid eye movement beneath the translucent lids. She cradled his head in the crook of her elbow, put the cup of coffee to his lips, and tried to get him to drink.

"You have to wake up now, baby," she whispered to him. "Open your mouth and drink some of the coffee. Please, baby."

But Barn was out of it, too far under, too much sedation in him. He could not even hear her, much less respond. She looked toward the man, who sat at a small table, writing in a notebook. The room itself was shabby, heavy with the smell of disinfectant, two beds, the remnants of a fast-food breakfast on the dresser.

With supreme effort, she stood up and made it to the dresser, where she finished off a hard biscuit and a cold sausage patty congealed with grease. She drank the remnant of orange juice at the bottom of a glass. She must have fuel to run; she must stay awake until Barn was revived, until his strength returned. She already felt better, drawing farther back from the edge of the abyss. She picked up the crescent remnant of a sugar doughnut, managed to get it down. He smiled vacantly at her from the table. "Come," he said. "Have a seat."

She sat down across the table from him. His smile was fixed; the eyes were ice, deep-set in his skull. "You have no idea how pleasant it is to have someone to talk to," he said. "Someone who can hear me."

"Would you mind telling me what's happening?" she asked. "Your name really isn't Agnew, is it?"

"No," he said. "My name is Gordon Oliver Desmond. My parents named me that so my initials would be GOD, and I was dedicated to his holy service. Not many people in my life have understood me. I was born to be the very essence of gentleness, and even as a harvester, I did my best to avoid causing pain." He put his hand over hers. She shivered from the touch of his cold fingers. "But I have also learned that I can be cruel when the work of God demands it." He removed his hand, looked over at Barn on the bed. "For instance, I could give him glory but I wouldn't hesitate to kill him, because I know what lies on both sides. The whole point is not whether you live or die but whether you slip into the presence of God or hurtle down the slope. Do you understand?"

"Of course. Yes."

"I've made a decision."

"Oh?"

"I've decided to keep you and your son instead of trading for your husband."

"You know what's best."

"I want your help."

"Yes, sir."

"You have a pleasant voice."

"Thank you."

"I'm going to give you your strength back," he said. He closed his eyes and placed one cold hand atop her head. She heard the hum of unintelligible words. Then he looked straight into her eyes. "You feel a whole lot better, right?"

"Yes, sir."

"And you can walk."

"Whatever you want me to do."

"I want you to look out the window."

She reached out and pulled back one edge of an oilcloth drape, looked out across a commercial street, a signal light at a crosswalk. There was a used-car lot directly across the street, next to a mom-and-pop diner with McDonald's Golden Arches farther down the street. He heaved a sigh, took an envelope from his jacket, counted out twenty-five hundred dollars in hundred-dollar bills. "Now, listen carefully. You see the used-car lot across the street?"

"Yes, sir."

"They have a seventy-nine Pontiac on the lot. You are to tell the man that you're interested but you want your mechanic to look at it. But you'll give him the twenty-five hundred dollars and tell him you'll come back in a couple of hours, after your mechanic checks it out."

"My mechanic, yes," she said. She had trouble absorbing the words. "A couple of hours."

"Once you have the car, you drive over here and around to the back of the motel. The police will know about the Lincoln. So you'll follow me until I can get rid of it."

"Please," she said. "My son needs help."

"He's perfectly fine."

"He needs solid food. I need solid food. May I stop at the diner and get something to go?"

The smile faded slightly. "I want you to look closely at the car lot. What do you see on the top of the office building next to it?"

She looked, saw nothing, knew he expected her to see something. "My eyes are blurred," she said. "I've never seen anything like it before."

He laughed. "You will. Heaven is full of them. But this one has been sent to me. His wings are darker than they appear to be in this light."

"An angel," she said in a hoarse whisper, a guess concealed in a sigh.

"He's going to be watching you closely, every second. He's going to be listening to your words and reporting them to me."

Desmond lifted the knife from his pocket, placed it on the table without opening it. "This is my little friend," he said. "He doesn't like it when people lie to me. You understand?"

"Yes, sir." With a hand on the back of the chair, she lifted herself to her feet, caught a glimpse of herself in the mirror. "May I freshen up? They will know something's wrong if I go in looking like this."

"Sure," he said.

She put on lipstick, combed her hair, tried to subdue the wild fright she could see in her own eyes. She had to do this precisely, follow his instructions to the letter, keep him placid. God, keep him from being riled to the slightest degree. She picked up the money from the table, put it in her purse, noticed that she had a ten and six ones of her own. "I'll get the car and then go to the diner," she said listlessly. "Then I'll drive around to the parking lot behind the motel."

"Okay," he said. "Remember what I told you."

She nodded dumbly, took one last look at Barn, who lay so quiet on the bed that a jolt of fear passed through her until she saw the shallow rise of breath in the frail chest. She went out the door into the warm afternoon air.

I can't do this. I can't bring it off. I'll burst into tears or collapse, she thought.

She caught herself. She could not allow herself to become weak now or he would kill Barn. She made her way to the street, breathing deeply, her eyes hurting from the bursts of reflected sunlight on car windows, glass doors, chrome bumpers. She kept one thought firmly in mind, a single image: Barn. Lying on that bed.

Were she to collapse or fail to do whatever Desmond required, Barn would die as certainly as if she had killed him herself. She pressed the walk button on the crosswalk pole, waited until the light showed her a green man with the word *walk,* and then she crossed the street, one foot at a time. She stayed within the white lines, her purse hanging from her arm.

When she reached the used-car lot, she looked at the two rows of cars and her heart sank. Her vision was too blurred to be able to tell one car from another. Desmond had said a seventy-nine Pontiac.

"Pretty, huh?" Feminine voice, a girl in jeans. How old? Eighteen, twenty, twenty-four? Voice not quite flint-hard yet but just this side of it. Smile half-genuine and Karen wanted to break into tears at this ounce of caring, but she did not. Her mouth was dry. "My husband sent me to look at a seventy-nine Pontiac," she said, managing a thin smile.

"We got a nice one," the girl said. "My name's Penny Masters."

"Karen . . . Jones."

The girl led the way across the lot. The Pontiac was obviously a blue coupe. Penny opened the door and began what sounded like a recitation. "You know Mrs. Falwell?" Doctor's wife. The car driven a very few miles with all the service records up-to-date. Abandoned only because arthritis had grounded Mrs. Falwell.

Karen only half-heard, felt dizzy, slightly nauseous, knew that the eyes were burning into her from across the street. She squinted toward the bright sky above the roof, saw a shadowy bulk, and thought for a moment it was the angel, after all. No, a chimney. Penny opened the hood, began the talk of valves and pistons and horsepower.

"How much does it cost?" Karen asked abruptly.

"A bargain," Penny said. "The boss is willing to take less than book. Say twenty-seven fifty."

"My husband can only pay twenty-five hundred," Karen said. "And he told me to take it to his mechanic first."

"No problem there," the girl said. "I know as a fact we'll let it go at twenty-five. But drive it first. If your mechanic doesn't say it's a cream puff, then it doesn't cost you a cent."

"I'll give you twenty-five hundred before I drive it," Karen said, knowing that her voice carried fear and sickness and hoping beyond hope this girl with bright and knowing eyes would pick up the desperation and the terror within her and call the police."

"That's not necessary," Penny said. "I trust you."

"You don't understand," Karen said, close to tears. "I have to do it like he told me."

"We better have a cup of coffee and talk," Penny said. "I know the crack you're in."

"No, please. I don't have time. Just give me a receipt. I have the money here."

"Come into the office," Penny said.

Once inside, she poured coffee into a mug that said LIFE'S A BITCH in Old English letters. "You take sugar, cream?"

"No, thank you. Black." She took the money out of her purse, put it on the faded oak desk.

"You don't have to put up with it," Penny said. "He's got you scared, don't he? So scared you don't dare cross him or he'll beat hell out of you. My husband was like that until I said, 'Clyde, you touch me one more time and I'll kill you. I'll wait until you go to sleep and you goddamn well won't wake up.' It lasted maybe a month until he got drunk and give me a black eye." She began to write out a receipt.

"The police," Karen said, about to risk the truth in the hope of reprieve.

"The police don't do a damn thing," Penny said, still on her problem. "They won't do you no good." She waved the receipt to dry the ink. "I had them on Clyde regular, but they don't pay much attention to women in this town. I had to leave Clyde. That's the reason I'm selling cars. Believe me, you have to do this yourself."

They were back on the lot again. The opportunity had passed. "It may take an hour or two," Karen said.

"Take all the time you want," Peggy said. "You left enough cash."

Karen started the Pontiac, the motor a low and throaty rumble, the transmission automatic. She inched forward cautiously, hands trembling. In her mind's eye, she saw herself aiming the car at the motel across the street, jamming it into gear, and pressing down on the accelerator with all her strength so the machine shot through the wall of the room and pinned the son of a bitch against a partition, where he would watch with glazed yet conscious eyes while she lifted her son and stumbled out into the street to take him to the hospital.

The fantasy faded. She would do as she was told. She drove off the used-car lot and parked in front of the diner, entering to sink down on a counter stool in front of a plastic dome that covered a coconut cake. The waitress was a heavyset woman with a wide smile. "You want a menu, ma'am, or just coffee?"

"I'd like some things to go," Karen said. "A couple ham sandwiches and a cheese sandwich, potato chips, two pieces of cake, three cartons of milk."

The woman hummed to herself as she turned back to the work counter, but Karen's eyes passed over the bread and smoked ham and fixed upon a small butcher knife the woman had taken from a rack of knives. This one had a worn wooden handle and a thick blade, honed razor-sharp. Snick! A smooth slice through the ham. Snick!

And Karen had the knife in her own hand and screamed and slashed out at the man, the blade miraculously slicing through coat and shirt and across his chest, cutting through bone and muscle, cleaving the heart in two.

She blinked. The woman was wrapping the sandwiches in paper napkins, piercing folded corners with toothpicks to hold the napkins in place. The knife lay on a cutting board. The woman put the two pieces of cake in a white foam box and the cartons of milk in a paper bag.

"My mother used to have a knife like that," Karen said. "When my mother died, my sister took it. I always resented that."

"Well," the woman said. She was jotting figures on a ticket.

"I'd like to buy it from you," Karen said.

"I wouldn't know what to ask for it," the woman said.

"Would five dollars do?"

"That would be more than plenty," the woman said. "It's really too much for an old knife like that."

"It's worth it to me."

The woman picked up the knife, washed it off, dried it, and then wrapped it in a paper bag. Karen put the knife in her purse. Her heart skipped a beat. She was aware of the lack of strength in her arms and hands. She paid for the food and the knife, knowing that salvation lay in her purse, but she must not even think about it now. She was afraid that her secret would be revealed on her face and Desmond would snatch the knife from her purse and cut her throat.

She drove the car down a block, then went into the parking lot behind the motel, and, finding that Desmond was not yet there, she took the knife from her purse and shoved it beneath the seat on the passenger's side, where it could be retrieved from the backseat. She locked the Pontiac, went into the motel. Desmond's eyes swept her like radar. She handed him the receipt.

"May I feed my son?" she asked.

He shrugged.

She opened a milk carton and dipped a piece of bread in it and tried to persuade Barn to eat it. He responded slightly, aware if not fully awake, and he managed to eat a bite of bread while she soaked another.

"Give me the new car keys," Desmond said.

"Where are you going?" she said.

"You'd like to know that, wouldn't you?" he said, quietly. "I might just be leaving you alone a minute to see what you'll do. He took out his knife, the blade springing from the handle as if it were alive. He lifted the telephone cord and slashed through it. "I'm going to lock the deadbolt from outside and it will be marked so I can tell if you've touched it." He closed the knife. "I test people," he said. "And I don't give second chances."

The memories of the Polaroid flashed before her eyes, the blur of blood leaping as his knife severed the little girl's finger.

"You don't have to worry about me," she said. "You've given me the chance to feed my son."

He left. Momentarily, she heard the roar of the Pontiac engine. She put her arms around Barn, testing her strength. She couldn't carry him and he couldn't walk. She would not chance leaving him here while she tried to get help. Desmond was perfectly capable of lying in wait until she left, and then, when she came back, she would find her baby . . .

She shivered at the thought and put it out of her mind. She fed Barn another piece of break soaked in milk.

"You have to be strong enough to run when the time comes," she said to him. And then she saw a pencil stub lying on the telephone table, and the idea came to her, and she did not know whether she had the necessary nerve to try it.

The car had power, a throaty roar, not like the quiet whisper of the Lincoln, and he drove up the ridge to the east and found a logging road where all the mature trees had been cut and replaced by seedlings. The road was in disrepair, infrequently used now. It would do. He got out of the car near the edge of a vertical bluff, a drop of fifty feet at least, straight down into the brush and rocks.

He drove back into town, found a pay phone beside a convenience store, dialed Stein's number, was pleased when Stein answered on the first ring. There was proper respect in Stein's voice. Desmond knew he was making no attempt to trace the call.

"You know who this is."

"Yes."

"I'm going to hold another demonstration and this time I want you there with television cameras, the press. And by all means, drag the police along. I'm going to expose them for what they are."

"I don't understand," Stein said. "What are you planning to do?"

"I am going to crucify Bar-nasha and bring him back to life."

There was a momentary pause on the line. "You don't have to prove anything to anybody," Stein said.

"That's not enough. The doubt would always be there. So I'm going to do something that can't be ignored."

"If we could just talk face-to-face . . ."

"I'll call you when the time is right."

"Who is this Bar-nasha?" Stein said.

"Your son," Desmond said, and put the telephone back in its cradle.

"I'm going to drive the Pontiac," Desmond said to Karen. "I'll have your kid in the backseat. You're going to drive the Lincoln. If the cops stop you, you're not going to say one word about me or this car. Understand? Because you know what I'll do to your son."

She nodded soundlessly.

He went out to the cars, transferred some of the equipment from the trunk of the Lincoln to the trunk of the Pontiac, then came back and wrapped Barn in a blanket and carried him out to the Pontiac as if he weighed nothing. He put Barn in the backseat, laid him down, then nodded to Karen and climbed into the driver's seat of the Pontiac, waiting for her to start the Lincoln.

I'm as crazy as he is, she thought. Crazy for taking the chance, still weak from the sedatives he had pumped into her.

She pulled the Lincoln in behind him, following, wandering with him as he drove down the street ahead of her. She wondered how people could possibly look at him without knowing what he was, instead of regarding that lopsided, fixed smile as benevolent because they could not see the jagged patterns of thought that flashed through his brain.

And as she drove, she flexed the fingers of her right hand, trying to build her strength. If she had a chance to use the knife, her hand wouldn't have the power to hold it. The polished wood would slide right out of her grasp. And the terror of that night, years ago, came flooding back into her, for she had been as helpless then as she was now. Life was unfair. For this murderous lunatic could kill them both without a second thought. He had the physical strength to murder them, while she was too weak to defend. But she swore as she forced her fingers to grip the wheel that when the time came, she would have both the strength and the resolve and she would kill him first.

He drove out of town and up a forested road. She knew what he was doing. He would dump the Lincoln and they would all get into the Pontiac. She wasn't hungry but she took a bite of ham sandwich, hoping the food would give her strength. She planned her moves. She would get into the backseat to take care of Barn; surely Desmond could have no objections to that. She would take the knife from beneath the car seat and with both hands raise it and plunge the blade into his back. She practiced it in her mind, visualized it. Consequences—his hands would drop from the wheel; the car would veer out of control. She would have to push his body to one side and turn off the ignition before she could guide the car to a stop.

They drove down the logging road until they reached the bluff. Desmond got out of the Pontiac and directed her to drive the Lincoln right up to the edge of the drop-off. "Kill the engine," he said as he walked up to her. "And leave it in neutral."

She did as she was told and then climbed out of the car. "Help me push," he said, and she approached the back of the Lincoln as he placed his wide hands against the smooth curve of the trunk and threw all his weight against it, forced it to move while she helped him. The Lincoln edged forward, paused on the edge of the bluff, then tilted forward, hung briefly, the underside dragging on the rocks before the car toppled over, end over end, crashing into the brush below with the squeal of metal against stone, to be swallowed by the undergrowth and a cloud of dust that rose to hang suspended in the warm air. Desmond was physically quickened by the violence and the destruction. His smile widened; his eyes sparkled.

He walked to the Pontiac, and when she started to climb into the backseat, he stopped her. "In the front with me," he said.

"I want to take care of Barn."

"He's okay. Get in the front."

She did as she was told, her small hope fading, frustrated. The knife lay beneath the seat, just behind her, and yet it was useless to her. She would have to wait, knowing that her odds were shrinking. If she delayed long enough, there would be no chance at all.

"Officially, your name is shit," Lieutenant Andrews said. "My God, Pete, you not only broke every goddamn rule in the book but you committed the cardinal sin. Jesus, you bypassed the department and made us look bad when this whole thing is on our turf."

"Then that means you won't help?" Stein asked.

Andrews leaned back in his chair, put an unlighted cigarette in his mouth. "No," he said. "But you're going to be making public apologies for the rest of your natural life. You're going to have to convince the captain that you're not trying to undermine him with the governor."

"I don't give a damn about any of that now," Stein said. "How much cooperation do I get?"

"Everything we've got," Andrews said. He stood up, flipped a light onto the wall map of the state. "But frankly, Pete, it's not going to do a hell of a lot of good. I've been in contact with our units in the field and it's going to take a long time to find out where all the crosses are."

"Desmond has the advantage as long as he's close in. It's my bet he's already scouted enough of the crosses to know exactly where he's going. And it has to be within fifty miles of here," Stein said quietly.

"You don't know that."

"I'm beginning to know him. He wants television cameras, newspapers. He only ranged out ten miles the last time. He knows he won't get half as much coverage if he chooses some remote place in the northern part of the state."

"It's a needle in a haystack," Andrews said. "No one ever mapped the locations of the crosses put up by the different individuals and groups. The guy upstate who started the trend is cooperating, but that won't cover half of them. Johnson's not available to help us here."

"Where is he?"

"Tour of the Holy Land. Or his sister says he may be in Greece if he's not in Hawaii."

"We only have to cover two counties."

Andrews studied him thoughtfully. "You know the logistics as well as I do. At least a hundred possible sites within a fifty-mile radius, maybe more. And we don't even have a time frame."

"He'll do it within twenty-four hours."

"You guess."

"I know the way he thinks. He knows the odds increase against him the longer he takes. He's got to move now."

Andrews shook his head sadly. "I know how you feel, Pete. . . ."

"You don't know how I feel. He doesn't have your family."

"Granted." He sucked on the unlighted cigarette. "You know the equipment we have. How would you use our resources?"

"You have a couple of helicopters and one fixed-wing aircraft."

"In the whole state."

"Then call them all in. Put your locals out to find the sites. We'll stake out those closest to roads, patrol the ones in rugged areas by aircraft. When we have a list of sites, we can patrol them all, every thirty minutes.

"The governor has one helicopter upstate at a coal strike that's threatening to turn ugly. We'll have two aircraft available now."

"I'll rent a copter on my own. I have to cut down the time. If I can't keep Desmond from doing it, I've got to move fast if I'm going to save my son. Desmond says he'll call when he's done it. My son's a strong little kid. He can survive an hour."

Andrews shrugged. "I'll start mapping patrols within the hour," he said. "And I'll set up some mobile teams and as soon as we get the locations, we'll start regularly scheduled patrols. But I just hope to hell we're wrong and the APB net gets him first."

"They won't," Stein said. "I'm on your frequency. Clue me in when you have something. And I'll let you know when he calls." He reached the door. "I won't forget this, George." He closed the door behind him.

The goddamn odds, Andrews thought, and none of these good things were going to happen, because even if they had put three in the air and a dozen teams on the ground, the crazy was going to work at night, and to try to pinpoint locations in these hills in the dark was going to complicate the hell out of things. They were going to need a lot of luck.

Stein drove to his office, saw the rented helicopter parked in the vacant lot next to his building, the pilot, a young man named Edwards, having a beer in the shade cast by the machine, snapping his fingers to the music wired into his ears from a Walkman. Thatcher and Picone were both on separate telephones in the office, Thatcher marking off locations on a map and Picone writing furiously on a piece of paper. He hung up, looked to Stein.

"Bingo," he said. "Your wife left a note in a motel room on the west side of town and the manager just called it in to the police."

Stein found it hard to breathe. "Are they all right?"

"Yeah," Piccone said. "She said Desmond's switching to a royal blue 'seventy-nine Pontiac four-door, dealer's license, no number. She says your son is still heavily sedated but she's talked Desmond into letting her stay awake. She's frightened but her spirits are good. She sends her love."

Quite suddenly, he could no longer maintain his calm, no longer keep his mind free from emotion. The picture was too vivid in his mind, the madman with Karen and Barn in the car. "The goddamned son of a bitch," he said. "He's got to move fast now or we've got him."

"I've got seventeen locations so far," Thatcher said, covering the mouthpiece of his telephone. "The churches are canvassing their members in rural areas."

"The telephone company has my helicopter patched in," Stein said. "When the call comes in from Desmond, patch him in."

"Will do," Thatcher said.

"When I get my family out of the way," Stein said, "I'm going to blow him to pieces."

Desmond had a half-smile on his face as he pressed down on the accelerator and the engine bumped into passing gear up the mountain road. "You ever been on TV?" he said to Karen.

"No," she said. "Have you?"

"Not yet, but soon." He remembered his father's face, the goddamn beatific expression, leaning in close to a client who was sobbing, his lips moving silently, counseling against pain. Whisper, whisper, whisper, while Desmond's mother was in the nuthouse. A shaft of sunlight broke through the trees, and Desmond glimpsed the angel up there in the clear, cloudless sky, having to wheel in a wide circle to keep pace with the car. Desmond squinted against the glare of the sunlight.

Where's my old man? he said to the angel without speaking.

Burning in hell, cool in heaven, the angel said, mocking him.

Desmond took the pistol out of his pocket. He slowed the car, took careful aim at the angel, and began to squeeze off the shots, one at a time. The first bullet clipped a shower of feathers from one wing and the second hit the angel dead center, and he began to trail a stream of silver blood behind him, like a contrail of glittering foil.

Don't destroy me, the angel said, screaming.

Where is my father, you son of a bitch?

Where do you want him to be?

In hell, where he belongs.

That's where he is.

And my mother?

In heaven.

He's lying, Desmond thought. The son of a bitch was inconstant, never to be trusted.

Desmond put his pistol back in his pocket. The angel wheeled away and disappeared behind a bank of trees to heal his wounds. Desmond looked at the woman, saw the pale fright on her face. "He wasn't worth a damn," Desmond said. "He thought he was above everybody else and my mama ended up in a padded cell because of him."

And Karen felt an opening, a crack in that warped psyche of his. "She must have loved you very much."

"No," Desmond said.

"I'm sure she wanted the best things for you."

"She'll get them back from me, that's for sure," Desmond said.

"I've done everything you wanted me to do," she said.

"You have to take care of your son."

"I try."

"Bar-nasha," he said absently. "Son of man." He whipped the car around a curve. "I'm going to make sure he's noticed, that people pay attention to him."

"What exactly are you going to do?"

He fished a cigarette from his pocket, then struck a wooden match with his thumbnail, a flare of sulfur. He touched the flame to the tobacco and in that instant his attention was diverted, the steering wheel under the control of the three fingers of his left hand resting on the bottom arc. She was tempted to grab the wheel and yank it sharply to the right, send it hurtling into a stand of new-planted trees just off the shoulder of the road, hoping that Barn would survive even as Desmond was smashed to death. But her mind was too dull, her reactions too slow. No sooner had the thought entered her mind than the opportunity was gone.

"I'm going to make your son divine," he said. "You won't ever have to worry about his dying again."

The slow realization of what Desmond intended took shape in her mind; she fought the truth even as she worked to find a way out. She had no idea how she could stop him but she would not allow him to do this to Barney, not as long as she was alive. She would have to watch her words carefully, weigh everything she said and wait for her chance.

He was driving with the window down. His head came up as he heard the percussive beating of the helicopter blades against the late-afternoon air, and as if by magic a rest area opened off the road to his right and he whipped the car into it, beneath a canopy of trees.

A red pickup was parked near a concrete picnic table, a hundred feet away, and a towheaded teenager was changing the oil, hood up, paying no attention to the blue Pontiac that had parked across the way. Desmond pulled the pistol from his pocket and laid it across his lap. He grimaced skyward as the helicopter chattered across the treetops. His eyes flicked from the teenager to her face and then skyward again, a clear warning to her. If she attracted the attention of the teenaged boy, Desmond would kill both of them. The boy looked across the rest stop at them idly, went back beneath his open hood. When the helicopter passed, Desmond pulled the Pontiac onto the road again. He hummed tunelessly to himself, a nonmusical sound that seemed to well up from his throat.

"You mentioned Las Vegas," she said, trying to filter the desperation from her voice. "Don't you think your plan would make a bigger impression there than it would here?"

"They had their chance," he said with sarcasm. "How much do you know about newspapers and the television stations?"

"Quite a bit," she lied. "I've worked in communications."

"You know how to deal with them?"

"Yes. And I have a suggestion."

"Go ahead."

"The things you do," she said. "They should be covered by national television, the networks. You shouldn't settle for local coverage."

"And you can arrange that?"

"Yes, I have friends in New York."

"I want a lot of coverage in Southern California next," he said. "I want all the networks there when I bring my father out of the grave."

"How long has he been dead?"

"Years and years," Desmond said. "Can you see it? Can you imagine it at all? The miserable, stinking son of a bitch coming out of the ground to snivel at my feet, begging forgiveness. He couldn't stand me, you know. I was too damned inferior for him. Always whispering, whispering, to other people but not to me, not to my mother."

He was working himself into a killer mood. His voice was honing itself to a razor edge; his eyes were sparking. She had to edge him away from that abyss. "The attention should be on you, not your father," she said quietly. "But I'm going to need some time."

"Time?"

"To arrange interviews with all the big talk shows."

Her diversion worked. As he could swing into murderous thoughts, he could be brought out of them. But quite suddenly, he reached out and slapped her across the face. It was a stinging blow, more startling than painful. He searched her face for a reaction. "You're trying to con me," he said. "You're stalling for time."

"Believe what you want," she said, keeping her fear under control. "If you don't want my help, fine."

"I don't have to arrange anything," he said. "Nobody gives a shit what you do in this country as long as it's big. I don't need you to make arrangements. I can snap my fingers and they'll all come running. You know they got a couple of guys on the Strip who make an elephant disappear? They get the attention, but they don't really do it. They just make it seem real. Well, mine isn't going to be any illusion. Mine's real. That's the reason they're going to cover me. Do you know how much publicity I got out of the little girl and the retired people in Nevada? A whole spread in *USA Today.*"

"You're right," she said, her ears still ringing. "You have it all figured out."

"No damn Mexican this time. That was my mistake. Nobody gives a damn whether some wetback comes back from the grave or not. But they'll care about your son."

She forced herself to remain coherent, easy, to react as if everything he said made perfect sense. "If that's the way you want it," she said, "then I wouldn't presume to question your judgment." She let the sentence hang between them until he responded.

"But?" he said.

"I'm sure you've already thought it through, decided against it."

"What?"

"Barney's a bright little boy, but when he comes through this experience, he won't be able to describe it. He talks in words like *neat* and *super.*"

"So?"

"If you use me instead, I can really let the world know what it's like," she said. She looked straight at him, unblinking. "As your press agent, I could tell them what it's really like on the other side. Where does the soul go when a person dies? What's it like? I could

270

really tell them, you see, and I'm an artist. I could make paintings. The paintings would be worth a lot of money."

"I already have money," he said. She wondered what went on within his head, whether the thoughts passed through his mind like windblown clouds, now dark and gloomy, now threatening, now suddenly bright.

"I sent an old man to glory for his money, but he had a miserable life anyway," Desmond said. "I set him free. It all belongs to me. Everything." He pulled a cigarette out of his shirt pocket, looked at her with a sharp frown, as if trying to catch an expression of disapproval. "My mother never gave a damn whether I smoked or not. She never even looked at me one way or another. It was always the old man and he wasn't worth the powder it would take to blow him to pieces." He lit the cigarette. "I have the right to do anything I want."

"Yes."

He looked ahead and she saw three crosses down a slope. She was suddenly frozen with fear.

My God, he really intends to do this and I'm not going to be able to talk him out of it.

She saw the ground fog beginning to rise from the deep hollows with the approach of evening. Even if the twilight lingered, the three crosses would soon be shrouded in fog and concealed by shadow. She had no doubt that her message had reached Pete, that the helicopter had come looking for her, but there was too much ground to cover and it was unlikely the helicopter would come this way again for a while. She had to stall, let time pass, cling to hope, pray.

He slowed the car, brought it to a stop on the narrow shoulder of a road beneath the leafy branches of a tree, sat and smoked, the blue smoke fuming out of large nostrils as he stared straight ahead. She had to derail his mind.

"What about it?" she said.

"What about what?"

"My taking Barn's place."

He cupped the cigarette in his hand, took another pull. "No way," he said.

"Why?"

"It's got to be a male. No, he's it." Stupid, stupid, stupid, he thought, all women were stupid by nature and his mother had been

271

the dumbest of the lot, but at least she had not been like his father, huddled with a patient in the den, mind feeding off other people. Whisper, whisper, whisper. Desmond had always imagined the whispers to be like invisible smoke. No, he was not going to explain anything more to this woman, because she was a female and far from being able to understand him. Just looking at her, he could see that she did not have the capacity to know, not at all like the Mother of God, who stood in the shadows of the church, forever silent, the baby held in the crook of one arm, her bare foot pressed just behind the head of the venemous snake on the ground. Now, there was a real mother, and he had no doubt she knew of his existence and perhaps had already come to admire him. He took another drag on his cigarette, compared this brown-haired woman with the mother of God. Impossible to do, he thought.

"Work to do," he said. He put the pistol back in his pocket. "You're going to help."

She nodded dumbly. He opened the door and watched her as she got out. She followed him to the trunk, where he took out the two short stepladders, folded for carrying, and the coils of rope. He ground the cigarette out beneath his heel, looked up at the sky. The dark angel was there, a blurred shadow soaring down to the center of the three crosses, where he perched on the transverse beam, hunched down, wings folded about him like a cloak.

You miserable son of a bitch. Desmond glowered at him without speaking. You've never been on my side, not since the beginning.

Wrong, the angel said silently. I tested you. You passed.

I don't trust you.

I'm here, the angel said.

Desmond looked to the woman. "You carry a ladder and a coil of rope," he said.

"I'll take care of everything," she said. "I'll make two trips. After all, you're going to be carrying Barn."

He was startled. He nodded, shrugged. "Okay," he said.

She slung a coil of rope over one shoulder and picked up a ladder. He took the limp body of the boy from the backseat, staggered slightly, not under the weight but from the cumbersome shape of his burden, all gangly arms and legs. He allowed the woman to precede him down the slope that descended gently for a few yards before it fell away into a steeper incline.

I must not fall, she told herself. She picked her way through the rocks and small trees and he followed carefully with the boy in his arms until they reached the small clearing dominated by the three crosses.

Desmond was out of breath. The boy was heavier than Desmond thought he would be. Too, the kid began to come around by the time they reached the clearing and Desmond's irritation was spiking. If the boy had come around fifteen minutes ago, he could have walked down the slope instead of having to be carried. To compound his irritation, the angel had disappeared once more. A useless son of a bitch, Desmond thought. Not even very bright. Desmond put the boy on the ground and then moved away as Barn sat up, the woman hovering over him.

"You have to wake up, Barn," she said, patting his cheeks. "You have to. Can you hear me?"

The boy moaned slightly.

"Go back for the other ladder and the rope," Desmond said to her.

But Karen just stood up and took a position between him and her son. "He doesn't even know what's happening," she said defiantly. "You're going to have to use me instead of him."

Instantly, his fist lashed out, caught her on the side of her face, and knocked her down. She lay dazed, stunned, her cheek compressed against the sharp rocks. A bright pain, no sense of balance. She had made a terrible mistake. He stood over her, the toe of his right boot moving back and forth, pivoting on the heel. "You want me to slice little pieces off of you? Is that what you want?"

She said nothing, paralyzed, the wavering toe of the boot moving back and forth like the head of a snake, ready to strike.

"You speak to me when I ask you a question," he yelled at her.

"I'm the boy's mother."

"His mother?" Desmond asked, incredulously. "His god-damned mother? You think that makes you special? And the Mother of God wasn't all that hot, after all. Did Jesus's mother bother to save him, I ask you? No, she stood around. Mine didn't even do that much. She just sat on her dumb ass. So don't tell me about mothers or fathers. Don't try to tell me anything at all." The toe of the boot slowed. "Now," he said, suddenly the voice of reason, admonishing. "Apologize."

"I'm sorry," she said instantly, quietly.

"That's not going to do it."

"I'm truly sorry I spoke to you like that. Will you please forgive me?"

She did not look up at him. The pain had spread over the side of her head. Maybe her cheekbone had been fractured. She was truly afraid of him and for the first time realized he would not hesitate to kill her. There was nothing in the world to protect her.

He gave her apology some thought. "Okay," he said. "But no more chances. That's it. Understand?"

"Yes, sir."

"Get the rest of the stuff down here. There's a canvas bag. Bring it with the rope and the ladder."

She nodded. Disoriented by the blow, she stood up unsteadily and began to stagger up the slope, rocks sliding out from under her feet, to clatter down the incline. She remembered the other madman from years back, an old terror overlaying the present pain, everything worse now because her son was down there in that clearing with a crazy who was going to nail him up and kill him. Not a vain threat, no, nor a *Grand Guignol* of a fantasy. Desmond would do it, kill them both unless she stopped him.

She fell once, caught herself on the rocks, skinned the side of her right forearm and bruised the palm of her hand. Her head swam; she was too dizzy to stand.

I have to get up, she thought.

I have to kill him. There's no other way. I have to kill him, and in order to do that, I have to stand up.

She regained her feet and her balance, managed to climb the slope to the car. The key was in the trunk lock. She canted her head to one side, tried to gauge the distance with her good eye, caught up for a moment in the same madness that possessed Desmond. God, let me find a way to send the car flying over the rocks to kill him, smash him beyond recognition. She could only see the distant shape of the man and the crosses. It wouldn't work. The car would crash into boulders and be stopped by the random picket line of small trees. God or no God, she could not make it happen.

She opened the trunk and removed the rest of his equipment, the second ladder, the rope, the heavy canvas bag that clanked with the sound of metal on metal. The hammer. The spikes. She sighed, heart banging away against her sore ribs as she opened the door and put her hand beneath the seat. But no sooner had she taken the knife from its hiding place than she dropped it. She picked it up again and immediately broke into silent tears. The fall had so bruised her hand, her fingers could not grip the handle or even hold it with any force. She grabbed it with both hands and raised it above her head, pretending that Desmond stood in front of her, and then brought the knife down with a rush. The momentum of the swing shook the knife out of her hands and it fell on the rocks beneath the front end of the car with such a clatter that Desmond looked up from the clearing below.

"What's going on?" he yelled at her.

"Nothing. I'll be right there," she called back to him, heart sinking. Hopeless. She would have no chance to retrieve the knife, no strength to use it if she could. She did not have the force to penetrate the back of his jacket, his skin, the muscles and bone that protected his heart. She was not strong enough to kill him.

She forced herself to stop crying. She must appear unflustered to him, calm. She must present no threat to his authority. She wrapped a handkerchief around her bleeding palm and examined her face in her compact mirror. His fist had smashed against the top part of her right cheekbone, and her face was swollen, the eye almost shut. But the skin had not been cut. She touched her own face gently with her fingertips, comforted herself. The bone was not broken. She was functional. Her appearance would not matter to him.

She made a decision. You will not kill my son, she thought. You will not crucify him. If the time comes when I see that's going to happen, I'll kill Barn first and then myself. She was startled to realize that she was not surprised by the predicament in which she found herself. For in some way, she thought, she had always known her life would end like this, in violence, from the moment she had married Stein. There was no way to contain violence, once you were close to it, and sooner or later, the violence with which he worked on a daily basis was bound to spill over into his personal life.

She looped the rope over her shoulder along with her purse, then put her hand through a rung of the small ladder, balanced the weight of it with the strap of the canvas bag in her uninjured left hand. She started down the slope, eased her weight from one foot to the other, being very careful. She walked into the clearing and thanked God to find Barn standing now, on wobbly legs to be sure, a glazed expression in his eyes, but standing nonetheless. His lips formed the word *Mama* without sound, and she wanted to be able to talk to him, to explain that death was passing into an unknown country, but that he should not be afraid if it happened because she would go with him so he would not have to be alone.

I don't know anything about death, baby, she thought. I have to keep you alive.

Desmond picked up one of the ropes, examined it with questionning eyes, then gauged the position of the sun that was hanging on the rim of hills to the west and would be giving way to darkness shortly. He glanced at the sliver of a red moon that rose like a scythe in the east. He opened the canvas bag, removed the hammer, and inspected one of the spikes. He tested a section of rope, yanked it sharply between his two hands.

Then, quite suddenly, he became motionless, chin thrust upward, listening, and he heard the distant chatter of the helicopter again. He responded immediately. "Get the boy under the trees," he yelled at her. He threw the rope out of sight, flipped the hammer and canvas bag toward the trees, and scrambled to drag the ladders toward the cover of the brush.

She put her arms around Barn, lifted him, carried him into the trees, where she put him down, the noise of the helicopter growing louder by the moment. Desmond was panting with the exertion of moving and the breathlessness of his excitement; his eyes searched the sky for the approaching helicopter in the dusk.

"This will be their last pass before dark," he said. She saw the spotlight from the helicopter now, the beam darting into the shadows of the trees. She saw Desmond's face in silhouette, lifted, a supreme confidence in his expression, a look of sublime concentration. She moved slightly. Her foot struck something and she looked down to see the shape of the hammer, and immediately the thought was there. She put her hand on Barn's sweating head and prayed for strength. The chance would not come again.

The helicopter was moving slowly, like a giant insect, absorbing Desmond's attention, and she reached down with her left hand, awkwardly, half-blind from the one eye swollen shut. Her fingers went around the handle of the hammer. She managed to raise it.

God, don't let me drop it. God, let me hang on to it.

And with her weak left hand, trembling, she waited until the helicopter had just passed the clearing and Desmond's eyes followed it away from her, and then she swung the hammer at his head with all her might. But he was in the process of turning toward her and the hammerhead only glanced off his shoulder, grazed his head, and knocked him backward.

He went sprawling into the clearing, dazed. The hammer slipped out of her grasp. She ran out into the clearing and waved her arms and screamed at the departing helicopter, but the roar of the machine was overpowering and her voice was weak. The machine continued to move away from her.

Her hope departed with it. Desmond was only staggered, not seriously hurt. He had risen to his hands and knees and was shaking his head as if to clear his mind and his vision. She ran back to Barn, grabbed his hand, and yanked him along a narrow trail through the trees, going away from the car, but his legs were too weak. He fell almost instantly and she tried to pick him up, half-carrying, half-dragging him along until, finally, her lungs hurt so much, she could not go on. She put Barn down on his feet and leaned against a tree. She listened for the sounds of pursuit in the gathering darkness. She heard nothing. She looked up the slope to locate the car and then knelt down beside Barn and held his face in her two hands, looking into his dazed eyes. "Barn," she whispered to him. "Can you understand me, baby? Can you hear me?"

He nodded vaguely.

"What's your name?" she said to him, testing.

"Barney Stein," he said, falteringly but clearly.

"All right, darling," she whispered. "Now, listen to me very closely. That bad man wants to hurt us, but I won't let him. Do you see the car up there?" With her two hands, she pointed his face up the slope. "Do you see it?"

"Yes, Mama," he said.

"I want you to go to the car. Can you do it? Are you strong enough?" Jesus, she thought, asking a small boy just emerging from a drug haze to gauge his own strength was crazy. "Darling, you have to do it. You have to crawl so the man can't see you. Do you understand me, baby? It's like a game. You mustn't let him see you. Understand, darling? Now, you go and I'll be with you after a while. When you get there, don't open the car door. Climb through the window and then lie down on the floor of the backseat. I'll be right there." She paused, listening. Frogs, night birds. "Now, go."

At first, she thought he had not understood, but then he moved away from her a step or two, looked back toward her as if seeking approval. "That's right, baby. You can do it," she said. "Go on."

He disappeared into the bushes. Let him make it, God. Let him get there.

She moved on along the path, the brambles skinning her legs. She took care to make more noise now, the mother bird decoying from the nest. "Watch out, baby," she said aloud to the child who was no longer there, hoping that Desmond's straining ears would pick up her words and not know they were meant for him.

Darkness now, pitch-black except for the blood color of the moon, and the earth had the faint smell of woodsmoke and summer leaves. She was certain he was on her trail, soundless with his supernatural powers, and perhaps he himself was the angel of death he fantasized.

Her right eye was puffed entirely shut, leaving her more vulnerable than ever, for even in the blackness of the night, there was some illumination, some difference in the shades of black. She could see the heavy trunks of trees and the deeper foliage of the higher branches, the pitch-black broken here and there by a slight reflection from the thin rind of moon. There was a difference in tone between the far mountain and the sky behind it, but with only one eye that could see, she had to keep her head in constant motion, for everything on her right was an unrelieved black.

She wanted to scream and yet she choked back even her normal breathing for fear that his keen ears would hear the sound of the air escaping from her nostrils and half-opened mouth. Finally, so short of breath she felt that she would pass out, she found a giant tree trunk and sank against it, her blind side toward the rough bark, and with her good eye, she sought the crescent moon, rising to the east. It gave her her a sense of direction. She listened for even the slightest sound of him, any trace of noise. She heard the faint distant cry of a night bird, the echo of a dog's bark so far away it was almost beyond hearing.

Where are you? You have to be making noise if you're moving at all. His vision would not be perfect; he could not fly. His boots were bound to scrape the rocks, set them whispering. Unless . . . she could not bear the thought . . . unless he knew what she was doing, had somehow read her mind and gone up the slope to the car. What if he really did have an angel up there in the night sky, if in his craziness he had somehow been able to move past the boundaries between this world and the next? She raised her good eye and blinked against the stars, looked for shapes, movement, anything. I'm crazy as hell. There are no angels. She looked, nonetheless. Was that flitting movement across one spike of the moon the motion of wings? Was the angel perched someplace above her, farther into the forest that covered a rugged terrain rolling toward an unseen valley and a river? Was he watching her?

Suddenly, a sound, crazier still than the thought of angels or boots that made no noise. She heard singing, a deep, relaxed crooning, wordless at times, not a Gregorian chant, no, but like it, a strong hypnotic sound, as if the madman searching out there was truly enjoying this, in his element. The search for blood. And then his voice, conversational, pleasant, as if it were asking her to do something she would certainly want to do. She was the child and he the parent, telling her it was time to come in, half-chiding, pleasant, even playful.

"Come on, now. Give it up. You know I can find you. I have all the time in the world, no hurry. But you're hurt and your little boy is tired. If things are bothering you, we can always talk."

More singing, humming, and she tried to fix a direction to it, but she could not tell whether he was close or distant. The trees, the crags, the hollows distorted the sound and its direction.

"He's there, you know. He can see you. If I gave him the word—not the word, no, only the thought, because he doesn't need words—he would shoot straight down at you like a hawk and gouge the eyes right out of your head. He wouldn't do that unless I told him to, and there's no reason for that. If you choose to wait, and if I choose to wait, we can enjoy the night for what it is. And come morning, you'll be able to see that there is no place for you to go, not in your condition, not with a son who needs good food and rest."

The voice stopped and she pressed closer to the tree, the bark rough against her skin. Her face was hurting, but the hope was there, the possibility. He was talking about time, talking about waiting, as if he were prepared to stay here until daylight, and when the sun came up, the helicopter would certainly spot the car and the activity around the crosses. And then the panic hit her. For if he stayed, it would not be in the clearing, no, he would go back up the slope to the car and a comfortable seat. And he would find Barn.

She had to move, but first she had to distract him again. She thought it through first, the route necessary to reach the car. She would go to her left, and then, when the trees began to thin, follow along a shallow ravine and up to the shoulder of the road. But first, the risk.

"Can you hear me?" she called out tentatively. She kept her voice soft, as if a strong sound would give him too much direction.

A wait. How long? Thirty seconds? A minute?

"It's time," he said pleasantly. Where is he? She listened intently. She could not tell. His voice floated in the darkness. "Have you hurt yourself?"

"Barn is sick," she said. "He's throwing up."

"Bring him to me. I can heal him."

"He can't walk. He's not strong enough."

"Then carry him. You're a strapping, healthy woman."

"You hurt me," she said, no accusation, an excuse to explain her lack of strength. "I can't see out of my right eye. I can't carry him."

He was silent a moment. "My angel says he picks up no vibrations at all from your son. Is he unconscious?"

She felt a crazy jubilation, an extension of his insane logic. There's no way you can have an angel. As if to contradict her, she felt the stir of wings, a plummeting rush, heard the squeal of a mouse in the bushes as the talons of an owl stabbed it.

You don't know that Barn isn't with me, she thought. There was nothing supernatural at work here. And now, despite her pain and her fear, her anger came back to her, and with it cunning. For Desmond was human and therefore limited. His ears were no better than hers, his mind no more facile. He had pushed her far enough.

"He's unconscious," she said. "I'll try to carry him. But show me a light, something to give me a direction."

"A light," Desmond said with playful wariness. "And suppose that a helicopter is looking for a light?"

"I don't hear any damn helicopter," she said. "Helicopters make a lot of noise. If you're going to help Barn, then do it."

Another pause. He was thinking. She could feel the force of

his thoughts, the scurry of an animal brain seeking to avoid traps. "All right," he said finally. "Tell me if you see this."

She heard a hiss and realized that he had struck a match. With her good eye she squinted through the trees and the rocks, everything fuzzy. See, dammit, see! For the light of the match would be short-lived, and she doubted he would strike another. Through the night fog, the dim flare registered on damp leaves, no more than a reflected glow. He was down the slope at least a hundred feet, and the flame was obscured by a tree.

"Do you see it?" he said.

"Yes," she said. "I'll do my best. You may have to help me."

All right, she whispered to herself. It's time. Get with it. And no mistakes. A game, herself against the madman. The goal, to reach the car before he discovered her deception; the stakes, Barn's life and her own. She moved from one tree to the next, arms groping out ahead of her, holding each trunk briefly before she abandoned it for another, keeping her good eye to the moon.

She lurched unsteadily, counting her steps, the distance increasing between the trees, and she knew she was going in the right direction. She moved toward a shadow she perceived as a tree trunk, reached out for it, and, off balance, fell heavily on the rocks. She lay motionless where she was, oblivious to pain. Did he hear? Is he moving?

Then his voice. "Where are you?" Desmond called into the darkness. Had he moved?

She did not answer. She stood up again, regained her balance, pushed on, more cautiously now. The rocky ground sloped downward into the shallow ravine. She made her way through the loose rocks and started up the slope on the other side. The crescent of the moon was blotted out by the embankment that formed the shoulder of the road.

Almost there. Only a little farther.

The embankment was steeper than she had thought. She was forced to crawl, inching upward like a mountain climber, biting her lip lest she make a noise, a moan, a gasp, an involuntary cry, as she cut herself on the rocks and still kept moving until at last the moon came into full view. She looked over the edge of the parking area and saw the shadowed island of the car sitting some fifty feet away. But now she was on level ground, on the road. She tried to run but her legs refused to cooperate. All used up. Nothing left. The side of her head had blossomed into a pulsing and continual pain. She knew she would be lucky to reach the car at all.

A breeze sprang up, light, fitful. A thin cloud scudded across the bottom hook of the moon. The island of the car grew larger and then she was there, leaning against the cool metal of the trunk. She allowed herself to breathe, great gulps of air. I made it. I did it. She ran her fingertips over the back of the trunk, found the ring of protruding keys, and moved up the side of the car to the door.

She could see nothing but shadows through the car window, but when she pulled the door open, the interior light blinked on and there was Barn, lying on the floor in the back, motionless as a fawn, his plaintive eyes fearful. He crawled into the front and she was about to slide into the driver's seat when the windshield exploded in front of her face, the safety glass shattering into a web of glittering lines around the bullet hole. And almost at the same moment, she heard the bark of the pistol.

Panic. She grabbed at Barn, pulled him out of the car, slammed the door shut. The light blinked out. She dropped the keys, grabbed Barn's arm, pulled him away into the darkness, her thoughts as shattered as the window. She heard the voice down-slope, the almost joyful craziness of the man, a low chuckle, as if someone had just told him a joke, and then the rambling monologue. "Wunnerful, wunnerful," he said. "God has a sense of humor, you know. All work and no play. Oh, you've done it now, all right, and I can harvest *you* and take my time. Oh, you've done it."

She forced her mind to settle down, pushed the panic away from her. Where are you? she thought, coming to rest with Barn in a stand of trees twenty feet behind the car. How far away are you? She rubbed Barn's shoulder gently, as if to reassure him that everything was going to be all right.

"Open the car door again," he said playfully. Where are you? she thought again. How far? "Give me a little light, not much, and I'll make you a deal. I won't use my supernatural powers and you know how reliable that goddamned angel is. I'll give you a fair chance and if I'm able to get you at all, I won't use anything except a nice, clean headshot. Instant glory. And who knows? You just might get away."

I'm dead, she thought. In the end he will kill me because I'm half-blind and terrified and Barn's in no shape to run anywhere.

The thought was there and she tried to push it away from her but it would not budge. True, true. He would kill her, now or later, and then he would have Barn as well. She felt Barn's hand squeezing her fingers. She put her other hand on his chest and through the fabric of his T-shirt felt the rapid beating of his heart. Suddenly, her head jerked up, almost reflexively as she heard the first faint sound of a distant helicopter, rotors beating the air.

"Go ahead, yell," Desmond said from the darkness. "They just might hear you. Never can tell. I'll give you ten seconds free. Just yell all you want to."

They would never hear. She cocked her head at the sky, scanning with her one good eye. Atop a far ridge, she saw the blinking lights, moving slowly, and a shaft of light shot down from the helicopter momentarily, probing, blinked off when it found nothing. Click. Click. A mile away. How long would it stay in sight? She willed it to move in her direction, but it did not.

"Hey," Desmond yelled at the helicopter. "Over here. You're going the wrong way." He chuckled and his voice was calm again. "You're not having any luck at all, are you, little lady? All right, I won't shoot you at all. How's that? God can be merciful, you know. He spares people. You can be useful, after all, the mother of the boy who came back from the dead, and I'll allow you to be a public witness, testifying . . ."

His voice went on but she tuned out. He was trying to keep her distracted until the helicopter disappeared altogether. She patted her pockets, found the book of matches from the motel. The searchers in the helicopter would never see the flare of a single match from this distance, but would they see the light if she ignited the whole match book? In any case, the flame would let Desmond know where she was. He would kill her. And then she thought of the possibility of a larger fire, knowing the risk was greater. She was unlikely to survive but Barn would have a chance. She leaned down, whispered in his ear. "Stay here," she said. "Don't move. Not a sound. I'll be back soon."

Remember your mother. When you grow up, remember what I was like and that I loved you.

She ripped a piece of cloth from the hem of her blouse, already torn by rocks and branches, and then half-walked, half-ran to the rear of the car, constantly checking the sky and the helicopter that was slowly moving away.

For the love of God, stay.

She ran her hands along the rear fender, found the gas tank, and with bleeding fingers, she unscrewed the reluctant cap. She stuffed half the cloth into the opening and then struck the first match, dropped it, struck another, quickly, then ignited the book and held it beneath the cloth until the fabric was lighted.

She could hear Desmond coming now, clattering up the slope, and she ran to the front of the car and fell to the ground, groping blindly beneath the front bumper. God, let it be there. God, let me find it. And then the tips of her fingers felt the cool wooden handle and she grabbed it. She managed to stand up.

Desmond was running now, yelling, heading toward the cloth and the reluctant thread of flame that clung to the edge of the strip. She had to stop him before he put it out. She held the knife in both hands, ran down the slope, weeping, saw the blurred and stocky silhouette of the man against the faint aura of the moon. She raised the knife, brought it down with all her might as he stepped aside. She sliced nothing but empty air. Losing her balance, she fell on the rocks and he rushed past her, and at that moment, the gas tank of the car exploded, a ball of flame. She saw the disbelief flash on Desmond's face as the helicopter tilted, swooped in a descending arc toward the burning car.

"Take it down," Desmond yelled at some invisible presence in the sky. "Destroy the helicopter, damn you." He yelled at the sky again and then turned toward her, his face filled with the bewildered hate of betrayal. Too late. The beam flashed down from the sky and he scurried away from the circle of light that illumined her, held her a long moment until it swept back to the road, the whirlwind of the rotors kicking up dirt as the helicopter settled down.

And almost momentarily, it seemed, the beam of a flashlight probed down the slope and Pete was there, his arms around her. She began to tremble, uncontrollably, weeping as he looked at her and saw the beating she had taken, the swollen face, the ripped blouse and skirt. He picked her up and walked back toward the road.

"You're going to be all right now," he said in a soothing voice. "I'm here. You're going to be fine. You're safe now. Where's Barn?"

She tried to control her crying enough to speak, but then

Thatcher yelled from the road. "Barn's here, Pete," he said, and Stein stumbled onto the level road, moving very quickly now to the helicopter and the pilot. "Call the hospital and get them ready." He put Karen in the helicopter and the care of a trooper. "You're safe now. He can't hurt you anymore."

Her voice croaked painfully. A single word. "Barn?"

Stein reached out to embrace his son, taking him from Thatcher. Stein felt a terrible anger within himself, palpable, with a force and life of its own. Growing. Barn was pale, dehydrated, hollow-eyed. Stein touched his cheek. "Take care of your mother, scout. I'll be with you later," Stein said to him and then allowed the trooper to put him in the helicopter with his mother. Stein turned to Thatcher, who stood in the light of the burning car. "I want your carbine," Stein said.

"You're not going by yourself."

"No time for argument. The son of a bitch is getting away."

"Chances are better with the two of us."

"I want him. Take care of Karen and Barn. Get the other helicopter out here, just in case. Have him watch for my signal. Three longs."

"Got it."

Stein took the carbine and plunged off down the slope, aware of the helicopter revving up again, lifting off, banking off toward the city and a hospital. The noise receded until it faded altogether, leaving him in a silence broken only by the hissing roar of the flames consuming the car, and then the tires exploding like pistol shots.

Something within him had switched on now, like a machine fueled by a cold hate that left his mind clear, unaffected by emotion. His wife and child were safe and he didn't have to worry about Phillips or business or Teddy's philosophical balancing act. There was something very clean and elemental about his position now, for never in his years on the street had he been allowed this clear and uncomplicated an act of tracking. He had always been called into the center of an inferno, with a crazy already raging, ready to kill again and therefore off-balance, but this time he was alone in a wilderness of trees with a killer out there in front of him who, because of the crazy pattern of his thoughts, was determined to destroy him.

Desmond was moving in darkness and Stein clicked off his

flashlight as well. He moved slowly, letting his eyes acclimate to the darkness and the pale cast of light from the sliver of moon. He had to pick his way along; the rocks were loose and treacherous on the slope. Once he reached the thick wilderness of trees, the underbrush clutched at his legs. To try to run would warn anyone within a quarter of a mile of his presence. He made his way carefully, paused to listen every few feet.

Ah, you bastard, it's a game of psych-out, isn't it?

A game, yes, because he heard no sound at all and that meant Desmond had either come to a stop, waiting, listening, or he was moving slowly and soundlessly away.

Where are you going? Stein thought. What are you up to?

He pushed past a low tree limb and found himself on a narrow deer path. He knew instinctively that Desmond, in his flight, would have followed it. The path ran transversely across the slope, and Desmond, moving away from the road, could not have missed it. It offered an even footing with a gradual gradient that would eventually wind downward to the Elk River, Stein guessed. He glanced up at the moon. It was in the east, high enough to silhouette the trees and make the descent easier to follow than the opposite direction with its slight upslope.

He went down the path, picked up his pace to a slow, loping run for ten minutes before he stopped again. He listened intently, held his own breath to still the sound of his breathing. His nerves jumped. A definite sound. The sharp crack of a twig breaking. Ahead of him? Behind? He could not be certain. He turned his head to one side, listened. This time the sound of a shoe against a rock. Definitely in front of him. He became aware of another sound, much farther away, the faint murmur of the distant river, a half-mile ahead perhaps.

I've got you now, you son of a bitch. A matter of time and you come up against the barrier of water.

He slowed his pace, much more cautious now. Quite without warning, he stepped onto a crackling pile of brittle twigs that had been placed on the path. He heard the bark of the pistol, the bullet whistling through the trees. He stepped off the path and froze, made no sound. He waited for Desmond to fire again. He raised his carbine.

"Stein," came the voice from somewhere in the warm darkness, the single syllable of his name spoken without malice, almost as if they were old friends. "I know it's you. My angel has been following you as you've been following me. It changed sides, after all. That means I have the power."

"There's no way out for you this time, Desmond."

"Nothing can kill me. You brought me back from the dead."

"Bullshit. I just dragged you out of the water like a dozen other kids. There's never been anything special about you. I didn't even remember your name."

"You're lying."

"Prove it. Come out if you think I can't touch you. I'll blow your fucking head off."

Ah, he had planted the doubt now and he could feel it, for Desmond fell silent, and then began talking in a voice so hushed that Stein could not make out the words. Delusion, yes, conversation with an imaginary creature. It sounded as if Desmond was having a discussion. Finally, he spoke aloud. "The angel says we're both equal," Desmond said. "And since we're equal, we've reached an impasse. Because I can kill you and you can kill me, but God doesn't want either one of us to die."

Stein kept his eyes on the path, the carbine up, his finger on the trigger. He was waiting for the slightest sign of movement. But something within him had begun to waver; the terrible sense of righteous anger that he had brought into the forest was fading slightly now as the training took over, the years of following rigid and specific rules of behavior. There was something new in Desmond's voice now, a tinge of fear, his bravado no longer as strong.

"I want a deal," Desmond said. "As your equal, you owe me that."

"I don't owe you a goddamn thing. You touched my family."

"I'm sorry for that," Desmond said. "I didn't want to hurt your wife. I just wanted to make your son immortal."

"What's the deal?" Stein said.

"I throw my gun away and come out. But you have to make sure that I go back to the hospital in Nevada. I trust the doctors there."

Stein shook his head. Impossible: he remembered the dead body of the little girl in the sand and the four senior citizens slaughtered in the casino and, most vivid of all the images, the priest wedged in the rocks, quite dead. And Desmond was following the pattern almost as if he knew it by heart, for he was certifiable, and now he would take advantage of it, just as the ax man had so many years ago. Stein had no real choice.

He clicked on the flashlight, stuck it in the crook of a tree so it bored a hole in the darkness, catching the ends of leaves, vines, the narrow path. Stein stepped away from the light, brought up the carbine. "Throw the pistol out in front of you."

The light caught on the pistol as it was thrown out, tumbling end over end into the brush.

"Now come up the path. Hands on top of your head."

In a moment, Desmond materialized at the far end of the light. He wore a gray suit, one lapel ripped and dangling, a side panel shredded and dirty. There were scratches on his wide face, his hair a disheveled thatch. But there was no expression on his face, as if the flesh had frozen, and only the eyes darted back and forth as if expecting something to jump out of the trees at him.

He approached Stein and then stopped. His face broke into a slow hint of a smile, a trace. Suddenly, faster than Stein thought he could move, Desmond's hands came off his head and a knife materialized in one of them, the blade springing out to glitter in the light, and without a sound he made a swing at Stein's face.

Stein pulled the trigger, a burst of shots, and Desmond stopped short from the force of the blows in his chest, the tracery of the smile fixed on his face. His hand descended slowly; the knife dropped from his fingers. Then he half-collapsed, half-sank to a sitting position against a tree while Stein grabbed the light and turned it on Desmond's beatific and peaceful expression.

"You think you won," Desmond said. He was running out of breath. "Not . . . much time." He forced the words. "In three days . . . the press . . . television . . ."

Stein looked down at him. "You won't be coming back."

"I . . . will."

"You'll stay here until you rot. I'll tell them I couldn't find you. You're a dead man, no glory, no resurrection, just another fucking human being like the rest of us."

"Wrong."

"Then here's your last big chance to prove it. You threatened me with your goddamned angel, so make him appear. Otherwise, we both know you're a liar."

And Desmond's eyes rolled upward. He let out a great and

violent roar, looked into the trees against the faint light of the moon.

"There's nothing there," Stein said. "Face it. There's nothing there."

Desmond made no further sound, and in his eyes, Stein saw the sober desperation, as if for a moment the truth was there and the hallucination was gone forever. A slow wag of the head, side to side, an exhalation of breath, and then he died.

Stein fixed the unseeing eyes in the beam of the flashlight and waited for the jubilance of triumph, but it was not there. No feeling at all for this son of a bitch who sat slumped against a tree. Perhaps that was the ultimate evil, to kill and stand in the presence of death and feel nothing. He heard the sound of a helicopter in the distance and he moved down the trail to the base of a dead tree, the bare branches giving him a clear view of the stars. He flashed his light three times toward the sky, waited, flashed again and again until finally the helicopter hovered high above the dead tree and returned his signal. The position of the body had been marked.

He stood quiet for a long moment, and he began to feel again, to smell the cool, rich air of the woods and to see the thin moon hanging in the sky. He welcomed the ache in his legs, the slight tremor in his fingers, the delayed reaction to the fear he had buried deep. Things to be done, he thought. He had let her down, badly, and now she was in a hospital, the old terrors renewed, and it was up to him to make it right, no matter how long it took. The money no longer counted, the business, the excitement of the hunt, the victory that meant nothing. There would always be another crazy in the world. Well, from now on someone else would have to deal with them, not him. He had things to do, a marriage to heal and the rescue of parts of his own soul that were in danger.

He started walking down the trail and then broke into a steady run, anxious to be out of the trees, tired of darkness and hungry for the light.